Bell
03/14

al Libra
R 86421

D0714676

*12

BROOKLYN
GIRLS

GEMMA BURGESS

Brooklyn GIRLS

ANGIE

Quercus

First published in the US in 2014 by St. Martin's Press,
175 Fifth Avenue, New York, N.Y. 10010

This edition published in Great Britain in 2014 by

Quercus Editions Ltd
55 Baker Street
7th Floor, South Block
London
W1U 8EW

A CIP catalogue reference for this book is available
from the British Library

ISBN 978 1 78206 736 8

1 3 5 7 9 10 8 6 4 2

Printed and bound in Great Britain by Clays Ltd, St Ives plc.

www.quercusbooks.co.uk

FOR **US**

CHAPTER 1

I was really going to be somebody by the time I was twenty-three.

Have a career. Be good at something. Be happy.

But here I am, less than two months before my twenty-third birthday, "catching up" with my mother Annabel over waffles and fruit juice in a tiny café called Rock Dog, because I am unemployed and have nothing better to do on a random weekday morning.

The waffles are organic, by the way, and the juice is organic lingonberry, a ridiculous Scandinavian fruit famed for its antioxidants. This is Brooklyn, where the higher the obscurity, the higher the cred. Personally, I haven't got a problem with SunnyD or good old full-fat Coca-Cola, but whatever fries your burger, right?

And of course the waiter—whom Annabel has already quasi-yelled at twice—rushes up with the jug for a refill, trips, and *boom*. Lingonberry juice all over me. So now I'm soaked. The punch line to an already (not so) delightful morning.

He's mortified. "Oh my! I am so sorry, let me clean that up—"

"You can forget about the tip!" My mother is furious.

"Don't overreact," I interrupt her. "It was an accident."

"But your top is ruined!"

"I was sick of it anyway."

"I don't know why you insist on coming to these ridiculous places." God, she's in a bad mood. Her phone rings. "Bethany! . . . No, darling, I'm still with Angelique. Somewhere in Brooklyn. I know, I know—"

The waiter has tears in his eyes, he's blotting frantically and whispering, "I'm so sorry. I keep spilling things because I'm so nervous. This is my first job waiting tables."

"Dude, it's not a problem," I whisper back. "Never cry over anything that won't cry over you."

He brightens. "That is such a good life philosophy! Can I take that?"

"It's yours. Get some T-shirts printed. Or a bumper sticker. Knock yourself out."

He starts giggling. "You are hilarious, girl! I'm Adrian."

"Angie."

Annabel hangs up and blinks at me till Adrian leaves. She blinks when she's annoyed. Making friends with the waiter is just the kind of thing that would irritate her. "Well. I have some news. Your father and I are divorcing."

What?

That's why she came all the way from Boston to see me? I'm so shocked that I can't actually say anything. I just stare at her, a half-chewed bite of waffle in my mouth.

"It's been arranged." She examines her glass for kiss marks. "The papers are signed, everything is done."

I finally swallow. "You're . . . divorcing?"

"It's not a huge surprise, is it? Given what he's been up to over the years? And you're too old to be Daddy's little girl anymore, so I don't see why you'd be upset."

"Right on." I take out a cigarette and place it, unlit, in the corner of my mouth. I find cigarettes comforting. (Yes, I know, they're bad for you.) "You're divorcing. Gnarly."

My mother blinks at me again. Princess Diana had a formative influence on her maquillage philosophy: heavy on the navy eyeliner. *They're divorcing* is playing on a loop in my head. Why didn't my father tell me?

Annabel clears her throat. "You broke up with Mani, I take it? Single again?"

I don't answer. Last year I told her about the guy I thought I was in love with in an unguarded moment of total fucking stupidity. Just before he dumped me.

"Unlucky in love, that's you and me," she continues blithely. "Perhaps we can go on the prowl, hmm? How's darling Pia? Why don't we all get together and have a girls' night out?"

I stare at her for several long seconds. She's out of her fucking mind.

The minute she goes to the bathroom I make eye contact with Adrian and mime the international pen-scribble sign for "Check, please."

He hurries over. "I am so sorry again! It's on me, I really—"

"Don't be crazy," I say, handing over a fifty-dollar bill as I stand up and put my coat on. "No change. The tip is all for you."

"Oh, Angie, thank you!" Adrian looks like he's about to cry again, but then stares at me in concern. "Wait, are you okay?"

I nod, but I can't even look at him, or I swear to God I'll lose it. I need to be alone.

While my mother is still in the bathroom, I leave. She'll find her way back to her hotel in Manhattan somehow. My mother is British, she lives in Boston most of the time, and her only experience in New York was the year they lived here, on the Upper East Side, when she gave birth to me. She got so fat during pregnancy that she wouldn't leave the apartment after I was born in case she saw someone she knew. So apparently I didn't see the sun till I was five months old and she'd lost the weight. And that, my friends, sums up Annabel's whole approach to motherhood.

The moment I get outside, I light my cigarette. That's better. It's late February, and goddamn cold outside, but I'm toasty. I'm wearing my dead grandmother's fur coat that I turned inside out and hand-sewed into an old army surplus jacket when I was sixteen.

They're divorcing.

Well, finally, I guess, right? Dad hasn't exactly been the best husband. Not that she knows about any of that stuff. I wonder if he'll tell her now. Probably not. Why rock a boat that's already sinking, or whatever that saying is. For a second, I consider calling him. But what will I say—congratulations? Commiserations? Better to wait for him to call me.

But how does this work? Like, where will we spend Christmas next year? How does divorce work when your kid is an adult? It's not like they can have visitation rights or custody battles or whatever, right? Will we simply cease to exist as a family?

When I was little, we spent every Christmas at my grandmother's house in Boston. I always emptied my Christmas stocking on my parents' bed. I sat in between them while they had coffee and I had hot chocolate and we shared bites of buttery raisin toast. I'd take each present out of my stocking, one by one. They'd get all excited with me and we'd wonder how Santa knew exactly what I wanted and how he got to every house in the world in just one night. Pretty standard stuff, I bet, but a happy warmth washes over me thinking about it. It just felt . . . good. I can still remember that sense of security and togetherness.

Now I can't imagine ever having it again. There's a hollowness in my stomach where that feeling used to belong.

Maybe I should grow the hell up. Our family hasn't felt good for a long time. Plus, I'm nearly twenty-three, the age that, to me at least, has always been the marker of true adulthood. It's the end of the carefree-unbrushed-hair-forgot-my-bra-I'm-a-grad-winging-it early twenties, and the start of the matching-lingerie-health-insurance-real-career-serious-boyfriend mid-twenties. And I'm nowhere near any of those things.

They're divorcing.

I take out my phone and call Stef. He's this guy I know, a trust-fund baby with a lot of bad friends and nice drugs. He's always doing something fun. But today he's not answering.

I live with four other girls in an old brownstone called Rookhaven, in Carroll Gardens, an area of Brooklyn in New York City. I'd love to live in Manhattan, but I can't afford it, and my best friend Pia hooked me up with a cheap room here after graduation.

I didn't think I'd stick around long, but it's the sort of place where you get cozy, fast. Décor-wise, it's a cheesy time capsule, but I've been living here since last August, and now I even like that about it. What bad things can possibly happen in a kitchen that has smelled like vanilla and cinnamon forever?

I let myself in and head up the stairs to my room. "Is anyone home?"

No answer. No surprise. Everyone's at work. Until a few weeks ago I was working as a sort of freelance PA to Cornelia Pace, the spoiled daughter of some socialite my mother knows. Basically, I ran errands (dry-cleaning, tailoring, Xanax prescriptions) for her and she handed me cash when she remembered. Cornelia's in Europe skiing for the next, like, month. She said she'd call me when she gets back. I've got enough cash to survive until then. I hope.

And no, I don't take handouts. My folks paid my rent when I first moved in last year, and always gave me a generous allowance, but between you and me, they don't have the money anymore. A few investments went sour over the past few years, and my dad told me at Christmas that they were basically broke, which totally freaked me out. I'd never seen him look that defeated, and I can't be a financial burden on him anymore. Especially with the bombshell my mother just dropped. *They're divorcing.* . . .

Do you think that an empty, cold, gray house at 2:00 P.M. in February, with nothing to do and no dude to text, might be one of the most depressing things in the history of the fucking universe? Because I do. I feel like my toes have been cold forever.

Oh God, I need a vacation. I want sandy feet and clear blue skies and hot sun on my skin and that blissed-out exalted tingly-scalp feeling you get when you dive into the ocean and the cool seawater hits the top of your head. I crave it. We had the best vacations when I was little. My dad taught me how to sail and fish, and Annabel would stop wearing makeup and not worry about her hair for a few weeks. It was the closest to perfect we came as a family.

I flop down on my bed and look around my bedroom. Closet, drawers, a bookshelf with back issues of *Women's Wear Daily* and Italian *Vogue,* an old wooden desk with my sewing machine and drawings and photos that I never get around to organizing, and clothes on every surface. Particularly the floor.

Clothes are my life, but not in a pretentious-label-whore kind of way.

I honestly love H&M as much as Hermès (and my only Hermès was a present from an ex, anyway). Making clothes—or styling clothes or thinking about clothes or mentally planning how I could pick apart and resew my existing clothes, my future clothes, my friends' clothes, and sometimes, to be honest, total strangers' clothes—is my favorite pastime. I can lose hours just staring into space, thinking about it.

Apparently, this sartorial daydreaming gives my face a sort of detached "fuck-off" expression.

I wonder how many of my problems have been created by the fact that I look like an über-bitch when I'm really just thinking about something else?

Sighing, I reach into my nightstand where there's always my latest Harlequin, M&M's, cigarettes, and Belvedere vodka. I read a lot of romance novels; they're my secret vice. But they're not going to be enough today. All I want—no, all I *need*—is to forget about everything that's wrong with my life. I need to escape.

And I know exactly how to do it.

Cheers to me.

CHAPTER 2

"What's up, ladybitches?" I stride into the kitchen and do a twirl hello.

It's just past 7:00 P.M., and everyone's home from work. They've all assumed their usual kitchen places: Pia's texting her boyfriend, Madeleine's reading *The New York Times,* Julia is answering e-mails on her BlackBerry and eating pasta, and Coco is baking. How productive. La-di-dah.

"Angelface!" exclaims Julia. "You're just in time. Deal me in."

Julia's the loud, sporty, high-fiving, hardworking banking trainee, former-leader-of-the-debate-team type, you know the kind of girl I mean? I think her hair automatically springs into a jaunty ponytail every time she gets out of bed. We didn't get along that well at first, but actually, I think she's pretty fucking cool. She really makes me laugh.

Maybe it just takes me a long time to get to know people. Or for them to get to know me.

"Oh, I'll deal you in," I say, picking up the cards I always keep over the fridge. "I'll deal you in real good, just the way you like it."

Julia snorts with laughter. "You make everything sound dirty."

"Everything is dirty," I reply. "If it's done right."

"What's on your top?"

"Lingonberry juice. Duh."

"Have you been drinking?" asks Pia, looking up.

Pia's my best friend, and she used to be a reliable party girl, a high-maintenance and hilarious drama queen lurching from meltdown to meltdown, but then she went and got her shit together. Now she has a serious career in food trucks and a serious boyfriend named Aidan. She even looks after his dog when he's away, that's how serious it is. Serious, serious, serious. I'm happy for her—no, I really am. I've known Pia forever, she's so smart and funny and she deserves to be happy. But I miss her. Even when she's right here, it sort of feels like she's not really here. If that makes sense.

Pia stares at me now. She's absolutely gorgeous: mixed Swiss-Indian heritage, green eyes, and long dark hair. "Seriously, ladybitch. Have you?"

"No! . . . Okay, that's a lie. Yes, I've been drinkin'. Actually, I've been drinkin' and sewin'," I say, shuffling the cards so fast they look like a ribbon.

Drinkin' and sewin' was actually kind of fun. One part of my brain was focusing on the sewing, the other part was skipping around my subconscious, thinking about movies and books and Mani—the fuckpuppet who dumped me last year—and what my grandmother taught me about pattern cutting and wondering when my father would call.

"Angie, it's a school night," says Pia. She's wearing her version of corporate attire: skinny jeans, heeled boots, and a very chic jacket that—wait a second, that's *my* very chic jacket. "Don't you have to work for Cornelia in the morning?"

"Cornelia doesn't exactly need me to be firing on all cylinders," I say. "Or any cylinders." I haven't gone into details about my current job situation with the girls. "Nice jacket, by the way."

"Thanks. I asked your permission this morning, but you were sleeping at the time."

"I think I'll take the rest of this lasagne down to Vic later," says Coco. Vic's our ancient downstairs neighbor who has lived in the garden-level apartment for longer than I've been alive.

"Good idea, Cuckoo," says Julia.

Coco beams. Such an approval junkie. Coco is Julia's baby sister, and a total sweetheart. She's a preschool assistant, and whenever I think of her, I think of Miss Honey from that Roald Dahl book *Matilda*.

I take a swig of my drink and look around. How is it I can still feel alone in a room full of people? "How were your days at the office, dears?"

"Shit," say Julia and Madeleine at the same moment Pia says, "Awesome!"

"I'm on a project so boring, I may turn into an Excel spreadsheet," says Madeleine. She's kind of an enigma. (Wrapped in a mystery. Hidden in a paradox. Or whatever that saying is.) Accountant, Chinese-Irish heritage, smart, snarky, does a lot of running and yoga and shit like that. Pia once described her as "nice but tricky." Recently Madeleine joined a band, as a singer, but she hasn't let us see them live yet. Who the fuck wants to be a singer but doesn't want anyone to actually hear them sing?

"At least your work environment isn't hostile. I sit next to a total douche who stares at my boobs all day," says Julia.

"To be fair, your rack is enormous," I point out. Julia frowns at me. Oops. That comment might have pissed her off. Oh well, if you can't laugh at your own norks, what can you laugh at, right?

"Well, I'm happy. SkinnyWheels Miami has doubled profits in under a month," says Pia. SkinnyWheels is a food truck empire she started a few months ago. You know the drill: tasty food that won't make you fat. Sometimes I think Pia has literally replaced our friendship with a truck. Well, a truck and a hot British dude who has his own place, so she practically lives there. But it's not like I can beg her to be my best friend again, right? I'm a grown-up. Adult. Whatever. The point is, we're not fucking twelve.

"Actually, I'm happy, too. My boss said 'great job' again today. That's the second time this year!" Julia looks insanely proud, and spills pasta sauce on her suit jacket. "Fuck! Every fucking time!"

"Does anyone want herbal tea?" says Madeleine, standing up.

I raise my glass. "Could you dunk the tea bag in my vodka?"

Madeleine gazes at me. "Is that a withering look?" I say. "Because it needs practice. You just look a bit lost and constipated. Maybe you should—Oh, no, wait. Now *that's* withering."

Madeleine ignores me.

"How about you, Coconut?" I look over at Coco. "Good day shaping young hearts and minds?"

She grins at me, all freckles and blond bob and oven mitts, and her usual layers and layers of dark "hide me!" clothes. "I got peed on."

"Someone took a *piss* on you?" I pause. "People pay good money for that."

"Ew! Gross! He is four years old! And it was a mistake. I hope."

No one asks me how my day was, and they all go back to their own things, so I get up and open the freezer, where I always keep a spare bottle of Belvedere, and fix myself another three-finger vodka on the rocks, with a slice of cucumber and a few crumbs of sea salt. My dad taught me this drink; we drank it together at the Minetta Tavern last time he was in Manhattan, about a month ago. But he didn't say anything about a divorce.

Cheers to me.

Several swigs later, I take a cigarette out of my pack and prop it in the corner of my mouth, and look around at the girls, so calm and happy together, so sure of one another and their place in the world. I can't remember the last time I felt like that. Is there anything worse than feeling alone when you're surrounded by your friends?

My phone buzzes. Finally! A text from Stef. *Just woke up. Making a plan. xoxo*

It's weird the way he ends texts with *xoxo,* I think, making myself another drink. He's like a chick.

"Oh, Angie, there's mail for you." Julia points at some packages on the sideboard. "What the hell do you keep ordering?"

"Stuff." I start opening them. Buttons from a little store in Savannah, a bolt of yellow cotton from a dress shop in Jersey, and a gorgeous 1930s ivory lace wedding dress that I bought for two hundred dollars on eBay when I was drunk last weekend.

Julia screws her face up at the dress. "Wow. That is fucking disgusting."

This riles me up for some reason, though the shoulder pads and puffed sleeves *are* a little Anne of Green Gables meets *Dynasty*. "This lace is exquisite," I snap. "And the bodice structure is divine, so I'm gonna take the sleeves off and make a little top."

"Good luck with that," says Julia, with a laugh in her voice, which annoys me more.

"I'm not taking fashion advice from someone who wears a double-breasted green pantsuit to work."

"This pantsuit is from Macy's! And who died and made you Karla Lagerfeld?"

"You mean Karl Lagerfeld."

"I know that! I was making a joke."

"Really? What was the punch line?"

"Kids, play nice," says Pia, a warning in her voice.

"I am nice," says Julia. "Angie's the one living in a vodka-fueled dream world. I can't even remember the last time I saw her sober."

"That is a total lie! I was sober when I saw you this morning! As you headed out the door with your pantsuit and gym bag and laptop like the one percent banker drone that you are!"

"Okay, that's enough!" Pia says. "Both of you say you're sorry and make up."

I stand up. "Fuck that. I'm out of here."

I slug my vodka, run upstairs, throw on my sexiest white dress from Isabel Marant, some extremely high heels, my fur/army coat, take a moment to smear on some more black eyeliner, and stomp down to the front door. I love wearing white. It makes me feel clean and pure, like nothing can touch me.

I can hear the girls talking happily again in the kitchen, ruffles smoothed over, conversation ebbing and flowing the way it should. Without me.

For a second, just as I close the front door, I'm overwhelmed by the urge to run back and apologize for being a drunk brat. To find my place as part of the group, with all the ease and laughter and fun that entails . . . But I don't fit with them. Not really. Pia was my only tie to them, and she doesn't even act like she likes me these days. Though I don't like me much these days, either.

Anyway, I already said I was leaving. I need to stick to my word.

I call Stef from the cab. This time, he answers.

"My angel. Got a secret bar for you. Corner of Tenth Avenue and Forty-sixth Street. Go into a café called Westies and through the red door at the back."

He always knows the best places.

I quickly check my outfit in the cab; this is a great dress. Short, white, with a sort of punk-hipster-Parisian attitude. I tried to copy it last week but failed; I can't get the arms quite right.

And by the way, I tried to get a job in fashion when I first got to New York. I sent my résumé and photos of the stuff I've made and some designs I'd been sketching to all my favorite New York fashion designers. No response. So then I sent all the same stuff to my second-favorite designers. Then my third favorites. And so on. No one even replied. I don't have a fashion degree—my parents wanted me to get (I quote) a "normal" education first—and I don't have any direct fashion experience at all. I thought maybe I could leapfrog over from my job with the food photographer I worked for last year, but then she fired me. (Well, I quit. But she would have fired me anyway.)

The problem is that when you're starting out, there's nowhere to start. And there are thousands—maybe tens of thousands—of twenty-two-year-old girls who want to work in fashion in New York. Girls who do little fashion illustrations and take photos and love clothes. I'm a total cliché. And I hate that. I feel . . . *different*. I can't explain it, I'm just sure I am.

So I never talk about my secret fashion career dream. It's easier that way. Secretly wanting something and not getting it is one thing. I can handle that; I'm good at it. But talking about wanting it, putting it out there, making it real . . . and then not getting it? I couldn't deal with that much failure.

The café, Westies, is in Hell's Kitchen, an area of Manhattan I'm not that familiar with, but it seems appropriate today. The streets are freezing and empty, heaped with filthy, blackened snow. Manhattan looks mean in February.

Stef's car is parked outside. Predictably, it's his pride and joy, a red Ferrari 308 GTS. It's a gorgeous car, I admit. A little "look at me!" for my taste, but he loves it.

I stride into the empty café—past greasy counters and scabby cupcakes on a dirty cake stand—to the back wall, open the red door, walk down some stairs that smell strangely like cabbage and yeast, past a dark red velvet curtain, and find myself in a warm, dark little room.

There's a ladder against a wall, where someone's been putting up dark red wallpaper. A handful of small round tables, a mirrored bar, candles, and the Ramones playing in the background. The perfect secret after-hours bar.

Stef's the only person in here, and he's sitting at the bar. He's cute, though a little simian for my liking. Overconfident and overintense with the eye contact. You know the type.

"What's up?" I greet him with a triple cheek kiss, the way Stef always does.

"Nothing, my angel," he says, running his hand through his hair and lighting a cigarette. Wow, this must be a secret bar if they let you smoke inside. "How's life with Cornie? It's so cute that you work for her. Does she say *yoo-hoo* every morning when she sees you?"

"She's away." Stef is part of that Upper East Side Manhattan rich kid crowd that all know one another, always have and always will, and so is Cornelia. "I need to make some money, fast."

"You wanna split an Adderall?"

"Sure." I look around. "So who do I have to blow to get a drink around here?"

"You're funny. This is my buddy's place. It's not open to the public yet, but the bar's fully stocked. Help yourself." Stef takes out his wallet, looking for his pills. He has a sort of cracked drawl, so he sounds permanently amused and slightly stoned. He probably is. "Fix me something while you're at it. I'm going to the bathroom."

Two dirty vodka martinis and half an Adderall later, the world is a lot smoother.

I like Stef, I really do. I think he's a nice guy underneath the slightly sleazy exterior. There's nothing between us, either, which is so refreshing.

And he's been good for meeting guys. That's how I met Mani last year. He's the one who bought me this dress, actually. He liked shopping. He also dumped me without a second thought or a follow-up phone call. I really thought we were in a serious relationship, so I guess

I was, um, stunned by that. The previous guy, Marc, had been married, and messed me around for a long time, but I thought Mani was the real thing. He wasn't. I sort of partied my way through November to get over it. Then just before Christmas I began sort-of seeing another friend of Stef's called Jessop, from L.A. But he only called me when he was in New York, which was rarely, and it fizzled out.

My love life is like a cheap match. Lots of sparks but the flame never catches. I pretend I don't care, of course. Even when I'm dying inside, I just put a cigarette in my mouth and say something stupid and flippant, and no one can ever tell. Well, Pia can. Or used to.

"You are very good at making dirty martinis, Angie," says Stef, taking another sip of his drink.

"One of my not-so-hidden talents," I reply. Alcohol always makes me cocky.

"I'll just bet."

"Hey guys," says a voice as two guys, one heavy and one skinny, walk into the bar.

"Angie, this is Busey and Emmett. Emmett is the owner of this particular establishment."

"Hey," I say. "Love the place. Does it have a name?"

"Not yet," says Emmett, the skinnier guy, fixing himself a drink in that self-consciously arrogant way that guys who own bars always do. "Why? Got any ideas?"

"Name it after me," I say. "The Angie."

The guys laugh. "Fuck it, why not?" Emmett smiles, holding my gaze just a fraction too long. "Maybe I will."

"Emmett, a word in my office?" says Busey. I look over. He's racking up lines on one of the little round tables. Ugh, I am so over coke.

"Angie? Ladies first."

"Not for me," I say. "Not my bag."

"I'm good for now, buddy," Stef takes out a little leather purse. "Let's have a smoke, and then I've got a couple of parties for us."

"Okay," I say. "What are we smoking?" It doesn't look like plain old weed.

"That's for me to know and you to enjoy."

For a second, I wonder if I should. I've been drinking since, what, 2:00 P.M.? And Adderall sometimes makes me a little crazy.

15

Then I think about why I started drinking. And about the fact that my father still hasn't called. I don't want to feel alone right now.

"My folks are splitting up," I say to Stef, accepting the joint.

"Mazel tov! Welcome to the club. Let's celebrate."

CHAPTER **3**

I wake up naked. And alone.

The first thing I think is: forty-one days till I turn twenty-three.

The second thing I think is: something is wrong.

I'm not sleeping on my pillow. I always have the same pillow. It fits my head perfectly. This pillow is higher, firmer.

I open my eyes and sit up real fast, my heart hammering with panic. Where the hell am I? Big bed, square windows, taupe blinds, huge TV, desk, one of those weird phones with the Line 1 and Line 2 buttons.

A hotel room. NakedinahotelroomIamnakedinahotelroom.

Okay, breathe, Angie, breathe . . .

On the nightstand there's a little notepad with SOHO GRAND printed on it. I know that hotel. It's in downtown Manhattan. And the clock says it's 10:00 A.M.

Fuck.

What am I doing here?

I try to remember last night.

We hung out in the bar with no name for a while, drank more, then we met some friends of his—an Italian guy? And was the chick Croatian? Something like that. Then we were in some new bar on Lafayette, or maybe it was Hudson? Or did we get a cab uptown?

Nothing. I remember nothing.

With a sick thud somewhere deep inside me, I see the indent of a head in the other pillow. I didn't sleep here alone.

Maybe the pillow just does that. Or maybe I started the night sleeping on that side.

I head to the bathroom to pee. The wallpaper has cool little cartoon drawings of birds. Nice. It'd make a cute fabric print actually.

Then, with an even sicker thud than before, I see something in the bottom of the toilet bowl.

A discarded condom.

Stef, probably. We've had sex before. It was years ago, at a house party in Boston, and it was not pleasant, but shit happens. At least we used a condom.

Goddamnit. I always end up sleeping with my male friends. A couple of drinks, I think maybe I have feelings for them, they give me that *look* and then . . . boom. It's totally wrong, I know. But I always seem to do it. I always think that this time it'll be different. I'm a sexual optimist.

I quickly shower, lathering soap all over my body to obliterate the sticky drunk-sex-morning-after feeling, and use the hotel shampoo and conditioner. My hair is pale blond, almost white, and very long, and it responds well to almost any hair product. As does my liver with almost any booze. Ha.

I wish I had a toothbrush. I look like shit, but I can make a quasi–smoky eye by rubbing yesterday's mascara and eyeliner around my eyelid. Part panda, part rock groupie. Fine.

It's when I'm getting dressed that I notice it, right over on the TV cabinet.

My cell phone, propped carefully over a Soho Grand envelope with "A xx" written on the front.

First I pick up my phone. Two missed calls and a text from Pia wondering where I am. She didn't even bother to get in touch until this morning. Thanks a lot, ladybitch. If she left the house drunk and upset, I'd sure as hell chase her. Though she wouldn't do that, of course. Not anymore.

Then I open the envelope.

It's full of hundred-dollar bills. Thirty of them.

Three thousand fucking dollars.

I count it again quickly, my skin burning strangely at the sight of so much cash. It's such a tiny stack of notes, but just imagine what I could buy with it. . . . Holy shit, that's a lot of money. That's more than Cornelia gave me every month. When she remembered.

Three thousand dollars.

I pause, looking out the hotel window over SoHo. I can see over the downtown rooftops, some with those funny Manhattan water thingies on top, and a bit of West Broadway, and people walking and shopping and going to Felix for brunch and leading ordinary days that probably didn't start naked, alone, and confused in a hotel room.

Why would Stef give me three thousand dollars?

Then my phone buzzes again.

It's Stef.

Hey kitten! Great night. Sorry for bailing, but hope you two had fun. . . . ;-) Heading to a party in Turks tomorrow if you want to come. xoxo

What does he mean "hope you two had fun"? Two who? Who two? And he bailed? So I didn't sleep with him? And the money isn't from him? Who is it from? Who the fuck did I sleep with?

I turn the envelope over again. No signature. Nothing else.

I feel sick.

I don't want to think about it, so I quickly throw my white dress back on, tie my wet hair into a tight little knot and secure it with the Soho Grand pencil, put the "A xx" envelope in my fur/army coat, and leave the room. I hope I don't see Mani. He used to hang out in the lobby here a lot. He was so—Urgh, *why* am I thinking about my ex-boyfriend at a time like this?

Five-inch heels before noon: not cool. The Soho Grand lobby, at least, is kind of sexy and dusky, so I don't feel too out of place, but once I'm outside, the freezing white glare of the February morning is horrific.

I feel like everyone is looking at me and thinking, *Slut*. I try my usual walk-of-shame trick of dialing up the attitude and pretending I'm too gnarly for this shit, but it doesn't work.

Deep inside my body I'm nauseous . . . in my soul, or heart, or brain, or something. Cold and itchy.

I always do the wrong thing. Always.

It's always an accident.

But it's always wrong.

A tall doorman with kind eyes puts me in a taxi, and I say, "Union Street, Brooklyn, please."

And then as the cab starts driving, I lean forward, bury my face in my knees so the driver can't see me, and cry.

CHAPTER 4

When I get home, I throw my dress and shoes in the very back of my closet so I don't have to think about them again. Then I put on my favorite old jeans and a pale gray rowing sweater that belonged to my dad when he was at Princeton. I saved it from being thrown out in one of Annabel's house purges years ago, and I wear it on special occasions, when my soul is cold and anxious and I really need comforting. It's like sartorial Xanax.

Three thousand dollars. Three thousand dollars.

Grabbing my latest romance novel, *Heart Crossing,* I glance at the back.

Angry, petulant Ivy hated the imperious Captain Drummond almost as much as she hated love. When the only way to save her invalid aunt is to marry the captain, she thinks she knows what to expect. But she didn't know she was about to meet her match. . . .

They always meet their match in the blurbs, have you ever noticed?

Yeah, I know it's seriously uncool to read romance novels, and yeah, I know that it's lame that the dude is always a rich guy and the chick is always a secretary and all that. I don't care. A good romance novel is simple, predictable, and makes me smile. Perfect escapism.

Except today, it's not helping me escape. I keep starting paragraphs and halfway through, I've already forgotten what I've read.

Three thousand dollars.

I can't bear to be alone with my thoughts today. And there's only one solution.

Cheers to me.

Swigging vodka periodically and smoking out my window when the urge takes me, I play around with some vintage silky scarves covered in faded gold Art Deco prints that I picked up last week at Brownstone Treasures, this little place on Court Street, and sew them into a cool little clutch bag.

I have to pick the bag apart and resew it four times, but by about 6:00 P.M. and after the rest of the vodka, it's just how I want it. Perfectly sized to fit my phone, keys, cigarettes, money, and lipstick, with a little flat handle so it sort of hugs my hand just right, and padded with extra layers of scarves so it scrunches softly. The rain is hammering down outside, it's freezing cold and dark and endlessly, endlessly February. But right now I don't care. I'm sewing something out of almost nothing, making the dreams in my head into reality, creating something new and real and lovely.

My phone rings. I glance at it and quickly press "Ignore." Annabel. My mother. Probably calling to give me shit for leaving the other day. I don't want to talk to her until my dad calls me. I haven't heard from him yet, but maybe he's waiting until we can talk in person. He usually comes to New York about once a month for work.

The combination of hangover and vodka suddenly has me starving. So I smile at my handiwork once more, and then head down to the kitchen for some raisin toast with extra butter, cinnamon, and brown sugar (one of the best things in the whole world, by the way).

Three thousand dollars. Three thousand dollars.

It's not like I'm a bad person just for blacking out, right?

My vodka stash in the freezer has run out, so I open a bottle of Merlot that someone brought home. It's pretty nasty—very acidic, which Merlot shouldn't be (I know I sound like a wine fuckwit, and I'm at peace with that). But it's wet and alcoholic and that is what I need to survive the rest of the day. I'll buy another to replace it. As I'm pulling out the cork, I notice that the old green curtains above the kitchen window are torn. Like, seriously torn. I could fix them! That would be a good peace offering for Julia. Maybe she'd like me again.

So I climb on the kitchen counter, slightly unsteadily, carefully take down the curtains, pick up my toast and wine, and with the curtains tucked under my arm, head back upstairs.

La-di-dah! Thank hell for booze, right? I bet it would be easy to make new curtains for my bedroom, too. Maybe I could—Oh . . . shit.

I tripped and spilled wine *everywhere*. All over the curtains, and the carpet and wallpaper outside Julia's and Pia's rooms. It's all one big, red stain.

I'll just hand wash the old curtains now and then fix them and then deal with the other cleanup later. The curtains probably need cleaning anyway, right? They're like a hundred years old!

I try to wash them. I really do. But the stain won't come out.

Wait! Brain wave! I'll make curtains out of that new yellow cotton I just ordered instead. It'd be an even better peace offering for Julia, and yellow would look great in the kitchen! Yes!

I should always drink and sew.

Because then, an hour later, when I head back down to the kitchen to hang our brand-new, beautiful yellow curtains, I feel warm and loose and absogoddamnlutely peachy keen.

I climb up onto the counter, wobbling slightly. The kitchen so looks different from up here! And I carefully reach up to rehang the curtains.

BANG!

The front door slams, surprising me. I lose my balance and instinctively grab at the curtains as I fall backward off the counter and *whoomp* hit my head on a chair or the table or something, ripping down the entire curtain rail off the window frame at the same time. I land hard on my back, plaster and paint and wood chips showering over my body like confetti.

The pain is immediate.

Like the shrieking.

Julia. Of course. "What the fuck are you doing!? You've destroyed my fucking kitchen!"

I can't move, so I just lie on the floor and close my eyes, my head *bangbangbanging*. It really hurts. I can feel the throbbing reverberating in my cheekbones, the shock of the fall bringing a painful lump to my throat and tears to my eyes. What kind of person cries after she falls over? What am I, some kind of sissy?

God, I feel so detached from myself. It's like I'm watching myself lying prostrate and alone on the kitchen floor. Alone. Always, always alone.

I wonder when my dad will call.

"You're drunk again," Julia says. "And you reek of cigarettes."

I move my arms up, slowly, over my head, so that I'm hiding my face in the crook of both elbows. Maybe if I lie here long enough she'll go away. I wish I wasn't here.

Then I hear the front door bang again. It's Pia. On the phone with Aidan, as usual.

"No, you pick a restaurant. Why? Because I am not the goddess of food! . . . Ha, you are a sweet talker. . . ." I hear her footsteps approach the kitchen. "Oh . . . *merde*. Aidan? I'll call you back."

Julia: "She's drunk."

Pia: "Angie, are you okay?"

Julia: "She's fine! She's like one of those alcoholics who survive tornados!"

Julia leaves the room; I can hear her *stompstompstomping* up the stairs. "Sort it out, Pia! This is your goddamn problem!"

I'm not Pia's problem. I'm not anyone's problem except my own.

"Ladybitch?" Pia says softly. But I don't reply. I don't even move. I can't. I just lie still, in my bubble of aloneness, my arms still covering my face, and listen to the *whompthump* of the pain in my head, and a weird rocking feeling in the base of my throat. A tear escapes my right eye and runs down to my ear. "Angie? Do you want to talk?"

Something warm and sticky is running down behind my ear, different from the silky tickle of tears. Blood.

"JESUS CHRIST!" Julia shouts. "The landing is trashed! What the hell is *that*?"

Oh God. The wine. I forgot to clean it up.

"This won't come out! It's dried on the carpet. And the wallpaper is stained. How dare that fucking ice queen treat my home like this!"

"Calm down, Jules," says Pia. I hear her open the cabinet under the sink and pull out cleaning products. "Angie, I love you, but you're going to have to start talking to me. *Now*."

Right. Because she'd totally listen right now. And stick around more than five minutes after I stopped talking. What's the point of ever sharing problems with anyone? People always just leave, and then they have your secrets, and you can never get them back.

"Angie. I mean it."

I ignore her, my arms still hiding my face. When she leaves, I slowly roll over to my tummy and feel my head to figure out where the blood is coming from. A little graze to the temple, that's all. The kitchen linoleum is cold against my face. From this weird angle I can see that it's gritty with dirt, it needs sweeping or Swiffering or mopping or something, and it's probably my turn. I haven't even looked at the stupid chore sheet in weeks.

Three thousand dollars.

Don't think about it.

"She's a fucking liability, Pia," I can hear Jules saying upstairs. "She's unreliable, she's selfish, she just does whatever the hell she wants to do and everyone else can go fuck themselves. I can't take living with her much longer."

"Would you give it a rest, Jules? She's been my best friend since we were born."

"And she's always drunk. She's got a problem, Pia."

"She is *not* always drunk. Sheesh! And you call me a drama queen. She's just . . . tough to get to know."

"Tough as nails and cold as ice, you mean."

I don't want to be here anymore.

I stand up, steadying myself against the counter. Woo! Head rush.

I grab a kitchen towel, hold it to my bleeding temple, and rush upstairs as quickly as I can—past the first floor landing where Jules and Pia are cleaning the carpet and wallpaper—to my room. I grab my big duffel and swiftly throw in my clutch, bikinis, summer dresses, heels, travel toiletry kit, makeup bag, and passport. At the last minute I add two packs of Marlboro Lights, take one cigarette out and put it in the corner of my lips, and grab my open bottle of wine. Then I change out of my dad's Princeton sweater and pull on a white cashmere sweater, my fur/army coat, and sunglasses.

Duffel over my shoulder, I head downstairs, lighting my cigarette as I go.

"Where are you going?" snaps Julia.

I exhale my cigarette smoke and take a swig of the wine, my face twitching with the effort of a cold smile. "I'm going to the fucking beach."

CHAPTER **5**

Good decision.

Coming to Turks and Caicos was a good decision.

Right?

Yes.

I called Stef the moment I left the house.

It sounded like he was in a bathroom. "Babe! Hosting a gathering at my place. And my friend Hal is throwing a party tomorrow. He's dying to meet you!"

I wanted to ask him who I slept with at the Soho Grand. I wanted to ask him if he knew why someone would give me three thousand dollars for no reason. But I didn't. I just shut up, drank my wine straight from the bottle, gave the driver a twenty to let me smoke in his cab, and tried not to think about it. Tried very, very hard.

Stef greeted me with a handful of pills and a bottle of Grey Goose. The next few hours became a blur. A party, a car, an airport, a plane charter, people laughing and shrieking. I just kept my sunglasses on and tried to look in control.

For a split second, as we boarded the plane, I wanted to turn around and run back to Rookhaven.

But I said I was going to the beach. And I hate going back on my word.

I sat in a corner and zoned out while everyone else partied, and next thing I knew, we'd landed. Everything had the glow of early dawn, and I could smell the ocean. We were finally in Turks and Caicos, a tiny, rustic, decidedly un–New York group of islands somewhere in the Caribbean. Sunshine and bare feet. Exactly what I need.

Forty days till I turn twenty-three.

Within minutes of landing, we're in open-top jeeps on the way to the party. I'm in the back of the smaller jeep, next to some Swedish guy called Lars, but he's been on the phone most of the time. Stef's sitting up front. He's hungover, I think, and very quiet underneath his straw boater hat. ("It's ironic!" he said, when I raised an eyebrow at it. "If you have to explain that it's ironic, it's probably not," I replied.)

I love—*love*—the Caribbean. I love sandy roadsides and paint-chipped houses and blue skies that look like they stretch forever. I love the big, strange blocky buildings that pop up now and again by the side of the highway, banks and hospitals and supermarkets, with parking lots that could fit hundreds, as though they're expecting a population boom any minute now. I love the eye-achingly bright light and the way the air feels so pure and warm when you breathe. . . .

I'm so fucking over New York.

And I'm *really* over Brooklyn.

The hot sun on my bare skin right this second is possibly the best thing I've ever felt. I'm sitting on my fur/army coat, wearing a little white sundress that I put on when we landed, and my studded Converse because I forgot to pack my flip-flops. With every breath of warm salty air, I can feel my bones thaw, my jaw relax, and the cold anxiety in my soul ease, for the first time in weeks.

When we arrive at Turtle Cove Marina, it's shiny and new and weirdly out of place in the shabby warmth of the rest of the island. Three young men wearing white polo T-shirts, shorts, and knee-high white socks—the kind of crew uniform that tends to indicate someone's working on a very, very, *very* big boat—come and grab our bags.

Everyone surges ahead, racing down the pier as though there's a prize at the end. There are eight of us in total: four other girls, all about my age, all gorgeous, all acting like best friends but ignoring me, all constantly reglossing suspiciously plump lips. Plus Swedish Lars, some guy called Beecher who kept cracking unfunny jokes about the mile high club while we were taking off in New York, and, of course, Stef. And me.

Three thousand dollars.

Don't think about it.

I look ahead and see a worryingly shitty-looking speedboat onto which our luggage is being loaded by the boat boys. The girls start squealing.

"Where the fuck did you find them?" I murmur to Stef.

"Old friends, babe, old friends."

Stef looks like shit. Pale and blotchy, with cracked skin in the corners of his mouth. It hits me that I've never seen him in daylight before. And I've known him for six years.

Wow. The realization stops me for a moment.

What am I doing here? Taking a vacation with Stef, the Jovial Medicated Playboy, and a cast of strangers?

Standing still, trying to gather whatever wits I have left, I watch everyone else surge ahead. The girls step from the pier into the speedboat, all squealing with excitement or fear or both, even though the boat is barely rocking at all and the boat boys are on hand to help them. One is offering them glasses of champagne.

But where are they taking us?

And where is the host? Hal, or whatever his name is?

Is getting on a tiny speedboat with people I don't really know the worst idea ever? Or the best, given my reality right now?

To stall for thinking time, I light a cigarette.

"Hey, you can't smoke on the marina," shouts a voice. I look over. One of the boat boys. Tall, tan, clean-cut, blond, ridiculously chiseled, as though he was bioengineered as an example of perfect all-American manhood. "Fire hazard. Gas spills."

I look around. The pier is totally dry beneath my studded Converse.

He reads my mind. "I know, it's not likely. I'm just saying, it's against the rules. You'll get a fine."

"The *rules*? Whose rules? What are you, some kind of nautical Nazi Youth?"

He raises his eyebrows in surprise, and then assumes the professional all-American mask again. "Something like that."

I take one last drag of my cigarette, stub it out, and walk toward the speedboat, ignoring him. How bad can a yacht party be when some angel-faced boat boy is freaking out about a stupid cigarette? This is just another rich guy's folly. Some loaded, insecure friend of Stef who wants to impress his friends and a bunch of girls by showing them a good time in the Caribbean sunshine. Bet you twenty bucks this Hal guy wears his shirt undone to midchest and says things like "island time, mon."

Once on board the speedboat, I grab a glass of champagne. Cheers to me.

And like I say, it's a good decision. Because the minute we clear the marina, the yacht—sorry, the superyacht—we're about to board comes into view. It's stunning, like something out of a movie, over 250 feet long, with three tiers stacked up like a wedding cake.

"A staff of eighteen for the comfort of up to twelve guests." A rote speech from one of the boat boys. I look around for my clean-cut goody-two-shoes. He's up front, staring into the wind. "Equipped with a swimming pool and a helipad, the *Hamartia* also boasts nine staterooms, including an indoor cinema and a fully equipped gymnasium with two state-of-the-art Pilates reformers."

"Oh, gnarly. I can work on my core," I say, to no one in particular. Which is good, because no one is listening.

"I am *literally* freaking out, you guys!" one of the girls squeals. "*Literally*. This is me, *literally* freaking out."

We pull up to the *Hamartia* and go on board. It's even bigger up close: shiny, white, and immaculately clean, like a bathroom turned inside out.

The other girls are squeaking and clapping their hands, and then accept yet more champagne from another boat boy. The crew is all men, I notice. And the host is nowhere in sight.

Something isn't right.

I turn to Stef. "What are we really doing here?"

He smiles, looking as unattractive as I've ever seen him. "Just good fun, babe."

Hmm.

Thinking, I gaze out at the view. We're a long way from shore. I can just make out the luxury hotels along Grace Bay beach, some with cabanas set up out front. People lined up working on their tans, or their marriages, or whatever people go on vacation to do.

There are three other yachts within swimming distance, and I can see a family running around on one, the daddy showing his kids how to do the mainsail, or some shit like that. My father taught me to sail, too. He taught me to sail but can't bother to call and tell me about the divorce.

My parents are divorcing. Wow. Every now and again it hits me, however much I try to ignore it. He hasn't called, and I haven't called my mother back. . . . It's like our family died or something.

I suddenly have a thumping headache that the champagne won't help. Caffeine. I need caffeine. And sugar.

"Could I please get some Coke?" I ask the boat boy offering the champagne, a short guy with a terrible cliché of a goatee.

"Si." Goatee draws a little one-inch-square plastic packet of white powder from his pocket and drops it into my hand. I stare at it for a second.

"No, um, a Coca-Cola," I say, staring at it. Cocaine. Fuck me, the crew is actually handing out drugs?

"I'll take that for later," says Stef, smoothly pocketing it. He swings an arm around my back. It's annoyingly ownership-like, but reassuringly protective at the same time. "I'm going to bed with Dr. Ambien and Dr. Dramamine, babe. See you in eight hours."

"Uh—okay—" I say, suddenly feeling panicky. Stef is my only link to quasi-normality.

"Just enjoy yourself, hon," Stef gives my waist a little squeeze and heads belowdecks.

I look over and see that clean-cut boat boy staring at me again, but I ignore him. I am in control of this situation. I can handle this. I can handle anything.

"I'll take you to your cabins," says Goatee, and we all follow him, the girls shrieking all the way down.

The décor below deck is sort of pan-Asian, with dim, sexy lighting, Chinese illustrations, Thai sculptures, and Japanese blossom prints on the bed. Interior decorators don't always care about the cultural sanctity of their creations, I've noticed.

The girls pair off to sleep in doubles together. I'm given my own room, a single with a tiny en suite. Three bottles of Coca-Cola are already waiting in a bucket of ice on my dresser. Wow. That's good service.

With the door shut and locked, I lie down on the bed, still wearing my Converse and sunglasses. I have that numb thoughtless inertia that I always get after a heavy night of meds and booze. I should really stop doing it. I will, I will stop . . .

The yacht is rocking gently, the bed is soft and clean and . . . I'll just close my eyes.

CHAPTER 6

I wake up alone to the sound of happy shrieks outside my cabin window (porthole, whatever). I can see a speedboat going around, trailing two of the girls in one of those blow-up donut things.

Man, I am going to get seriously sick of hearing those chicks squeal.

It's just past 3:00 P.M. I should let Pia know where I am . . . but I don't have cell reception out here on the goddamn ocean. And she probably doesn't want to talk to me after my behavior last night. She's at work right now anyway. And I'm all the way down here in the Caribbean. Weird. The world is so big. It's easy to get lost.

I drink one of the Coca-Colas, take a long shower, French braid my hair and tie a red ribbon on the end just for fun, and throw on my white bikini, sunglasses, and my white sundress. I forgot to bring sunscreen, which is a drag. (My skin is so white it's nearly translucent. I swear to

God, I can't even fake tan, it's like my epidermis rejects it.) I have a little blister from wearing my Converse for too long without socks, and I have a feeling that heels are not appropriate on deck, so I go barefoot.

I look at myself in the mirror one last time before I leave my cabin.

"No drugs, and no meds," I say sternly to my reflection. Angie in the mirror nods back obediently.

When I get upstairs, the party is in full swing. Beecher is making out with one of the girls, Lars is drinking margaritas with another, and the squealers are back from their donut excitement, self-consciously wringing out their hair in the sunshine so they can dry off their personal-trainer-and-surgeon-sculpted bodies without resorting to something as unsexy as a towel. Stef isn't here. No one even looks up when I arrive.

"Could I get a margarita, please?" I say to the guy manning the bar. "Where is the host?" I ask. "Hal, isn't it?"

"I'm right here," says a voice. I turn around and am greeted by the sight of a swarthy dude wearing huge wraparound shades, white pants, and a white linen shirt (undone to midchest, ha, I knew it!). He's hotter than I imagined. "Angie, right? Finally, we meet. I'm so glad we both dressed to match."

I flash him my best smile. "Virginal white. That's totally my thing."

"I'll bet it is." Hal looks around. "Lars! Take it easy, my friend! Beecher, whoa there, big fella. Get a cabin."

He's normal! Well, rich-kid normal.

I can relax. It's just a bored, insecure rich kid's party. I can play this scene like a fucking guitar. (Well, okay, I can't play a guitar. Like a harmonica. Whatever.)

My margarita and I follow Hal down to a shaded lounging area where mellow trance music is softly playing.

"This music is seriously annoying," I say.

"What do you want to hear, Angie?" Hal grins lazily at me. He's definitely cute.

"I'm going through a nineties electro dance phase." I look him straight in the eye and play with my hair in the unaffected-yet-sexy-I-hope way that I always do when I like a guy.

"The Prodigy okay? Hey! Carlos!" Hal shouts up to the drug-dealing goatee boat boy. "Put The Prodigy on! And can we get a couple more drinks? What is this, island time, mon?"

Two for two.

We both light cigarettes, lie back, and look at the view. It's stunning: the calming blue of the sky and sea meeting in a perfect line far, far into the horizon, and sunshine that floods your brain with feel-good endorphins. I'm glad I came to this party. I pick up my margarita, smiling. Cheers to me.

"I love being by the ocean," Hal says. "When I'm away from it too long, I physically crave it. I have no idea how those people in the Midwest survive. Like farmers and cowboys."

"Yeah, I bet farmers and cowboys wake up every day and crave the ocean."

"The prettiest girl on the yacht is funny, too, huh?"

"I'm the whole package."

Gradually, everyone else from the party, except Stef, comes and sits around us. We're the center of attention for some reason. Even the girls who ignored me the entire flight are suddenly trying to start conversations. All of their sentences end in exclamation marks. Including the questions.

"How do you French braid your own hair!" asks one excitedly. "I find it, like, totally hard to see the back of my head!"

"I just close my eyes and feel my way around it," I say.

"That's totally my motto in life," says Hal, stretching out one arm behind my neck.

I turn my head to make eye contact with him, and we smirk at each other for a moment. Boo and ya. It is in the bag, baby. (Isn't that the most awesomely arrogant thing to say about a dude? Pia and I used to say it a lot as teenagers, and then normally had way too much fun just being with each other to bother with said dude. Damn, she was fun to be around. I miss her.)

Hal is lightly stroking one finger up and down the top of my arm. I think he's trying to be sexy, but it's just making me shiver uncomfortably. . . . Maybe we could go out for dinner or something, back in New York. Or maybe we'll make out later. Nothing more than that though, I've had enough meaningless-sex remorse for one week. (Urgh, don't think about it.)

I love kissing. Actually, no, you know what I really love? I love that moment right before you kiss, when the guy looks into your eyes, you know, and you feel that *spark*. That funny tingle, all over your body, when you know you're just seconds away from touching lips. It's so romantic, so mind-blowingly perfect. . . .

It's the prekiss. The moment when you know you're really, truly connecting with the guy. And it's almost always better than the kiss itself.

"What's your sign, Angie?" asks one of the girls, a sweet-faced brunette wearing last season's DVF.

"Aries," I say.

"Fire sign," says Hal. I find it weird when guys are into horoscopes, don't you? "And it's your birthday soon. How old are you turning?"

"Twenty-three."

"You don't look it!" chorus two of the other girls in unison.

"Wow, thanks," I say. "I'm going for the preteen look right now. Like a tween, you know, but stacked."

The girls are not sure if I'm joking.

Ignoring their confused looks, I take a cigarette out and Hal lights it for me. I stare up at him while he does it. Ah, flirting.

"Another margarita?" asks the goateed bartender a few minutes later. It's the same one who offered me cocaine. He's been bringing the drinks out fast, potent as hell. I should probably eat something. Then, as if someone's reading my mind, great platters of food arrive, and a giant jug of iced water.

"Conch fritters, a local speciality." It's that pain-in-the-ass clean-cut boat boy again. "And snapper sandwiches."

"Thank you! I am starving!" I grab a plate. The conch is kind of weird, but the sandwiches are amazing: soft bread, salty butter, and hot, crispy fish. None of the other girls are eating. I always wonder if girls like them don't eat in front of guys so that they'll think they don't have a digestive system and never poop or something. Not me. I'm an eater. And I poop. Deal with it.

I look up, halfway through my third sandwich, and catch the clean-cut boat boy's eye again. He's staring at me intensely, kind of disapprovingly. Unused to seeing girls eat, I bet.

So I take the rest of the sandwich and jam it into my mouth, all at once, edging it past my molars on either side, and look back at the boat boy, my cheeks stuffed with sandwich, my face bulging like a cartoon. Then I blink a few times like Bambi. His entire face lights up with an ear-to-ear grin. Ha! I snort with laughter, crumbs blowing out of my mouth, and the boat boy ducks his head and turns away to hide the fact that he's cracking up.

"Wow, *that* is attractive," says Hal, looking at me. Like the others, he's barely picked at a couple of conch fritters. He's on coke, I suddenly realize, chewing through the half-sandwich in my mouth. They all are. That's why they're not eating. And actually, Beecher and two of the girls have disappeared belowdecks. Oh, well. All the more food for me.

When my mouth is finally clear of sandwich, I take a slug of water and smile at Hal. "I have an appetite. Is that a problem?"

He grins. "Absogoddamnlutely not."

Another margarita or two and more Euro trance music later, and the sun begins to set. Lars and another one of the girls disappear, and the other girl passes out on one of the daybeds. They're all kind of strange, and I'm used to Stef's freak-show friends. I can't even figure out how everyone knows one another.

Hal turns to me. "You should come check out my cabin. It's ridiculous. There's a bar and everything."

"Really," I deadpan. Wow, is he really going to be that obvious? It's so transparent, it's almost adorable. "Are you going to make me a cocktail?"

"Yes," he says, grinning at me. "Yes, I am."

We get down to his cabin, the blast of the air-conditioning assaulting my sun-warmed skin. As you'd expect on a megayacht, it's ridiculously big and glossily immaculate, with a gigantic bed, a full sofa area with a bar, and even a diving terrace.

"Wow," I say. "What a dump."

Immediately, Hal disappears into the en suite. You know, I don't think I will make out with him after all. He's clearly more interested in taking drugs than talking to me.

Maybe I'll wake Stef and find out when we're leaving tomorrow. Brooklyn suddenly seems really far away, and not in a good way. This whole yacht scene feels a little . . . I don't know, creepy. And I really do want to make up with Julia. And everyone else, too. Now that I've relaxed a bit, the situation at Rookhaven doesn't seem so dire. Everything will be fine. It has to be. Right?

Hal shuffles out of the bathroom, wiping under his nostrils.

"How was the powder room, dear?"

"You want?" he says, pointing his thumb in the direction of the en suite.

I shake my head. "I'm gonna go find Stef."

"Make me a martini first? Stef tells me you do a great dirty martini."

"Um, sure. Why not."

I walk over to the bar and am reaching up to get the martini glasses from the top shelf when WHAM, I'm slammed up hard against the counter, Hal nuzzling the back of my neck.

"Whoa, dude, slow down," I say, trying to push him off me. I hate it when guys mistake force for passion. "Stop it. I mean it."

"I've got a surprise for you," he whispers, slowly turning me around so I'm facing him.

I look down.

Hal's penis.

Is out.

In his hand.

Small, pink, and erect.

Oh. My. God.

Hal smiles at me, and then at his penis. "Do you want to touch him? He likes you."

I laugh out loud. "No!"

"No?"

"No . . . thank you?" How do you refuse an erect penis politely? "Sweet of you to offer, but, uh, no. Let's get back to the party."

Hal tucks his penis back into his pants, thank fuck, but as I go to push past him he grabs me, hoists me up so I'm sitting on the bar, pushes my knees apart, and pulls up my dress.

"Stop," I snap, but he's pinning me down, kissing my neck, his hands grabbing at my thighs and this isn't funny anymore, but he's not even looking me in the eye, he's just dryhumping like a fucking crazed teenager. "Hal, stop. Now. Stop it!"

I shove him away, get down from the bar, and push past him. I'm out of here.

"Sorry!" he says. "Listen, Angie, I'm sorry, I really am."

I pause in the middle of the room. "You should be. Jesus."

Hal sniffs. "Listen, let's just be totally open, okay? We're grown-ups. Maybe I went about it the wrong way. You're different."

I frown at him. What does he mean? Different from what?

"Let's set the boundaries now, and open a bottle of Veuve, go to the diving terrace, and figure it out from there."

"What boundaries?"

"Three thousand, right? Full sex, and I want head first."

I stare at him. If I was a cartoon, there would be a little exclamation mark above my head.

"What?" Hal looks surprised at my reaction. "Fuck, do I have that wrong? Is it four thousand? Stef said—"

In that moment, everything becomes crystal clear.

I'm suddenly sober.

And.

I.

Am.

Angry.

CHAPTER 7

I turn around, stalk out of Hal's cabin, and storm through the yacht. I'm so furious, I feel like sparks are exploding from my body.

"STEF!" I scream. "STEF, YOU PREPPY PIECE OF SHIT! WAKE THE FUCK UP!"

I get to the first sleeping cabin and kick it open. Lars and another girl, doing coke.

"STEF! WHERE THE FUCK ARE YOU?"

I kick in the next cabin door. Beecher and two girls, naked.

"STEF! SHOW YOURSELF!"

I kick open the next cabin door. Empty. But I can see Stef's ridiculous little hat. This was his room. Which means he's up.

My fists are clenched so hard that my nails are cutting into my palms. On my way up the last set of stairs I run into that clean-cut boat boy again.

He frowns at me. "Are you okay?"

"No. I am not okay!" I push past him angrily.

"Can I do anything?"

"Yes. Stay the fuck away from me."

I stomp above deck, look around wildly, and see him. Stef. Sitting at the bar, looking completely normal, the goateed drug-dealing boat boy serving him a chilled glass of rosé. I walk right up to him.

"Why the fuck did you bring me here?" My voice is suddenly shaking. "Hal thinks I'm a fucking hooker, Stef!"

"Labels are very ugly, Angie." Stef's drawl is even more pronounced than usual.

"You told him I'm a hooker?"

"You need cash. Hal needs a girl. Maybe he upset you by being too up-front, but c'mon. You must have been expecting it."

"I was *not* fucking expecting it," I hiss. "How dare you. I asked you what we were doing here, you said, 'Just good fun, babe.' You LIAR! I thought—"

"Mani took you shopping, right?" Stef interrupts. My ex? Why is he bringing him up? Stef introduced us, but—"Did you get an extra-nice present after the first time you fucked him? I bet you did. How about Jessop? A weekend in Aspen and a charge card for a couple of grand at Bergdorf Goodman, right?"

"That was . . . he said it was a freebie from his work, he said—" I'm stuttering now.

"Sex in exchange for what you want."

"No." Suddenly I can't breathe. "That's different."

"Is it? And does it even matter?"

"It matters to me. They were just . . . generous . . ." My voice trails off as I realize how ridiculous I sound.

"And you woke up yesterday morning in some hotel room with a stack of cash next to the bed, I'm guessing." Stef's voice grows eerily controlled. "Come on, tough girl. You're smart. You really think you're here for your conversational skills? Hal needs a girlfriend for the weekend. You told me you needed to make some money. Everybody wins."

"No—" My voice is a whisper.

Stef's eyes are glinting with controlled fury, and he's talking super-low, through gritted teeth. "Just sit the fuck down and play nice. I went to a lot of effort to make this party happen for my friend Hal. You're embarrassing me."

Total silence.

We stare at each other.

Suddenly, I'm very, very scared.

I don't know Stef, not really. I don't know what he's capable of doing to me. And I'm alone. Completely alone.

Panic rises like bile in my stomach. I stumble backward away from Stef and look around wildly.

The sun is setting, and the other yachts that surrounded us earlier have left. They're just gone, swoosh, vamoosed. I didn't even notice! Or did we sail somewhere? I wasn't paying attention, have we been sailing into the middle of the fucking ocean? I turn again, desperately trying to see land.

It's there. Thank God. Off the stern, I can see the long white beach of Grace Bay, and, in the soft dusk light, the twinkling lights of all the hotels. How far is it? A mile? Half a mile?

I look back at Stef for a second. He stands up and opens his mouth to say something.

Before he can speak, I look him in the eye. "Go fuck yourself, Stef."

Then I turn around, run toward the back of the yacht, take a deep breath, and dive.

CHAPTER **8**

The moment the water hits my head, I have a weird flashback to my wish the other day. When I thought I was so miserable, back in freezing gray Brooklyn, and all I craved was the blissed-out feeling of diving into seawater.

Be careful what you wish for.

My dress is wrapping around my legs, making it hard to swim, so I quickly remove it. Then, wearing nothing but my bikini, I start swimming toward the shore.

"Angie!" I can hear Stef screaming at me from the yacht. "Get the fuck back here, you crazy bitch!"

There's no point in shouting back—I need to save my breath—so I tread water for a moment, and without turning around, raise my arms out of the water to give him the finger from both hands.

Then I keep swimming.

Fuck you, Stef, I think, with every single stroke. *I'm going to pay you back for this.*

I'm not exactly the running-around-the-soccer-field type, and the years of compulsory team sports in school just stressed me out because I was really uncoordinated and dreamy and forgot things like which direction to run if I ever actually got the ball. Swimming, however, is the perfect exercise for creative loners. And I'm pretty good at it.

Every few breaths I look up to make sure I'm still heading in the right direction. I think I am, but it's hard to tell. The land is a lot farther away than I thought. All I want is to get back on land, and then somehow I'll find my way to Brooklyn. I want my home.

Five, or maybe ten minutes later—I can't tell—I hear a voice.

"Hey you!"

I turn around. It's that fucking boat boy again, the clean-cut one who was watching me all day. He's in a tiny blow-up dinghy. They've sent him to collect me.

"Go the fuck away," I shout. "I'm not going back there."

"I'm not going to take you back to the *Hamartia,*" he calls. "I'll take you to shore. I promise."

For a split second I consider it. But then reality hits: how many times do I have to be screwed over before I realize that everyone lies?

"I'm not going to trust some boat boy from a fucking superyacht," I say. "Go back and tell them I've drowned."

He laughs. "They don't know I'm here."

"Why the hell should I believe you?" I say. "I'm flying back to New York tonight. Leave me alone."

"There is no flight to New York tonight."

"Then I'll fly to Chicago and catch a fucking bus."

Before he can reply, I take a deep breath and keep swimming. Talking is making me breathless, and it's a waste of time.

A few minutes later I glance back again. He's still behind me. Just floating in that stupid little dinghy, using the oars to keep pace.

Whatever.

My arms and legs ache, but I don't stop. I figure this pain is my punishment for being such a moron. For trusting a guy with the morals of a vulture. For not realizing there's no such thing as a free lunch. (Or dress. Or trip to Aspen. Or charge card at Bergdorfs. Or . . . anything.) At one point, thinking about everything I've done, by accident and on purpose, but always with total stupidity, tears build up behind my eyes.

The last three men I slept with—Mani, Jessop, and whoever I was with at the Soho Grand—thought I was a hooker. Or something close to it.

But I thought they liked me. I really did. I thought I was just unlucky in love.

What would my parents think? What if my dad knew? How could I be so *stupid*?

I start sobbing, and my mouth fills with water, so I have to tread water for a second, making dramatic strangled choking sounds.

The boat boy stalker is right behind me. "Listen, it's Angie, right? My name is Sam, and I—"

"Please fuck off, Sam!" I am trying as hard as I can to sound normal and tough.

Stop crying, I tell myself sternly. *You can get through this. Just get away. Keep swimming.*

And so that's what I do. I swim, and breathe, and force every other thought out of my head.

"Angie?" Sam the boat boy calls out again. "Are you okay?"

"What are you going to do about it if I'm not, Sam?" I call over my shoulder. "Save me? I don't need to be saved. I just need to get home."

About two hundred feet from shore, just as the sun has finally set, swimming suddenly gets easier. It feels like the tide is helping me. I'm aiming for one of the smaller hotels, which I'm hoping will mean it's an exclusive luxury-type place, where everyone keeps to themselves and you tend to not know the other guests. My arms and legs are almost cramping now, and I am exhausted, but I won't stop. I'm determined to make it.

Finally, my feet hit sand. I turn around and see Sam, the boat boy, still twenty feet behind me in his stupid dinghy. God, what is he going for, some kind of Mr. Perfect medal or something?

"You can go now, Sam," I call. "I'm safe and sound."

"I don't think you're ever safe."

Ignoring him, I keep swimming until I can easily stand up, my body more than half out of the water. Then I walk out of the sea. When I'm on the beach, I look back. Sam has finally left, already halfway back to the *Hamartia*. Sayonara, annoying boat boy.

It's at that moment that I remember my passport, clothes, shoes, and money—the three thousand dollars—are in my cabin on the yacht. Oh shit, my phone! How could I have left everything behind without a second thought?

Fuck it. I'll manage. I can't go back now. I'll figure something out.

With as much dignity as I can fake, I walk across the sand toward the hotel. I'm wearing my white bikini and nothing else, but it's a beach resort, so it's not like I'm out of place, right?

In front of the hotel is a faux-shabby beach bar, with reggae playing quietly. It's a chill scene that stinks of money. The guests are predictably self-satisfied: the men are a little bit too sunburned, with the ubiquitous fat guy ostentatiously smoking an expensive cigar. The women are all wearing quasi-Ibizan tunic tops and deep conditioning their sea-and-chlorine-fried hair, pretending they're going for the slicked-back look.

And they're all gazing out, with restless boredom, at the ocean, at the pale twilight sky and the only yacht in sight. The *Hamartia*. It's so weird looking back at it, like it's a toy. A tiny, stupid toy.

Trying to look like I know exactly what I'm doing, I walk up to the bar. "I'll have a Coke, uh, a Coca-Cola, please," I say. "And I'll start a tab."

"Room number?"

"Um, I forgot!" I laugh gaily, trying to look dumb and charming. "My boyfriend will be down any second."

The bartender nods, and serves it up in a huge chilled plastic cup.

Taking big frantic gulps—ah, sweet sugar rush!—I glance around, hoping I look like I belong. I need Internet access so I can e-mail Pia, beg her to get me on a flight home, maybe help me get an emergency passport. . . . God, I wish I'd talked to her more lately. She's my best friend, but I never tell her what's going on with me. I don't even know why. I just always keep everything secret.

"Hey, can I buy you a drink?"

I turn around. Older guy, early thirties, accent. South American, maybe Spanish. Supermacho, in that almost pretty way Spanish guys often are, with dark brown eyes, ridiculously thick eyelashes, and perma-stubble.

"All good here." I hold up my drink.

"Shame," he says. "All I've wanted to do since I got here was meet a blond girl in a white bikini, and buy her a drink." He makes a sad puppy face.

"Oh, okay. I'll have another Coca-Cola." And maybe he'll pick up my tab.

"I'll have the same." The guy nods at the bartender. "I'm Gabriel," he says.

"Angie."

"I'd love to ask you out for dinner, Angie. But I have to go back to New York tonight. My sisters have to be back in the city for some school thing."

I turn around. Two petulant-looking teenage girls are sitting on the sofas behind us. Both have long, swishy brown hair, deeply tanned skin, and are texting furiously.

Then I remember something.

"I thought there were no flights to New York tonight?"

"Ah," he says, picking up his drink. "Well, I have my own airplane."

CHAPTER 9

A few hours later, I'm sitting on board a Gulfstream, halfway back to New York.

For some reason, taking a stowaway back to New York isn't fazing this family at all. I borrowed a pair of jeans and a sweater from Gabriel and a pair of fluffy slippers from his sister Lucia. I look baggy and weird, but it'll keep me from freezing until I get back to Rookhaven. Gabriel has been on the phone for the past half hour, and his sisters and I are tucked up in the corner under blankets, all cozy with gossip magazines, herbal tea, and plates of peanut butter cookies. Being around the girls, and listening to their chatter, has put me at ease for the first time all day. It's almost like being at Rookhaven.

"I am completely over Bieber," says Amada. She's twelve, wears braces, and though she says things with total self-importance, her eyes dart around nervously when she talks. It's adorable.

"Bullcrap. Bieber was practically your first word! You cried at his concerts!" says Lucia, who's fourteen. She's incredibly shy, and talks to Gabriel and Amada loudly and sarcastically to, I think, impress me. I admired her customized jean jacket earlier—she layered a vintage Jordache sleeveless denim vest over a leather jacket, and the result is unbelievably stylish—and she blushed for about ten minutes. God, I would not go back to being a teenager for anything.

Then again, being twenty-two isn't exactly working out that great for me, either. My birthday is coming up way too soon. I really thought I'd have a real career and a serious boyfriend by now. A life, in other words. A life that didn't include being invited to parties and paid to sleep with the host.

Ugh. Don't think about it.

"Where are your things?" asks Gabriel, coming over to talk to me for the first time since takeoff. "How can anyone travel in just a swimsuit?"

If you ever get the chance to hear someone from Madrid say "swimsuit," I highly recommend it. I shrug and try to act nonchalant.

"I'm just that kind of girl, I guess."

"Cool, calm, and collected."

"Mm-hmm." If he only knew the chaos inside me. I turn back to my magazine. "Wow, does anyone actually like Angelina Jolie? Because I just do not get that whole thing."

"She is a goddess, a statue," says Gabriel, looking over my shoulder. "For worshipping. Not for loving."

How can Spanish guys get away with saying stuff like that?

Oh, here's the downlow on Gabriel. I got it all before we left the hotel. He's thirty-four, Spanish, never married, no kids of his own, sold his first tech company when he was twenty-five, works between New York and Silicon Valley, and has an apartment on Columbus Circle. Basically, he's your average run-of-the-mill very rich guy. The girls are his half sisters from his dad's second marriage to an American woman. I get the feeling they're growing up with wealth, and he had to make his own.

Gabriel sits down and picks up *Us* magazine and, for a few minutes, we all read quietly.

"Are you hungry?" he asks.

"Almost always."

"The hotel made me these. Not quite as nice as the avocado and prawn salad I usually get to go when I'm at Eden Rock on St. Barts, but not bad."

Gabriel pulls out some sandwiches that the hotel must have made for him. Freshly cooked fish sandwiches on soft, buttered white bread. Like the ones I ate just a few hours ago on the *Hamartia*.

Suddenly, I've lost my appetite. But I take a sandwich anyway and force myself to eat it. The girls are chattering away.

"St. Barts is boring. I like Turks way more."

"I liked Antigua the best."

"No way!"

Eventually, they calm down and go back to their magazines, and Gabriel turns to me with a little grin. I smile back. His hair is still messy, probably from being on the beach all day, and he has a nice face, if a little pouty-pretty for my taste.

"So, we have to work out what you owe me for this trip."

A cold fear spikes through me. "What?"

"I fly you to New York, smuggle you through passport control, and you think it's all for free?"

My heart is beating in my mouth. Holy shit, not again. . . .

"In return, you have to buy me dinner sometime."

Oh. That's all he meant.

I smile glassily up at Gabriel, trying to look composed, my mind racing.

What *was* I doing, really, walking into a hotel bar in a bikini like a goddamn Bond Girl, confident that somehow, I'd find a way home? I'd just swum God knows how far, all the while thinking how stupid I was for walking into such a horrific situation, how clever I was to not trust that goddamn boat boy who followed me . . . but how stupid was it to trust the next total stranger I met? Just because Gabriel had his sisters with him, just because he seemed nice and polite, I decided to get on his private jet? What the fuck is *wrong* with me?

I keep making the same mistakes. That's why I'm stuck in this ridiculous, destructive holding pattern. I make the wrong choice. Every single time.

I glance up at Gabriel. If it was this time a week ago, I'd date him until he dumped me. I know I would. But that's not what I want anymore. And it's definitely not what I need.

"I'm sorry, Gabriel. I didn't mean to give you the wrong impression. I'm not . . . looking for anything. Uh, romantic." Interesting choice of words.

"Okay," he says, with an "easy come, easy go" shrug. "So you just want to get back to New York and say good-bye, is that it?"

I feel bad. Why do I feel bad? Like I owe him dinner. Like he gets to be with me in exchange for giving me a ride home. Why the fuck am I thinking like that? Sex in exchange for what I want. That's what Stef said. Is that how I think? It's not, it's really not. I accepted those gifts because I never had much spending money and the guys always did. Because I like clothes and nice things, and they liked buying them for me. Because I thought they liked me and I really, really liked them, especially Mani. And most of all, because I thought that when they gave me something, it meant that I was worth being with.

I was wrong.

That's it. My life has been all about guys for far too long.

I want my life to be about me.

I want to be single. I want my home. I want a real job. I want my friends.

And by the time I turn twenty-three, I want to be doing something that *means* something. Either I have a life that I can be proud of, that I earned on my own merits, or . . . or . . . or I don't know what.

Twenty-three is my deadline.

"You sure that's what you want?" repeats Gabriel.

I look up. "I am."

CHAPTER 10

When we land, Gabriel offers me a ride home in their car. He gives me his business card, though I have no intention of calling him, and I thank him and his sisters profusely for being such Good Samaritans. They drop me at the corner of Smith and Union before continuing on to his apartment on Columbus Circle and, shivering from the cold, I walk down the street to Rookhaven.

It's past midnight. Everyone is asleep, and for a moment, as I walk up the stoop of my house in the darker than dark, freezing-cold February night, it feels like the whole sun-filled superyacht experience was just a dream. Or a nightmare.

With the hidden spare key, I open the front door and inhale the warm, comforting Rookhaven smell. Vanilla and cinnamon from the kitchen, the wood polish Coco uses on the furniture, all mixed with everyone's shampoo and perfumes and a sort of papery scent that I always think of as old wallpaper.

I have never been as happy to be in Rookhaven as I am right this second.

Minutes later, I'm tearing through my bedroom like that Tasmanian devil cartoon. Wrenching dresses off hangers, taking jewelry out of drawers, grabbing shoes and underwear, every gift from an ex-boyfriend, ex-flings, ex . . . whatevers. All my labels, all my most expensive clothes . . . Touching them, knowing now why I got them, gives me a cold, scared feeling in the pit of my stomach.

I'm so stupid. How could I have ever thought they actually liked me for me?

I will never trust a man again. Ever. They all lie. They lie and lie and lie. My father lies, Stef lies, Mani and Jessop and Marc and, oh God, all of them. Liars.

Now all that's left in my closet is stuff from H&M and Urban Outfitters and other cheapish places, stuff I borrowed from Annabel and never gave back, and secondhand pieces found in vintage stores and flea markets that I customized to suit just me. I bundle all the designer clothing in a bag to take to Goodwill tomorrow.

But I can't even bear to have the white dress from the Soho Grand night in the house anymore. It was from Mani, the guy I really thought I might be in love with, the guy who took me out for dinner and talked to me like he *cared*. . . . The dress was bought with bullshit.

So I grab it, head downstairs, out the front door, down the stoop, and throw the dress in the garbage.

"Watch out there, girlie, you'll break the lid," says a voice. I turn around. It's Vic, the old guy who lives in the downstairs apartment. I haven't seen him in ages.

"Vic! Hey! What are you doing out here so late?"

"Just sitting." He's all bundled up in an old coat and scarf and hat, perched comfortably on the chair outside his apartment. I can hardly see him, his voice is just rumbling out of the darkness as though it came from Rookhaven itself. "Sometimes I like to get some air. What about you?"

"Um, yeah, air." I don't even know why, but suddenly, I want to tell him everything. "I've made a mistake, Vic. A few actually, really huge mistakes, and I, um, I don't know if I can ever forgive myself."

God, I sound dramatic. Pia would be proud.

"What mistakes?"

"I don't . . ." I take a deep breath. "I don't want to talk about them. Ever. To anyone. But I don't know if I can deal with them alone, either."

"I understand that." Vic and I both sigh into the silence. My breath is coming out all misty, and I'm not even smoking. I'm so tired of being cold. I'm so tired of winter.

Then Vic pipes up again. "Regret . . . it'll kill you. Out of all the negative emotions, regret is the one that will get its claws into your soul."

My throat suddenly aches with the desire to sob, and tears well up behind my eyes. I blink them away quickly. I never cry in front of people. Ever.

"You tried talking to your friends? Your parents?"

"No," I say. "No way."

"You gotta let it go, girlie. Otherwise you'll spend your whole life thinking about it. Trust me. I know. And it's much easier to let go of problems when you share them with the people you love."

"But what if they judge me? What if they hate me for it?"

"Friends don't judge. Friends just listen."

The crying feeling threatens to engulf me again. "But I feel like . . . like this thing . . . this will never leave me. Like there's a permanent mark on my record. A stain on my soul."

"Nothing is permanent. Everything changes. You can choose to let that comfort you, or depress you. Once an event is in the past, it's just a memory."

"A bad memory."

"Sure, sometimes it's a bad memory. You can choose to remember it and hold on to it forever, or you can forget it, and it's like it never happened. You're in control."

"I'm never in control." I start laughing, though the lump of tears in my throat is so big and square it hurts. "I am, by nature, out of control."

"That's your choice, girlie." Vic stands up. "Night night. Sweet dreams."

CHAPTER **11**

"Stef is an evil cockmonkey," announces Pia. "I hope he rots in hell."

"I hope he gets an STD!" says Coco.

"I hope Hal gets an STD," says Julia.

"I can't believe Hal told you his *dick* liked you," says Madeleine.

"Diving into the sea was the best idea ever," says Pia.

"You're so lucky that guy had a private plane!" says Coco.

"And your parents will have a much better relationship now," says Pia.

"Totally. No more fighting, no more problems. Divorce is great!" says Madeleine.

"I wish my parents would divorce!" says Pia.

"Being single is the best! Most of the time," says Julia.

"And you'll get a job in fashion in a heartbeat. Who wouldn't want to hire you?" says Coco.

Don't you just love girls? It's so simple: I walked into the kitchen two hours ago, apologized profusely for being such a nightmare, confessed everything, and received total acceptance, affection, and absolution in return. It surprised me, but this is how they've always treated one another, so it's how they're treating me. I'm part of the group. That probably shouldn't be a surprise, but it is.

Well, I didn't confess *everything*.

I didn't tell them about waking up in the Soho Grand with three thousand dollars in an envelope. I just can't. I told them about the yacht, that Hal had assumed I was, erm, someone who'd take money for sex, that Stef had set me up, that it was a one-off, the culmination of bad luck and bad decisions. They are shocked enough at that. If they knew I've accidentally been playing the part of the happy hooker for the past few months with Mani, Jessop, and whoever the dude was from the hotel room . . . well, I don't want to think about their reaction. How could they not judge me? *I* judge me.

I told them about my parents divorcing. And about being unemployed and my money issues, i.e., that I don't have any.

"And I am sorry for going so wild with the vodka," I said, looking each of them in the eye. "I know I've been, um, unreliable, and unpredictable. And a bad roommate. And I'm sorry. I was feeling crazy, I guess, and I acted accordingly. I'll be different now. I swear."

And then they all started talking at once. It was an orgy of emotional support, a total validation binge.

Just like Vic told me last night, the moment I shared my problems, I felt better. That cold, itchy feeling in my soul started to thaw and ease. I felt lighter, as if the weight that had been pressing down on me, keeping me from laughing or even smiling for the last few weeks, had magically disappeared. Secure is the word, I guess. I felt secure.

Who knew sharing felt so good? I mean, I hated all those late-night compulsory deep and meaningful heart-to-hearts at school, remember them? When all the girls eat junk food and one girl talks about her parents and another talks about her abusive ex-boyfriend and another talks about her body issues and another talks about whatthefuckever and at the end everyone has a Care Bears hug and then the bulimic sneaks off to puke. I wasn't really invited to those talks, mind you. But I was in the dorm when they happened.

Anyway. During my confession, Coco got tears in her eyes, Madeleine frowned, Pia gasped, and Julia clenched her fists and muttered "*Those fuckers*" a lot.

It should have been the easiest to confide in Pia. I've known her, literally, since I was born. But somehow, I felt most scared about her reaction. Maybe because she was always having her own crises, maybe because my parents aren't exactly the pull-up-a-pew types, but I've never really burdened her with my problems before. I always kept everything to myself. Sharing things felt, I don't know, like complaining, like asking for help, like saying I couldn't handle life, like I was weak. Keeping my secrets to myself felt like the only thing I could do . . . well, keeping my secrets, drinking, and falling for the wrong men.

Letting my friendship with Pia drift is just as much my fault as hers, I'm finally realizing. Maybe more my fault. How can she be around for me if I never tell her I need her?

"So that's that," I say finally. "From today, I'm just going to stay single and concentrate on my career. Get a damn job."

"No you're not," says Julia. "It's Saturday. You can get a damn job on Monday. Today you're making up for the whole curtain thing by coming with us to Smorgasburg."

"You're all going?" I don't want to be alone, not when I've got so much to think about. And to try not to think about. "Pia? Even you?"

"Yep. Aidan's in San Francisco till tonight, he had some work thing," says Pia. "It's a special presummer preview event. I'm going as a corporate spy."

"She means she's checking out the competition," Julia explains to a confused Coco. "We're going for the dudes."

"Smorgasburg doesn't worship at the altar of SkinnyWheels?" says Madeleine, making a pretend sad face. SkinnyWheels is Pia's food-truck business.

"Apparently my salads don't cut the Zeitgeist gourmet hand-cut mustard," Pia says sarcastically, but I can tell she's genuinely kind of pissed about it. "So let's go eat quail's egg quiche and banana-cheddar spring rolls and fig-studded mozzarella balls and crazy shit like that."

"And meet some dudes!" Julia cheers. "It's Meet a Dude Day! Angie, are you in? High-five me! Fivies! Come on!"

I'm not the high-fiving type, but Julia grabs my hand and forces me to high-five her.

"There. Doesn't that feel good? Next we'll work on hugs."

At that, I laugh out loud, and suddenly feel happy endorphins flooding my body. Laughing! Who knew it felt so good? Fuck it, why not go with the girls and help them meet dudes? It'll take my mind off . . . everything.

Smorgasburg is a weekly open-air festival of unique foods that grew out of the Brooklyn Flea. By midday, in the interest of getting as many tastes as possible, we've shared fried anchovies, spicy beef noodles, chicken and waffles, chili mozzarella balls, a caramelized-onion-smothered hot dog, a buttery porchetta sandwich, a lobster roll, teriyaki shrimp balls, and a basil-and-raspberry popsicle. Yeah. There's some funky food here, all right.

Julia and I are by far the most enthusiastic eaters. Madeleine is picky and sniffs everything distrustfully before taking a tiny bite, and Coco is staring at the food longingly and talking about it a lot, but hardly touching it. (Between you and me, I think she might have a guilty-secret-eater thing going on, based on the number of times I've come home to find her scarfing Cheerios at midnight.) And Pia is frowning thoughtfully with every bite, taking notes. Apparently it's called "competitor analysis."

"I could do something with basil and raspberries, if they're really going to be the next big thing," she's muttering to herself. "But, *merde,* I need some protein in there, too. With what? Low-fat feta, maybe? Ricotta? Would chicken be too overpowering?"

"Remember when Pia used to be fun?" Julia says to me, handing over a gigantic maple-frosted bacon donut.

"I think I do," I say, taking a bite. "Da-yam, that's good. . . . Was that the Pia who applied Captain Morgan topically to all of life's woes? The same Pia who is now permanently attached to her iPhone and says shit like, 'Let's action that'?"

"Yes! And 'Get back to me by EOP!' "

"What the fuck is EOP?"

"Exactly!"

"So now you're bonding over making fun of me?" says Pia, arching an eyebrow. "Whatever. I don't care, as long as you're getting along."

"Are we getting along?" asks Julia. "Ladybitch? Can I call you that?"

I arch an eyebrow at her. "That's *Sir* Ladybitch to you."

Julia giggles and chokes on some frosting, making a strange quacky-bark sound, and I crack up.

"What are you laughing at?" Pia sounds annoyed. Like Julia and I shouldn't be allowed to have private jokes.

"At Julia," I gasp. "She gagged on some frosting."

"That sounds like a euphemism," says Julia.

"What, like . . . he frosted my mouth?" I say. "Mmm. Glaze me, you stud. . . ."

Julia shrieks with laughter. Pia rolls her eyes.

"Exsqueeze me, but there are no *guys* here," says Coco, looking around plaintively.

Oh, yeah. I nearly forgot. It's Meet a Dude Day.

I do a quick survey of the area. There are hundreds, probably thousands of people here, but she's right. Hipstery girls, young families, older parental types, and bewildered tourists. This is not a target-rich environment for the single girl. You need two or three guys, alone, who are up for some flirty conversation over a drink. Or in this case, an artisan farm-reared slow-pulled-pork organic-sourdough sandwich.

"You could talk to the food dudes," I suggest.

Madeleine laughs. "Ugh, they'd be all obsessed with their work like all food people in Brooklyn."

I glance over at Pia to see if she heard, but she's too busy making notes. What is with Madeleine and the snide comments?

"That guy over there is gorgeous," says Jules. "See him? Next to the chick in the hat?" We all look over. "Don't look now! Jeez, you guys! Oh, shit, he just kissed her. What a dick."

We all sigh in supportive disappointment.

"I think the flaw in the Meet a Dude Day plan is that you need an excuse to talk to guys," says Madeleine. "Like, you know, an activity, a conversation starter. Maybe you should take a cooking course or something."

"Yeah. All hot single guys just love a cooking course," says Pia, deadpan.

"I'm not a joiner. And the flaw in Meet a Dude Day is that we're treating this like an excursion to the dude zoo," I say. "They're not wild animals waiting to be observed."

"No, the Meet a Dude Day flaw is that it's practically impossible to pick up a guy sober," says Pia. "You know, unless you work with him, or you're, like, religious or something."

"So true. Alcohol is a social lubricant," I say. "It makes everything slip just that little bit easier."

"Ew, gross." Madeleine wrinkles her nose.

"You're a sensitive little flower, aren't you?" I say. And a raging bitch, I don't add.

My phone rings. I glance at it quickly. It's Annabel, my mother. But I'm not talking to her until Dad calls me and tells me the full story. So I quickly press silent.

"Excuse me?" asks a voice. We all turn around. A dude! Slightly chubby, has not quite mastered the art of the clean shave, but a dude nonetheless. "I was wondering if you've seen the headcheese? One of my Twitter followers said it was going to be here, but we can't find it."

"Headcheese?" I repeat. "That sounds . . ."

"Fucking disgusting," finishes Julia. "What is it?"

"It's kind of like meatloaf made from the parts of a pig no one else wants to eat. The face, the feet. Sometimes the heart."

We all gaze at him in total horror.

"I think I might be sick," I whisper to Julia.

"I hope I will be," she whispers back. "That shrimp is really repeating on me."

Coco is fascinated. "Wow! Are you a chef?"

"No, I run a food blog called the Hungry Geeksters! You gotta meet my cobloggers, hang on—"

We all turn around as two guys—one tall and flabby, one short and squat—come over. They're not bad-looking, and they seem friendly. For a second, it looks like Meet a Dude Day might actually work out.

Then they start to talk.

Normally, I kind of like geeks. I hung out with them a lot at boarding school. They're easy to make blush, they're smart, they let you sit with them at breakfast. But these geeks are a different breed. Big-city geeks. Boring know-it-alls with superiority complexes who aren't making eye contact and just talking to one another *around* us, if that makes sense. Maybe they have a touch of Asperger's—hey, it's not unlikely, let's be honest—or maybe they just never hung out with people with real live breasts before. Whatever. It's boring me.

". . . and remember that time you ate jellied eel, Gary?"

"That was great! It tasted like river trout cooked in Vaseline."

"You're such a gourmand! That was still our most successful post ever."

After a minute or two Coco is the only one still smiling at them hopefully. Madeleine surreptitiously started texting someone. Pia muttered something about making notes and wandered away. Julia is giving me "get me the fuck out of here" eyes. (You know the look: a stare, into a sort of eye-widening glare, back into a stare.)

Time to take charge. I clap my hands together, hoping it makes me look authoritative. "Well, boys, it's been great, but it's time for us to get home before we turn into pumpkins."

"It's two-thirty in the afternoon," says the chubby geek.

"And I believe that it was Cinderella's coach that turned into a pumpkin, not Cinderella herself," says the spectacled geek.

"Right on." I put a cigarette between my lips and walk away. The other girls follow me. "Why do I always have to play the bitch?" I mutter.

"Well, it just seems to come naturally to you," says Julia, and we both start laughing again.

I think Coco and Madeleine have that slightly dejected feeling you get when you were hoping something would be the highlight of your weekend and it turns out to be totally not. But as we walk home through the frosty afternoon, Jules and I are actually having a good time.

"You have such a cool walk, you know that? You sort of swagger like a cowboy," says Julia.

I arch an eyebrow. "Like I have a dick?"

She cracks up. "No! You just . . . look like you own the world."

"Ha." Yet another thing about my outside that doesn't match my inside. "I'm sorry Meet a Dude Day didn't work out, Jules."

She shrugs. "I haven't met any guys in forever. You know what we need? Some platonic male friends who can introduce us to a continuous flow of new single men," says Julia thoughtfully. "Only dudes know dudes."

"Like a dude dealer?" I say.

"Yes! Exactly like a dude dealer. Or a pimp."

I flinch. Fuck. Stef is a pimp, I guess. A casual rich-kid high-end pimp with a "he needs a girl, you need money" mentality, and hopefully without a switchblade and a sideline dealing meth, but essentially a pimp nonetheless. All day, I've been trying not to think about how I was on the boat this time yesterday, or what was happening to me. . . .

"Sorry," whispers Julia. "I was only messing around."

I turn to her and smile. Man, she's a nice person. "It's okay," I say. And all of a sudden, it is. Just like Vic said: it happened, now it's in the past. I have to let it go. Or at least try.

Coco skips up next to us. "Why did we leave? I liked them!"

"You liked the fact that they were male, Coco. Aim higher," says Julia.

"Harsh," I say, seeing Coco's face fall, before she plasters on her usual "everything's great!" smile.

"Is it? I don't mean to be harsh. Coco, honey, next time you decide you truly like someone, I swear we will all be one hundred percent behind you. Right, Angie?"

"For sure," I say. "I'll get his name printed on a T-shirt with an 'I heart' in front of it."

Coco is trying to act flippant. "Well, I will never meet anyone. I work in a preschool. My job is the least guy-friendly job in the world."

"What about all those hot dads?" Pia finally tunes in to the conversation, though she's still texting someone. Aidan, I bet.

"Are you *serious*? They're old. And married."

"Can you imagine being a wife and having, like, children?" says Julia. "Right now I think it would be easier to learn Russian."

"I could learn Russian in six weeks if I tried hard enough," I say. "But find a dude who might like me for *me* in six weeks? Not a chance."

"Aw, do you have low self-esteem?" Julia pulls my ponytail affectionately.

"No, I really don't," I say. "I just know what guys see in me. And it's never . . . me."

Julia is quiet for a moment, suddenly serious. "I know exactly what you mean. Sometimes I would kick a puppy just to have an interesting conversation with a good-looking guy who also happened to find me attractive."

We stroll along in silence, Julia's words echoing in my head.

An interesting conversation with a guy.

You know, I can't even remember the last time I actually talked to a guy. Like, really *talked*.

Take any of the guys I've dated (please! *Boom, tish*). Mani, Marc, Jessop, Hugh, the guys I met at college, in bars, on vacation . . . My entire life, it's always the same.

They talk, I listen. They joke, I smirk. I never reveal anything about myself, I never trust them enough to show them who I really am or how I really feel, so it's just chase, flirt, party . . . and then sex. Which is always shit, anyway, the kind of sex where afterward I feel inexplicably like crying, and I go to the bathroom alone and look in the mirror and wonder what the hell I'm doing and why I feel empty inside. (Urgh, sorry. Drama, I know. But it's true.)

And then in the morning I always wake up next to them and feel more alone than ever. But I stick around in the hope that next time, they'll try to see past the tough shell I've built over the years. That they'll suddenly *know* me, and I'd understand them and feel a connection. A real connection.

It never happens, of course. Why would a guy bother to get to know me? So I act flippant and cool and tough, and eventually they dump me, and I never hear from them again. They even defriend me on Facebook. Like there is no point in keeping in touch. Like I am disposable.

No wonder I've always liked that moment before the first kiss so much. The prekiss. That is the moment when there is still a chance that this time, it will mean something. Like I might meet someone worth trusting, someone to whom I can show my true self. Like there might be a happy ending.

Never again. Never, ever again. I'm staying single. Forever. I'm staying away from all dudes. Especially rich kids and liars.

And I'm going to get a job in fashion.

CHAPTER 12

I'm never going to get a job in fashion.

In the past week, I've tried everything. I've scoured *WWD*, talked to the few recruitment agencies that specialize in fashion, searched Craigslist and every fashion website and blog. I e-mailed my resume to all my favorite Manhattan-based designers yet again, just in case the last time I sent it last August, when I first got to New York, it was misplaced. I told them I loved creating clothes; I asked if they needed a junior designer, an assistant, a receptionist, a coffee flunky, shoe polisher, anything.

Nothing.

I called everyone nice who I met via my old boss The Bitch food photographer; I phoned Cornelia's contacts that I used to call to pull samples when she was on her way to some gala. I Facebooked, I IM'd, I tweeted. I called back and back and back.

Nothing.

I asked about internships, but they're booked up months or even years in advance, and the problem is that they don't pay anything and I need *money*. I guess this means that every intern in New York either still lives with their parents, or has an enormous salary-type allowance that enables them to pay for a New York apartment and, you know, eat. Which means that only rich kids get fashion internships, and therefore, are first in line and the most qualified for the best jobs. Doesn't that seem fucking stupid to you, by the way? Shouldn't it be the hardest working and most talented people who get the best jobs? Sometimes it seems like being in your early twenties in New York is not survival of the fittest, it's survival of the richest.

So I applied for sales positions in my favorite designers' stores. If you work in a Marc Jacobs store, you've got to meet him at some point, right? I spent all day yesterday going to all the best stores. I filled out forms and left my perfect Julia-approved résumé and smiled so much that my face ached.

Nothing.

Getting a job is the only thing I've thought about, the only thing I've focused on in the past week. When my thoughts slip back to Stef, and Hal, and the yacht, and everything else, I force them forward. *Get a job. Get a life.*

But I'm not getting anywhere. I'm failing.

New York City is rejecting me.

Today it was cold and rainy, a typical March day, so I hid in my bedroom, reading romances and drawing and sewing little bits and pieces. Throwing out all my high-end clothes the other night also ripped a hole in my wardrobe, and obviously I can't afford to go shopping right now, so I decided to take my cheap-ass basics and make them more interesting. For example, I ripped the sleeves off all my shirts and T-shirts. Yes, it's still cold as hell outside. Yes, I should have thought it through a bit more.

Anyway, when Julia found me moping in my room earlier ("Are you sick? I have never, ever seen you in the house on a Saturday night before"), she suggested I get the girls together to "brainstorm a solution." Pia isn't here, of course. She's with Aidan.

But that's okay. I'm in the warm, cozy kitchen at Rookhaven, eating pizza from Bartolo's and drinking wine while it rains outside.

"What the hell is this? I asked for triple pepperoni, this is, like, double at the most," says Julia, peering at her pizza.

"I think there's more than enough processed pig on there," says Madeleine through a mouthful of spinach and ricotta.

Julia sighs. "I guess." She looks up at me. "Pepperoni, Angelface?"

I grin at her and take a slice. There's nowhere else in the world that I'd rather be right now than right here.

"I don't know when I started drinking wine, but I like it," comments Julia. "It just tastes so fucking sophisticated."

"I started drinking wine about the time I got my first period," I say.

Julia cracks up. "You know, I would think you were joking, but I know you too well now. I was drinking Malibu and milk until I was, like—"

"Twenty-two," interrupts Madeleine. Julia flicks her the bird.

"I was allowed watered-down wine at dinner," I say. "Annabel thought it was the mature, European thing to do."

"Well, I'm glad that didn't backfire on her," Madeleine says snarkily. I'm not sure what she means by that, but I'm pretty sure it's not nice.

"Okay. What's the latest with the job search?" asks Julia.

The others look up, waiting for my response. It feels weird—but kind of nice—to be the center of attention in the group. In the past, that's always been Julia, the loud one, or Pia, the drama queen. (I'm probably the one sitting on the sidelines with a drink and a cigarette making comments.)

"Helmut Lang, A.P.C., 3.1 Phillip Lim, Opening Ceremony, Rag & Bone, Acne, Maje, Sandro, Alexander Wang, Marc Jacobs, Steven Alan, Intermix, Scoop . . ." I tick off all the names on my fingers as I chew my third slice of pizza. "I have applied for retail jobs with all of them. Not even a design job, just *retail*! But they still want someone with retail or fashion experience."

"So, plan B," says Julia.

"That was plan B! Plan A was getting a job with the actual designers! Plan B was to be humble. Start from the ground up . . ." I sigh, and look around the table at the girls. "I'm not even eligible for the ground. I'm somewhere below sea level."

"Just keep trying," says Julia. "Madeleine, if you don't man up and finish that fucking pizza I will never talk to you again."

Madeleine picks up her half-eaten slice and takes a tiny nibble. "Look, Angie, it's not like you're the only person looking for a career. The job market is a nightmare right now. Remember that *Newsweek* article? We're Generation Screwed."

"What happens to us, then? What will happen to Generation Screwed? The grads that can't get a job?" I look around the table. "Like, seriously. What if we *never* get jobs? Will we all become homeless? Destitute?"

"What does destitute even mean, anyway?" says Coco.

"It means to not have the basic necessities of life," says Julia. "None of us are in any danger of that."

"So you'll ask your parents for money," says Madeleine.

"Like fuck I will." The words come out far more vehemently than I want them to. The girls all look at me in shock. I mumble out an explanation. "My dad lost a lot of money, you know, in the last few years, the economy and everything . . . and with the divorce, I just, um, I don't want to make his life more difficult."

Everyone is quiet for a moment. No one wants to ask if I've heard from my father. They probably guess that the answer is no. Annabel, meanwhile, has called at least three more times. I still haven't answered. I'll call her back after I speak to my dad.

"What about volunteering at New York Fashion Week?" says Julia. "I just read something about girls who do that to get started in fashion. They dress the models and assemble gift bags, stuff like that."

"New York Fashion Week just finished," I reply. "The next one is months away. Plus, I can't volunteer, I need to earn money."

"Bartolo's is looking for a bartender. Jonah wants to cut his hours back because he got a part on that big lawyer show," says Coco. Jonah is one of Pia's friends, a Williamsburg acting/bartending/beekeeping hipster, you know the type. I think Coco has a crush on him.

"But I want *something* to do with fashion. I need to learn."

And I do. During the interviews last week, store managers kept asking me questions using all these fashion terms I didn't understand. I mean, I know the difference between a bugle bead and a seed bead—I've been reading *Vogue* since I was eight, you pick that shit up—but there's a whole world of other stuff I don't know. Sales terms, merchandising terms, industry acronyms . . . I panicked and bought a bunch of fashion business books. Probably not the best use of my credit limit right now. Oops.

Madeleine speaks up. "What did you study at college again? You were at UCLA, right?"

"Um, yes," I say. "I went to the University of Pennsylvania first, but I transferred because it was too cold in the winter."

"You left an *Ivy League college* for *sunshine*?" Madeleine is stunned.

"Yeah, but . . . it was really cold."

Actually, I left because I thought I was in love with a guy I knew from Boston who went to UCLA, but when I got to L.A. he just dated me—i.e., slept with me—for a few weeks and then didn't talk to me again. But I don't want to tell the girls that right now, not on top of everything else. They'd just feel sorry for me . . . and just because I've been dumped by every guy I've ever been with doesn't make me a loser. (Right?)

"What's this?" says an icy voice, and we all look up. It's Pia. "Having a house meeting without me?"

"It's just an impromptu pizza night!" says Julia.

Pia looks from Julia to me and purses her lips. "Right."

I suddenly realize that Pia is threatened by Julia and me becoming friends. God, I never thought she was that the jealous type. Then again, I don't think she's ever had two of her best friends independently make real friends without her, either. I would know: I've been her best friend forever, and I sure as hell never made an effort with anyone else before Julia.

"Pia, I'm so glad you're here," I say. Pia looks at me with a little more warmth. "I'm having a total career crisis, you know—"

"A lack-of-career crisis," interrupts Julia.

"Totally," I say. "And I really, really need your advice."

"Okay!" Pia sits down happily and grabs the bottle of wine and a slice. Quick to forgive, that's my Pia. But wait a minute—

"Why are you here? Why aren't you with Aidan?" Julia asks the question the same moment I think of it.

"He has a work thing," Pia says, through a mouthful of pizza. "I don't like his coworkers. They're all, like, forty. They patronize me like I'm just a stupid little girl. I'd rather be with you guys."

"Good. We'd rather you were here with us, too." Julia turns to me. "Angie. Let's start with education. What was your major?"

"Anthropology at Penn," I say. "And theater at UCLA."

"Theater!" exclaims Coco excitedly. "I could totally see you as an actress."

"They were cliquey asshats," I say. "I just kept to myself and took as many of the design-led things as I could. I barely passed. Then I applied to the Fashion Institute of Design and Merchandising and to the Art Institute of California. I didn't get in."

"You never told me that." Pia is always shocked when she discovers things I haven't told her. But it's not personal. I never tell anyone anything.

So I just smile. "Rejection is not a good look for me."

"What about *Project Runway*?" exclaims Coco excitedly.

"Like hell."

"I think you should go back to college," Madeleine says. "Apply to FIT or Parsons or something. If this is really what you want, and there are no jobs out there right now, then study more so you can get the advantage over every other fashion wannabe."

"I agree, but I can't," I say. "College costs money."

"No shit," says Pia. "Have you heard from Stef?"

"No," I say. "Hopefully the yacht capsized."

"Do you want to get revenge?" asks Julia hopefully.

I shake my head. "I just want to forget about it. Sweep it under the rug, pretend it never happened. That's the way I was brought up." I'm kidding, kind of, but no one laughs, so I get up to grab my sea salt caramels from the fridge and toss two to Julia. I found out this week that she shares my sea salt obsession. "Anyway, I have bigger things to think about. Like my career. Or lack thereof."

"You should start a blog," says Julia. "A fashion blog."

"Everyone has a fucking blog," I reply, through a mouthful of caramels. "I want a *job*. I want something I can feel passionate about."

I flush slightly, embarrassed to hear myself talk so emotionally about wanting something. Being this open isn't really my style.

"You should start your own line," says Pia, reaching over for a caramel.

"My own line of what?"

"Accessories," she says thoughtfully. "Leather bags, or bracelets, or something like that. Something that's one size fits all, right? So you don't need to worry about fitting models and stuff like that, and women of all body types can buy them."

"You are a terminal entrepreneur." Another snide remark from Madeleine.

"All I'm saying is, every woman wants at least one new bag every season," says Pia.

"I don't," says Julia.

"It's a great idea, ladybitch, but I don't know how to do leatherwork," I say. "I wish I did. I wonder if I could take a class . . . Wait, that would cost money. So would materials to start my own line. And I still need to pay rent, remember? And have a life."

It always comes back to money.

"Anyway, I don't want to run a business," I add. "I just want a job." Silence. I guess my career crisis talk is over. And we didn't find a solution. I take a cigarette out and prop it in the corner of my mouth. "Well, thanks again for listening, you guys. I'm not sure how the whole group-hug thing works but let's just pretend I instigated one."

"Poker time!" says Julia, throwing me the deck of cards we always keep in the kitchen. "Shuffle up, Angelface. I'm gonna wipe the floor with you guys. That's why they call me the Swiffer."

"I think you mean they call *us* the Swiffer," I say. "If we're the ones you're wiping the floor with, you know? If you're *doing* the wiping, we should call you the maid or something."

Julia snorts. "The maid. Hilarious."

Coco leans over and gives me a huge hug.

"Thanks," I say.

"You don't have to thank people for hugs," says Julia. "You just have to hug them back."

"Oh, my God, I've got it," says Madeleine. "Look."

She throws *New York* magazine open on the table in front of me.

It's an ad. For salespeople.

At the Gap.

There's silence.

I stare at Madeleine in slight disbelief, my cigarette wilting in the corner of my mouth. She stares back, a sunny "isn't this hilarious" smile on her face.

Suddenly, I don't want to play poker anymore.

"I'm going upstairs."

I stomp up to my room, flop down on my bed, and stare at the ceiling, trying to fight the tears pooling in my eyes. Hello again, empty gray bedroom. Hello again, empty gray life.

I'm so lost.

I automatically reach into my nightstand, shove aside my Harlequin and M&M's. There's no vodka, but then miracle of miracles, at the very back, I find half a bottle of Wild Turkey I'd totally forgotten was there. It's not my favorite tipple, but it does in a pinch. Guaranteed escapism.

As I'm unscrewing the lid, cigarette propped in the corner of my mouth, it suddenly hits me.

This is the moment that everything always goes wrong for me.

The moment that I walk—or dive—away from my problems. That I leave the restaurant, bar, house, car, party, conversation, or, let's not forget, yacht. The moment that I press the self-destruct button and bury myself in booze, or drugs, or men, in order to pretend that I'm feeling better than I am. That I'm not alone.

I swivel up to sitting, placing my feet on the floor with a thump, and put the alcohol back in the nightstand, the cigarette back in the pack.

At that moment, the doorbell rings.

Then there's a *thumpthumpthump* of Coco running up the stairs, screaming my name.

"Angie! Angie, it's a guy, he says he wants to see you, something about the yacht, I didn't ask him in, I didn't know if you'd want me to—"

Hal? Stef? Heart hammering in fear, I jump up and run out of the bedroom and downstairs, almost before Coco has finished talking.

The guy waiting politely outside the front door in the freezing cold is so bundled up in a huge coat, boots, and hat that you can barely see his face. But I recognize him immediately.

It's the tall, annoying dude with the intense frown. The clean-cut one who laughed when I was stuffing my face with sandwiches and followed me in the dinghy all the way to shore.

It's the boat boy.

Sam.

CHAPTER **13**

"What do you want?"

"I . . . Wow, really? That's how you say hi?"

I take a deep breath. *Calm, Angie, calm*. . . . What the hell is Sam the boat boy doing at my house in Brooklyn? Thousands of miles away from Turks and goddamn Caicos?

I look up at Sam and try to maintain eye contact. He's at least six foot four. I hate the way men being taller than us automatically puts us at a conversational power disadvantage, don't you? But I can feel the girls hovering protectively behind me in the hall, which gives me the confidence to just talk normally rather than slam the door in his face. "Hi. What do you want?"

Sam smiles, all perfect teeth and effortless confidence. "I've got your stuff. Your weird coat. Your bag. Your—"

"My stuff!" I'm delighted. "Thank you thank you thank you! Ahh!" My fur/army coat! My makeup! My passport! The clutch that I made out of vintage silk scarves! I already replaced my old phone, but I got to keep my number, thank God.

"Also I wanted to see . . . see if you were okay." He frowns, as if not sure how to say it.

I frown back. "I'm just peachy."

"Really? That was pretty wild."

This guy is a living reminder of a memory I'd do anything to erase. I just want to get rid of him, though I can feel the burning curiosity of everyone in the hall.

"Yes, thank you." I affect my coldest voice. "It was a difficult situation, but—"

"From what I could see, you handled yourself perfectly."

"I screamed a lot and dived into the sea."

"Exactly. By the way, we weren't formally introduced. I'm Sam Carter," he says, holding out a hand. "And you're Angie James."

"Yep." I open the door wide, so he can see the girls, or more to the point, so they can see him. "And these are my roommates. Julia, Pia, Coco, and Madeleine." I turn to them to explain. "He was working on the yacht. For the dude. Hal. The party guy—"

"Really!" Julia struts to the door. "Listen up, buddy. You tell your coke-addled cockmonkey boss—"

"He's not my boss," interrupts Sam. "He just chartered the yacht for a week. Like a rental. He's gone, and the crew guy, Carlos, who was supplying the drugs for the—cockmonkey, did you say?—to get addled with, he's gone, too."

"This is the guy who followed me in the dinghy," I say to them. "The boat boy."

"Oh! Hi!" The girls are delighted. They loved that part of the story.

"Aren't you gonna ask him in?" says Pia.

"You should totally come in," agrees Julia.

Madeleine and Coco pipe up in unison. "Totally!"

I look around at them in surprise, then back at Sam. Oh. They've decided he's hot. He does look pretty good, I guess. Tan and healthy and rested, a novelty at the end of an extra-long New York winter when everyone else looks like an anemic sneeze.

But I'm not interested in dudes right now. And I'm definitely not interested in him. I don't like blond guys, I don't like outdoorsy guys, and I never, ever like guys who saw me being treated like a . . . well, you know. In fact, I'd like to never see him again. Effective immediately.

"Sam has to go home." The girls make disappointed noises, so I turn around to give them a "quit it" face. Then I turn back to Sam. "Thanks again, man. Sayonara—"

"May I trouble you to use your restroom?" Goddamn, is this the politest dude in the world? "I walked all the way here from the place I'm crashing in Fort Greene, it was farther than I thought, and—"

"Oh, my God, you must be freezing!" exclaims Julia, before I can say no. "Come on in!"

And boom, next thing I know, Sam's coat is off, Coco's handing him hot chocolate, Julia's leading him into the living room, Pia's grinning at the whole spectacle like it's the Rookhaven puppet show, and even Madeleine, who I've *never* seen act gaga over a guy, is putting on some French Nouvelle Vague music.

"I was singing this song, last night, uh, I've been singing with this band? You should come see us. . . ." Madeleine is saying. She and Julia have sandwiched him down between them on the sofa. Real cozy.

"I've got to call Aidan." Pia heads upstairs, leaving the single girls to their prey.

"So, um, Sam? You're a sailor?" asks Coco, blushing pink. She's hovering around the bookcase, trying to look busy.

"I am." Sam seems remarkably unperturbed by all of this. "Some people call us boat boys." He glances at me with a smirk. "We call ourselves crew."

I roll my eyes. *Some people.* I heard someone call them boat boys once, how was I to know?

Coco is impressed. "And working on yachts is your, like, career?"

"Looks that way. Though I'm looking for a new job right now."

"We're having a party next Saturday," Julia blurts out. "You should totally come."

I stare at her. "We are?"

"Yes! The dinner party, remember? For . . ."

"For Pia's twenty-third birthday!" says Coco quickly.

"Yes! It's a surprise dinner party. Right, Angie?"

I arch an eyebrow. "Right. Because who doesn't want a surprise dinner party." The fact that I share the same birthday as Pia, and that it's not for weeks, hasn't crossed anyone's mind.

"It's going to be sick," Julia adds. "And, and, and Madeleine's gonna sing!"

"I am? I am!" says Madeleine.

"And um, and Coco's gonna cook—Coco, what are you going to cook?"

We all turn to Coco, who is pink under the pressure of having to lie on the spot. ". . . Food?"

"Right, Coco's cooking food and I'm making this awesome punch."

"Sure," says Sam. "Sounds great. I'm crashing at my buddy's house, but he's away right now. Is it okay if I come alone?"

"You're new here? Oh, my God! Then you have to come!"

Please, God, don't let Julia hump his leg.

"I'd love to. What time should I be here?"

"Oh, seven-thirty. No! Eight. Yeah. Eight o'clock."

"Sweet," I say. "Can't wait. A dinner party. Right on. Well, Sam, thanks for stopping by—"

"Guess I should get going." Sam stands up, to the obvious disappointment of everyone else.

"And thank you, again, so much, for bringing back my stuff," I say, opening the front door for him as he puts on his coat. Then something occurs to me. "How did you know where I live?"

"Easy," he says. "I waited until that Stef guy was totally out of it, then I asked him. He would have told me anything."

"Wow. Crafty."

"Yeah. Weird thing, though. That same night, his phone and his wallet and passport fell overboard." Sam puts his hat on, his gray eyes looking very serious. "He doesn't remember what happened. He said he had them one minute, the next . . ." Sam mimes throwing something really far away.

"You didn't."

Sam grins and then turns and walks down the stoop. "It seemed like the right thing to do. See you Saturday."

When I get back upstairs, I remember.

The three thousand dollars. That envelope of cash that, though I hate its existence and the quasi-mystery of its origins, would come in pretty handy right now for paying for rent and, you know, life.

I reach into the inside pocket of my fur/army coat.

It's gone.

There's nothing in there but a little note, folded up.

Go fuck yourself, Angie.

Stef.

CHAPTER 14

I'm in a Starbucks on Seventh Avenue, just off Thirty-seventh. The throbbing heart of the Fashion District of New York City. Not that you'd know it by the streetscape: it's pretty fucking depressing, especially on a rainy March day like today. A lot of cheap bead shops. Everything is happening off the street, in the offices upstairs. That's where the production facilities and showrooms are for most big designers.

I'm (sort of) reading today's issue of *WWD*, the fashion industry newspaper, and (mostly) looking out the window.

My plan is to sit here, make my coffee last as long as possible, and look like I work in fashion.

Maybe a fashion person will come to Starbucks and we'll start talking about my semi-ironic Hello Kitty umbrella and that will lead to a job. Maybe I'll be reading about someone in *WWD* and look up and, boom, there they'll be and I'll be like "wow!" and they'll be like "aw shucks" and that will lead to a job. Maybe I'll meet someone, and they'll know someone, and they'll know someone, and that will lead to a job. You know the six degrees of separation, the theory that you're only six people away from anyone else in the whole world? It's just like that: I'm six degrees away from getting a job.

Where did this crazy hopefulness come from? Rookhaven, I guess, particularly Julia and Pia. They're so fucking can-do and optimistic, it's worn away my natural cynicism.

A young guy in a fedora, carrying a huge white umbrella, wheels seven dressmaker's dress forms tied together past on the street—you know, the headless, limbless soft mannequins that you pin dresses to—and my heart jumps. I wonder where he's going! I bet he's wheeling them somewhere for a designer. Maybe Anna Sui or Michael Kors is going to be touching those dress forms in, like, five seconds. My grandmother had one of those dress forms. She called it Elsie.

Suddenly, the rope breaks, and the dress forms spill out from the plastic sheet covering them, careening all over the sidewalk. I can see him panicking, so I jump up, grab my stuff, and run outside.

"I'll help you!" I say.

"Thank you!"

Most stayed under the plastic sheet and are damage-free, but one dress form rolled straight off the sidewalk into a huge black puddle. As I pull it out, fumbling with my Hello Kitty umbrella and my bag at the same time, I notice a shard of glass has somehow embedded itself in the side, and the wire frame at the bottom is bent.

"Oh noooooo!" The fedora guy is freaking out.

"Drowned and then stabbed," I say. "Fashion kills, huh?"

"Shitballs! What am I gonna do? She's destroyed!"

"She's fine!" I say. "You could spray and soak the mud off. Good as new!"

He's really freaking out. "Don't touch her! She's revolting!"

"It's just a little mud!"

"No! She's only fit for the garbage now. My boss is going to *kill* me! Fuck it, I'll throw her in the Dumpster."

He reaches out, but I snatch the dress form away from him. "No, don't, I'll take her!"

"You will?" he says, smiling and tilting his head to one side. "Who are you? And what do you do?"

"Angie James," I say, holding out my hand. "I'm a fashion designer."

That's the first time I've ever said those words. They feel good coming off my tongue. Even though, strictly speaking, I don't think they're true. Yet.

"Philly Meyer," he replies. "I'm a milliner and DJ, but I'm interning right now for Sarah Drake."

"Nice," I respond, smiling. Sarah Drake! I know about her. She was a protégé of Narciso Rodriguez and then they had some sort of huge bust-up. She just started her own label creating one-off pieces that are more like avant-garde art than fashion.

"Yeah. She's a stickler for time, so I have to run."

Before I can say anything, he turns and herds the six remaining dress forms around the corner.

Quickly I write his name down. *Philly Meyer.* Wow. One degree of separation from Sarah Drake, two degrees from Narciso Rodriguez. I'm so going to Facebook him later.

I turn and look at the dress form. She's pretty high-end: the kind you can make bigger or smaller, thinner or fatter, so you can fit whatever you're making to any specific size. She's covered in a rough cream canvas—though now, of course, it's stained with filthy New York puddle water, and the gash in her side is fairly unsightly, too.

But I can fix her. Underneath all the stains, she's still good.

I walk back into Starbucks, wheeling the dress form as I go, and as I'm lining up for another coffee I notice the woman in front of me.

Candie Stokes.

She was a stylist, got lucky with an Oscar winner a few years ago, and now runs a website called *What to Wear Now.* It's one of those fashion blogs that somehow rode the first blog success wave and just got bigger and bigger. Last time I checked, she was working with Neiman Marcus and Piperlime to create some über-fashion-blog empire. She looks a little tan-and-smoke-addled, and she's the size of, like, an elf, but damn! She's a fashion person! I knew my plan would work!

Okay. So what do I say?

Let's just go with the old reliable.

"Candie Stokes!" I am too nervous to sound anything but hyper. "I'm a huge fan!"

She turns, sees my muddy dress form, and instantly smiles. Heavy makeup and four-inch heels. "I don't think we've—"

"Angie James. I'm a fashion designer." It's getting easier and easier to say that. "I'm also an illustrator and photographer." Where did that come from? Well, it's true. Kind of. I draw. I take photos. Sometimes.

Candie's smile disappears. "Really. Ever been paid to design clothes?"

"Um, no."

"Ever been paid for an illustration?"

". . . No."

"And your photography? Ever been paid for that?"

I can hardly get the word out. "No."

Candie's eyes flick up and down. I'm wearing jeans, white studded Converse, layered sweaters, my fur/army coat, and an old trapper hat. My face is smeared with yesterday's eyeliner, because I forgot to take it off and left the house without bothering to do anything about it, and my hair is dirty and gathered in a topknot. I thought I looked kind of punk and tough, but now I wonder if I look like someone you see drinking cans of beer outside a train station.

"What, exactly, do you design?"

"Um, I'm just starting out. I want to work in fashion though, and I, um, I would love to talk to you sometime." I try to sound professional and enthusiastic, like Pia would. I grab my Moleskine sketchbook. "You can see my ideas—"

"No," she says decisively, picking up her coffee.

"Could we maybe swap numbers, or I could Facebook you—"

"No." She walks away, then pauses, and comes back, lowering her sunglasses, her bloodshot eyes staring hard at me. "You ever see that movie *Working Girl*? Melanie Griffith? Before your time, I bet. Well, there's a line in it. 'Sometimes I sing and dance around the house in my underwear. Doesn't make me Madonna. Never will.' Think about it."

She puts her sunglasses back on and walks away.

"Bitch," I say under my breath, in an attempt to master the panicky fear inside me. She treated me like I was nothing. Like I was totally worthless.

I'm never going to get a job.

I turn and face the barista, just as he hands over my black coffee.

He smiles, whispering loudly, "I'm launching a Navajo-inspired jewelry line in the fall! You should check out my blog! We could collaborate on something!"

Suddenly I just want to go home.

I wheel my dress form out of Starbucks. She looks as dejected as I feel. I'm going to call her Drakey. As a reminder to myself that the Sarah Drakes of the world probably didn't get their first job hanging out in Starbucks.

I walk toward the subway along Seventh, along the Fashion Walk of Fame. Do you know it? It's like that Hollywood thing, only instead of dead movie stars, each star honors American design legends. From Mainbocher to Diane von Furstenberg to Donna Karan to Norma Kamali. They've all walked this exact sidewalk. They all started out with nothing more than a love for fashion and a desire to create clothes, just like me. And they all made their lives happen.

Just like I can't.

CHAPTER 15

"SURPRISE!"

"Pia's not here yet. More to the point, Sam's not here yet."

"I'm practicing, and I'm, I'm—Oh, gotta go. Nervous pee."

I'm sitting on the sofa reading an old issue of *W*—because I can't afford the new one right now—while Jules and Coco snipe at each other in an affectionate sisterly way and put the last touches on the dining table for Pia's so-called surprise dinner party.

Pia's birthday is the same day as mine, and it's not for ages. Our mothers met in the maternity ward, for Pete's sake; they became friends so we became friends. But I'm glad everyone's forgotten. I don't want a big deal about a birthday that I always thought would be a huge milestone of adulthood and is turning out to be a reminder that I'm failing my twenties.

Madeleine screams from upstairs. "The freaking hot water is gone again!"

"Give it twenty minutes!" Julia shouts back.

"I don't have twenty minutes!"

Coco skips back into the room. Her face is unusually flushed.

"Are you okay?" I say to her.

"I'm great!" she exclaims. "I'm so excited. I asked this guy Ethan I met at my friend from work's birthday drinks? He's her roommate's friend from college's coworker? He's nice! He's said yes."

"Have you been drinking already?" I look at her closely.

"I pregamed!" She stands up and does a twirl. "WOO!"

I think the pressure of throwing a party is getting to all of us, but we've managed to prepare perfectly. Coco has been cooking individual chicken pot pies all day. I picked up some cheeses from Stinky. Pia bought Brooklyn Blackout from Steve's Ice Cream. Madeleine has been cleaning all day, including vacuuming the inside corners of the sofa and Q-tipping the fridge. Julia bought a bunch of early hydrangeas, her favorite flower, to put on the side table in the front hall. And we've invited one "date" each, to make it seem "totally normal."

"Like a trash-or-treasure party!" Julia said. "Bring a dude you haven't ever been involved with, and he might be perfect for someone else!"

Coco defied Julia's trash-or-treasure rules and invited this Ethan guy she's crushing on, Madeleine asked Heff, a guitar player from the band she sings with, and Jules asked Lev, some coworker from the bank. I literally could not think of a single man to bring that I haven't ever been involved with. (How depressing is that?) So I just decided my contribution is Sam. Whoever wants him can take him.

Julia is frantically polishing the wineglasses. "These things are refuckingvolting! How do you clean ancient glass? This one has lipstick marks from, like, before I was born."

"Baking soda and vinegar!" says Coco, running out of the room again. "Soak and scrub!"

"That seems like a lot of work." Julia puts the glass down.

I look over at her for the first time tonight. "What the *what* are you wearing? Those pants are wrong on, like, eight levels. Were you drunk when you bought them?"

"No! I was fifteen. Fuck! What should I wear then, fucking fashion guru of awesomeness? I hate all my clothes."

"Come on. I'll find you something."

Julia stomps behind me, up to my room. God, she's tense. She must really like Sam. Is he genuinely that good-looking?

I open my closet and frown as I skim the racks. "Let's see, you're bigger than me in the boob department—"

"And the ass department—"

"This is killer." I pull out a little black dress that I got from the Brooklyn Flea. "Black tights, borrow these shoes. And take your hair out of that damn ponytail."

Julia takes the clothes obediently. "Turn around. I don't do the public nudity thing like you and Pia. And I like my ponytail. I get a headache when I take it out."

"That's your hair follicles going, ooo, finally! We can stretch!" With my back to Julia while she changes, I do an imitation of hair follicles stretching, and she cracks up.

"You are not the cool bitch I always thought you were, Angie James."

"And you're totally the tactless sweetheart I always thought you were, Julia Russotti."

"Okay, you can turn around now. Is this right?" She's trying to tie the dress, but she's doing it all wrong. I take over. "Thanks," she says, suddenly relaxing a tiny bit. "I'm not good with the whole fashion thing. I fear change. You won't believe me, but I wore the same jeans every single day in high school. I washed them at night."

"I believe you, trust me. . . . So who's this Lev guy?" I ask, arranging Julia as though she were a doll.

"Lev? No one. I mean, he's my friend, kind of. I sit next to him at work. I like him, but I don't *like* like him. . . . Apart from him, I don't like any of the guys I work with at all. There are twenty guys on my team, and all of them except Lev treat me like I'm invisible and don't have a voice, like nothing I say is worth listening to." She's babbling now, her nerves kicking in. "Do you know what it's like to say something and have everyone act like no one has spoken? It fucks with your mind. Um, but I like Sam, I really do. In fact, he's the first guy I've liked since Mason, remember him?" I don't, but I nod anyway. "Sam is so fucking gorgeous, don't you think?"

I shrug. "He's a bit . . . clean-cut, isn't he? You know. Preppy. Square."

"Classic, you mean! He's like a Ralph Lauren model. Or Abercrombie & Fitch."

"Julia, Abercrombie & Fitch models are like, twelve years old."

"Well, whatever. He won't like me, I know he won't, they never do. I'm going to be single forever and I will never get any action ever again. My sugar is never going to see another wang."

"First, if you call them wangs and sugars, then, fucking hell yes, you're never going to get any action."

"May I call them both junk? Just generically?"

"No, you may not. Let's start with penis and vagina and take it from there. Or you can say dick and p—"

"Don't say that word! I hate that word."

"Fine. Second, of course he'll like you! Just be yourself."

Pretty rich coming from me since I've always found my personality at the bottom of a vodka bottle, but whatever.

"Really?" she says. "I just, ugh, it's so weird. . . . Putting myself out there is totally out of my comfort zone."

She's never talked to me like this before. In the past I would have assumed it's because her go-to confidante, Pia, isn't around much, but actually, I know that's not true anymore. Julia and I are friends now. Real friends.

"I haven't liked anyone like this in ages. What if he doesn't like me back?"

"Of course he'll like you back!" I say. "Sit down. You need eyeliner. When you look tough, you'll feel tough."

"Is that your secret to success?" she says, sitting down and closing her eyes.

I take out my eyeliner bag. "Right on. My success."

Julia glances down. "Whoa. You have, like, sixteen black eyeliners?"

"Yeah. It really depends on my mood. Gel, cake, liquid, pencil . . ."

"Just make me pretty. Prettier, anyway."

"You have amazing eyelashes."

"Why do chicks always say that to each other?"

For a minute or two, while I draw punk-yet-pretty eyeliner around Julia's eyes, we sit in silence. I'm good at eyeliner. The secret is getting it right into the lashes and waterline, and if you mess it up, just smudge it a bit. Perfect eyeliner is too amateur makeup blogger, you know?

"Look up. Okay, close your eyes."

"How's the job stuff going?" asks Julia.

"Hashtag fail. I have officially been rejected by every fashionista in New York City. Okay, open your eyes, look up."

"You can always get a job at the Gap."

"Double ha," I say.

"Madeleine was just kidding, you know," says Julia. "She thinks you're still pissed at her."

"I am, a little," I say. "That Gap comment the other day was so bitchy and demeaning."

"She's lovely, she really is. You just have to get to know her, that's all."

"I don't want to get to know her. She says that shit and it just . . . it cuts."

Julia looks at me funny.

"What?" I say.

"Pia told you," she says in a low voice.

"Told me what?"

"About Madeleine and the . . . Oh. She didn't."

"What?" I cast my mind back. What did I just say? "Cuts? Madeleine *cuts* herself?"

"Not anymore," says Julia quickly. "Please, forget I said anything."

I can't believe Pia didn't tell me something so big. . . . Though really, it figures, it's not like she talks to me lately anyway. But if Madeleine doesn't do it anymore, then it's not a problem, right? And why should I worry? She's not even nice to me. She's always so goddamn standoffish and sarcastic. I guess I can be, too, but . . . never mind.

"Look! Beautiful!" I say, handing Julia a mirror.

She takes a moment to gaze at herself. "Wow. If I could press a 'Like' button, I would. Thank you, Angelface."

"You're welcome, Ju . . . Ju . . ." I try to think of something cute to do with her name. "Juicy Fruit?"

She wrinkles her nose at me.

"Don't make that face or you'll never get laid."

At that moment the doorbell rings. Coco whizzes past my door heading upstairs.

"Oh, my god! It's Ethan! I know it is! Sugar! I'll be back in a minute!"

"What if it's Sam? I need to brush my teeth!" Julia runs to the bathroom.

I walk downstairs just as Madeleine opens the front door. It's Sam and Madeleine's date, Heff the musician guy. He's hot, in a skinny, put-the-crack-pipe-down-and-eat-a-fucking-burger kind of way.

"Mad!"

"Heffy!"

Madeleine and Heff hug, leaving Sam and me awkwardly not hugging.

"Sam."

"Angie."

Sam leans down to kiss me hello on the cheek. I'm not expecting it, so I sort of jump, and then frown because goddamnit, I am cooler than that.

"Don't you look all cute when you make an effort," I say. Sam is all stubbly and scruffy, very different from my first impression of the Nazi Youth, slick, boat-boy (sorry, crew) hair.

"I was just thinking the same about you," he says.

Yeah, right. I am not looking my best. I'm wearing a secondhand blouse I customized by cutting the sleeves off, the only cheap-ass jeans I could find that weren't too wrinkled to wear, and Converse, and I braided my hair instead of washing it.

Compared to all my roommates in heels and shiny blowouts, I look boring as hell. Which is new for me. And kind of nice. I realized today that I used to make clothes do the talking for me. I let my leather pants or four-hundred-dollar jeans tell people that I was a tough, important bitch they'd better not fuck with. But for the way I'm feeling at the moment, I don't want to be noticed at all.

And I don't own any four-hundred-dollar jeans anymore, anyway.

Sam hands over two bottles of wine just as Coco and Julia bounce downstairs, flushed with excitement, and immediately attack Sam with giggles and bashful questions. I look over at Madeleine, who is talking to Heff about some new band in Williamsburg, but he's one of those cool types who talks in a low monotone drawl so no one farther than fifteen inches away can hear a goddamn word.

God, where is Pia already? She's one of those people who makes a party work. She's the ultimate mixer, like tonic and lemon. I usually hide in the corner at parties, ignore everyone, and drink until I find my personality and/or a guy chats me up. But not tonight.

Julia claps her hands like a headmistress. "Right! Who's thirsty?"

We dole out Julia's punch—vodka, canned peach juice, sparkling white wine, and crème de cassis. Sam takes one sip, chokes slightly, and wordlessly accepts the beer I slip him.

Coco is positively flying. "Woo! This punch is punchy! Am I right?"

The doorbell rings, and she leaps to get it.

"Hiiiiiiiiiiiiiiiiiiii!"

Coco leads Ethan into the room like a proud owner at a dog show.

"Everyone, this is my date!"

"I'm Ethan," he says in a Kermit the Frog voice. "*Enchanté*."

Ethan is a short, stocky guy wearing a blue plaid shirt and red plaid trousers. Without irony. (You always need to check for sartorial irony, especially in Brooklyn, but trust me, I know this guy is not being ironic.)

And his conversation is worse than his fashion sense. "So I thought, well, I'll take the L train, and descended a stairway that led me to a train heading in the wrong direction! I had to ascend to street level and cross to find the train that would take me to the correct destination! Now, take it from a Chicago man: there's a flaw in the system! In fact, as I was—"

That's it. I'm having a smoke to kill some time. I sneak out to the front hallway, pull on my fur/army coat, and head outside to the stoop. I can almost-but-not-quite feel the thaw in the March air. Time to lose the fur/army coat soon. Yay. I mentally start going through my jackets and blazers. . . . Ah, clothes. Always a comfort, especially when I'm feeling alone.

"You know, smoking is bad for you."

I glance over. It's Sam, standing next to me, looking out at the night.

"I heard that." I take a drag and frown. "I don't actually like cigarettes that much unless I'm drinking."

"You're not drinking?"

"Not really. I mean, I haven't officially 'quit' drinking or anything. I hate it when people do that."

"Yeah, it's so annoying."

"I'm just dialing it down for the foreseeable future. Vodka applies pressure to my self-destruct button."

"Good to know."

Sam glances over at me, a tiny smile on his face. He's very self-assured, but not arrogant. An unusual combination, at least in the dudes I've known. His nose is ridiculously straight. Like something from a coin. Regal. Or whatever you call noses you see on coins.

At that moment we see Pia and Aidan walking up Union Street toward us, gesturing intensely. Pia looks upset. They're fighting?

"I can't believe you'd do this to us—" she's saying, then glances up. "Angie?"

"Um, hi!" We have to continue the surprise party charade. "Pia, pretend to be shocked, okay? Just count to thirty, come in, and be like, 'Holy shit!' Dial up the drama, okay?"

"What? A surprise party? It's not my birthday!"

Before she can say anything else, I stub out my cigarette on the stoop, grab Sam's arm, and pull him back into the house. Pia and Aidan might be fighting, but I'll find out more later.

Sam raises an eyebrow. "It's not her birthday? This is a *pretend* surprise party?"

I smile at him and shrug, just as Julia lurches around the corner and pounces on Sam. "There you are! Would you like some more punch?" Then she cocks her head. "I hear them! Everyone hide! Hide!"

We all scramble to our assigned hiding places. Julia's date, the guy she works with, hasn't even turned up yet, I realize. Not that she's noticed. Sam and I are both behind the sofa. Our eyes meet, and he gives an incredibly dorky pretend-excited face. I try not to laugh and make a bursting sound.

"Angie!" hisses Julia.

Sam shakes his head at me and makes a "shh!" sound.

A few seconds later, as we're all crouched in the dark, Pia and Aidan walk into the living room.

"SURPRISE!"

"OH, MY GOD!" Pia screams, jumping up and down in pretend shock.

"Great acting skills," says Sam under his breath, as Julia and Coco yell and clap in delight.

"You should see her do an anxiety attack, seriously," I reply.

"She's a faker?"

"Oh, no," I say. "I think her emotions are real. I'm just saying that she really lets you know what she's feeling. She's highly expressive."

"Jeez, I could be collapsing inside and my face would look just the same to everyone around me," says Sam.

"Me too," I say. "It's my curse."

Sam's perma-frown turns into a grin, just as Julia walks up to us and downs her punch in one gulp. "Let's eat!"

Coco's face falls. "Oh, my god, the pies."

At that moment the smoke alarm goes off.

CHAPTER 16

Okay, the kitchen stinks of smoke, the house is now freezing because we opened all the windows for fresh air, and the pies are charred beyond saving. But the party is going strong. There was a team decision to have ice cream and cheese for dinner, and as a result, everyone is shitfaced and acting—to use a phrase I was fond of in my teens—totally wack.

Pia is ignoring Aidan. This never happens, they're usually sparkling at each other all night like two little birthday candles. I am waiting for the right time to ask her if she's okay, but right now, she's ranting at Madeleine and Heff, who are so stoned they can't respond. That never *ever* happens. I'd bet money Madeleine's experience of drugs up to now doesn't even extend as far as Midol PM.

Julia has stopped talking entirely and is just staring at Sam like he's television.

And Coco is hopping around like a big-boobed fairy on ecstasy, dancing to one of her favorite CDs (Will Smith's *Greatest Hits,* of all goddamn things), turned up to eleven. Sam and Aidan are the only people actually talking: they're discussing some scandal involving a Yankee or a Jet or something.

"What do you think of Ethan?" Coco whispers, hiccupping into my ear. "I asked Jonah? But he said no, he said no."

"He was probably just busy," I whisper back.

"No, he doesn't like me." Coco suddenly looks incredibly sad.

The doorbell rings. I head out to answer it.

It's a tall guy wearing a human-size Mighty Mouse outfit. What the?

"Tricksh and treatsh?" Ah. He's drunk out of his skull.

"Dude, it's March," I say, closing the door.

"I'm Lev." His eyes are crossing with the effort of getting the words out. "I'm here for a party dinner?"

"Dinner party."

"There was a party bachelor last night? In City Atlantic? So I'm . . . late. Where am I? You're pretty. You're so pretty. Are you my date?"

"No."

"Will you go out with me?"

"No."

I lead him into the living room.

"Jules. Your date is here."

"He's not my date! He's, he's just my friend from work, uh, a colleague, um, Lev, this is—"

Julia introduces him to everyone, but Lev ignores her, sits on the sofa, and goes straight to sleep.

"Get up, Lev!" Julia is freaking out. "You're missing a totally sick party!"

"Julia is shouting again," mumbles Lev. "I'm telling HR."

Sam catches my eye again and does his ducking-head laughing thing.

"Have you tried the Oregon Blue? I'm something of a cheese aficionado," says a froggy voice at my elbow. It's Ethan, Coco's date. "I once spent a summer making cheddar in Wisconsin."

"That must have been so exciting for you," I say.

"It was, it was," he says. He's very drunk. "You see, the secret with cheddar is the rennet—"

Ethan the Cheesemaker works for the Department of Health, but so far tonight has revealed himself to be "something of an aficionado" of wine, bicycles, fly-fishing, yachting, James Bond movies, headphones, the Battle of Brooklyn, typography, hip-hop, and Gothic architecture. He's the kind of guy who likes to teach people things, i.e., a dick. Worse? Coco thinks he's amazing.

"Wow!" Coco says now, suddenly standing next to us. "I never knew that about cheese, did you Angie? Did you? Hey! We should get matching tattoos! Saying 'Rookhaven Forever'! Because we are super awesome!"

If I didn't know better, I'd think she was on something.

"Lev!" Julia is prodding Lev. "Wake up!" She looks at Sam and smiles nervously. "He's really a nice guy, usually."

Lev opens his eyes. "Julia, can you go to the vending machine for me? Hey? Is that Ruthy?" he says, looking at Sam. "Ruthy! Ruthy!" And then he rests his head back, collapsing again.

Across the room, I see Aidan whispering to Pia.

"No, Aidan, we cannot talk about it!" she snaps. "You're moving to San Francisco. What more is there to say? Fucking awesome, dude. Awesome!"

"You're being a baby," says Aidan.

"You're being a baby," she mimics.

"Call me when you want to talk about this," he says in a low voice, and turns and walks out of the room. The front door slams.

With a loud sob, Pia gets up off the sofa and runs after him. "Aidan! Wait, oh God, wait!" The front door slams again.

Julia runs after Pia. Julia comes from the-more-the-merrier school of drama.

"Bad idea," I call. "She wants to be alone with him!"

"Pia is a princess," says Madeleine loudly.

I narrow my eyes at her. Madeleine and Pia have never been that close, but no one bad-mouths my best friend. "She is *not* a fucking princess, she's just a bit of a drama queen, and it's adorable."

"Adorable?" Madeleine snorts.

Before I can administer the verbal bitch slap I'd like to, Sam is at my side.

"So, Angie, what do you do?"

"What do I do? What DO I do, hmm, let's see. Well, I am unemployed, Sam. I am trying to get a job and I am failing." I pause and take a sip of punch. "Miserably. Any advice for me?"

Sam shrugs. "Find a passion, talk your way in, then impress the boss."

"Talk my way in? Like how?"

"Well . . . okay, I'm about to talk about me here, so, sorry if it's boring—"

"Apology accepted."

"Oh, thanks. So . . . I never sailed, you know, growing up, but I'd always wanted to. And I didn't have any other burning ambitions and I really wanted to, uh, get away for a while. My life was kind of . . . imploding. So I bought a one-way ticket to Trinidad, made some friends at bars the sailing crews all hung out in, and talked my way onto a yacht that was being delivered to the Bahamas. I just copied everyone else and learned on the job. Then, the new owner liked me, and that was that. Three years at sea and counting."

"And you love it?"

Sam thinks for a second, his gray eyes staring into the distance. "When I am sailing, I wake up looking forward to the day."

"Huh," I respond thoughtfully, frowning.

"You frown a lot."

"So do you! You're gonna need Botox by thirty."

"That's so sweet of you to say." He pauses and takes a sip of beer. "This whole thing is to set me up with Julia, right?"

"No. Maybe." Pause. "Yes."

He laughs, his face lighting up. "Really? I was only kidding. The entire night? Just for me?"

"Not exactly," I lie, suddenly feeling disloyal to Julia. "It really is Pia's birthday. Soon. Ish."

He raises an eyebrow at me. I raise mine back.

"There's something I've been wanting to ask you," says Sam. "How did you end up with that crowd, on that yacht, at that party? You didn't exactly fit in."

I smile, but my face suddenly feels locked with tension. Didn't fit in with a bunch of girls who tread the fine line between fun and fuck-for-money.

Even thinking about it makes me shudder.

"You okay? You look like you're about to ralph."

"I'm fine. . . . Do people still say 'ralph'?"

"Oh yeah. All the time. . . . Seriously, though, what were you doing there? Right from the start I knew something wasn't right. You swagger up, looking hungover and lost and pissed as hell, smoking a cigarette and wearing studded Converse. Unlike the other girls, you had no fake tan, no fake breasts, no fake teeth. . . . Are they your friends?"

"Hell no, I'd never met them before. It just sort of happened. I've known Stef a long time, I trusted him, I shouldn't have. End of story." I take a swig of my drink, hoping Sam will say something. He doesn't. And for some goddamn reason, I find myself gabbling. "So from now on, I'm avoiding rich kids forever. You know, they're all entitled asshats who just lie to get what they want. Um, enough about me. Where are you from, Sam?"

I know nothing about him. Except that he works on yachts and is living on a friend's floor in Fort Greene, broke and between jobs.

"Ohio."

"Ohio? Are you serious? Tell me more."

"Do you really need details? I'm Sam. Just Sam."

"And I'm Angie. Just Angie."

"So, how about I set you up on a blind date dinner party with one of my buddies, Just Angie? See how you like it."

"Oh . . . no. I'm not dating right now, Just Sam. I have made too many bad decisions with, uh, the dudes."

"If you can't date anyone nice, don't date anyone at all, is that it?"

"Something like that. I want to be single. But I totally think you should ask Julia for a drink or something. She's really hilarious." I pause and see Julia on the other side of the living room shouting "Fivies!" and forcing Heff to high-five her.

"She seems great, but really, uh, I'm not looking for anything, either. I just broke up with someone."

"Details, please."

"Her name's Katie. We went to college together and sort of did a long-distance thing, but it got complicated, you know. It's hard to stay in touch when you're at sea for weeks on end. . . . She's in Paris right now. Studying."

He shows me a photo on his phone.

I'm impressed. "Her friends are all doing that duckface-kiss pose but she's just smiling normally. She looks like the kind of girl I could have a drink with."

When it's his real smile, Sam's entire face is taken over by it, like a little kid's drawing. I grin back, and get the strangest, nicest, warmest feeling. I like this guy, I realize. As a friend. Purely as a friend. Which has never happened before in my entire life.

What a novelty.

"Do you want to be friends?" I say, the words out before I can assess how weird I sound. "I mean, seriously. Let's just not do that whole sexual-tension thing. No drunk kissing, no one-night regrets, no Dawson Does Joey. Let's just be friends."

"Friends?"

"Friends. Tomorrow, you should come over here and we'll have a *Freaks and Geeks* marathon or something."

"I love that show," Sam says, his face totally serious. "It was a travesty they canceled it. . . . Are you asking me out on a friend date? Is this what grown-ups do?"

"Yeah," I say. "I guess I am. And I guess it is."

I look around at everyone. Madeleine and Heff are lying on the floor giggling helplessly at Julia, who is doing the worm dance move, Ethan the Cheesemaker has passed out on the sofa next to a still-sleeping Lev, Pia and Aidan are missing, presumably fighting, and Coco is standing on a chair, singing and prancing like a pony on speed.

"They're usually not like this," I say to Sam. "Someone must have spiked the ice."

At that moment Coco shouts "WOO!" jumps off the chair, and falls on the floor.

That's a strange dance move.

Then she starts convulsing, throwing her head back violently, her entire body going rigid like she's being electrocuted, and starts making choking sounds.

Holy shit. Coco is overdosing.

CHAPTER **17**

We all stare in shock for a few seconds until Sam takes charge. "Call 911. Now."

He crouches down next to her while I kneel, get out my phone, and dial 911. I put my hand on her forehead: her skin is boiling hot and damp with perspiration.

Julia is freaking out. "Coco! Coco! Oh my God ohmygodohmygod . . ."

"Calm down," says Sam. "She's fine, she'll be fine. Coco? Can you hear me?"

He puts his ear to her mouth, then feels her neck for a pulse.

The operator answers. "We need an ambulance—" I start talking her through what just happened. The operator instructs me to put Coco in the recovery position, which Sam has already done, and then check her vitals.

"She's, uh, she's breathing, but she's not a great color, and she's still unconscious," I say, as Sam instructs me. He seems to know exactly what to do.

"What has she taken?" asks the operator.

"I don't know," I say. "She's been acting weird tonight, but I've only seen her drinking alcohol—"

Coco starts convulsing again, puke bubbling out of her mouth. Sam turns her on her side, and, still unconscious, she retches a foamy mess of booze and cheese and crackers.

"Jesus," I murmur.

Sam rolls her back and puts his ear to her mouth again, trying to hear or feel her breath.

"She's breathing, but she's out cold," he says. "And her pulse is racing."

I'm talking to the operator calmly on the outside, but inside, I'm freaking out. This is my fault. I've been totally neglecting Coco. And I haven't talked about it before now because, well, it's her business, not mine, and I never tell other people's secrets, but she had an abortion a few months ago and confided in Pia and me. We helped her go to Planned Parenthood, the whole thing. She was sort of quiet and sad over the winter, but hell, everyone's quiet and sad over the winter, right? And she had an abortion, I mean, that'll make you feel pretty goddamn sad for a while. I've had one, too. About eight years ago. The guy was a bartender from a vacation I took with Pia and her family. I try not to think about it, ever. I guess I figured Coco would be the same.

"I need to know what she's taken," says the operator.

How the hell would I know? I never have any idea what's really going on with anybody else!

But maybe I should have asked, I realize, looking at Coco's little body lying on the floor. She's younger than me, she's infinitely more naive and inexperienced, she's just a baby, really. . . . We should be looking after her better.

We should all be looking after one another better.

Suddenly, Coco opens her eyes, convulses, and starts puking again. Sam quickly turns her on her side.

The operator is talking again. *"Ma'am? Drugs, alcohol, prescription medication?"*

"Um, I don't know, I'll find out, I'll find out." I hand the phone to Sam and stand up. "I'm going to search her room."

He nods, wiping away her puke, and turns to Julia. "Get me a wet towel."

Julia nods frantically and runs away, completely freaking out the way that über-bossy people always do in a genuine emergency. Madeleine and Heff are staring at Coco in stoned shock. Ethan the Cheesemaker is passed out on the sofa, totally useless, next to a still-sleeping Lev. And I guess Pia is still outside fighting with Aidan. The only people here who can really help are Sam and me. Fuck.

I hurry up to Coco's room, taking the stairs three at a time. It's an adorable room: all sloping ceilings and book-lined windowsills. Feeling like a thief, I open the drawers to her nightstand: books, lip balm, tissues, an old keychain, photos of her mom (she passed away when Coco was nine or something). Then I try her desk drawers. Pencils, pens, scissors . . . nothing else.

I look around. If I were Coco, where would I hide drugs? I wouldn't have drugs, comes the answer right back. Unless they were prescription. And I'd think of them as medicine, so I'd keep them with my Band-Aids and cough medicine.

Where the hell are her toiletries? I look around and finally see that hanging on the back of Coco's bedroom door is one of those plastic shoe storage things, you know the kind? With all the little pockets? But she's using it for toiletries, not shoes. I go through each pocket one by one. Moisturizer, face scrub, razors, deodorant, hairbrush, hair bands, sunscreen . . . and finally, pills.

Demerol and Xanax.

Of course.

I grab the pills and head back downstairs. The paramedics have arrived; they're in the living room asking Sam questions. Coco's eyes are open now, and her skin is a pale gray-blue, like someone has bled the color out of her with some faulty Photoshop app.

"I'll go to the hospital with her," I say to Sam.

"I'll come, too," he says.

"I'm going, too!" says Julia. "She's my sister."

So, somehow, the three of us end up in the ER.

Coco is put straight into a hospital bed, and the three of us sit around her, curtains drawn. Doctors come in and out, calm and preoccupied, concerned and cold. She's having palpitations, so they want to monitor her heart. And she's still not breathing properly, so they've attached an oxygen mask to her face, plus a drip in her arm to replenish her fluids. She's conscious again, but the oxygen mask means she can't talk. Her eyes look even bigger and more blue than usual, and tears are running down her face and pooling around the edge of the mask.

I've never been in an ER before. It's not like on TV and in movies: a lot quieter, more mundane. No gunshot wounds, no stabbings. Just ordinary, run-of-the-mill people who hurt themselves. I can hear the family at the next bed whispering to one another in Spanish, and an old lady talking in Russian down the hall. How scary it must be to be in a hospital speaking a foreign language.

The three of us are sitting in silence, sipping the sweet, metallic-tasting hospital coffee Sam bought, murmuring to one another in that intimate shorthand you use in the wake of an emergency. Strange how a crisis can fast-forward a friendship. Right now, I feel like Sam is one of us.

I take out the bottles of Demerol and Xanax that I found in Coco's room.

"Xanax?" says Julia. She hadn't noticed it before. "Oh God, poor Coco, this is my fault, it's my fault, it's my fault. . . ."

Sam reaches out and grabs Julia by the shoulder. "It's not your fault. These things happen. Drink your coffee."

Julia obediently picks up her coffee and takes a sip.

"Good girl," says Sam.

"Don't 'good girl' me, my friend," says Julia. "I'm twenty-fucking-three-years old."

"Good . . . woman?"

"That's more like it."

We sit there in silence a while longer.

"I hate hospitals," says Julia finally.

"Me too," says Sam. "I think everyone does."

"No, I really hate them. My mom died in a hospital. They wouldn't release her, even though she really wanted to go home for the last few days. Isn't that mean? It was so mean." Julia is talking in the tiniest voice

I've ever heard from her, and her breath catches. "I think about it all the time."

Sam pauses. "How . . ."

"Breast cancer."

"I'm really sorry," he says, and rather than sounding rote or formulaic the way those words usually do, it sounds real. Then, in a strangely paternal gesture, he reaches over, pulling Julia into a half hug, their little plastic hospital chairs clanging together. Like a daddy owl pulling a baby owl under his wing. "But you know Coco will be fine."

Julia looks over at Coco, now sleeping quietly. "Why would she need a prescription painkiller?"

Oh, my God. Coco never told her sister about the abortion. I never even thought about it, really. I was too busy thinking about Mani, who'd just broken up with me, and partying every minute that I could to obliterate all the emotions I didn't want to deal with. . . . Coco and Julia are incredibly close, how could she not tell her only sister something so important?

Because Coco thought she wouldn't understand. That she'd disapprove, and judge, and make Coco feel even worse. It's Coco's secret. Of all people, I can understand that.

So I just shrug. "Who knows? They hand those things out like candy. Didn't she get her wisdom teeth out last year?"

"Uh, yeah, I guess." Julia frowns. She doesn't seem surprised about the Xanax. She must have known about that.

Then a doctor comes back in and checks on Coco again. They decide to keep her overnight, for observation.

"What's really scary is that she was so out of it," says Julia to the doctor. "What if we hadn't been there? What if she'd been doing that with a bunch of people she didn't know? Anything could have happened to her!"

Three thousand dollars. The Soho Grand hotel. And I still don't know what happened that night. I shake my head, as if to clear it, getting a strange look from Sam.

"About a quarter of our admissions are related to alcohol and prescription abuse," says the doctor. "Sometimes more. With your permission, I'll dispose of those leftover pills safely. If she doesn't need them, it's best not to have them in the house."

Julia hands over the pills and the doctor leaves. Then she turns to us.

"You guys should go home, get some sleep. Thank you so much, Sam. Thank you."

Sam leans forward and gives Julia another hug, rumpling her hair as he does it. Her face changes from stress to bliss when she's in his arms. Wow, she really likes him. I hope he does ask her out.

"You sure you want to stay here by yourself?" I say to Julia.

"Totally," she says, and surprises me by grabbing me for a hug, too. I'm a non-hugger, I come from a long line of non-huggers—but I hug her back out of instinct. It's like putting on warm socks straight out of the dryer. A sort of *ahhhh* feeling.

"Angie, I'll escort you home," Sam says, as we're walking out of the hospital.

"Dude, I'm fine. I don't need a chaperone."

"That wasn't really my point. We're outside a hospital in the middle of the night, in one of the not-so-nice areas of Brooklyn. You'd probably get home fine, but you might not. Why take a risk?"

I sigh. "Fine. Have it your way. Jesus, do you do everything right? And how do you know what's nice and not nice in Brooklyn? You've been here, like, a week." Sam makes a snorting sound and doesn't answer.

The air outside is cold and crisp, but sort of sweet. A nice change after the stale chemical smell of the hospital. I pull my fur/army coat tighter around me.

"So, talk me through your friends," says Sam as we walk. "Coco's younger than the rest of you, right?"

"Yep," I say. "She's twenty-one, Jules is twenty-three. They're from upstate New York."

"Julia is the overprotective big sister. Coco is the little one looking for approval, huh?"

"More or less. God, I hope she's okay."

"She will be," says Sam. "She just made a mistake, that's all."

"Do you have any brothers or sisters?"

"One brother. And Pia's your best friend? The drama queen?"

"Um, yeah. Our moms met in the hospital when they were having us, we have the same birthday."

"The same birthday . . . that was not the reason for tonight's surprise party. Because I was that reason." He pauses. "I feel so important."

I start to giggle. "Um, well, yeah, so, Pia and I both turn twenty-three in April. And Madeleine is . . . I don't know, actually. We're not that close. She's hard to talk to. Unfriendly. Sometimes downright bitchy."

"I thought she was just shy," he says. "Whenever someone is sort of cold and controlled like that, making weird little comments, I figure they're shy and awkward. Trying to impress people."

This idea surprises me. "You might be right. I assume that what you see is what you get."

"That's a nice theory. But it can backfire in all sorts of ways."

I think about Stef, and the yacht, and all the mistakes I've made in the past by not bothering to look below the surface of anything, by not getting to know guys before I . . . Well, by not getting to know guys. That will never happen again.

"I'll keep that in mind."

"You do that, missy."

I smile at him, feeling that same easy warmth I felt with Julia before. The warm-sock *ahhh* feeling. Security and friendship. This guy is a good guy.

"They're a great group, anyway. Most of my friends are all over the country right now, some studying, some working. . . . You really fell on your feet in Brooklyn, huh?"

"Yeppers," I say. Actually, that's not exactly true, but I don't want to tell him everything about me.

"Did you just say 'yeppers'? What are you, nine?"

"Yes. I am nine"—I pause—"kinds of *awesome*."

Sam cracks up. I don't even know why I said that. It's the kind of dumb shit I would say if I was hanging out with just Pia.

"Do you have your favorite childhood toy hidden somewhere in your bedroom back at Union Street?"

I frown at him. How did he guess? "I have six of them," I say finally. "Big Ted, Little Ted, Grace, Rose, Ralph, and Pinky."

Sam laughs out loud again. "Six! Are you an excessive person by nature?"

"Shut up! Don't laugh at my toys!"

"I'm not laughing at them! I have one toy that I take everywhere with me. I just hide him in the bottom of my toiletry case."

"*Him?* Name, please?"

"Panda . . . He's, uh, he's a panda."

"You were obviously a highly inventive child."

"I was indeed." Sam pauses and smiles at me. "It's nice. Having Panda with me. It's a link to the past, you know? A nice one."

"I know what you mean. I guess I just like knowing that they're around," I say.

We smile at each other, and again I get that warm-sock feeling. A male friend I'm not going to sleep with. How bizarre.

When we get to Rookhaven, Sam turns to me. "Well, good night. Don't try to kiss me or anything, okay? It'd just be awkward, because of how I only like you as a friend."

I start laughing and punch him lightly in the arm. "Thank you for everything with Coco tonight. You kind of saved her life."

"Hey, it was nothing. And it's part of the platonic friend code, right? It's in the fine print: *save roommates from overdosing.*"

"Right on. So . . . I'll call you. About our friend date."

"You better."

When I get inside, Pia and Madeleine are sitting on the living room floor, around the wet shadow of a recently cleaned puke stain. The guys have all disappeared.

Pia looks up. "Angie, we need to talk."

CHAPTER 18

This is weird. Pia, my best friend in the house who I've grown apart from recently, with Madeleine, her former frenemy and my least favorite person in the house, sitting down and enjoying a 2:00 A.M. bottle of Malbec.

"What do you want to talk about?" I ask, suddenly feeling exhausted.

"Well, first, tell us about Coco," says Pia.

"How is she?" Madeleine pulls her sleeves down over her hands, looking at me anxiously. She's permanently covered up. Suddenly, I remember what Julia told me earlier. About the cutting. Maybe she is still doing it. Or maybe she has scars. Now probably isn't the time to ask. "That was so awful. . . . I've never seen someone collapse before."

"She's fine," I say. I tell them what happened. "It was a stupid mistake. She just didn't know not to combine them with alcohol."

"Where the heck did she even get those drugs?" says Madeleine. "Seriously. Coco is as straight as they come."

Pia and I exchange a look. I don't think we should tell her. It's not our place.

"She had an abortion," says Pia. "About three months ago."

Clearly Pia disagrees.

Madeleine sighs but doesn't seem shocked, which, though it sounds strange, sort of shocks me. I thought she'd be the judgmental anti-abortion type. "Poor, poor Coco. I thought she'd been a little withdrawn lately. I bet she hasn't told Julia, either."

"Nope." Pia shakes her head. "And you can't tell her, either, okay? If Coco wants to tell her, she will. . . . Anyway, so, the Demerol came from there. The Xanax . . . I don't know."

"How did you find out?" asks Madeleine.

"Angie found her crying in the kitchen one day, when she thought she was alone in the house."

I nod, remembering that day back in December. I thought Coco was just reading another goddamn Nicholas Sparks book. She's always crying over something like that. But she was sobbing—this scared, sort of intense, desperate sobbing—and I knew something was really, seriously wrong. I didn't know what to do, so I called Pia. She was on her way to see Aidan but came straight over. She guessed immediately. I think she'd suspected for a while. Then Coco told us everything.

Madeleine sighs again. "That's so awful. Of all the people for it to happen to . . . Who was the dude?"

"That guy Eric." Pia wrinkles her nose up with distaste. "The little fuckwipe."

"Urgh," says Madeleine.

We all sit in silence for a moment.

"Well, Coco will be home tomorrow, good as new, right? And it was a mistake!" I say. "I think we should just . . . let her forget about it. Not bring it up. That's what I would want."

"Coco might be different," Pia points out. "Maybe she'll want to talk about it."

"Well, if she does, then we'll listen," I say. "We'll be here for Coco if she wants to talk about it. But she's probably really embarrassed, you know. She'll be ashamed, because it's not like she does it all the time, it was an accident. She didn't really know what she was doing, it's not like she's a bad person! It was a weird situation, and it just sort of snowballed, and next thing you know, boom! She had no control over what was going on, she didn't know what was happening, but it was a mistake, a one-off, it won't happen again! You know?"

Pia and Madeleine stare at me. I try to catch my breath. Was I ranting?

Finally, Pia speaks. "Are we talking about Coco or you?"

I've nervously torn a tissue into tiny little pieces in my hand while rambling. I jump up and put it in the trash.

Time to change the subject. "Anyway, what happened with Aidan?"

Pia sighs, tears automatically springing to her eyes. "He's got a work project. In San Francisco. He might be there awhile. . . . Like, a year. Or longer. And I just, I, um . . . I don't know what to do."

"You'll be fine!" says Madeleine.

"He'll be back every weekend!" I echo. "You work so hard anyway, you'll just have more time to spend here at Rookhaven. With us."

"No, he won't be back," she says. "He's subletting his place here. He's taking his dog, Angie. His *dog*." She pauses dramatically, letting the dog factor sink in. "He's basically . . . he's leaving. And he didn't even discuss it with me. He didn't ask me what I thought, he just took the project. I thought we were about to move in together and he was just thinking about his job! What does that say about our relationship?"

"Nothing!" Madeleine and I say in supportive unison.

"He's career-focused! So are you!"

"And it's not like you're married!" I add. "You practically just got together!"

"You can do the long-distance thing. You can text and IM and Skype and FaceTime and—"

"No!" Pia shakes her head adamantly. "The long-distance thing never, ever works. You both know it as well as I do. It's like couples that take a trial separation, or a 'break.' What's the fucking point? It's just the beginning of the end. He's the first guy I've ever truly, truly loved, but I'm just trying to be a realist here. I think . . ." Her eyes well up again. "I think we're going to break up."

"Don't plan for a breakup before it happens." Madeleine pauses.

"Listen to me, giving relationship advice. I've never even been in love. Not really."

"What about that dude at Brown? The math major?"

"Sebastian? Pia, that was three years ago."

"What about Heffy? The guy from the band tonight?"

Madeleine shakes her head. "The same total disconnect I've felt with every guy I've ever known. Heff said he's got a girl back in Florida but he'd be happy for a 'casual bang' now and again. I was so stoned I didn't even know what to say. I just stared at him."

Pia cracks up. "I was hoping you'd bring that up! Dude, I *literally* never thought I'd see you stoned."

"I thought maybe it would give me a reason to laugh," says Madeleine. She looks up and meets our eyes. "Wow, how pathetic does that sound?"

At that we all crack up and laugh for such a long time that Madeleine starts drooling. Which makes us laugh more. I have an endorphin rush from laughing; I feel heady and good all over. I actually like Madeleine right now. Amazing what a crisis and a lot of booze will do.

Later on, I'm lying in bed thinking how I've never had a conversation that long with Madeleine before. Ever. And I've been living with her since August last year. I never thought about her at all, really. I never really thought about Coco, or how she was dealing with her problems after Eric and the abortion. I never thought about how Julia felt about her job. I never thought about how Pia and Aidan's relationship was going or if they'd move in together. I never thought about anybody else.

I only thought about me. My relationships, my problems, my life.

From now on, I'm not going to be the loner in the corner, smoking cigarettes and drinking vodka and shuffling cards. I'm going to be a good friend, I really am. To Pia and Julia and Coco. Even to Madeleine. I'm going to be single, always, no matter what. And I'm going to get a job.

(This time, I mean it.)

CHAPTER **19**

I'm trying again.

That's how success works, right? You get knocked down, then you get up, dust yourself off, and try again. That's what Pia's always saying, anyway. And that chick had some knocks from hell last year.

There's a fashion PR agency called Maven in SoHo. They are my (new) ideal employer (if I can't work with a designer, then work with people who talk about those designers all day, right?). Their accounts are my favorite labels, they have satellite offices in London and Paris (Paris!), and they have a really cool website. I sent them my résumé by e-mail and snail mail, I tried to start conversations with them on Twitter, Facebook, and LinkedIn, and I've called. Every day. For weeks now.

Nothing.

So now I'm trying it the old-fashioned way.

Bribery.

Sam is helping me out. He texted to see what I was doing a couple of days after the dinner party, and I replied "seeking gainful employment." There's less than a month now till I turn twenty-three, so time is running out. Anyway, he offered to help.

And that's how we ended up standing outside the Maven office building on Broome Street. I'm holding twenty coffees on a tray and shouting, "Free nonfat lattes with every CV!"

My aim? Just to make someone look at me twice as a potential employee. If they even gave me one chance, just one day of work, I *know* I could prove myself to them. (Well, I don't really know that for sure. But I'm not going to show my self-doubt now, right?)

Sam is next to me, holding twenty copies of my CV, which has been written, edited, and proofed to within an inch of its life by everyone at Rookhaven. So far, the only people to take a latte have been the doorman and someone who I'm pretty sure was going to a different company entirely. (No one wearing Crocs works in fashion, it's just a fact.)

"Free latte with every CV!" I say, as a guy takes a latte, who almost-but-not-quite looks a bit like that famous sleazy British photographer who makes everyone look slutty.

"The latte is free! The CV'll cost ya!" shouts Sam.

"No ad-libbing," I hiss.

"Not helping? Okay. I'll shut up now. How about I stand on the lower step, like I'm your personal assistant."

Sam smiles winningly at me. He's dressed up in a very sharp suit and a crisply ironed shirt. He's lost that annoyingly innocent clean-cut look that was my first impression of him and instead looks sort of aloof and sharp, like a young Wall Street bloodsucker. He's been getting a lot of attention from passing women.

"Nice shoes," I comment. "J. M. Westons, right? My father wears them. How the hell did you afford them?"

"My roommate is the same size as me, he works in finance. Where did you get those sexy little things?"

I look down at my feet. Manolos that once belonged to Annabel. "My mother."

A stunning woman saunters past. She has perfect caramel-highlighted hair trailing over one shoulder and long, long legs in tight jeans, and stares at Sam so hard I think she might trip.

"You are getting some serious eye fucks, Samuel," I comment. "You should dress well more often."

"Eye fucks? Oh, that's nice. That's real nice. Well, you're getting a lot of stares, too, Angela."

"My full name is Angelique, bitch. I hate being called Angela."

"Yes, ma'am."

I stepped it up today, after my grungy errors with Candie Stokes. I'm wearing white Theory pants that I bought for my job interview with a photographer last year, a white turtleneck, and a little slim-sleeved leather jacket that came from Zara but could be designer. (I hope.) Plus that gold clutch I made from secondhand scarves, and my usual out-for-the-day oversize white tote with everything I own in it. There are girls like me all over New York, all lugging sofa-size bags with our lives inside, like glossy little snails.

Finally, around 9:30 A.M., the fashion girls start arriving. I can spot them a mile off: they're wearing some of the hottest items from the last five seasons with casual "this old thing?" aplomb, as though they were wearing something from Gap. Acne, Lanvin, Equipment, Alexander Wang, Current/Elliott, A.P.C., and a lot of Rick Owens. I even see four women carrying the Proenza Schouler PS1 satchels, which go for a couple of grand a pop, minimum. But I also see recognizable pieces from H&M, Topshop, J.Crew, and American Apparel. Real fashion people mix high and low. Only wannabes do head-to-toe labels.

Sartorial observances aside, I can see that the arrival schedule demonstrates the hierarchy. The younger ones come first. Mostly my age, mostly smoking, mostly gorgeous, as though they could have been models but something tiny—a too-long chin, a too-snub nose, or a too-traditional prettiness—kept them from achieving supermodel success. They're mostly in flats, and some pause at the front door and throw on a pair of heels.

"Take a latte!" I exclaim, while they're shoeless and defenseless. "My name is Angie James. If you need an intern or assistant or someone to fetch you coffee, please remember me!"

"This latte is cold," says a chic, pointy-faced girl about my age, wearing one of the Marni for H&M skirts from a few years ago.

"Well, put some ice in it and pretend it's summer," I say.

She grins, revealing a snaggletooth. "I wish." Why does imperfect dentistry always make someone seem more likeable?

"Great skirt," I say quickly. "Marni for H&M, right?"

"Right," she says, looking surprised. "I slept outside the store overnight to get it. I'm obsessed with Marni."

"I missed the best pieces from the Marni collaboration, but I got the jacket from the Versace one," I say. "I'm obsessed with Versace, like, 1990 to 1992."

"Oh, me too! Hey, *love* the clutch, whose is that?" Her phone beeps. "Shit, I gotta run. Good luck!"

I turn back to Sam, who gives me the thumbs-up.

Then the midlevel women come, most of them intimidatingly glossy-haired, some shouting on the phone, some quietly texting. All too busy to stop and talk, though three of them take a latte and a CV. One, a brunette with a dark bob, says "Thank you," and actually appears to read over my CV as she walks into the building.

And finally, a town car pulls up, and out steps a black-haired woman wearing Lanvin (I think)—and a mink coat. It's the owner and director of Maven PR, Cynthia Maven. (I Googled her.)

"Ms. Maven, I have a latte for you?" I say, with my best and brightest smile. "It's free with my CV!"

Her head moves slightly toward me and she takes a latte and a CV, barely breaking stride, and disappears into the building.

I turn to Sam and sigh.

"Well, so much for that idea. I am never going to get a job."

"Of course you are."

"No, I'm really not, Sam. I'm underqualified, underexperienced, and probably underdressed. I just . . . I can't compete."

"You think that now, but then, one day, you'll get your break. And that's when your future begins."

"Wow. That is some serious Hallmark card shit right there."

"Thanks. Now it's my turn," he says. "Do you know how the subway system works? I need to get downtown."

"You don't know Manhattan at all?"

"I prefer Brooklyn."

"God, really? I only live in Brooklyn because I can't afford Manhattan," I say. "Manhattan is way more glamorous."

Sam laughs. "You think? Well, from what I've seen, Brooklyn is kinder. Manhattan can be a total bitch. Come on, help me out. I gotta go see a man about a crew job."

"A blow job?"

"A *crew* job. I'm straight, Angie. You know that."

"Do I?" I say. "You suit up pretty well for a straight dude. And you're still refusing to ask Julia out."

"Dude, you've got to get over the Julia thing. Not gonna happen."

"Why not? Give me one good reason."

"Maybe I'm still hung up on Katie."

"Your ex? She's in Paris! One date! What's the difference? Come on. Grow a pair."

"This from the girl who has sworn off relationships."

I ignore him, and we take the subway downtown. Then, as we're sitting side by side, and I'm looking at everyone around me and wondering why fluorescent lighting was invented when it's just so uglifying, Sam turns to me.

"So what happened with the last guy you fell in love with?"

"What?"

"Just making conversation, Angela. Wondering why you don't trust men."

"What?" I say. "What kind of a dude talks about love, Samuel? You're like a chick. Why don't we just make some fucking s'mores and swap our traveling pants?"

"I was wondering why you seem a little bitter."

"Ouch."

"Just tell me. I mean—" Sam checks himself, as if wary of being too arrogant. "If you want to talk about it."

I pause. Fuck it. For once I do feel like sharing. "The last guy I thought I was in love with was named Mani. But he was just using me. I think maybe . . . dudes have always used me. But it's my fault."

"How is it your fault?"

"Um, because I choose to let them treat me that way. I just sit back and hope everything will be perfect and real and lasting if I behave just right." I take a deep breath. I don't know why I'm confessing all to Sam, but I can't help it. "I make the wrong choices. I put myself in situations where . . . where these guys treat me like nothing, you know, like shit. But I'm not shit." I suddenly hear a break in my voice. "I'm *not* nothing." Stop talking, Angie, Jesus.

Sam turns and looks me right in the eye. "It's never your fault if someone is an asshole and treats you . . . in a way that you don't want to be treated. It sucks, but it's not your fault. It's theirs. Fuck those people. Okay? You just . . . shake it off, pretend they don't exist, and move on."

This is a slight variation of Vic's "let regrets go" speech, but somehow, I'm not sure I agree with the fine print in Sam's approach.

"Pretend people don't exist? Isn't that kind of harsh?"

Sam stares into space. "Probably."

It occurs to me that I'm basically pretending my mother doesn't exist. And my dad still hasn't called me either. Sam's approach suddenly isn't looking that out-of-the-ordinary.

We're both silent the rest of the journey, and fifteen minutes later we're on the very edge of downtown Manhattan, at North Cove Marina. It's a square-cut marina for just a handful of incredible yachts, all nestled peacefully together, surrounded by the architectural beauty and chaos of the Financial District.

"It's totally surreal to see a yacht next to a skyscraper. Looks like drunk Photoshopping," I say.

"I know," says Sam. "But they balance each other perfectly, don't you think? I never even knew this place existed until recently."

"Why would you? You're from Ohio."

"Right. Anyway, there was a job I saw on CrewFile, the guy said he was interviewing in person down here today," Sam says, as we walk along the pier. "It's a six-man crew, sailing from here to Greece next month. So I need to make a really good impression."

"Wow, these are some amazing boats," I say.

"They're not boats. They're yachts. Never boats."

"Sheesh, touchy. Which one is the one you're interviewing for?"

"She's over there."

"She? Oh . . . right."

Sam points to a long yacht, easily the biggest in the marina, at the end of the pier. It—sorry, she—is truly beautiful, like something out of an old movie. Black body, white detailing, and immaculately clean and shiny, with masts reaching far into the sky. When we get to the end of the pier, I see her name. *Peripety*.

Why are real sailing yachts so romantic? I don't know why, they just are. Way better than the money-monster megayachts favored by sleazy types like Hal.

"She was built in the 1950s as an ocean racer," says Sam. "See how she's made from wood, not aluminum alloy? It makes for a smoother ride. Really old-school."

"How big is she? Is it okay that she's so old? I mean . . . is she safe?"

"She's one hundred and four feet. And she was restored a couple of years ago, she's in perfect condition. She's got the most amazing history, she's a work of art, really, she's . . ." Sam trails off, running his hands through his hair, suddenly nervous. "I really want this chance, Angie. It's all I've wanted for a long time."

"You'll get it," I say, trying not to show how surprised I am to see Sam shaken out of his customary cool. "That job is totally yours."

He nods, his voice low and intense. "This is the yacht, Angie. This is the one."

"You'll be fine!" I say. "Go get 'em, tiger. This job is your bitch and you are its daddy."

Sam's too tense to even smile.

"Okay," he says. "I'm gonna go talk to the guy. Back in twenty."

CHAPTER 20

While Sam is away, I play Let's Pretend with the boats. I wonder what it's like to be able to afford a yacht of your very own. To just have it here, waiting for you, whenever you feel like getting out on the open sea.

Pretty goddamn great, I bet.

I bet someone saying "you're hired" would feel pretty good right now, too.

Sighing, I sit down at the end of the marina and check my e-mail. Nothing, nothing, nothing. I've e-mailed hundreds of people about jobs, and I haven't had one single reply. Since when are job applications spam? And why is everything good in life so hard to get?

I get a text from Julia: *Yoo-hoo. Fashion Guru. Should I get green or purple panties? Ordering online.*

I grin to myself. Julia has been saying "yoo-hoo" a lot, ever since I told her it was my old boss Cornelia's favorite saying.

I reply: *Black.*

She replies: *Black feels kinda whorish.*

I smirk to myself. Jules is hilarious, and I never knew it before. I reply: *Maybe that means there's a chance you'll get some action.*

She replies: *BOOM. Okay. You win. Black panties it is.*

Julia is fast becoming one of my favorite people. I've barely seen Pia in days; she and Aidan are deep in crisis talks. I'm getting used to her not being around, to the point where I feel almost awkward when I *do* see her. Don't get me wrong; I still totally love her and everything, but it's a bit weird right now. Female friendship is so much more complicated than any dude relationship.

I pull out my latest romance novel, *Secrets of the Sahara.*

After being jilted at the altar, Suzanne goes on her honeymoon alone to Africa, attracting the attentions of big game hunters: arrogant, hateful Ty Hunter and his flirtatious brother, Rock. At first, her romantic preferences are clear, but soon Suzanne's feelings become tangled, and when their plane crashes in the desert, there's a choice she'll have to make. . . .

I admit, this one is pretty goddamn lame. But it is still somehow calming, you know? When I open a romance novel the real world, all my real world problems just disappear.

Sam comes back after about twenty minutes. I quickly hide my book.

"Fucking washout," he says angrily, walking down the pier. "It's always who you know, who you are. Where you goddamn come from."

"You didn't get it?"

"No. I didn't fucking get it." Sam is striding so fast I have to run after him.

"There are more boat jobs, right?" I say.

"That's not the point! I wanted *that* job!" Wow, Sam has a temper.

"Calm down. Why don't you just fly to fucking Nassau, or whatever, and bullshit your way into a crew again? I would totally employ you as my boat boy."

Sam stops and turns to smile at me, his face softening slightly. "You have such a way with words. *Boat boy.* Jeez."

"Crew member. Whatever."

"Yeah, whatever." Sam's all laid-back cool again, his anger passing like a storm.

Calling Sam a boat boy immediately reminds me of Turks, and I get a sick sour feeling in my stomach so fast that I feel dizzy. I wish I could take a scalpel and cut those memories out of my brain. Or swap them to find out what happened to me at the Soho Grand that night. I wince at the thought and turn to Sam to clear my head.

"Why do you want it so badly?"

Sam sighs. "I started from nothing, you know? No sailing experience, no training, no contacts, nothing. So if I were to get picked for the crew on something like the *Peripety* . . . I'd know I did it all on my own. Sailing across the Atlantic, forging my way on the open sea . . ." Sam smiles at me. "Like it when I wax a little lyrical for you?"

"Okay, so then you'll be like, oh, yay, I sailed around the world, woo for me. What the hell do you do after that?"

Sam gazes at me for a few seconds. "That's the big question."

I frown at him. "There's something you're not telling me." He doesn't respond. "You are a stubborn bastard, anyone ever tell you that?"

"Actually, yes," says Sam. "I'm hungry. Let's go to the Village and drink beer and eat burgers."

"I'm eating pasta and Cheerios for, like, every meal this week," I say. "We're both unemployed, remember? Why waste the cash?"

Across the street, I see a Duane Reade.

"Quick pit stop, Sammy," I say. "Tampons."

"Dude . . ."

"Oh, grow a pair. Girls get periods. It's not exactly breaking news. You're coming with me." I grab Sam's arm and pull him into the drugstore. "Hey! Where are the tampons, please?" I ask a Duane Reade guy stacking shelves.

He doesn't bother to turn around. "Back of the store to your right."

"Back of the store. Great. Well, it's not like fifty percent of your customers need them once a month, so why make it easy for them?" I mutter as I stride through the store, a deeply reluctant Sam beside me. "And while we're there, why not make it fucking expensive, too? Yeah. Nine bucks for a box of tampons. That seems reasonable. Asshats."

I grab the tampons off the shelf. Sam raises an eyebrow.

"Super plus?"

"Damn straight, super plus. Girls only buy regular tampons so guys will think they have teeny tiny vaginas," I snap over my shoulder as I stride toward the cash register.

Sam laughs so hard he stops walking for a moment and leans over with his hands on his knees.

"I'll pick up the new *Us* magazine for Coco, too," I say. "She's been a bit down after her dinner party meltdown. It might cheer her up. Oh, and some hand soap for the bathrooms; we're running out. And one for the kitchen; I hate getting food on my hands and just rinsing them, don't you? Oh, and body moisturizer. My legs are so dry and cracked right now. Nivea? What do you think?"

"When we met, I thought you were the tough, silent type," says Sam, as we line up to pay. "Now I know you have heavy flow and your legs are like the floor of an old church."

I feel the giggles coming on. "I am tough and silent, Samuel! You just bring out the chatterbox in me."

"That comes to $52.96," says the woman behind the counter.

Yikes. That's more than I expected. Giggles canceled.

I take out my credit card and zip it through the machine.

It makes a BA! sound.

I try again.

"It's not working, ma'am. May I see the card?"

She types in the numbers. Waits a few seconds, shakes her head.

"I'm sorry."

Burning with shame, I quickly take my card back and look through my purse. I thought I had some cash in here, but there's nothing. Just coins and one-dollar bills. I also thought I was nowhere near my overdraft limit.

"I'll pay," says Sam. "I have cash."

"No!" I exclaim. "No, no. I don't want your money. I don't want you to pay for me. Ever."

"Angie, don't be crazy. I have it right here—"

"No," I say, suddenly fighting the urge to cry. "I'll . . . I'll have to come back," I say quickly to the woman behind the register.

She sighs with annoyance and picks up my shopping bag, putting it on a counter behind her.

The thing is, I really do need the tampons. I can see them through the cheap plastic of the Duane Reade bag. I could probably afford them if I scraped together all my change. But I'm too embarrassed. Who pays for tampons with fucking quarters?

Sam and I take the train back to Brooklyn in silence. God, the journey to Brooklyn is depressing on a cold weekday afternoon. I'm broke. I'm unemployed. I'm too broke to buy tampons. I'm unworthy of anything except, apparently, something I really don't want to do. The kind of job that starts with a night out with friends and ends with an envelope of cash on the dresser.

We get out at Carroll Gardens, both eye the Momofuku Milk Bar with hunger but don't even bother to stop since we can't afford it, and silently trudge toward Union Street and Rookhaven. Wait, why is Sam still here?

"You're coming to my place?"

Sam looks embarrassed. "Is that cool? I like Rookhaven. . . . My friend's place isn't as cozy."

"His place is a disgusting shithole, you mean. How long is he going to let you sleep on his floor like some kind of vagrant bum, hmm?"

Sam laughs. "We're pretty close. I don't think he'll kick me out anytime soon."

"How do you know him again?"

"Old friends," Sam says.

I can tell he's being evasive, but before I can interrogate, we run into Vic, my downstairs neighbor.

"Well, hello, girlie." Vic's face creases into a craggy smile.

"Hi, Vic!"

I introduce them quickly. Sam shakes Vic's hand with a sort of earnest intensity. Such a goddamn Boy Scout.

"Where you kids heading?"

"We've been job-hunting," I say. "I want to work in fashion; Sam wants to work on a yacht."

"On a yacht!" Vic looks impressed. "That's hard work."

"Yes, sir," says Sam. Such a kiss-ass. I guess they teach good manners in Ohio.

"Brooklyn was a huge naval center, for decades," says Vic.

"Really?"

"Mm-hmm. When I was young, everyone worked on the docks. But manufacturing dropped, the factories closed, and that was that." Vic sighs. "There's a yacht club out in Sheepshead Bay, you know it?"

"Yes, sir, I do."

"We used to go out there sometimes." Vic stares into space for a while, his eyes looking sort of watery. Then he blinks and looks at us, as though only just remembering we're still here. "Never mind. Say, Sammy, I don't suppose you'd like to earn a little extra cash? I wanna knock through the wall between my sister's old room and my room. And re-paint the kitchen and update the bathroom. I'm tired of looking at the same damn tiles every day. What do you say?"

"Sounds great, sir!"

Vic starts walking toward Union Street. "No time like the present. Let's go."

Sam follows obediently. "I've done a little grouting before, and I can do basic plumbing. I also spent a couple of months helping a buddy build a bar on Canouan Island. It was pretty basic stuff, but I'm a fast learner, sir."

Vic turns and looks at him. "I can see that. And don't call me sir. Call me boss."

Now everyone's got a job but me.

CHAPTER 21

Being broke has a way of fucking with your mind.

The night after the Duane Reade incident I dreamed that I called Stef. Asked him for a couple of grand in exchange for a night of, you know, partying.

In my dream, I knew what I was doing. I felt guilty. And sick. And I tried to stop myself, I tried to tell myself it was the wrong thing to do, but part of me—in my dream, a *big* part of me—felt relieved to know that I'd have cash. That I could survive another month in New York.

The next day I found two hundred dollars in an old purse. Enough to tide me over until I find a real job. In the week since then, I've only spent seventy-five dollars. It's amazing how little you can spend if you do absolutely nothing except hang out with Sam. He's been working for Vic, but that's only three or four hours in the mornings. The rest of the day, we mooch around Rookhaven, watching TV and playing cards and eating pasta. If it's nice out we go for walks around Brooklyn and try to find the bars that offer free food with a two-dollar can of PBR.

It's fun, it's an easy way to spend the day, and I feel like I've known Sam forever. . . . But somehow, I still lie in bed every night feeling tense and worried about the future and sort of, I don't know, unsatisfied. Like I'm still hungry and I don't know what for.

In the past, when I felt this way, I'd drink or sew or both. But I'm pretty sure that drinking myself into obliteration isn't the answer anymore, and I think I've lost my sewing mojo. Last night I dressed Drakey the Dress Form in a 1990s silk slip dress that I picked up from the Brooklyn Flea and stared at her for an hour. And I could not think of anything to do with it.

Tonight, while Madeleine's band is writing songs in the living room (and Pia is with Aidan and Julia's working late and Coco is seeing Ethan the Cheesemaker), we're lounging in my bedroom, reading magazines that Sam brought over as a special treat (magazines are one of the first things to go when you're broke), surfing TV, and generally being silly.

"Pass the M&M's, *Angela*."

"I think you've had enough, *Samuel*. You're getting jowly. I'm doing you a favor."

Sam reaches over and grabs the bowl off of me. I try to stop him, and a tug of war ensues, followed by the inevitable bowl upheaval and M&M explosion.

"See what you did?" Sam sighs with pretend annoyance.

"You're cleaning that up, sonny. I'm not sleeping on M&M's all night," I say, surfing the channels.

"I'm a guest. How dare you ask me to clean up? That is shocking."

"Oh, shut it."

"No, *you* shut it."

"Oh, gnarly. *Reality Bites*." I stop flipping.

Reality Bites is an awesome movie from the '90s. Though, slightly depressingly, the Janeane Garofalo character has to get a job at the Gap.

At one point, Winona Ryder tells Ethan Hawke, "I was really gonna be something by the age of twenty-three." I raise my eyebrow to myself and make a little snorting sound. I'll be twenty-three in less than two weeks, and I'm nobody. Sam glances at me and I quickly try to look normal again.

And I know what you're thinking. But there's nothing between me and Sam. Nothing. I swear. It's purely platonic. There's no frisson, no spark, none of that bubbly-tingly sexual tension, just a funny insta-friend easy intimacy. You know? It's like I've known him for years, not weeks.

I've never had a platonic male friend before. We never really talk about our personal problems, or our families, or anything like that. We just hang out. I can be myself with him—be relaxed and silly and loud and bitchy—the way I never am with actual boyfriends. It's incredibly nice. He's like Pia. But with a penis. And he doesn't borrow my clothes.

Right now he's wearing one of the two fleeces he wears constantly. One is navy, one is dark gray. The gray one looks nice with his eyes. But that's not the point. They're fleece. They're fucking disgusting.

"You need to buy some new clothes. No one is ever going to date you when you're wearing a fleece."

"This fleece is thermal insulated for optimal warmth!"

"That is all the more reason not to wear it."

"I should have never followed you when you jumped off that yacht." Sam crunches another M&M. "Should have let the sharks eat you. Lesson learned." He closes his eyes and nods reverently to himself. "Lesson learned."

I laugh until my attention is stolen by a feature in *Vogue* on the latest Rodarte collection. "God, those girls are amazingly talented," I comment enviously. "The Rodarte sisters."

Sam glances up. "Show me?" I hold up the magazine. "You could do that. Your drawings are better than that, the stuff you make is better than that."

I smile at him and shake my head. "How do you know? You haven't even seen my stuff."

"That dress on the doll thingy is nice," he says. "Sexy."

I look at Drakey the Dress Form, still wearing the black vintage silky slip dress. "I didn't make that. I haven't touched it."

Sam cracks up. "Oh. But still, I've seen the stuff you wear, you never look like everybody else. You don't really believe in yourself, that's your problem."

"Thank you for diagnosing my problem, Doctor Sam."

While Sam stretches his long legs out across my bed and grabs the latest issue of *New York* magazine, I check him out over my *Vogue*. His hair is growing out of the goody-two-shoes crew cut, and he's stopped shaving, so his cheeks are all stubbly. He looks scruffier. Older. And kind of sexy.

"Hey, Sam?"

"Yes?"

"I think you should ask Julia out."

"No."

"One date! Would it kill you?"

Julia keeps asking, with shy hope in her voice, if Sam ever talks about her. Given my newfound friendship with her, I would really like to make her happy. Anyway, why shouldn't they date, right? She's the clean-cut wholesome type, she's sporty, she's funny, she frowns a lot. She's just like him. She even wears fleece sometimes.

I take another M&M, peering into the bowl. I always eat the yellow ones first, I don't know why. So I take out five and line them up on my thigh, like little planes ready for takeoff. Then I zoom one up toward my mouth.

I look up and see Sam looking at me with a little grin on his face.

"What?" I say.

"You're so different from how you . . . seem on the outside."

"You thought I looked like a bitch?" I say, sighing. "I get that a lot. It's just because I'm thinking about something else. And, you know, it doesn't tend to be the person in front of me."

Sam cracks up again.

After *Reality Bites,* we flip channels till *Kramer vs. Kramer* comes on.

Sam is thrilled. "The young Meryl Streep. Totally my perfect woman. Icy-cool on the outside, dynamite within."

"Oh, God. Seriously? Okay, move over, let's watch it."

Sitting side by side—though Sam's shoulders are so wide I have to arrange my pillows around him and lean on his arm so that I'm not totally falling off the bed—we watch the movie. I haven't seen it before, so I have no idea what it's about, but basically it's about divorce and families.

At the very end, just when Dustin Hoffman and Meryl Streep are getting back in the elevator to tell their little kid that he doesn't have to leave his home and his daddy, and Dustin tells Meryl she looks terrific, I find myself crying hysterically, tears streaming down my face.

"Angie?" Sam asks. "Are you okay?"

I try to talk, to stop crying, but I can't even breathe. I'm just wailing and hiccuping, snot and tears covering my face, my chest shuddering with misery. I can't stop, I can't control myself, and I'm so embarrassed, so I curl up, burying my face in a pillow and hiding in my long hair.

"Angie, shhh . . ." Sam strokes my head and makes some slightly awkward mothering sounds, which makes me giggle through my tears. "I can't believe I'm saying this, but . . . do you want to talk about it?"

It all chokes out in a rush. "My parents—my parents are divorcing. My mother told me last month, and I haven't spoken to her since." I'm crying even harder now. I can hardly get the words out. "And my dad, we're really close, or we were, anyway, and, he, he hasn't even called me."

"That's terrible. You must feel like shit."

The fact that Sam is agreeing it's terrible, rather than the proactive hey-girl-high-five-sing-it-sister-you're-amazing-positive-thinking diatribe I've been getting about it from the girls, shocks me out of my incipient hysteria.

"You are not good at this supportive friend stuff, dude."

"Sorry." Sam frowns, propping his elbow on the pillow next to me, resting his head on his hand. "I just meant, uh, that's a shitty situation. And you must feel . . . sad."

"I do," I say, rolling over on the bed to face him. "I feel so sad. I try to ignore it and cover it in other thoughts, you know, but I can't. And when I think about talking to them about it, especially my dad, I just feel, um, scared." I exhale, feeling a strange, painful relief, like I'm stretching out parts of me that have been tight forever. "I ignore all my mother's calls, and my dad hasn't even tried to get in touch. They don't want to be a family anymore, they don't want—they don't want what we had. Even though what we had wasn't exactly the fucking Waltons, you know? It wasn't perfect."

Sam nods. I get the strangest feeling he understands exactly what I mean. "Why wasn't it perfect?"

"I saw my dad making out with his secretary." The words are out before I can stop them. I've never told anyone about this, ever, not Pia, not anyone. "When I was twelve. Her name was Alyssa. He made me promise not to tell Annabel—that's my mother—because it would hurt her feelings. I think he broke up with Alyssa, but then I became his alibi. . . . He'd tell me to tell Annabel that he'd been visiting me at boarding school when he was obviously with other women."

"Wow. What an asshole."

"He's not! He's not, he's . . ." I stop, trying to think how to describe my dad. "He's charming and funny, he dresses immaculately, he knows all about wine and history and the world. He always took my side against Annabel in fights and treated me like I was a grown-up and said I could go out without a curfew. In exchange, I helped him keep his affairs secret. . . . But maybe he is an asshole. A lying, cheating asshole, who just used me to lie to my mother and get what he wanted."

And boom, the tears start again, and with them an ache deep inside that I'd almost forgotten. . . . Whenever my dad asked me to lie for him, I felt nauseous, with strange blunt pains in my torso, like something was pressing on me, stopping me from breathing properly. It was stress, I guess. What kind of a kid gets stress pains?

Sam reaches over and grabs a Kleenex for me. "Are you close to your mom? You never wanted to tell her?"

"I guess I thought I had to keep his secrets." I'm now getting a strange heady feeling from crying so much. "And she should have guessed. It made me so angry that she never figured it out! He was so obvious sometimes!"

Sam frowns. "Maybe she was ignoring it. You can't tell what's going on in a marriage from the outside. Even the kids can't tell."

"Maybe."

A new thought occurs to me. What if she knew I knew about the affairs and that I never told her? It's almost the worst idea of all.

"Was she happy?"

The idea is so strange that for a moment I just stare at Sam in total surprise. "I don't know." How can I never have wondered that before? I try to think. "She wasn't around much. She just hung out with her rich friends, even though we're not rich like them. I mean, don't get me wrong, I know I grew up, um, privileged, but we were never crazy rich, and my dad lost a lot of money in investments in the past few years. I always worry about them being broke, isn't that nuts?" My face is wet with tears, my thoughts zigzagging erratically around my brain, finding everything about my parents that makes me unhappy. "But I bet Annabel still acts like she's loaded. And I hate that. I hate . . . that pretension. I hate rich people. They just use people to get what they want."

"I know," Sam whispers. "I hate that, too."

Everything is silent for a moment. We're both laying on our sides on the bed now, heads on pillows, facing each other. Sam is staring at me so intensely, it's like he can see right into me.

"So these days, Annabel and I don't really get along. I mean, we don't fight, you know, we just don't . . . we don't talk. I haven't answered her calls in weeks. Oh, and she sent me to boarding school without consulting me about it."

"She sent you to boarding school against your will?"

"No! I mean, it was fine, I sure as hell wanted to get out of the house, you know. Dad was never around, and I was avoiding her because it was so hard to keep those secrets from her, she's my *mother*, you know?" Tears threaten to overwhelm me again. "She just didn't ask me. I had no say over what happened in *my* life."

"That'll make anyone angry," Sam says. "Everyone wants control over their destiny."

"She sent me to this expensive all-girls school that all her friends' daughters went to, it was really sporty and outdoorsy and there was only a tiny art faculty. It was totally cliquey. I didn't fit in. And Pia's parents sent her to different schools, um, I think my mother convinced them that we'd be a bad influence on each other or something. But I needed her. And I think she needed me, too. I was alone all the time. Even in the middle of a crowded dining hall, I was alone. I was so alone, it was like I could *taste* it."

"Not fitting in somewhere makes you stronger," says Sam, leaning over to push a strand of hair out of my eyes. It's stuck to my skin with tears, and it takes him a few tries to get it off. The feeling of his fingertips on my skin is surprisingly lovely.

"That's true," I say. "I became tougher and more independent. I decided that if I was going to be alone, I was gonna look like I enjoyed it. I'm alone because I choose to be, you know? But then sometimes I think I can't break out of feeling alone, like I'm in a perma-bubble of aloneness."

"Don't you mean loneliness?"

"No. I don't feel lonely. I like my own company, most of the time, I like drawing and sewing and being by myself. I just feel . . . *alone*. Like I can't rely on anyone. Like the world and I speak a different language."

I sigh deeply, breathing out all my sadness and worry. I've never told anyone this stuff. God, talking really does make me feel better. Even better than when I confessed to the girls. Why have I always kept everything to myself?

As I look into Sam's eyes, I realize something. Right now, right this exact second, for the first time that I can remember, I don't feel alone.

Instead, I feel like I belong right here with Sam. Together.

Sam gazes at me across the pillows, his gray eyes steady and sure. "Angie, I'm sure your folks are dying to hear from you. Both of them."

I want to believe him more than anything. "Would you contact them if you were me?"

Sam doesn't say anything.

"I'm just so sick of their lies, you know?" I say in a tiny voice. "I don't want to give them the opportunity to lie to me more. It seems sometimes like everyone lies. Everyone lies, and everyone's got secrets. I hate it."

"There's a difference between secrets and lies, Angie," says Sam.

"Is there?" I say. "It seems to me like they're interchangeable."

"Mmm." Sam doesn't agree, but he's too well-mannered to argue.

"I just, um, I want life to be . . . simpler."

Sam nods slowly. "I completely agree. My life before I took off was complicated. Sometimes I felt like it was overwhelming me. More than I could handle."

"Exactly," I whisper.

We're still lying on the pillows; our faces are just inches away from each other.

For a few seconds, there's total silence, the only sound our breathing.

My heart is beating so fast that I'm trembling, and I close my eyes for a few seconds, a fizzy tingle in my stomach.

Then I open my eyes again. Sam is still staring at me. He's so close that I can see his individual eyelashes, brown at the roots but white at the tips from sun, the tiny tan-free mark on his nose from wearing sunglasses, the fledgling stubble on his chin. He's staring at me, too, and it's making me self-conscious. I don't know what to do with my lips, I wonder if I have eye snot, if I look stupid, if . . .

Then Sam locks eyes with me again.

We're going to kiss.

I know it. I can feel it, that prekiss moment, the tingly tension, that almost unbearably sweet torture of anticipation. I can imagine the feeling of his lips on my lips so strongly it's like I'm craving the taste and feel and touch and smell of him, like he's the only thing that will satisfy me right now.

Sam leans in a tiny fraction, oh, my God, we're actually going—

No!

I jerk my head away and turn over to break the moment while my mind races. No! No. It's wrong. Sam's my friend. I can't fuck up this friendship by giving in to a base impulse that is the reason I've never had a male friend longer than two weeks. I only like him as a friend. I'm sure of it. Being friends is safer and easier. Take a deep breath. Yes. Another one. Good.

This is transitory sexual tension that is inevitable when you put two people of the opposite sex on a bed and give one of them a crisis. Right? Right. Friends. Safe.

So I get up, go over to my window, open it up, and light a cigarette. For a minute, neither of us says a word.

"My parents divorced when I was twenty-one," Sam says finally. "Then my mom decided she wanted to move to New Mexico and live on a ranch, and my dad, uh, he didn't. Boom. Family over."

I'm so surprised Sam is being so open with me, instead of his usual cryptic self, that all I can think to say is: "Where does your dad live?"

Sam doesn't answer, or doesn't hear me. He's just gazing into space, quiet and serious. "The thing is, it's just another change. You know? Not an ending, just a change. Everything changes, all the time, you move on, your life changes. You graduate from school, boom, change. Go to college, boom, change. You date, you break up, you move in with your buddies, people get sick and die, change change change. So divorce is just another change in life, which is constantly changing anyway."

"But what if you don't like what life changes into?"

"Then you do something to make it change again. Life has to change. If it didn't, then what would be the point? You'd always know what was going to happen next."

"That's pretty good," I say. "You should be a therapist."

"That's what my therapist says."

"You're in therapy? I thought you didn't like talking about yourself."

"Ha." He pauses, and then it all comes out in a rush. "I'm not in therapy anymore, I was in therapy, um, I was kind of angry about the divorce and stuff that happened around that time. . . . You know. And it was such a fucking waste of time, all that anger, people are just gonna do what they're gonna do, you know, you can't change them, not really, you just have to accept them and love them for who they are. I shouldn't have . . . Some of the stuff I did, I was kind of a dick. I wish . . ." He shakes his head, as if to clear it. "Sorry, we're not talking about me."

"We can talk about you if you want to."

"I don't want to. I just want to watch TV and not talk. That's my prerogative, as a dude."

"Where are you from?"

"Ohio. I told you."

"Ohio? I kind of thought you were joking about that. You just don't seem very . . . Ohio-like."

Sam makes a "huh" sound. "I really don't want to talk about it, Angie."

"Too bad, tiger, I do. Is your dad still in Ohio?"

A long pause. "My dad is dead."

"Oh, God, I'm so sorry."

"Don't be."

"Where'd you go to college?"

"New England. I dropped out."

"What did you study?"

"That's all for today."

"Talk," I say, poking him with my toe.

"Nope."

"Talk!" I poke him again.

"Don't poke the bear, Angie, or I will tickle you so hard you will yelp."

"Tickling is just an excuse for teenage boys to accidentally-on-purpose get some tit," I say. "And did you just refer to yourself in the third person as 'the bear'?"

"Did *you* just say 'get some tit'? Wow, you are some lady."

I giggle, overwhelmed with relief that the whole sexual-tension thing is over. He doesn't like me as anything more than a friend. Everything is back to normal.

"I call it like I see it," I shrug.

"Fine. I won't touch you. Not even if you beg me. Can we just watch the next goddamn movie?"

He flicks channels until we find another movie. It's *Rear Window,* an old Hitchcock movie with Grace Kelly and Jimmy Stewart. The sexual tension seems to have been broken, and I feel safe getting back on the bed now. We're just friends. Yes. It's fine.

"God, I love Jimmy Stewart," I say, snuggling down on my pillow.

"Yeah? I thought he'd be a little straight for you."

"Nah. He's perfect. . . . I'm getting under the covers. You can join me if you want, but no funny business."

"Yes, ma'am."

And so, side by side, snuggled up together in a purely platonic way, Sam and I watch the movie. And pretty soon I'm so warm and cozy and comfortable that I fall asleep.

CHAPTER 22

I'm in bed with Sam.

No, not like that, we really did just fall asleep while watching *Rear Window*.

But I'm all curled up into a little ball on my side, with my head over Sam's arm, and he's nestled into me.

We're fucking *spooning*.

For a few minutes I just lie here, listening to Sam breathing. . . . He still smells like soap, even after a night of junk food and no teeth brushing. What is that about?

And why is it so different, sharing a bed with a dude, even if he's just your friend? I'm fully dressed, and Sam's wearing a T-shirt and jeans, it's not like we're indecent. Pia and I have shared a bed a gazillion times, after nights out or on vacation, and during a weird period when this fuckpuppet Eddie broke her heart and I had to carry her home every night, shitfaced and weeping. She always puts her freezing feet on me and snores, I tell her it's goddamn annoying, she says it's freakish that I sleep either starfished out and facedown, or curled up into a tiny ball like a little porcupine. That kind of sleepover is funny and silly.

But with Sam, it's different. I'm so aware of his body next to mine, it's all I can think about. I'm conscious of his feet sticking over the end of my bed, of his deep, even breathing, of the size and strength of him.

There's such a vulnerability and sweetness to sharing a bed with a man, too. Awake, Sam always looks like he's got something very serious on his mind. Asleep, he seems, I don't know, peaceful.

And between you and me, well, sharing a bed with Sam is kind of sexy. Sam is so big, like a giant bear, heat is radiating out from his body, enveloping mine. I'm conscious of the warm, smooth strength of his arm I'm using as a pillow, I can feel the rest of his body pressed against mine all the way down to his feet, and I can see one of his hands: tan, very clean nails, big calloused fingers and palm. He's missing his little fingernail entirely; it was ripped off during a regatta last year. Right now, even that looks kind of sexy. Goddamnit. Why am I having these thoughts about Sam?

And then Sam puts his other arm around me and pulls me in closer against him. He's still asleep, his breathing hasn't changed, he's just hugging me tightly, like it's the most natural thing in the world.

"Angie," he mumbles.

I grin to myself. Sam's talking in his sleep.

"Yes, Sam?"

No response.

Hmm.

I'll try a trick my mother once told me about. Ask people questions when they're sleeptalking, and sometimes their subconscious will understand and respond. Apparently they'll tell you all kinds of stuff. So I wriggle around, still wrapped in his arms, until I'm facing him.

"Hey, Sam," I whisper, pulling my head back so I can see his face. "Sam, what do you think of Angie?"

He smiles in his sleep. "Angel . . ."

I find myself relaxing into him. God, this is lovely. I can't remember the last time I snuggled like this. And yeah, I just used the word snuggle. There's no other way to say it. Sam is wrapping me into him tightly, I can smell his neck, I feel warm and comfortable and safe and just a teensy bit tingly. . . . It's bliss.

Suddenly, Sam takes a deep breath and holds it, for what feels like forever but is probably only about ten seconds. Then he exhales, holding me even more tightly. I fit perfectly into him. I can hear his heart beating. For a second I lie there, listening to it.

Then I try again, craning my head back so I can see his face. "*Angie*. Tell me about Angie. Do you think she's funnier than you are? I bet you do."

Sam gives that little half-sleep smile again and, in one swift move, shifts his arms tighter around me and rolls onto his back, pulling me with him, so that I'm lying almost on top of him and my face is right over his. Holy shit, if Sam was awake right now, we'd be an inch from kissing, literally a *moment* from it. . . .

If I just turned my head a fraction of an inch, I could—

No.

For the second time in twelve hours I pull away from Sam almost violently, half jumping, half falling out of bed in my hurry to escape. This is wrong, this is all wrong.

I'll shower and dress, and then this whole weird intimate sleepover thing will be finished and we can go back to just being normal plain old friends. Right? Right.

I take a long time in the bathroom, washing and scrubbing and conditioning and shaving and moisturizing. I actually love shaving my legs, it's an art form to get each swoop perfect. And the money I used to spend on waxing! What's the point? I'm blond, I'm not exactly hairy, and that whole growing-back-thicker thing is a myth made up by the wax union. (Yes. They have a union.)

Then I shuffle back to my bedroom and check quickly to see that Sam is still asleep. I throw on some very comfortable old jeans, and, after reflection, my dad's Princeton sweater. So what if he hasn't called me in forever? It's still a good goddamn sweater, though it has a couple of small bloodstains from that night I fell off the kitchen counter. That feels like a very long time ago.

Then I turn around, see Sam smiling at me, and let out a little shriek.

"What the hell!? Were you watching me change the whole time?"

"No." Sam looks guilty. "Okay, yes. But I didn't see anything, like, R-rated. Just the beautiful PG parts of you."

"Really." I avoid his eyes. Let's get this conversation back to friend territory. And get the hell out of my bedroom. "How about some breakfast?"

"Buttermilk Channel? Or Café Luluc?"

"I don't have any money, Sam. And no, you're not paying for me. You must be broke by now."

"Right, sorry. Well, I can make you breakfast, how about that? I owe little Coco about sixty meals, too, she keeps feeding me. She's like a very young and innocent grandma. . . . I'll do it for the whole house. I'll fry up some bacon, eggs, pancakes. . . ."

"That would be great!" I say. "But can you grill the bacon, not fry it? I don't like it too oily."

"Oh, really?" Sam says. "I thought you'd like oil."

"What? Why would you think that?"

"Well, you like oil tycoons!" Sam grins widely, and brings out from underneath his pillow . . . *Her Secret Desire*! My latest romance novel!

"Give that back!"

Grinning, Sam leans away from me and starts reading the blurb on the back. *"Shy Millicent had always been unlucky in love. But when oil tycoon Rod Rockson moved to town, she thought her luck was changing. Till she discovered his secret past. . . .* I wonder what his secret past could be?"

"Shut it!" I jump on the bed and reach for the book, just miss it, and find myself straddling Sam, furiously trying to grab the book back. "Give that to me! That's fucking private! I'm not kidding! Sam! I mean it!"

"Now, Angela! Play nice!"

"My name isn't fucking Angela!"

I finally snatch it out of his hands, jump off the bed, and throw it under Drakey the Dress Form.

I'm so upset, I can't even look at Sam, so I pretend to be looking for something in my closet. I'm mortified to be caught reading something so uncool. I feel even more embarrassed than I did last night after my *Kramer vs. Kramer* meltdown! God! And why can't I read whatever I want? Who cares if it's cool? Why do I have to pretend to be tough all the time? Why is it so important to be cynical and unromantic, to not like happy endings and kisses and people saying I love you? Why?

Sam stands up, looking very apologetic, his hair sticking up at crazy angles.

"I'm so sorry, it was under my pillow, Angie. I just thought it was funny—"

"Well, it wasn't." I open my sock drawer and rifle through it pointlessly. He must think I'm such an idiot. "You know what, I've got shit to do," I say over my shoulder. "You should go home."

"You want me to leave?"

"Yes."

There's a long pause while I stare at my socks. Where the fuck do socks come from, I ask you? I don't remember ever buying any in my entire goddamn life.

Sam clears his throat.

"Angie, I'm really sorry, okay? I was just fooling around."

"Yeah?" I finally turn to face him. "Well, I'm sick of fooling around. I don't want to waste my life hanging out like this anymore. It's fucking depressing. I need to get a job. That's what I'm doing today. I'm gonna get a job."

Sam nods. "Right."

I stand up and head for the door, my face still burning from the shame of being busted as a romance reader, and pause quickly to snap at him over my shoulder.

"See yourself out."

CHAPTER **23**

Less than a week before I turn twenty-three.

And I could not be further away from having the adult life I always imagined I'd have by now.

I'm working at the Gap.

Stop laughing.

I need money. I need to pay rent. I need a job, something to focus on, a reason to get out of bed in the morning. Especially since I haven't seen Sam since the whole romance novel sleepover fiasco last week.

He texted the next day: *I'm sorry . . . Forgive me?*

I replied: *Totally. Not a problem.*

And he hasn't tried to get in touch since. I haven't called him, either. I'm too embarrassed; I still feel a hot flush of mortification when I think about him holding up the book with glee. He probably thinks I'm such a romantic. A total cockeyed optimist loser. I hate that. It makes me feel weak. I don't know why, but it does. And I was already feeling so exposed after telling him all that stuff about my parents. . . .

You know what? We became such close friends so fast, it was too intense. I needed space. That's all.

And a full-time job at the Gap has certainly provided it.

In some ways, the Gap isn't all that bad: it turns out my folding skills are kind of gnarly. Who knew? (I never folded anything of my own before; I just pretended the wrinkles were part of my unique style.)

But the hours are long, the salary is terrible, I'm getting blisters from being on my feet all day, and wow, it's boring. I'm so bored I almost can't keep my eyes from closing. Sometimes I fantasize about making a bed out of T-shirts in the changing rooms and curling up for a nap, like a little puppy.

Also, people never look you in the eye when you work in retail. Don't they realize it's my job to ask them if they need help finding anything? It's what I am paid to *do*. And one of the managers, Shania, has told me off twice for not having a "pleasant expression." I can't help it if I look bitchy when I'm preoccupied. She looks bitchy because she's a bitch.

But the best part? The clothes. Gap isn't exactly my style, but I genuinely like helping customers choose the right clothes. Sometimes someone asks me what style of jeans would suit them, or if this shirt will go with that skirt, and I get to style them. The smile when that person comes out of the changing room and sees they're looking better than they expected . . . I *love* that. I never upsell, either. I make sure that they stay in their budget. And I've pointed a few people in the direction of Urban Outfitters or Zara, to pick up something that will just make their outfit. (Usually a bright belt, clutch, or pair of shoes. Pretty textbook stuff.)

But no matter what, my mind still paces back and forth, trying to think of ways to get out of here, get a real job in fashion. . . . I know I can't be a designer, that dream is just that—a dream. It's out of reach. Impossible. But I could be an assistant, right? Or a receptionist, I could work for a fashion label or a PR company or a stylist.

I am sure I could do *something* better than this, if only someone would give me a chance.

But no one will.

Goddamn, I'm lost.

Right now, it's nearly the end of the day in this soulless part of Midtown Manhattan, and there's a particularly bleak cross section of society in the store. Sticky little whiners in strollers who just want to be home playing with toys, backpacked tourists shell-shocked from a day sightseeing, overweight solo shoppers eyeing merchandise like a potential foe. . . .

Humanity. Urgh. Pia always says how much she loves working with people; she gets energized by it. I'd rather just be in a quiet corner thinking about clothes. But not my parents. Or my future.

My phone vibrates in my pocket, and I immediately duck to the floor, pretending to rearrange some sweaters so I can check it. A text from Julia.

Just letting you know that my boss just invited everyone except me to a strip club tonight to celebrate a deal. My job is worse than yours.

I grin to myself and reply.

This morning, I found a shit in the mens' changing rooms. Not a dog shit, not a kiddie shit. A man. Took a shit. In the middle of the changing room. My job is worse than yours.

I get a reply a moment later.

You win.

Ha. Jules and I are still texting a lot. Mostly competing to see who has the worse job. It's so cute that she's even pretending working at an investment bank is anywhere near as terrible as working at the Gap. Pia was right all this time: Julia is kind of awesome. I'm so glad we've become real friends. I don't think Pia is jealous anymore. . . . Though, to be honest, Pia hasn't been around to be jealous. She's spending every minute she can with Aidan before he leaves for San Francisco. They've decided to give the long-distance thing a try.

I'm surreptitiously stretching out my hamstrings—why they're so tight from just standing around all day doing nothing, I don't know—when an older lady comes over and starts scanning the wall of jeans.

"Hello! May I help you find anything in particular?"

She nods. "I want a pair of jeans that don't make me look like a hoochie mama."

I grin. "Right . . . hooch-free denim. Well, this pair is really well cut around the thighs, so they're supportive but not too snug. They've got a ten-inch rise, which is so much more comfortable around your tummy area, and the dark shade is classic, no hoochie whiskering or wash. . . . It's almost like a pair of pants, but with the comfort and ease of denim."

"Wow. You're good."

"Thank you," I say, taking down the jeans. "I love clothes. Here, just for comparison, you should try on this pair and this pair, too."

"Thank you. . . . I used to love clothes. Now I just wear them." She takes the jeans I offer her and frowns. "This is my size. How did you know?"

"That's why they pay me the big bucks. Can I put them in a changing room for you?"

"I'll take them myself." She takes the jeans off to the changing area.

Suddenly, I'm in a much better mood. I *do* like this job! And I'm good at it! I helped that lady find jeans and she'll look *great* in them, I know she will, and it'll make her happy all day. All because of me. An old Rihanna song comes on over the music system, and without even thinking about it, I start bobbing my head and singing along, then do a teeny tiny twirl on the spot.

At that moment Derek, one of the guys who usually works the register, walks past. He frowns at me and shakes his head.

"This isn't a nightclub, Angela."

He's gone before I can reply "It's Angie, dickface," so I just flip him the bird behind his back. Real mature, but that's what retail does to you.

At that moment, I hear a familiar drawl behind me.

"What the fuck are we doing here, Blythe? You know my rules: no moms, no hugs, no chain stores."

I freeze, my heart suddenly hammering in my chest. I'd know that voice anywhere.

It's Stef.

The Blythe person giggles.

"Stef, baby, I told you, I need some tanks and Gap ones fit me best."

"Can't we go to James Perse or Splendid or, fuck, somewhere decent? I'll pay."

"Maybe later. I have to hit Intermix."

Their voices are getting louder and louder. Keeping my head down, I drop to the floor, pretending to adjust the chinos on the bottom level. No chinos have ever been this perfectly symmetrical in the history of casual pants. I look for an error, anything that will give me something to do. . . . Aha! A size six in the size eights! My face still turned away from their voices, I pull out the entire stack and start realigning them, very slowly, praying that Stef just walks away, that—

"Well, look at this," says a soft voice. Suddenly, inches from me on the floor, I spot Stef's shoes. John Lobb. Of course. "If it isn't the infamous Angie."

I slowly stand up, feeling a strange combination of fear and fury. "Stef."

Our eyes meet. He's looking his standard privileged, oily self.

At that moment the Blythe girl comes over. She's one of those tall, expensive brunettes that the Upper East Side breeds in litters. She's wearing DVF shoes, dress, bag, and coat. Style by numbers.

"What's this?" She cocks her head to one side, looking at me like I was a funny little painting.

"This is Angie," says Stef. "An old friend."

Blythe gives me a little fake smile. "How sweet." She saunters away.

"I'm not your friend," I hiss at Stef. "And I'll never forgive you for what you did to me."

"What I *did*? Chill out, Angie. You love rich guys. I just introduced you to some of them. Your behavior on the boat was really uncool. You totally overreacted."

My fists clench. I want to slap him. I want to scream and make a scene and quit this stupid job and run away and drink vodka and laugh all night and pretend everything is perfect. I crave it so badly, I can almost taste the joy of that escape.

But I'm not going to do it.

I'm not running away from my problems anymore.

Because I can't make them go away like that. Not really.

"You're a worthless scumbag." My voice is shaking with the effort of keeping it low. "Stay away from me. And get out of my store."

Blythe has sauntered back toward us and overhears me.

"I don't believe this! Where is your manager?" snaps Blythe. She looks around, her voice high and demanding and Upper East Side-y. "I need a manager here!"

"No, Blythe, leave it." Stef is staring at me, a half smile on his face. "I have a feeling I'll be hearing from her soon enough. When reality hits, a night of fun in the Soho Grand won't seem so bad."

I can't meet his eyes, so I stare at his nose instead (an old trick my dad taught me when I was little). *A night of fun in the Soho Grand . . .* What the fuck happened that night? I feel sick.

For a few seconds, there's total silence.

Then, I smile at them both. "Can I help you with anything? No? Then please excuse me. I have work to do."

Trembling, I walk away and start refolding T-shirts, following their progress through the store out of the corner of my eye. Stef stares at me, till Blythe starts sniping at him. He snaps back. She immediately shuts up, and they leave.

And I don't run away. I don't give in. I just focus on getting through the day.

That night, on the subway home to Rookhaven, the sick feeling slowly subsiding in my stomach, I can't help staring at every other worker drone, all of us jammed in side by side on the way home from our shit jobs, and everyone is doing something to distract their brains from reality. They're either listening to music with their eyes closed, or reading the *New York Post,* or staring at BlackBerrys or iPhones, thumbs frantically tapping away.

I always thought people did that stuff when they were bored and trying to kill time. But now I know it's because they're all trying to forget whatever it is they had to do that day to earn a living. Because it probably sucked.

This can't be what my life is meant to be like. It just . . . it *can't* be.

But I don't want my old life, either.

So I guess I'm stuck here. And suddenly, I know that the only thing in the world that will cheer me up is my friends. Pia, Coco, Julia, and Madeleine. And Sam. I miss Sam. It's only been a few days since I spoke to him, but it seems like forever. I don't care that he knows I read romance novels. I don't care if he thinks I'm a loser. I just miss him.

When I get off the subway at Carroll Gardens, I take out my phone and call him.

"Are we friends again?" he says, instead of hello.

"Affirmative. I'm sorry I kicked you out."

"I'm sorry I made fun of your book. Do you know that I love Harry Potter? I do. I'm crazy about that little wizard geek."

I can't help cracking up. "Okay, we're officially friends again."

"Our first fight! Man, I feel special. Do you feel special?"

"I feel hungry."

"I'm at Vic's, finishing off the bathroom. We're heading up to Bartolo's for pizza. You want in?"

"Yes."

"Where have you been, anyway, lady? I knocked on your front door, like, four times this week."

"Uh, I got a job."

"Oh yeah? That's awesome! Where?"

"If I tell you, will you promise not to laugh?"

"Yes."

"The Gap."

CHAPTER 24

Sam is still laughing when I get to Bartolo's. It's a real old-school Brooklyn Italian joint, the kind of place with mismatched plates and menus that haven't changed in forever. Vic's family started it decades ago, and it's still run by one of his nephews. It has that family feeling, you know? At least half the tables have kids, and tonight, most have kids, parents, and grandparents. I gaze around at them. Real live happy families. I wonder how my dad is.

"Okay, Angie, what'll it be?" asks Vic, interrupting my reverie.

I don't even look at my menu. "The margherita pizza, please."

Sam looks over at me and cracks up again.

"Shut it!" I say. "Vic, Sam's picking on me. Just because I got a job."

Vic grins at me, his face all gnarled and happy. "I think it's great, girlie. Work gives life meaning. Makes you feel fulfilled."

Working at the Gap is supposed to give my life meaning and make me feel fulfilled? The idea is so insanely depressing that for a moment I can't say anything. Then the bartender, Jonah, comes over with our drinks. A beer for Sam, a club soda for Vic, and a vodka on the rocks for me.

"You sure you want straight vodka, honeybunny?" asks Jonah.

"I'm sure, sugarnuts, I'm sure," I say.

Jonah winks at me and walks away. I grin after him. Cute guy. Not so bright.

Then I look back and see Sam staring at me with a strange look on his face.

"What?" I say. "He's a friend of Pia's! She worked here for about four and a half seconds last year."

"Right," says Sam. "So tell us about the Gap."

So I do, a bit. And then Vic tells us about a department store that his sister used to work at in Park Slope. It was called Germaine's.

"She hated it," Vic says. "Especially during the holiday season. She'd come home with dozens of mismatched gloves, you know. People would drop them on the ground when they were shopping. I didn't wear a matching set of gloves until I got married." Vic cracks up, and it's so weird and nice hearing him laugh like that that Sam and I crack up, too.

When our food arrives, we get lost in chewing and appreciative eating noises. I love margherita pizza. I like the constancy of it: you always know what you're getting, each bite is exactly like the last, no nasty surprises. And eating with Sam and Vic feels natural, like we're family. I think Sam's thinking the same thing. This is just so happy and peaceful.

I wonder who Vic eats with these days. His sister passed away last year, his wife died a long time ago. He must feel very alone.

"We should do this more often," I say. "Dinner, here, I mean. Every Thursday! Would you like that, Vic?"

"Me? Sure." Vic goes to take another leisurely bite of pizza, then stops, as though a thought just occurred to him. "You think I'm a lonely old man, Angie?"

"No," I say, slightly defensively.

"I never feel lonely," he says. "I'm very busy. I got my bocce ball, I got my social club, I got a million goddamn nieces always calling up and nagging me, I got cable now and that HBO is a whole lotta fun, I can tell you. . . . I got things to look forward to. Keep your life full of things to look forward to, and you'll never feel alone."

"Roger that," I say. More pearls of wisdom from Vic. We should start a goddamn blog.

The thing is, he always does make sense. It's just that it's never the answer I really want to hear. I don't think working full-time at the Gap qualifies as having a fulfilling life. But I know that's my problem. A lot of people probably love working at the Gap.

I look down at my little gold clutch. It's been the most incredibly useful purse. I usually get sick of bags and change every two or three days, but I love this one. I might make one with a long shoulder strap or a wrist strap, and a larger size for days when I need to take more with me but don't want the full snail-tote. I'm sure I have about fifteen more of those secondhand Art Deco scarves stashed away somewhere. And I've been tailoring that slip dress that Sam liked to suit me, too. (Four inches off the hem, natch.)

Suddenly, even just thinking about sewing makes me feel happy, awake, and excited, like I have something to look forward to. If I can just pretend sewing is my job, then my life does have meaning.

I look up at Vic and grin. "You are absolutely right."

At that moment my phone beeps.

A text from Pia: *Where are you? EMERGENCY.*

Bartolo's, I respond.

Ten minutes later, just as we've finished eating, there's a screech of brakes outside. A huge pink food truck has parked in the middle of the sidewalk. Pia.

She strides into Bartolo's, banging the door behind her dramatically, sees us, and comes straight over.

"Oh God, Vic, Angie, Sam, help me! Aidan and I broke up." She bursts into noisy sobs and throws herself down next to me. "We're not doing the long-distance thing, we're not even going to try. He just flew out tonight. It's over, it's really, seriously over." Pia is crying so hard that I can barely make out the words, and I automatically pull her into me, into Sam's baby owl hug where she's nestled under my wing, drenching me with her tears.

I look up at the waiter. "Check, please."

Pia drives me back to Rookhaven, wailing the whole way. There's nothing I can do except be a good friend and listen right now, so I try to make out words among the wails and hope like hell we don't crash. Sam and Vic decided to walk back, ostensibly to get some air but clearly to avoid Pia's crisis. She *does* cry pretty loudly. It scares men and small animals.

Coco and Madeleine are in the kitchen eating stir-fry chicken and broccoli, and Pia stops sobbing long enough to tell us all the whole story.

"We started breaking up last night, and then we went to sleep, and then we had, like, four A.M. sex—"

"Overshare," mutters Madeleine.

"—and then we woke up and didn't discuss it, you know. Like if we just drank our coffee and ate our bagels it would just be like any other day. And then we met up after work and broke up for real. We have done nothing but talk about it for weeks, you know, and the thing is, we were going to do long-distance but we know it'll never work! It's like a slow death rather than, uh, a swift stab to the heart." Nice. "And now Aidan's on a plane to California, and I can't believe it's over.... But my life is going this way, his life is going that way, and neither of us should sacrifice our careers for each other, right?"

"Right!" Coco and I say firmly.

"What if I end up old and alone? Choosing my career ahead of love! I'll be that woman with cats! I fucking hate cats!"

"Ladybitch, you're not even twenty-three yet. You don't have to worry about being old and alone."

"I'm gonna miss him so much!" Pia isn't listening to anyone. "Our relationship is like that movie *Dead Man Walking*!"

Madeleine frowns. "Uh, I'm not sure that—"

"I can't believe it's over! It's over." Pia stares into space, whispering, "It's really over."

"It's not over!" says Coco. "It's not like you've been fighting or fallen out of love, you're just forced apart by, um, by unforeseen circumstances, that's all! He'll be back one day!"

"Yeah!" I say. "And in the meantime, you can date!"

"No! Do you know how hard it is for me to meet guys who really, truly *get* me? With whom I have a genuine connection? It's just ... it's impossible."

For a second, tears spring to my eyes. I try to imagine what it would be like to finally fall in love, *real* love, and then have it ripped away from me. It would be like a bitch slap from the universe, that's what.

Pia's ranting now. "Guys always think I'm weird, or stupid, or both. They think my upbringing is strange, that moving so much must mean I'm a basket case, or that being Swiss-Indian means I eat nothing but fucking cuckoo clocks and curry!"

I start laughing at this. "Ladybitch, calm down. . . ."

But Pia isn't listening. "And they think I'm great for a good time, but not for conversation, not for anything real. I am really good at talking, goddamnit! I could talk for hours if you wanted me to! Now I'll be single forever! And ever and ever! Oh God! I'm going to have a panic attack!" Pia closes her eyes and makes a sound that can only be described as "WAHHHH."

At that moment, Julia walks in the kitchen, still in her suit from work, little gym bag glued to her shoulders, as always.

"What the fu—?"

"Pia and Aidan broke up," says Madeleine.

"Holy shit!" says Julia. "I thought you guys would get married for sure. And we'd all be your bridesmaids."

That sets Pia off again, naturally. Five minutes later, she's still crying, and we've run out of calming platitudes.

So I put on my strictest voice, the one that has worked with a hysterical Pia in the past.

"Pia! Stop wailing and breathe," I say. "Now. I mean it. You're making yourself sick." Pia closes her mouth, her chest still shaking from hysteria. "If Aidan is the man you are meant to be with, then you'll get back together in the future. In the meantime, you get to enjoy your life. You love your job, you love Rookhaven. . . ."

"I love drinking," she says, sniffing. "Let's go out Saturday and get really shitfaced. I need attention from pretty boys. That will make me feel better."

"Um, I can't," says Julia, turning pink.

"Why not? Hot date?"

Julia looks around the room, a coy smile on her face, until she has all of our attention exclusively on her. "Well, yes actually. I just ran into

Sam on my way in, he was outside Vic's place . . . and he asked me out!"

"Woo!" shouts Madeleine. "How did that happen?"

Julia is pink with pleasure. "We were talking about Bartolo's, and I said it's my favorite place in Brooklyn, then he said his favorite Brooklyn restaurant was this Mexican place near his house, and then I said, 'Oh, my God I totally love Mexican,' and then he said, 'We should go sometime,' and I said, 'How's Saturday?'" She turns to me with a huge grin. "Isn't it awesome, Angie?"

Oh. My. God. Julia is going out with Sam.

CHAPTER **25**

Five days until my birthday.

And another boring day at the Gap.

Fact: being bored changes the space-time continuum. As in, space starts to close in on you, and time stops moving. It seems like a month since I got up this morning. I can't even remember what I ate for breakfast. Or what I had for dinner last night.

Wait. Yes I can. I ate pizza at Bartolo's with Sam and Vic.

And then Sam asked Julia out.

I'm still so surprised. I'm like a little Angie cartoon with an exclamation mark above her head.

I'm also annoyed at myself for being surprised. Julia really likes him, and I've been bugging him to ask her out for weeks. It's just what I wanted, right? It's totally fine!

Well, whatever. I'm trying not to think about it. It's only weird because he's my friend, and we've been spending so much damn time together. We had that strange sleepover, though nothing happened, and, you know, it's just one of those friendships that you make sometimes when you're between relationships. I usually end said friendships by sleeping with the guy, and then find out that we weren't actually friends at all. But that won't happen this time.

Because he's going out with Julia Saturday.

So that's that.

And in thirty-two minutes, I can leave for the day.

(And then go home and put salve on my blisters and eat and sleep and get up and come in here and do it all over again. Argh.)

Suddenly, there's a tap on my shoulder.

"Angie! It's me!" Coco jumps up and down with delight. "Surprise!"

"Hey! What are you doing here?"

"I was in the neighborhood, um, going to the Museum of Modern Art."

We hug hello quickly.

Weird, I don't think I've ever been alone with Coco outside of Rookhaven. With Pia and Coco together, yes, but never just the two of us. I look around, trying to think of something to talk about, and see my coworkers Derek the dickface and Shania the bitch staring at me.

"Want to try on some clothes?"

"Sure!"

"You should wear blue." I have been dying to get Coco out of those baggy, faded black threads ever since we met. "Pale blue. To bring out your eyes. And gray. And white. Sharper shoulders, tighter waists, no more high-neck sweaters. . . . How much money do you want to spend? I'll buy it all for you and use my fifty-percent-off employee discount, and you can pay me back. It's kind of bending the rules, so we have to be real sneaky about it."

Coco's eyes light up. "Your job is so cool!"

I guess it is pretty cool. Kind of.

Coco and I spend the next half an hour enjoying a full-on makeover montage. All that's missing is the eighties music. By the time my shift ends, she's bought three pairs of jeans, four tops, an actual dress (I have *never* seen Coco in a dress before), and a really cool trench coat that's perfect for spring. I've managed to get her out of her oversize, baggy, hide-me look. She has enormous boobs so unless she wears something really fitted, she can look a little frumpy.

"Wow, Angie, thank you so much. This is going to be so great for my next date with Ethan."

"You're seeing that guy again?" I say, the words out of my mouth before I can stop myself.

She pauses. "Yeah . . . I mean, I thought I would. Why? You don't like him?"

"Of course I like him! Anyway, it doesn't matter if I like him. What matters is if *you* like him." God, I hate it when people say that shit, and here I am, saying it anyway.

"I think I do. . . ." She pauses. "Can we grab a coffee after this and talk?"

"Let's get a drink instead. Go to P. J. Clarke's on the corner of Fifty-fifth and Third, and I'll finish my shift, buy these clothes, and meet you in fifteen minutes."

P. J. Clarke's is an old bar with a Sinatra-Rat-Pack pedigree, but I like it because you can sit at the bar, eat tiny burgers called sliders, and drink martinis. I don't have the cash for sliders and martinis, of course, but I got my paycheck today, so I can totally afford a couple of beers for Coco and me. (I wonder if I'll ever be able to make social plans without mentally going through my bank balance.)

On the way, I call Pia quickly. She answers, but all I can hear is snuffling.

"Ladybitch. It's me."

A small choking sound comes out.

"I'm having a drink with Coco near your office in Midtown. You wanna join?"

"No." Pia's voice is barely a croak. "I have to work late. I'm way behind because of all this fucking crying. It's really hard to read a computer screen with tears in your eyes, you know?"

"Love you, ladybitch," I say, surprising myself. I never say shit like that.

"Love you, too."

When I get to P. J. Clarke's, Coco is sitting at the far end of the bar, drinking a cosmopolitan and staring at her phone, looking incredibly self-conscious. The rest of the bar is filled with the usual Friday night happy-hour crowd: suits, tourists, and some nervous daters.

"Voilà. Fashion delivery," I say, handing over the Gap shopping bag.

"Thank you! Wow. This is really so awesome of you!"

"Do you want another cocktail?" I ask Coco, praying she'll say no because I can't afford it.

"No, it's kind of nasty," she says, wrinkling her nose.

I nod. "Cosmopolitans taste like crap. That's the weird thing about them." I catch the bartender's eye. He's a huge hulk of a guy, in a perfectly pressed shirt and tie. "Two Heinekens, please."

The first sip of a supercold beer is always the sweetest. I take a sip and sigh. What a long, boring day. My blisters are throbbing, but I guess it would be kind of gross to apply fresh blister thingies right here at the bar.

Coco has started tearing pieces of her beer's label off with her fingernails. Nerves? I never have any idea how she's really feeling, since she's always sweetly smiling. Maybe it's time I found out.

"Do you want to talk about the dinner party med meltdown, Coco?"

"No," she says, and then looks at me and forces a little laugh out. "I just had a headache before the party, you know? So I took the Demerol they gave me at the clinic back in December."

"Have you told Julia about it?"

"She would never understand," Coco mumbles.

"Okay. Where did you get the Xanax? Was it prescribed to you?" I feel like a school counselor.

"I found it," she says carefully, ripping off another tiny shard of her beer label. "I just found it lying around."

Well, that's obviously not true. But I won't push her. "So why did you take it?"

"I thought it might make me less nervous," she says. "It's an anti-anxiety med, right? And I was feeling very anxious before the dinner party, about the cooking, and about Jonah, you know, because I asked him to be my date and he said no, and then I felt nervous about Ethan."

"Right. Ethan."

"My therapist thinks he sounds like he'd be very positive for me," she says, slightly defensively.

"You're in therapy?"

"Yeah. Um, they offered it, so I said yes," she says in a very low voice.

"Do you want to talk about it?"

"No."

"Are you sure?" Vic's words of advice from the night I got back to Rookhaven spill out of my mouth. "It's much easier to let go of your worries when you share them with the people you love."

Coco looks at me, her eyes filling with tears, and she puts her face in her hands. As usual, when faced with a crying friend, I'm not sure what to do, and particularly not in the middle of a crowded Midtown Manhattan bar. I get her a big wad of cocktail napkins from the bartender, who doesn't seem fazed to have a girl crying hysterically in his bar, and then stroke her arm in what I hope is a comforting manner. After a few minutes, she dries her eyes.

"Sorry," she says. "Sorry, Angie, you must think I'm such a freaking loser."

"Trust me. I don't."

A slick, suited guy is suddenly standing almost on top of us. "Ladies! Don't cry, I'm here now."

I stare at him, hoping he can read the fuck-off message in my eyes.

Apparently he can't.

"I was thinking—"

"No."

"You haven't even heard what I—"

"No."

His smile drops. "What's your fucking problem?"

"My problem is that my friend and I are not in the market for a date rape tonight, thank you."

"What the fuck? Are you getting your fucking period or something? I—"

"That's enough, buddy," calls the bartender. "Leave the ladies alone."

He slinks off, and I wink at Coco. She is giggling helplessly. "I can't believe you just said that."

"I know," I say. "Sometimes I open my mouth and shit like that just comes out. Are you okay?"

"Yes . . . no . . . I mean, yes, I'm fine like, right this second, but when I'm alone, I don't feel okay . . . and I've been having trouble sleeping, and it's so hard to feel happy when you're tired all the time, and I know it's a process, it's a process, my therapist keeps saying it's a process, but you know, I just . . . can't imagine . . . feeling normal again."

"Of course you will!"

"I've been thinking about antidepressants, what do you think about that?" Before I can say anything, she continues quickly. "I went on them after my mom died, but then they made me gain weight and gave me crazy dreams, which kind of made me more depressed, though I guess I could try another kind, you know?"

"Um . . . so you just keep trying different kinds until you find one that fits, like Goldilocks and the Three Medicated Bears?"

But Coco isn't listening. "My dad says everyone needs to feel sad sometimes, that it's part of being human, you know? He says that all great art and literature is created by people who feel things deeply, who experience love and hate and heartbreak and jealousy and loneliness and, you know, everything, so people taking antidepressants are cutting themselves off from real human emotions. They're making themselves, like, nonhuman. That's why I went to MoMA tonight, I thought maybe art would make me feel better. . . ."

"Did it?"

"A little. But then I think about the future, I think about going home for another sleepless night, and getting up tomorrow and going to work again surrounded by children and having no adult conversations, and I feel so alone and so exhausted." Coco takes a deep breath. "I don't want to keep feeling this way. I want to feel *better*."

I chew my lip, hesitating. Fuck it. "I had one, you know. An abortion."

"You did? Why didn't you tell me?"

"I don't know why I didn't tell you before. I guess, um, oh, I don't know." I pause, not wanting to tell her the truth: that sharing secrets, or problems, or issues, has always made me feel weak. "He was the first guy I slept with. A bartender while I was on vacation with Pia and her parents. I didn't plan on having sex with him, you know. I was really drunk and feeling sort of crazy. I don't even remember it really."

"Why were you feeling crazy?"

"I'd gone home at the start of the summer and my dad had moved out. Annabel—that's my mother—she kept saying he was away on business, but I didn't believe her, and he wouldn't answer my calls." I stare into space, remembering. "And then she sent me on vacation with Pia and her folks without asking me. I felt . . . I don't know. Crazy. I wanted to go completely out of control because I had no control over anything in my life, you know?"

"But your parents stayed together."

"Dad came to see me at school the next semester and told me everything was fine, and by the next vacation he was back in the house."

"And you got an abortion. . . ."

"In a town near my boarding school," I say. "I had a fake ID so they thought I was twenty-one. It wasn't hard."

"That makes me feel so much better, is that weird? Did you feel bad afterward?"

"I felt sad, but it was the right choice for me," I say. "Mostly I was relieved."

"I did some reading online, and I got so upset—"

"Never read about anything controversial online, Coco," I say. "That's where all the freaks come out to play. It's your body, it's your choice. If they spent half as much energy helping people in need as they do condemning them, the world would be a better place."

Coco nods. But she doesn't look convinced. "Abstinence is the only form of birth control that works," she says, clearly repeating something she's read.

"Abstinence is a myth," I say. "Humans fuck, Coco. It's the way the world works. We always have, we always will. And women have always tried to prevent conception. . . . Ancient Egyptians, Romans, Greeks, people in the Middle Ages, in Shakespeare's time, they all had birth control, and when it failed, they had abortions, though they were incredibly dangerous and women died, like, all the time." I put a cigarette in the corner of my mouth. "It's part of human nature. We fuck."

"Oh," Coco says in a tiny voice. She looks slightly shocked. I need to tone down the swearing.

"Sorry, honey. I'm just saying . . . sex is sex. The urge to do it is what has kept the human species alive for millions of years. But now we have the right and the ability to choose when and where we have babies. We're not animals."

Coco nods. "That makes sense. I guess."

Then I remember something else Vic said. "You've got to let regrets and worries go, honey. Otherwise you'll spend your whole life thinking about them."

"But *how* do I let them go?" Coco stares at me, willing me to have an answer. *"How?"*

I don't want to disappoint her, but I don't want to lie, either. So I shrug. "I wish I knew."

Coco sighs and picks up her beer. We clink a little silent cheers.

"So, are you gonna see Ethan the Chees—I mean, Ethan again?"

"I hope so!" She smiles. "He's so smart and nice! And my therapist says I have, um, self-esteem issues, so he'd be great for me."

"We all have self-esteem issues," I say. "They come with tits."

"You don't. You're gorgeous. Men always look at you. Right now, I can see, like, seven guys in this bar looking at you."

Sam pops into my head. Sam asked Julia out. Weird.

I force myself back to the present and shake my head. "They don't like me. They just like . . . my outside. They like my shell."

"How many times have you been in love?"

"Oh, Coconut. I don't know. A dozen times . . . and also never."

Coco stares at me. "I don't understand what you mean."

I take a sip of my drink, thinking. "I mean . . . I always think I'm in love . . . but if you're in love, you should be happy, right? I wasn't. I was always trying to please these guys who could never be pleased. I was always stressed, always putting them first, and doing anything I could to make them not break up with me, but trying to act really cool about it all. It was exhausting. That can't be love. Sometimes I even felt . . . a little psycho. And I don't even know if I was myself around them, not really. I don't think any of them ever really knew me at all."

Coco nods thoughtfully. "I don't think Eric knew me, either. Or Jonah . . . Maybe Ethan does, or will. . . . I think you need to be friends first, like Julia and Sam!" she says. "I hope they fall in love. Julia really wants a relationship."

"Yeah, totally, me too," I say, staring at my drink. Julia and Sam. Sam and Julia.

"I'm so glad you and Julia have gotten to know each other better," says Coco. "You're both so cool. You're the leaders of the house, you know?"

I laugh out loud. "I am not the leader of anything!"

"Yes you are," she says insistently. "Pia is never around anymore. But you and Jules are the ones who make everyone laugh. Plus, you're the cool one."

I smile. Only Coco would see the world in terms of cool and not cool.

"And you're really good for Julia. You know, the makeover stuff, and introducing her to Sam. You're a good friend."

"Really?"

"Really."

Coco's uncomplicated approval, and the idea of me being a good friend, makes me feel happier than I have in a long, long time. "Let's go home," I say.

"Okay!" She hops off her stool obediently. "Thanks, Angie. You really made me feel better about everything."

"Anytime, ladybitch."

"You've never called me that before!" Coco is beaming. "I love it . . . ladybitch."

On the subway home, I reflect on the ever-been-in-love question. I don't think I've ever been truly, madly, deeply in love. Or in a real relationship, one that really meant something, one that made me truly happy. Maybe I'm simply not capable of it. Which just makes me thank God, yet again, that I've decided to be single now.

So I'm glad Sam's going out with Julia.

I hope they'll be very happy together.

CHAPTER 26

"When can we see your band?"

"Never." Madeleine calmly looks at her cards. "I get stage fright when people I know are watching."

"Maybe we should blindfold you."

"Maybe we should gag *you*."

Julia takes a slug of wine. "Angie, are you sure I look okay?"

I glance at her. "Perfect."

It's Saturday night, and we're all in the kitchen at Rookhaven, having wine and playing poker before our Celebrate Pia's Singledom Night Out (subtitled Make Her Stop Crying Just for a Few Goddamn Hours for Fuck's Sake).

Well, almost all of us.

Julia is going on her date with Sam instead.

"I'm not nervous." Julia flicks her perfect blowout-by-Coco.

Madeleine smirks. "That's why you made Angie spend four hours shopping in SoHo with you for the right outfit?"

"I liked it," I say. Which is mostly true.

The shopping part was fine. And Jules bought me lunch at Café Habana to say thank you. But then she kept asking me questions about Sam. And really, all I know is he's from Ohio, he dropped out of college, he learned how to sail on the job, he's currently sleeping on his buddy's floor, he's my friend, and I've been avoiding his calls ever since he asked Julia out. But I don't own him! He can do whatever he wants. Right?

The rest of today, I've just been sewing and trying not to think about him. I altered Drakey's little slip dress, the one Sam liked, and I'm wearing it tonight. It felt so good to *do* something again, to be creating things, to take myself outside my head . . . The only time I've felt at peace in days is when I've been sewing. Just like Vic said.

"I feel . . ." Julia takes a deep breath, waiting for everyone to pay attention to her again. "I feel certain, in my soul, that it's going to be good. That's probably a sign, right? They say when you know, you know."

At this, Pia, who has barely spoken all day, makes a gulping sound, her huge brown eyes filling with tears. Any mention of romance, men, or breakups, and she loses her shit. Seriously, it's like every dramatic soap opera meltdown you've ever seen, in one woman. She came into my bedroom at 4:00 A.M., weeping, saying that she couldn't sleep alone, that the universe was against her, that she'd never love again. She was asleep and snoring within six seconds. Even Sam didn't snore . . . argh. Don't think about Sam.

"Oh God! My makeup . . ." Pia tilts her head back to stop the tears from ruining her eyeliner. "Damn you, Aidan, for breaking my heart," she whispers at the ceiling. "Damn you to hell."

"Have you talked to him today?" asks Madeleine.

"He keeps calling. I keep not answering." Pia slaps her palm on the table. "Fuck Aidan! Tonight is about my ego-driven, God-given right to drink hard spirits while enjoying the restorative power of the male gaze."

"Hey, you guys. Look at this," says Julia, pinging the leg of her black tights. A cloud of dust, or skin cells, or something, billows out.

Madeleine looks like she might puke. "Julia! That is disgusting!"

"I know!" Julia looks fascinated and does it again. "It's like a scab. I can't stop picking at it."

"You pick at scabs?"

"Everyone picks at scabs." Julia waves her hands dismissively. "Anyone who says they don't is lying. That's my whole philosophy on life."

"I don't *get* scabs," says Pia, shocked out of her Aidan-induced misery. "Do I look okay, too, ladybitch? No post-breakup sartorial errors?"

"You look perfect, too," I say. She's wearing supertight jeans and an extremely cool silk top.

Me? I'm wearing my newly altered slip dress with my Zara leather jacket and mean-looking boots. It's April, so it's a little chilly out, but I'm bare-legged anyway. Amazing how subversive bare skin can seem after months of bitter winter. All in all, I look like no one should fuck with me. Which is kind of how I feel right now.

Still haven't heard a word from Annabel. Or my dad. Maybe he'll call me on my birthday in a few days. No one forgets their only child's birthday, outside of a goddamn John Hughes movie, right?

Pia turns to Julia. "Where's your date with Sam, by the way?"

"Some Mexican joint in Fort Greene," Julia opens her purse and shows us a toothbrush, toothpaste, floss, and perfume. "But I will *not* smell—or taste—like quesadillas." She looks at her watch. "Oh, my god! I gotta run! I'm meeting him in twenty minutes! Wish me luck!"

"Ah, young love," Pia says with a weary sigh, as the front door slams. "So full of hopes and dreams. But it never lasts." She takes another dramatic slug of wine. "Ever. Love just rots and dies. Like a dog. In a ditch."

Two hours later, the four of us are at Pijiu, a bar in Williamsburg. It's one of those places that looks paint-peelingly nondescript from the outside during the day, but sparkles with attitude at night. One wall is taken up with a long wooden bar and, at the back, a stage is lit by hundreds of little red Chinese lanterns. The rest of the space is littered with old brown sofas covered in seventies-style plastic and a cluster of secondhand mahjong tables with mismatched chairs. Sort of Beijing disco farmhouse.

There's live music later, an up-and-coming Brooklyn band called Spector that Madeleine wants to check out. But for now, a vintage 1950s jukebox is playing Guns N' Roses, and the crowd is the usual mix of hipsters, yupsters, and normal people (i.e., us).

Since we're without Julia, who, whatever Coco thinks, is the real linchpin of Rookhaven, and since anything personal is off-limits due to Pia's propensity for breakup-related hysteria, we've turned to a subject that not-quite-perfect social gatherings employ to kick-start engaging conversations all over the world. Yep. We're talking about blow jobs.

"Use your hand to cup the balls," says Pia. "The balls are totally the secret."

"I also like to use one hand to work this bit—" I start miming.

"Stop it! Stop it!" Madeleine is scandalized.

Coco, surprisingly, is fascinated. "What do you mean? The helmet-y bit?"

"No, the helmet-y bit is in your, um, okay. Look—" I start drawing on a napkin. "See, there's that bit, and that's the shaft. That's a vein, by the way—"

"No! No cock diagrams! Jesus!" Madeleine snatches the napkin from me and rips it up into little pieces as Pia and Coco and I collapse into giggles.

"This is just what I needed," says Pia, after we calm down. "I've been weeping—weeping!—about Aidan for days, and the bastard is probably having sex with some Californian bimbo right now."

"Of course he's not, ladybitch," I say, placing a comforting hand on her arm. "California is three hours behind. He wouldn't screw a bimbo in the midafternoon. He's probably just masturbating now."

Coco collapses into hysterics again.

Pia rolls her eyes. "Too far, Angie. I swear you're like a dude sometimes."

"A dude with a great rack, you mean."

Actually, I'm feeling weird and wired. Alcohol, instead of calming me down, is stirring me up. And acting crass and drawing cock diagrams helps me pretend that I'm okay. The truth is, I'm worried about my birthday, I'm worried my parents will contact me and even more worried that they won't, I'm worried about what Stef might do after our meeting in the Gap the other day, I'm worried about my job and my future. And most of all, I'm worried about Sam and Julia's date and whether it will go well. Though I know it's none of my business.

Sigh.

I have enough cash for another two rounds of drinks, and then I'll go home. (I worked out that it's all I can afford on my salary from the Gap once I take out what I need to pay rent and kitty, till I get paid again on Monday. I know, how fucking responsible am I? Seriously. High-five me.)

I tune back in to the conversation.

"Of course you should text him," Pia is saying. "If you want to. Are you sure he's the guy for you though, honey?"

"Yup," says Coco. "All I want right now is someone who is kind and stable and smart."

"You make him sound like a horse you're investing in," says Madeleine.

"It is an investment!" says Coco. "I went with my heart with Eric, and that backfired. So this time, I'm going with my head."

It strikes me that boring little know-it-all Ethan the Cheesemaker isn't the right choice for her heart *or* head, but none of us will say that, of course.

Madeleine stands up and calls to someone on the other side of the bar. "Heff! Over here!"

It's her date from the dinner party, the perma-stoned musician. He ambles over, all beaten-up clothes and overgrown eyebrows.

"I'm having a fucking nightmare, man." Wow, Heff is unusually lucid tonight. "I'm filling in on bass for my friend Amy's band, but her lead singer has flaked."

I turn to check out the band. They're setting up, and a tall girl with pink hair is shouting into her cell phone. She looks pretty tense. For someone with pink hair.

"Amy is freaking. This is the first time Spector has played here, they won't book her again."

Madeleine looks over at the girl. "Okay. I'll do it."

"You will? Fuck, I was too scared to even ask you! That's totes rad, man!"

"You were scared of me?" Madeleine is stunned.

"*Everyone* is scared of you." Heff swings an arm around her shoulders as they walk away. "Everyone."

We all turn to watch Heff introduce her to Amy with the white and pink hair.

"I'm a bit scared of Madeleine," says Coco.

"Me too, sometimes," says Pia.

"I'm not," I say.

Coco sighs. "Yeah, but you're not scared of anything."

I snort. Right. I'm not scared of anything. Except for my past and my future.

"My round," I say, to change the subject. "Same again?"

"Make mine a double!" says Pia, taking a photo of the stage, one eye squinting shut to help her focus. "I am totally Facebooking this so Aidan can see what an awesome life I am having without him."

The bar is packed three-deep with young Billyburg hipsters all drinking Yuengling or PBR and talking passionately about their socially engaged graphic design skateboard business or urban farming co-op or karmic slam poetry or whatever. So not my bag, you know? I appreciate a bit of alternative entrepreneurship as much as the next girl, but come the fuck on. "What's your order?" the waitress asks, one of those short henna types with a lot of tattoos.

"Uh, four gin and tonics."

She slams them on the bar and I pay, just moments before the drunk hipster next to me stands up and knocks over one of the drinks.

"Whoopsh," he says, waffle crumbs in his beard, and wanders off.

"Sorry!" His friend stands up, a tall guy with gravity-defying hair and an air of pharmaceutical confidence. "I'll buy you another."

I want to say don't worry about it, but it's also a waste of my limited cash to replace them myself. So instead, I try to smile. Is there anything worse than worrying about money?

"Thanks. Gin and tonic."

"Any particular gin?"

"No, any gin will do. You know, your garden-variety, bathtub-produced, boring, ordinary old gin."

"Mediocre gin, got it. Something . . . unimpressive. Just my style."

Cute response. I focus on his hands. Long fingers, square nails, lots of little leather and fabric bracelets. Sam's hands are like ancient gardening gloves, all worn and battered from sailing.

Argh! Don't think about Sam.

"Here you go," Square Nails says, handing me the drink. "I didn't slip anything in it, I swear."

"Actually, I roofie myself these days, it saves time," I say.

He doesn't laugh. One of those arrogant pseudo-easygoing dudes who doesn't expect a woman to be funny. Instead he pats the vacant stool next to him, expecting me to sit on it. I don't sit down. He starts talking anyway.

"Let me ask you a question. So, my buddy and I are creating a morning coffee delivery service around Williamsburg and Brooklyn Heights. It's like a bespoke food truck service. Your cup of joe, however you like it, whatever time you like it, and you order it online the night before." While he's monologuing, I take a cigarette out of my purse and place it between my lips and stare at him. "Naturally, it's all free-trade organic coffee that's hand grown by farmers we know personally in Colombia. And you can choose from organic milk from our buddy's farm upstate, or non-GM unsweetened soy or almond milk. It's called MyJoe."

"So what's the question you wanted to ask me?"

"Would you use it?"

"I usually get coffee on my way to work."

"Oh yeah? Where do you work?"

I pluck the cigarette out of my mouth. "The Gap."

His jaw drops. I think he would be less horrified if I told him I made kitten porn.

"Thanks for the drink, big guy. Check you later."

I stride away, drop off Madeleine's drink at the stage—where she's going through the set list with Amy and Heff and looking extremely stressed out—and then walk back to Coco and Pia.

Pia is in full five-drinks-and-this-is-what-I-think-about-everything-goddamnit mode. "Fuck Aidan! And fuck California! I'm gonna start fucking dating as soon as I fucking can. Rip that fucking Band-Aid right off and get right the fuck back up on that fucking horse."

"That's a lot of fucks," comments Coco.

I raise my hand as if to ask a question. "By 'horse,' you mean 'penis,' right?"

Coco cracks up, sputtering her drink everywhere.

"Here are my new dating rules." Pia ignores us. "If they're rude to the waitress, walk away. If they order before me, walk away. If they leave their phone on the table during dinner, walk away. If they would rather live in California than New York City, walk the fuck away."

"Wow, that rules out, like, every dude I've ever met," I say, and Coco cracks up again, slapping the table with her hand. She's pretty tipsy. Her phone vibrates, and she grabs it, shutting one eye slightly to read a text, and then smiles a secret little smile.

"Is it Ethan?" I say. "Do you want to share something with the rest of the class, Coco?"

She smirks and ignores me to reply, and Pia continues her Aidan rant.

"Fuck love. You know? Fuck it! Fuck men! They're all just fucking cock-monkeys. I'm just gonna use and abuse from now on. Abuseorama." She tries, unsuccessfully, to hide a tiny belch. "What about you, ladybitch?"

"I am not using or abusing anyone," I say.

"What's your ideal man?" asks Coco.

I stare at her, my mind a blank. My ideal man? Does that even exist? "I don't know. Every guy I'm ever attracted to just ends up a lying, cheating sack of shit out for whatever he can get."

There's a pause.

"Wow. You want a little lemon to go with that bitter?" says Pia. "I thought I was fucked up, but seriously, dude . . ."

I shrug. "I call it like I see it."

"You guys, Ethan and I haven't even kissed," says Coco worriedly. "Do you think I should make the first move? Oh, shush, don't answer! He just walked in! I invited him along, is that okay?"

Pia and I exchange looks. Even without having talked about Ethan the Cheesemaker with her, I know we have the same opinion: he's a dick. And then when I see his sweaty face, I almost flinch with dislike. I can't help it. But that's bad, right? It's Coco's decision. Not mine.

"Ethan!" exclaims Coco. "Hi!" She leans in to give him a big hug.

"Do I have a story for you!" Ethan says. "Prepare for a twist in the tale that will shock and surprise! Now—"

Oh God. Ethan doesn't converse, he lectures. Thank hell Coco accompanies him to the bar, and I turn to Pia.

"Looks like it's you and me, ladybitch."

But it's not.

Because at that exact moment, Pia's jaw drops, her eyes filling with tears, and she stands up, unsteadily clutching the back of her chair, staring toward the front of the bar.

I turn to follow her gaze.

Aidan.

Jesus, is everyone's fucking love life turning up at this bar tonight or what?

Aidan strides right over to our table, carrying a huge duffel bag, as though he came straight from the airport, staring right over me at Pia like a man possessed. "Pia, I love you. I can't live without you."

"Oh, Aidan, I can't live without you either!"

Fucking drama queens.

And boom, they start to kiss, squishing my head between them. I have to duck down and crawl under the table to get away. I pause under the table for a moment. It's so quiet and calm. I just want to hide here. Forever.

CHAPTER 27

But I don't. Of course. I just get up and find another chair like a normal person.

Then, while Pia and Aidan continue to kiss passionately and tearfully like the last scene of a romantic comedy, and Coco listens eagerly to Ethan at the bar, Madeleine steps up to the microphone, and one of the shaggy-faced bartenders introduces the band.

"Ladies and gentlemen, may I present . . . Spector!"

The music starts, and within a few bars, I realize it's a metal-pop cover version of a 1960s song by The Ronettes, "Be My Baby." They're playing it very rough and sultry, with a lot of angry guitar. Heff is on base, pink-haired Amy is on lead guitar, and some dude with a ringletty beard is on drums.

Then Madeleine starts singing. God, I forgot how good she is.

"The night we met, I knew I . . . needed you so . . ."

Somehow, her voice is whispery and husky at the same time, and every word sounds sad but sort of sexy. Like she's promising you something.

"And if I had the chance, I'd . . . never let you go . . ."

Pia and Aidan are kissing so hard there's a fighting chance one might collapse from oxygen deprivation.

"Get a room, you two!" says Ethan the Cheesemaker, coming back from the bar with a glass of red wine. He didn't bother to get anyone else a drink.

Coco giggles, skipping behind him. "Yeah! Ooh! Aidan! Hi! Madeleine's singing! Yay!"

Pia and Aidan stop kissing, and he whispers in her ear. She nods, then turns back to our table quickly, grabs her bag, and smiles at me, her face lit up with happiness.

"He flew back last night. He's been trying to find me all day but I've been ignoring his calls, then he saw my Facebook update that I was here." She smiles, happy tears filling her eyes. "God, I love Facebook. We're out of here. Tell Maddy I'll make it up to her. Love you, ladybitch."

And boom, just like that, I'm left with Coco and Ethan the Cheesemaker.

Ethan clears his throat loudly. "Angie, do tell me all about your family. I understand your mother is British? Now, the British healthcare system is fascinating, deeply flawed, but some would say, better than our own. Or it was. These days—"

And off he goes. I can get away with ignoring him, if I gaze at the stage. "Be My Baby" finishes and the bands starts playing "The Wanderer" by Dion.

"Well, I'm the type of guy who'll never settle down . . ."

Madeleine has such a beautiful voice, but she lacks confidence onstage. Her eyes are almost shut; she's practically singing to the floor. And the rest of the band is thinking the same thing: Heff is exchanging looks with Amy, and the ringlet-haired drummer is hitting the shit out of his drums in an attempt, I think, to make Madeleine give the song a little more energy.

"I gotta go to the little girls' room! Excuse me!" whispers Coco, hurrying off with her head down, as though we were in a movie theater.

I don't want to talk to Ethan the Cheesemaker, so I pretend to be enthralled with the band. Actually, I don't have to pretend: they are really good. If only Madeleine would give it a little oomph. . . . If only she'd smile. Watching someone not-really-enjoying singing is kind of excruciating.

A minute later, I feel a warm, slimy hand on my bare knee.

Ethan!

He's touching me!

"Angie . . ." he says, his voice low and froggy.

I instinctively jerk my knee away, look into his little eyes, and just have time to hiss *"Don't touch me"* before Coco returns from the bathroom, smiling happily.

"The bar snacks here look great! I got us each a menu!" She sits down, oblivious to the tension at the table.

Oh God, why, *why* does she like Ethan the Cheesemaker—hereafter known as Ethan Wonderslime—so much? In her current vulnerable state, she really doesn't need to fall for a fuckwit who will inevitably disappoint her. On the other hand, he seems to make her happy right now, and maybe that's more important. On the other hand (uh . . . the third hand), he just came on to me.

Ignoring them, I stare at the stage, where Spector is now playing a pretty awesome cover of "Peggy Sue" by Buddy Holly.

The ringlet drummer dude is really enjoying his little drum solos in this song, but Madeleine still looks nervous and uncomfortable as hell. If she wasn't onstage, if I didn't feel like she might need my support, I'd leave. Run away from this whole messy Coco-Ethan thing, from annoying know-it-all hipsters. But I know that impulse, that almost overwhelming urge to escape that I always get, isn't the answer.

Instead, I put myself in Madeleine's shoes: a bar full of strangers, songs she's not sure about and maybe doesn't even know that well, no one smiling, no one applauding, no one even dancing. . . .

Hang on. Why *don't* people dance in bars anymore? They should. Right? Why the hell is everyone here too cool to dance?

Without even thinking about it, I stand up and walk to the bar, where the Square Nails hipster coffee business dude is still sitting.

"Would you like to dance?"

"Say what?"

I stare at him. "You heard me. Let's go."

Square Nails gazes at me for a second before standing up. "Okay."

I hold my hand out and pull him toward the space in front of the band, suddenly very aware of everyone in the entire bar looking at us.

We start dancing, doing those semi-twist-n-shout moves that you do when you're too self-conscious and not drunk enough (pretty much the same thing in my book). Dancing wasn't my strongest talent, even in my vodka-fueled days of yore—a lot of nonchalant nodding, a lot of shoulder shapes—but right now, I give this dance floor everything I've got.

"You're a great dancer," says Square Nails.

"Thanks. I was professional when I was younger, but I had to give it up. Steroids, you know?"

Square Nails stares at me for a few seconds, confused. Sigh. My kingdom for a dude who thinks I'm funny. (Yeah, I totally have a kingdom.)

The song finishes, and the band segues straight into "Then He Kissed Me" by The Crystals.

I look up at Madeleine and wink, and she returns the most brilliantly huge smile I've ever seen. And then, something magic happens: her voice is louder, her words are clearer. Madeleine is shining.

More people join us on the dance floor, and within thirty seconds, it's a churning mass of twisting, turning, jiving couples. Halfway through the song, I glance back at the table where Coco and Ethan Wonderslime are sitting and suddenly, behind them, I see Julia and Sam walk in just as Square Nails grabs my hand and spins me out in the other direction.

"Dipping you!" he exclaims, and I make the involuntary "whoop!" sound that I always do when I'm dipped. I'm such a cliché.

Then he twirls me again.

Mid-twirl I glance over to our table and see, through the crowd, Julia and Sam.

Kissing.

A split second later, he spins me back into him, but I can hardly see where I'm going and land against his body with a bang.

Julia and Sam are kissing.

Julia is kissing my Sam. I mean, my *friend* Sam. That's weird. Why is that weird? It's normal! They were on a date! I quickly try to arrange my face into some kind of happy serenity and keep smiling as Square Nails pings me around the dance floor. He's getting pretty confident with the dips and turns.

But my brain is racing. Julia and Sam. Julia . . . and *Sam*. All I can see is that image of them kissing, like a snapshot that's been burned into the back of my eyelids. I feel strange, as if I've been punched, or winded, like when you're a little kid on the monkey bars in the playground and you fall off and land hard on your ass. Yeah, that's how I feel. Like the breath has been whacked out of me.

Julia and Sam were kissing.

By the time the song has ended, I've pulled myself together. It's totally normal to feel weird when your friends kiss. Right? Right. But it's only a thing if I make it a thing. It's totally fine for my friends to like each other! They went on a date! What did I expect? I don't want to be one of those people who won't share friends, or who gets jealous when their friends start a new relationship. It's fine. It's so fine.

I walk back to our table, smiling as wide as I can, focusing on nothing.

"Hey!" I say, trying to sound supernormal and happy. "How are you guys? How was dinner? Was it great? That's great!"

"Hey, stranger," says Sam. "You lose your phone or something?"

I haven't returned his calls since he asked Julia out. I mean, it's no big deal, I just had nothing to say. "No, just busy, you know, working. . . ." I can't even look him in the eye; instead I pretend to be really interested in the dance floor.

"Hey, you're wearing the dress!" Sam says. "The Drakey dress. It looks great!"

Turning around so I can avoid replying, I notice that Square Nails has followed me to our table. I turn to face him. "Thanks for the dance. You can go now."

Looking shocked, he walks away.

Julia and Sam are laughing.

"You're right! She is so goddamn harsh!" exclaims Sam.

"Told ya," says Julia. "She goes through men like water."

"That sentence doesn't mean anything," I say. Since when do Julia and Sam talk about me?

"We were wondering where you guys were so I texted Maddy, and she told me about her surprise gig," says Julia. "She's amazing!"

"She is," I agree. I don't know where to look. If I focus on Julia's smiley face I feel angry and guilty about feeling angry, and I can't even look at Sam.

I think I might cry if I see how happy he is with Julia.

I guess it's just because he won't be my friend now. Now that he's dating Julia. I mean, we won't be unfriends or anything . . . but it won't be the same.

And that makes me want to cry even more.

Thank God for the band. I turn to face them, trying to look serene and tough and normal and conceal the chaos inside me, just as they start playing "Do You Wanna Dance?" by Bobby Freeman.

"WOO! Madeleine, you ROCK!" screams Julia.

"Let's dance!" says Coco. "Me and Ethan, and you and Sam!"

"Yeah!" shouts Julia.

"Oh, no . . ." says Sam. "Angie, help . . ."

But I ignore him, and Julia grabs his hand and pulls him after her like a recalcitrant child, followed by Coco and Ethan. They're quickly swallowed up by a mass of churning couples on the dance floor.

And here I am. Alone at the table. I wonder again if I can just crawl under it and hide.

This is why people don't dance in bars. Because being the only person not on the dance floor makes you feel like a fucking loser.

I'm out of here.

I grab my bag and head for the exit without turning back. Sam didn't even think about the fact that I'd be left all alone at the table when he went off to dance with Julia and Coco and Ethan Wonderslime. Even though Sam and I have been practically inseparable for weeks. What ever happened to bros before hos? Not that Julia is a ho, exactly, but you know what I mean. . . . Does everyone just dump their friends when they fall in love or what? Fuck!

Once I'm outside, I angrily light a cigarette and take out my phone. There must be someone I can call, no not Stef, no one like that, but someone to distract me from everything . . .

Gabriel.

The nice guy from Turks. The one with the plane.

Done.

I tap out a quick text.

I think I owe you a dinner for the plane ride. How about a hot dog and a beer?

CHAPTER **28**

Thegapthegapthegapthegapthegap.

You wouldn't think it, in a city the size of New York, but the entire store has literally been vacant since I got here. Midtown Manhattan is not shopping central on a rainy Monday morning. So I've been counting the seconds while arranging and folding and generally trying to look busy whenever a manager cruises by.

I have *literally* been counting the seconds, that's not a figure of speech. I count to sixty, and then hold out one finger behind my back. Then I count to sixty again and hold out another finger behind my back. Every time I use up all my fingers, I move location and try to look busy again.

It's seems like such a long time since I walked out of Pijiu on Saturday night, and yet nothing has happened. On Sunday morning I got up extra early—6:00 A.M.—and got out of the house, and then had a long, silent breakfast alone down at the New Apollo Diner. Great pancakes, bad coffee.

I tried to read the Style section of *The New York Times,* but the words just swam in front of me. So then I stared into space, wondering if Sam had slept over and whether it upset me more to imagine them having sex or to imagine them just kissing and whispering and giggling together in bed, and then getting annoyed with myself for caring when it's none of my business, and then thanking God that I wasn't at home to run into him as he walked out of Julia's room. Because it would be weird. Why? Because it just would, that's why. My thoughts ran around and around and around. I tried to ignore them, but they chased me.

Then I took the subway to work and stared into space and felt my blisters throbbing and tried not to think about anything.

I'm so stupid! Sam and I were always just friends. I know that. I guess I just haven't had a platonic male friend before, so I don't know how to handle it. Of course he's going to date. And Julia has liked him for ages. I need to get a grip. And not think about my twenty-third birthday tomorrow. *Bonjour,* adulthood.

I haven't seen any of the other girls since Saturday night, which has to be a record. Pia texted this morning that she and Aidan commenced some kind of sex marathon after he showed up at the bar, and both took today off work as a "personal day" so they can "try to come up with a solution" (i.e., have more sex). And no one else has been in touch. I guess Coco's been with Ethan and Madeleine's been with Heff. And Julia's clearly been with Sam.

Whatever. I'm not really feeling that social, anyway. I'm just going to meet up with Gabriel tonight for a hot dog, go to bed early, wake up tomorrow, avoid everyone, and pretend it's not my birthday. And work at the Gap.

Argh.

"Excuse me, blondie!" says a voice, and I turn around. It's a gorgeous spike-haired guy wearing such skinny jeans that he absolutely has to be gay.

"How may I be of assistance, sir?"

"I need help with sizes. We need to get my boyfriend, Adrian, a pair of white jeans for a Euro-trash party, and his budget is forcing us here! No offense!"

"None taken. So, what size is Adrian?"

"I'm a twenty-eight regular!" says a voice. I turn around. It's the little hipster waiter from Rock Dog, who spilled lingonberry juice all over me!

"Don't I know you?" Adrian frowns, cocking his head to one side.

"Rock Dog!" I say. "Lingonberry juice!"

"Oh my Lord!" Adrian looks like he's never been so happy to see anyone in his entire life, and quickly introduces me to his boyfriend, Edward. "This is the girl! The girl who gave me that amazing tip on my first day! Wow, honey, you shouldn't be giving out tips like that if you work here."

"I kinda fell on hard times just after that."

"Ugh, retail is *such* hell," says Edward sympathetically. "I worked at Urban Outfitters when I first moved to New York, and it was the longest three months of my life. I nearly got fat because the only joy in my life was Dunkin' Donuts. I am not even kidding."

"Okay, so how about these?" asks Adrian, holding up some white jeans that will be six sizes too big for him.

I look over. "They're good, but I'd recommend trying these and these, too. You never know the perfect fit till you're in it, you know?"

"That is totally my motto in life," deadpans Edward, and Adrian cracks up.

"Okay, boys, come with me. . . ."

Half an hour later, they're both overjoyed. Adrian found four pairs of jeans that fit him perfectly, and Edward got jealous and started shopping, too, and has two pairs of pants and three blazers.

"It's been so much fun helping you guys," I say.

"I never knew I'd love it here so much!" says Edward joyfully. "The fit is totally amazing!"

"So much for coming to the Gap to save money," says Adrian, combing worriedly through the price tags.

"Listen," I say, lowering my voice, "I can get you fifty-percent off if you just hang around twenty minutes. It's coming up on my break, so I'll buy this stuff for you with my employee discount and meet you at the deli on the corner. Sound good?"

"Oh, honey, is that allowed?" Adrian makes an anguished face.

"He's so naive! Of course it is," hisses Edward. "We did it all the time at Urban Outfitters!"

"This feels wrong. . . ." says Adrian.

"No! It's perfect! Angie, honeybun, we'll see you at the deli on the corner in half an hour, okay?"

They head off, and I try to look busy until my break. Then I grab their clothes, head to the register, and flash my employee card.

That dickface Derek is behind the counter.

"This is for you?"

"Affirmative," I say.

"Men's clothes."

"Yep. I'm going to customize them. Make a fabulous long patchwork denim skirt. It'll be sister wife meets Amish wife. A sort of Utah-Pennsylvania hybrid." I give him my smarmiest grin.

He remains uncharmed. "I don't believe you. I think you're buying this with your employee discount and selling it for a personal profit to those two men who were in here before." He pauses dramatically. "You're stealing from the Gap."

"What?! I am not!" I'm genuinely shocked. I mean, yeah, I'm buying this stuff for someone else using my employee discount, but I wouldn't even think about charging them and making money off it. I'm just doing them a favor! I'm bending the rules, not breaking them! "I'm not stealing! I swear to God! I'm not!"

Dickface Derek smiles, revealing very yellow teeth. "I think you are. I've called Shania."

A moment later, Shania, my manager, walks over, flanked by two security guards.

I decide the best defense is offense. "This is outrageous! How dare you suggest I would sell these for a personal profit! I wouldn't do that! How could you accuse me of that?"

She narrows her eyes. "We've had complaints about you from customers, so security has been keeping an eye on you. We were willing to overlook this the other day with your blond friend, but you were clearly cavorting with those two men today."

She must mean Coco. And the complaints could only have come from Stef. Or his bitchy girlfriend, Blythe.

But *cavorting*? Sheesh.

"Shania, I promise," I say, looking her right in the eye. "I swear I wasn't going to sell them for a profit. I was just, I was trying to help them out—"

"By abusing your employee privileges," she interrupts, with an evil little smile. "Angie, I'm going to have to let you go. Employee discount abuse is illegal. It's theft. You're a thief. I could have you arrested."

"I am not!" I respond angrily, and they all just stare at me. Judging me. Ready—no, *wanting*—to believe the worst.

And that's the moment I snap.

"I did nothing wrong! I didn't! I swear! Fucking hell! I wasn't stealing! What the fuck is with the universe? When the fuck am I gonna get a break? THIS IS BULLSHIT!"

CHAPTER 29

A few minutes later, I'm escorted off the premises.

I go straight to the deli to meet the guys, trying not to weep with shock and shame. I fight the tears back, and they all ball up in a lump in my throat. Ah, unshed tears. I wish I knew how to quit you. And of course it's freezing cold, windy, and raining, which just increases my misery. The media has been talking about a superstorm all week, but ever since Hurricane Sandy, they like to freak out about the weather. A little rain does not equal a fucking hurricane, you know?

Edward and Adrian are waiting for me.

"Those bastards," says Edward. "I'm totally boycotting them now. And I hate their ads."

"I am so sorry," Adrian keeps saying. "This is all my fault. I'm, like, your bad luck charm."

"No, no, you're not," I say, my voice unnaturally high, the lump in my throat aching. "I hated working there anyway. I really did. But I just . . . I need money." To try to fake the toughness I don't feel inside, I take a cigarette out of the pack and prop it in my mouth. The perfect accessory to a bad mood. "I'm so fucked."

"Angie!" Adrian claps his hands to get my attention. "First, come work at Rock Dog with me. Screw Gap! Rock Dog is totally fun, you can eat all day for free, and you could still job-hunt for something in fashion. They always let me have time off for auditions."

"You're an actor?"

"You think I'd waste a face this pretty on anything else? And second, I bet Edward can help you network. He's a floral event designer for the biggest names in fashion! You know Donna Karan? Diane von Furstenberg? Candie Stokes?"

I look up. "That bitch?"

Edward cackles. "She is *such* a bitch! But she spends so much on flowers, it's almost sinful. I'm, like, best friends with all her assistants now. They fucking hate her."

"She was so mean to me." I tell them about the day I talked to her in Starbucks and realized, to her, I was nothing, nobody.

My throat-lump dissolves into tears again. That feels like so long ago, and I still don't have a job. I'll never get a job. I really won't. I look down, blinking hard to get the tears to go away.

"Well, good for you for trying, girl!" says Adrian. "Now, I have a piece of advice for you." He takes a deep breath. "Never cry over anything that won't cry over you."

I smile, remembering that day, the bombshell Annabel dropped, everything that happened afterward. . . . God, that feels like so long ago. That was the moment that my life began spiraling out of control.

Oh, let's face it. It's never been in control.

"I know," I say eventually. "I'm just so tired of trying and failing. I'll never get a job in fashion. Never. I'm . . . I'm nothing."

"You are *never* nothing!" Adrian grabs both my hands. "Never, never say that! I'm deeply psychic, and I can tell that you're very kind and honest and loyal and talented. Your future is bright, okay? You just need to hang on. Just hang on, keep trying, and everything will be okay."

I really do start crying at this, but quickly pull myself together. Jeez, I hardly know these guys, but I can't help it. I feel like I've been so close to crying for days, like I'm a cup full of tears and this was just the little prod I needed to tip over. . . .

"Sorry," I say, wiping my face. "I'm such a loser. I can't do anything right."

"You are *not*. Just one break, that's all you need," adds Edward.

"I've been here since last summer!" I exclaim. "And I don't want my life to be like this anymore. I've made too many mistakes here. . . . I want to start over."

They look at each other and sigh.

"You can never start over," says Edward.

"Never," agrees Adrian. "No matter where you are, your problems follow you, so you may as well deal with them. Take it from a man who spent the first five years of his twenties running from city to city, looking for the meaning of life in empty hookups. God, I was such a little slut."

"*Plus ça change,*" says Edward, raising his eyes to the ceiling.

"My tip? Hang on to your friends," says Adrian dramatically. "The only thing that will give your life meaning is the people around you. Create a circle of support that will keep you afloat when you feel like you might drown. A life raft. That's what your friends are. A life raft."

"And remember, you may feel like no one will give you a chance right now, but your dream job is out there, so keep trying," says Edward. "When you're intellectually and creatively stimulated by your work, the world is a different place. You feel valued. And valuable. Not just in terms of money, but in terms of what you're contributing to the universe."

"Oh my God! Oscar speech! Goose bumps!" says Adrian.

I nod slowly. Everything he says makes sense. But I don't know if I can keep trying.

Somehow, Adrian and Edward know I don't want to talk about it anymore, and they start chatting about accessories for the Euro-trash party. (Loafers with snaffle-bits and fake tans.) I'm numb as their conversation washes over me.

I was just fired.

From the Gap.

The day before my twenty-third birthday.

Reality really does bite.

No matter how you cut it, this is rock bottom. After we finish our coffee, we exchange numbers and air-kisses, and I head for the subway.

On the way, I automatically take out my phone to call Sam. Weird, right? In just a few weeks he's gone from being an annoying boat boy to being my go-to phone call after I get fired. . . . But I don't want to hear about how the date with Julia went or how much he likes her. I just . . . I don't want to hear it. It shouldn't bug me, but it does.

Then, as I'm sitting on the subway back to Brooklyn, it hits me.

I'm not going to make it in this city. I'll be chewed up and spit out like every other loser who tries to create a life here and doesn't have what it takes. It's obvious. It's so obvious, I can't believe I didn't see it before now.

So why waste any more time?

Next thing you know, I'll be in my late twenties, and then I'll be fucking thirty. Thirty!

I don't know what else is out there in the world, but I know it's got to be better than getting fired from the Gap and living in Brooklyn where everyone I know is happy, in love, and going somewhere with their lives.

Tonight, I'll see Gabriel, just so I can get out of Rookhaven and avoid everyone for one more night.

And to celebrate my birthday tomorrow, I'll book a flight to L.A. I know people there from college; I can crash with them until I get a job. They have the Gap there, right? (That's a joke.) (Kind of.)

And I know what you're thinking. But I'm not running away.

I'm moving on.

CHAPTER **30**

"See? Best hot dog in the city," I say. "It's a New York classic."

Gabriel takes a tiny bite of his hot dog and chews like it might have thorns.

"This is not good." He looks around for a napkin, spits his half-chewed hot dog into it. "Not. Good."

We're at Gray's Papaya, a legendary hot dog joint, on the corner of Sixth Avenue and Eighth Street in Manhattan. You can't really sit down here, which means that when we finish our hot dogs in about five bites, this will have been the fastest date in the history of dates. I think that might be a good thing. Gabriel is not quite the guy I remember, and tonight might not be the easy killing-time exercise I thought it would be. Gabriel is acting all sorts of precious. He could barely contain his horror when he saw where we were eating and keeps grabbing paper napkins to wipe everything down before he touches it. I mean . . . grow a pair.

Worse? Outside there is torrential rain. Not April showers, but dude-where's-my-ark rain. The kind of rain that makes you want to hide in a dark bar and drink wine and eat cheese and then have crazy dreams all night. But I'm not on a red-wine-and-cheese budget. I'm on a hot-dog-and-papaya-juice budget. So here we are.

And I'm just here for the food. I made it clear to Gabriel this wouldn't be the start of anything romantic or sexual or whatever, plus I'm wearing flats, so it's clearly not a *date*-date. I'm obviously not capable of having a functional relationship, just like I'm not capable of having a functional career. Fuck. What am I going to do with my life?

"What's the deal with the papaya juice?" says Gabriel. He pronounces it "pappa-yah."

"Pa-PIE-ya," I correct him. "It's traditional to have it with hot dogs. I don't know why." I take another bite. God, I love hot dogs. "You didn't put mustard on it," I say. "That's your problem."

"The mustard is not my problem," says Gabriel. "The hot dog is my problem." He looks so serious that I crack up.

Gabriel waits for me to stop giggling, pouting slightly. He doesn't have much of a sense of humor.

"Sorry," I say finally. "Sorry. I know. The mustard is not your problem."

"Okay, that's enough," says Gabriel, throwing his hot dog-filled napkin down. "I take charge now. We go to Minetta Tavern."

"You don't like the dog?"

"I don't like the dog." How to piss off a European dude: don't take dinner seriously. "I want wine and steak and a chair on which to sit. *Sí?*"

"*Sí, señor.*"

"You, stay here."

Gabriel pulls out a mammoth black umbrella and goes to hail a taxi while I wait inside. I think he might be a control freak. He tucked a napkin into his shirt to protect it from ketchup, and then tried to get me to do the same. Um, no. I'm pretty good at not getting food on my clothes since I stopped being able to afford dry-cleaning.

"Angie!" shouts Gabriel. "I have one!"

He runs back with his umbrella to escort me to the taxi.

"Man, it is insane out there!" I say, looking out over the street. The water is running up the gutters and over the sidewalk, and coming down so hard that you can hardly see out the front window.

"Helluva rainstorm," says the driver. "This storm is hitting the whole Eastern Seaboard. They're predicting serious flooding all over the city. We've had three inches of rain in the last two hours."

Gabriel's phone rings. "My sister," he says apologetically. "Lucia? *Qué pasa?*"

I wish I'd paid more attention to Spanish in school. My French is pretty good. Well, my dirty French is pretty good. To kill time, I check my phone. I've been texting some of my friends in L.A., hoping one of them has a place I can crash until I get on my feet.

But it's a text from Sam. It's the first time I've heard from him since Saturday night.

The text reads: *So are we talking yet or what?*

What the hell is that supposed to mean? I reply: *Why wouldn't we be talking?*

He replies: *Aren't you pissed at me about Julia?*

Wow, that's direct. How does he know how I'm feeling? I reply: *Dude, I'm the one who set it up. I'm delighted it went so well.*

He replies: *Uh, have you spoken to Julia?*

I reply: *I've been working.*

He replies: *The night was a total bust.*

I reply: *I saw you kissing in the bar. Didn't look like a bust.*

Sam replies: *Put the crack pipe down. That did not happen.*

Why the fuck is he lying to me? I reply: *Sam, you don't have to lie. I saw it.*

Sam replies: *Angie, we didn't kiss. She whispered in my ear at one point— telling me that guy Ethan is a dick. But we did not kiss. Pinkie swear.*

I frown. Why would he lie about something like that? But I didn't imagine it. Did I?

He sends another text: *Talk to Julia. Total fiasco. We have nothing in common. I figured you were giving me the silent treatment because she was pissed about what a bad night she had.*

The strangest, sweetest feeling of relief floods through me, and I look out the window at the rainstorm, smiling so hard I think my face might crack.

Sam doesn't like Julia. He didn't ditch me. He can still be my friend exclusively. Totally immature, I know, but hey, that's me.

"Angie, we are here." Gabriel nudges me, bringing me back to reality.

Yes! Dinner! Totally!

I shake my head to clear it of thoughts and put my phone back into my bag, just as we pull up to a corner on MacDougal Street.

Gabriel gets out first and walks around the cab to hold up the umbrella for me, though the wind-rain combination means I'm covered in an icy spray in seconds anyway.

Then he pulls open a heavy door and I push past a curtain, into the Minetta Tavern.

CHAPTER **31**

"Now *this* is a New York classic," says Gabriel.

It's true. The Minetta Tavern is how Hollywood would imagine classic New York décor: a long bar, black-and-white-checkerboard floors, dark red leather booths, hundreds of frames on the wall, and the sort of yellowy sepia lighting that makes all the beautiful people glow just a little more beautifully. This is one of my dad's favorite places when he's in New York. He took me here back in January.

And hasn't called since.

Whatever.

Even though it's not yet 7:00 P.M., Minetta Tavern is packed with patrons talking, eating, drinking: all with the kind of animated, joyful gusto that you only see in people who have made a success of their lives. The place is throbbing with self-satisfaction. I don't belong here.

But I want to be successful. I want to get a job. I want to stay in New York. And I want Sam—

Stop! Where did that little voice come from? No, I don't. I want to leave. I want to start fresh in California. I want to get a job in a place that doesn't chew up and spit out its young. I want to go somewhere where I don't feel completely worthless, useless, and restless. Where my life isn't just me, always by myself, ricocheting off everything around me like a tiny pinball trying to hit the jackpot. And Sam has nothing to do with anything.

"Angie!" a voice calls from across the bar, as we're following the maître d' to our table. "Yoo-hoo!"

Only one person I know says *yoo-hoo.* . . . I turn around and see Cornelia, my old sort-of employer, standing at the bar, glass of champagne in hand.

"Cornie!" I immediately assume my perfect fake Upper East Side face.

We air-kiss three times, *mwah-mwah-mwah,* to show how Euro we are. Cornie is a SoHo transplant from the Upper East Side: skinny, blond, pale to the point of translucent, and overly groomed. She models herself on Gwyneth Paltrow, not that she'd ever admit it.

"The notorious Angie!" she says, tilting her head slightly, showing her small white teeth in a tight little smile. "Up to no good, as usual?"

"*Moi?* Straight and narrow, darling," I reply.

The man she's with, a much older silver-fox-type gentleman, smiles at me. He has cold gray eyes and perfectly capped teeth. "I'm Roger Rutherford," he says. "Clearly, Cornie won't introduce us. She's the jealous-in-advance type."

I give my best "how charming" smile and quickly introduce Gabriel.

"Haven't we met before?" says Cornelia, narrowing her eyes. "That fund-raiser at the Boathouse last year?"

"Ah, yes," says Gabriel politely. "We did. I go every year."

Cornelia, Gabriel, and Roger make small talk about the fund-raiser for a moment, while I replay Cornelia's greeting in my brain. Up to no good? What's *that* supposed to mean? I was never late to work for her. I was the model personal assistant. And she said she would call me when she got back to NYC from skiing!

"So good to see you again, sweetie," says Cornelia. She leans in to kiss me on the cheek, and whispers, "Well done on catching such a big fish! Clever girl!"

So I smile and say all the right things and then follow Gabriel through to our table. *Well done on catching such a big fish. Clever girl.* I'm clever for dating a rich guy? If I were really clever, wouldn't I be making my own money?

We sit down at the table and look over the menu. Suddenly, I feel like an imposter. I would never come to the Minetta Tavern if I were the one paying. I can't afford it.

"I'm really not hungry," I say.

"I thought you were always hungry," says Gabriel. "You must order something."

God, I hate being told what to do. But I don't want to cause a scene, not with Cornie nearby.

"Bone marrow," I say. "Followed by the burger. Not the Black Label one, the normal one."

I had the burger here in January with my dad. Maybe I'll just call him when I get to California. He's obviously been too embarrassed to get in touch. And maybe I'll call Annabel back, too. She's been calling me at least three times a week. I know I need to do something about my relationship with my parents . . . I just don't know what that something is.

Gabriel is in a fantastic mood now that he's gotten his own way. He starts waxing nostalgic about the first time he ever came to New York, about what he thinks about the American restaurant scene, about the restaurant his cousin owns in Madrid, about his favorite hotels in the world.

He's is a total name-dropper, but not in the star-fucker sense. He drops names of restaurants and hotels he's been to as if he's qualifying for a Rich Guy Experiences Championship. Per Se, Babbo, Cipriani Downtown, Daniel, Mr. Chow, Hotel Arts in Barcelona, Ushuaia in Ibiza, the Capri Palace in Capri, the Hôtel de Crillon in Paris, the Hôtel du Cap on the French Riviera, Le Club 55 in St. Tropez. Does he ever truly enjoy anything, or does he just do certain things because it's the *thing* to do? A way to show the world that he's made it?

You know, now that I think about it, this aspect of his personality was evident from the start. He missed the salad from his favorite hotel in St. Barts, he had a private plane, an apartment overlooking Central Park . . . I just missed the signs. Or ignored them. Another self-involved rich guy. Well done, Angie.

I glance at his watch. It's a Patek Philippe, i.e., costs more than most people earn in a lifetime. He's wearing a gold signet pinkie ring that I don't remember noticing on the plane, and his clothes—a navy jacket, a white shirt, slim oatmeal jeans—have a casual Euro-fied pressed perfection, topped off by an Hermès belt. His cuticles are flawless, his hair is slicked back with studied nonchalance, his skin is suspiciously supple, even his eyebrows are freshly trimmed.

Money, money, money.

The real question is: why is Gabriel here with me? He never asks me anything about myself; he doesn't know what I want to do with my life. I've never been funny or interesting or, hell, anything around him. He doesn't *know* me. So why would he like me?

He doesn't like me, is the answer. He just likes my shell. A nearly-twenty-three-year-old blond girl in a dress that you hopefully can't tell that I made myself, and a face that looks okay when I've smeared black eyeliner over half of it.

I can't believe I'm in this situation again.

Why did I think he was different from every other guy I've dated? Because he was nice to his sisters?

I don't want to be here.

But I don't want to cause a scene, either.

So what do I do?

My cocktail arrives—a vodka martini with four olives—and I take a massive slug.

"Easy, tiger," says Gabriel, laughing as though he just made the funniest joke in the world.

My phone beeps again. I look quickly: it's Pia.

We need to talk. I'm moving to San Francisco.

I look back up at Gabriel. "Would you excuse me?"

I walk through the restaurant, to the tiny ladies room in the very back, and call Pia. There's no answer: either she's screening and she thinks I'll be too upset to talk to right now, or she's having sex (ew), or—most likely—she texted Julia at the same time and Jules called her first.

I leave a quick message.

"Ladybitch, call me. I think—I mean, I *am*—I'm leaving, too. I'm leaving New York. I guess that's the end of Rookhaven. . . ." I feel a stab of sadness. No more Rookhaven? No more *us*? I clear my throat and force myself to keep talking. "Um, see you later? Maybe?"

Then I get another text, from Sam.

Being ignored makes Sam sad.

I reply quickly. *Not ignoring you I swear. Am on a date with a guy who I think might be a pompous fuckpuppet.*

Sam replies immediately.

Name, vital stats?

At that moment, Cornelia walks into the bathroom.

"Angie, what a surprise," she says archly, quickly looking around to make sure we're alone. "Are you holding? Let's be naughty."

"Am I—What? No. Sorry," I say, quickly realizing she means co-caine.

"Don't worry. My guy is on the way. I need it to get through a night with the Rog."

"He seems nice," I say. Considering he's at least thirty years older than you.

"He'll do. He's divorced, knows *everyone*, and is richer than God, so all those bitches from Spence will be impressed." Cornelia shrugs, her gaze falling to my gold clutch. It's the soft, perfect, hand-hugging one I made all those weeks ago from secondhand Art Deco scarves. "Love, love, *love* the clutch. Who is it?"

"It's, um, it's me," I say. "I made it."

"Bullshit."

"No bullshit. Look, no label. Uh, I need to get back to my date."

"Of course you must. Duty calls!"

She turns her head. I'm dismissed again.

I head back to our table, where great sticks of bone marrow are waiting for me. They really are bones, I realize, slightly belatedly. I sort of thought they'd scoop the marrow bits out of the bone for me and make them pretty. Apparently not. I'm supposed to do it myself.

"Ah, Angie, you're back," says Gabriel, who ordered a very boring goat cheese salad. "Bon appétit."

I smile at Gabriel, take my fork, and look at the great sticks of yellowy bone stretching out in front of me on the plate. What animal is this again?

I don't want to eat it, but I don't want to look like I didn't know what I was getting myself into, either. I ordered it; I'm damn well going to eat every bite.

Then I'm gonna get the fuck out of here, go back to Rookhaven, and start packing.

So I dig out the marrow with my fork, smear it on my buttered bread, sprinkle some salt on it, and chow down. It's a strange, strong, meaty taste. Sort of rich and fatty. I take a slug of martini to cleanse my palate.

"Taste the wine." Gabriel is way too bossy. Who cares? Just get through the meal and go home.

So I take a sip of wine. It's delicious, a pretty standard Châteauneuf-du-Pape. My dad knows a lot about French wine, and somehow, I picked it up. It dawns on me that practically everything I know came from my dad. Except for how to sew.

"It's great," I say.

"Can you taste the earth? The berries? There is a chocolaty edge in this particular year, I always wonder why, and I always order it when I come here. . . . I keep studying wine, and I love it. But I will never truly understand it."

Oh for fuck's sake. Who *says* shit like that?

At that moment, Gabriel reaches across the table and places his hand over mine. I stare at it, unsure whether to snatch my arm away or just let my fingers go limp in the hope he gets the picture.

Then he starts talking.

"Angie, I know you said no romance, nothing serious. But I have to tell you . . . I've been thinking about you ever since we met."

"No kidding." I haven't thought about him. Not once. Not until I needed a distraction. An escape from reality.

"My last girlfriend was very . . . challenging," he starts talking again. "She was Spanish. Passionate, beautiful—"

Gabriel goes on about how amazing his ex was for a few *really* long minutes while the waiter clears our dishes.

"So, Angie. Tell me about you," he says finally.

I blink. Did he really just ask me about myself? That's the first time tonight.

"Um, you know. I'm . . . me. I'm trying to get a job in fashion, I work in, uh, in retail, I live in Brooklyn. . . ." How typical that the moment someone actually asks me about myself, I have nothing to say. "Your average twentysomething struggling to make ends meet in New York."

"You need money?" he says.

"Everyone needs money," I reply, taking another slug of wine. "You can't survive in this city without it."

"Where do you work?"

"The Gap. Well, I did. I was fired yesterday." I look him right in the eye, daring him to judge me.

"That did not pay very well."

"Nope."

Our burgers arrive, and I concentrate on salting my fries and arranging my burger.

I'm feeling kind of *woo* from the wine. Red wine always makes me feel a little funky. The heavy ones make me feel like going to sleep. Something to do with the histamines. And I had the worst insomnia last night. I kept thinking about Julia and Sam. How silly I was to be so jealous! Of course he's still my friend. They just had a friendly meal together, that's all. It's no big deal.

Gabriel clears his throat. "Angie? What are you doing?"

"I'm arranging my burger so the first bite is perfect," I explain, looking up at him. "It's really important. The first bite is like the first kiss, you know? It's everything that the rest of the meal will be."

Gabriel smiles at me. "You are a romantic."

"I am."

"I am a pragmatist."

"Really."

I take a big bite of burger, just as Gabriel reaches in his pocket, pulls out a card, and puts it next to my wineglass.

"This is my financial manager. He'll have ten thousand dollars waiting to transfer to your account on Monday."

"What?" My mouth is full of burger, but suddenly, I've forgotten how to chew.

"You shouldn't have to suffer without money. Life in New York is hard enough already. It is a gift. From me to you."

I swallow my food and stare at Gabriel.

Ten thousand dollars. That would mean I wouldn't have to leave Rookhaven. I wouldn't have to get another job in retail hell. With ten thousand dollars, I could try to get unpaid internships in fashion without worrying about rent and money, I could take a course in fashion design, I could survive for months, I could—I could—

But I can't. I can't do it. I can't take money from a guy in exchange for . . . whatever this would be in exchange for. I can't knowingly walk into a life that exists on the fine line between a girlfriend with spending money and a girlfriend for hire.

I look at Gabriel as he takes a bite of his trout, totally unconcerned. As if he hadn't just tried to buy me. He glances up. "My sisters would love to see you, by the way. Would you like to come to our house upstate this weekend?"

I take a deep breath. "No."

"You have plans? You can change them. It's Lucia's birthday, we're having a family party—"

"No."

I push my chair away from the table, stand up, drink all of the wine in my glass, grab my clutch and coat, and hand him back his financial manager's business card.

"Thank you for dinner. I don't want your money. Good-bye."

And with that, I stride out of the restaurant, past Cornelia and her ancient suitor, past all the crowds of beautiful people at the bar, feeling a sort of sick euphoria.

I just walked away from ten thousand dollars.

I could have solved all my problems; I could have made my life easy. But I didn't.

I did the right thing, instead.

Then, just as the door to the restaurant closes behind me, I bump into a couple sheltering from the rainstorm.

Oh. My. God.

My father.

And a woman I've never seen before. Thirtysomething, brunette, slim.

They're kissing.

CHAPTER **32**

"What the fuck is this?" I say.

My father's face lights up. "Angelique? Sweetheart! I didn't—"

"Didn't know I'm living in New York now? Didn't know you were going to run into me? Didn't know that maybe you should call your daughter to tell her you're getting a divorce?"

Suddenly I'm furious, really truly spitting with anger that my father could be passionately kissing some strange woman outside a New York restaurant, sheltering from the rain like something out of *Breakfast at fucking Tiffany's*.

"And who's this? Some slut you picked up in a bar? Or does she work for you like all the others?"

The woman recoils as if I've slapped her. She's dressed very Midtown chic, you know, not quite flawless enough for Uptown, nowhere near edgy enough for Downtown.

My dad stares at me in shock. "Now, wait just a minute—"

"Annabel told me you were getting a divorce weeks and weeks ago," I interrupt him. "And I heard nothing from you. Not a word. After everything I did for you, after keeping all your fucking secrets for all those years—"

"Your mother told me you wanted to be alone—"

"Bullshit!" I snarl. "You didn't need me anymore, so you didn't bother. Do you even remember that today is my birthday?"

"Oh, God!" My father looks dismayed. "Honey, I swear—"

"Stop LYING!" I scream as loud as I can, and everything around us goes very still and silent.

My father stares at me, mouth open, unable to say anything. I thought he looked like George Clooney when I was little. I don't anymore. I think he looks like a fucking circus showman.

"It's true, your mother told him you didn't want to hear from him," says the slut. "I was there when we all met up to discuss arrangements."

"And who the fuck are you?"

"I'm—I'm Veronica," she says, her eyes suddenly wary. "I thought you knew—"

"Knew what?"

My father puts his arm around her and smiles proudly. "Veronica's pregnant. We're getting married."

I don't really know what happens next.

I think I scream, because my ears are ringing and my throat is raw and I can't breathe and I start running away from them, but they don't follow me anyway, then I'm running and running into the black night. There are no cabs and I don't know where I am but I keep going anyway, through the storm, through the rain and the wind that feels like it might blow me away entirely. My brain can't hang onto any thoughts, and I think I'm hysterical but I don't know because I feel, I honestly feel like I might be losing my mind, like I want to run away, out of myself, out of my life.

I wonder if my mother knows, and how she feels about it, and if she's upset, and I think back to those Christmases when the three of us opened my stocking in bed together with raisin toast and cuddles and everything was warm and good and simple.

I miss simple.

I fall down at one point, into a giant filthy gutter puddle, and force myself up and walk and walk until I don't know where I am. The rain is so heavy I can hardly see across the street. Store awnings are banging in the wind, the gutters are thick furious rivers, there's not a single other person on the street, and it's so dark and crazy, it feels like the end of the world.

My head hurts and my stomach hurts and I have these weird blunt pains in my chest. Oh God, where am I?

Eventually I'm too tired and wet to walk anymore. I sit on a little children's climbing frame in a playground, in the freezing darkness and pouring rain, shaking from the cold and crying because my life is fucked. I'm lost and cold and I don't have a job or any money or any future or any family.

I have nothing. Nothing.

At that moment, my phone rings. It's Sam.

"Hey! How's the date?"

"Sam—Sam—" I can hardly speak. Immediately his voice changes.

"Where are you? What happened? Angie. Stop crying. Tell me where you are and I'll come and get you. You shouldn't be out in this storm—"

I look around, trying to see a street sign. "The corner of Spring and Mulberry, in the playground. I'm fine, I'm fine, it's just, my dad—he's getting married again, he's having another baby, I know, I'm a fucking loser for crying, I can't—"

"Stay there. I'm coming."

I don't know what to do with myself, so I stay here, in the playground, feeling every last inch of me get soaked all the way through. Right this second New York feels empty, totally empty, and I am completely alone.

Then minutes—or hours—later, Sam turns up, jumping out of a black town car, and I stand up and look across the playground.

Our eyes meet, the rain still hurtling down, like a million tiny shooting stars lit by the streetlights.

And in that split second, everything becomes clear.

I love Sam.

I loved him from the moment I saw him on the pier in Turks and Caicos. I loved him when he followed me all the way to shore, I loved him when he brought back my stuff, I loved him when he saved Coco's life at the surprise party, I loved him when he helped me hand out lattes and CVs, I loved him when he comforted me after my *Kramer vs. Kramer* meltdown, I loved him when I woke up in his arms, and I loved him when he walked into the bar after his dinner with Julia. I love everything that he does and everything that he is. He's honest and real and true. He's everything I want to be.

For several long seconds, we stare at each other through the rain.

Then I run over to him, to my Sam, my gorgeous Sam with his perfect frown. Everything about him that I know so well. Everything that I love. And I know, *I know,* that he loves me, too.

"Sam—"

I tilt my face up to his. Our lips are nearly touching, so close that even the rain isn't coming between us. It feels, for a second, as the storm rages around us, that the wind is buffeting us together, like we're the only people in the universe.

"Angie—"

I shake my head. "Shut it. Just . . . just shut it."

He grins down at me, and we stare at each other.

This is the prekiss.

This is the moment that I always wish could last forever.

And for several very long seconds, I think it might.

But I want to know what happens next. So I reach my arms around his neck and pull him toward me, and our lips finally touch.

And *bang.* My brain is empty, but I feel like I'm going to burst, and everything bad that's happened to me, everything bad I've done, everything I'm always worried about, just disappears. Like magic.

We kiss and kiss and kiss. Then I pull back and I cover his face in frantic kisses, as though I'm trying to blot up the rain with my lips, until Sam grabs me, kissing me properly again. Oh God, our mouths were made for each other, and we're sort of giggling into each other's faces, laughing and shivering, and his lips are so warm, and his cheeks are so cold, and he smells just *right.* Like rain and soap and sugar and coffee and everything I like most in the world.

I pull back, gaze at him again for a second, and out of nowhere, I say it. "I love you."

"You do?"

I pause for a second, shocked at myself. I said it out loud. But I *know* it. I know it's true. I've never felt this sure about anything in my life. I've never loved anyone, ever, like I love Sam. I had to tell him.

"Yes. I love you."

"I love you, too."

"You do?"

"I promise. Cross my heart."

Sam smiles at me, the kind of smile I've never, ever seen on him before. And I feel a funny bursting feeling in my chest. I love Sam, Sam loves me. The world makes sense.

He pulls me to him and we kiss again, kiss and kiss and kiss, until my lips are chattering so hard that it's no longer possible.

"You're freezing. Let's get out of here."

"Your place," I say. "Not Rookhaven." I only want to be with him tonight. Not the noise and drama of Rookhaven. Pia is leaving, I'm leaving, the entire house is imploding . . . but I'll deal with that tomorrow.

Sam leads me out to the street, where the car is waiting for us.

Such a strange sensation: I'm holding Sam's hand. But everything about this just feels *right*. Exciting, safe, and lovely. Like Christmas morning.

He opens the door for me. It's a high-end town car, little Evian bottles in the back, Kleenex, magazines, the whole deal.

"How can you afford this?"

He shrugs. "My roommate, Pete, has an account. Don't worry, he's away."

"How thoughtful of him."

Before climbing into the car, Sam looks back at the playground quickly and sees something.

"Just a second," he says.

Then he runs over to the climbing frame, picks something up, and runs back to the car. It's my gold clutch. I must have dropped it. It's soaked through, but it's still good.

"My clutch! Thank you!"

Sam closes the door. "Back to Fort Greene, please," he says to the driver. Then he turns to me, and I think, for the hundredth time in the past minute, *I love you*.

I lean in and we start kissing again, but I'm shivering from the cold, and my clothes are heavy with rain, so Sam helps me take off my sodden coat. Then he leans back to take off his soaking-wet fleece, and as he pulls it up I get a flash of his brown, muscled torso and my stomach buckles with lust. Holy shit, he's sexy. I grab him and we kiss more, as the car speeds through the storm, shivering with cold and excitement and lust, the rain and wind battering the roof, kissing all the way, until finally the car pulls up outside a nondescript ten-story building. It's the kind of place you wouldn't look at twice from the outside.

Once we get into Sam's building, it's a different story: expensive-looking high-gloss interior, and an elevator that requires a key to take you to your floor.

Sam inserts a key and presses the top button.

As the elevator whooshes up, I turn to him and frown. "Your friend lives in the penthouse?"

He takes a deep breath and nods. "Come on in."

CHAPTER **33**

"The penthouse?" I repeat. "Seriously?"

Sam just shrugs and smiles.

The elevator opens straight into the apartment, and my jaw drops. A huge loft-like space with wall-to-wall windows looking out over Brooklyn and Manhattan and the raging storm.

And it's decorated with the kind of understated, comfortably masculine touches that you only get from a professional interior designer. This is one hell of a place to sleep on the floor while you're trying to find a job. Why did Sam want to spend so much time with me at crummy old Rookhaven when he could have been hanging out here?

"Holy shit. What is your friend? A captain of goddamn industry?"

I look up at Sam to see if he's laughing, but he's suddenly frowning at me so intensely that my stomach drops and my heart races and oh, God, every cliché I've ever read in any romance novel, ever, and he's just so sexy and this is really happening, he really loves me, too, he wants me, too. . . . I want to kiss him again, but I feel paralyzed with, I don't know, shyness, or fear, or something.

Then Sam pulls me in to him and kisses me again.

And so we kiss. We kiss, standing up, against the closed elevator door. Then take a step toward the sofa, then stop, kissing more, then one more step again. My clothes are drenched and I'm freezing, but all I can feel is Sam's warm lips on mine and his arms around me, all I can hear is our breathing and the storm outside. This is perfect.

When we finally get to the sofa, there's a clap of thunder so loud that we both startle, and pause to look at the awesomely violent storm currently at play over the city. The thunder is making the entire building shake every few minutes, and the rain is coming down in hard, angry sheets hitting the windows with an audible *crackcrackcrack*. The strangest thing of all is that the clouds over New York City are purple and gray, furious-looking and illuminated every few seconds by lightning. It looks almost like CGI.

"Crazy . . ." I murmur. "This must be the best view in the city."

"It is," says Sam, and I look up and see he's looking only at me.

"Cheesy," I say.

"Yeah. That was a little cheesy." Sam kisses me again.

"It's like that hurricane," I say. "Sandy. The one that lasted all night and gave half of New York a blackout for days."

"Actually, this is a derecho, rather than a hurricane," Sam says. "A derecho is a series of storms. All of them pounding across New York City."

"Tell me more about the weather," I say. "You're so interesting."

"And you're such a smartass." Sam grabs me and I give a little involuntary shriek, and we get lost in kissing again, till another clap of thunder draws our attention back to the storm. There are over a dozen lightning storms right now over different patches of the city, like tiny rain gods are fighting wars in the clouds.

"Why did you ask Julia out?" I say, out of nowhere. "I mean . . . seriously. I was so shocked."

"I didn't ask her out." Sam looks surprised. "I thought you knew. She asked me out. We were talking about this Mexican place and I said 'We should go sometime.' I meant all of your roommates, especially you. . . .'"

He leans forward and kisses me again. "Next thing I knew, she was texting me about what time she could meet me and that I should pick her up and that she was having first-date nerves and all this stuff, and I just . . . didn't know what to do."

"Oh . . ." I say.

"I tried to call you about it, but you weren't answering your phone. So I just went to the dinner. It wasn't romantic, at all. And the moment we finished our burritos, we came to find you. Trust me, Julia doesn't have any feelings for me. We're just friends."

Sam looks so serious, and so honest, and so fucking gorgeous, that all I can think about is how much I want to kiss him again. We kiss for a few more minutes, until a gunshot-like crack of thunder interrupts us and we both flinch.

"Man, that was loud," I say.

"Did you know you can count how many miles away a storm is by counting between the lightning and thunder?" says Sam.

"Is that true? I thought that was one of those mythical things. Like Santa Claus. And the Tooth Fairy."

"Yeah, right. Like the Tooth Fairy is a myth."

At that moment, lightning whites out the sky, and our eyes lock on each other as we both count silently. Eleven seconds later, a deafening clap of thunder makes me jump, even though I knew it was coming.

"Eleven miles," says Sam.

"It feels like Armageddon," I say. "Not the Bruce Willis one. The biblical one. Hey, Sam?"

"Yes?"

"Kiss me again."

We kiss more, stopping only when I start shivering so violently in my wet clothes that I can't kiss anymore.

Sam gives me a T-shirt with RUTHERFORD written across the front and a pair of green Dartmouth sweatpants. I go to the bathroom to change, but my skin is so cold and drenched with rain that I'm shivering too hard to dress, so instead I decide to take a quick, very hot shower. I wash my hair with his roommate's shampoo and conditioner (Aveda, nice) and wipe away the last inevitable residue of mascara and eyeliner with spit and toilet paper.

Then I look in the mirror. My lips are chapped and swollen, my chin is red and raw with stubble burn, my hair is wet and draggly, I'm not wearing any makeup, and I'm in boy's clothes. I'm a total mess and I don't care. It doesn't matter, because Sam knows who I am no matter what I look like. And he loves me.

I am so happy right now.

I look down and see an open toiletry case. Sticking out the side is an ancient, battered panda toy. Sam's Panda. I smile, thinking about the night he told me about Panda, on the walk back from the hospital after the dinner party. It feels like so long ago.

Holding Panda, I pad back to the sofa and pause for a second, gazing at Sam. He's changed into dry jeans and a long-sleeved T-shirt and is stretched out along the long leather sofa, eyes closed, arms crossed behind his head, a happy smirk on his face. God, he's gorgeous. (And may I just say, his guns are sick.)

Then lightning flashes around the night sky, and I count in my head. One . . . two . . . three . . . four . . . five . . .

"Five miles," says Sam, opening his eyes.

We stare at each other for a few long, silent seconds.

"Is there room for two more?" I hold up Panda.

"Panda! Oh, my God, he's been dying to meet you."

I leap onto the sofa and attack him with kisses, feeling like I'm, literally, physically craving him, like I want to lick and nibble and taste his lips for hours, and even then I won't be satiated. Kissing Sam again, after a period of just a few minutes, feels like coming home. Like every bit of his face and lips and neck and jaw belong to me.

"We should move Panda. He's really too young to see this sort of thing," murmurs Sam.

I grin and place Panda on the coffee table, facing away from us.

"We kiss extremely well together," I murmur.

"I know. Thank God. Imagine if you'd done that whole I-love-you speech in the rain and then I'd discovered you were all tongue or something."

This feels different from any make-out session I've ever had, and I think I know why. He's not grinding an angry hard-on against me. Or frantically clawing at my top or grabbing my ass. I know he's turned on, and I sure as hell am. But unlike every other dude I've ever been with, I don't have the feeling that he's racing against the clock in the endless battle to get laid.

"Why aren't you pawing at me like an oversexed puppy?" I ask at one point.

"Uh . . . do you *want* me to paw at you like an oversexed puppy? And how sexed should puppies be, anyway?"

I laugh, and then think for a second. "I guess not. I'm enjoying the kissing."

"Me too." Sam frowns for a second, as if deciding whether to say anything. "Don't get me wrong, I'd love to do . . . all kinds of things with you. And I will. But I always told myself that if I were ever lucky enough to kiss you, I'd enjoy it as long as I could. Before sex. Before anything else."

"You've thought about kissing me? Since when?"

"Oh, Angie." Sam looks at me and smiles. "Since always. Since you stubbed out your cigarette, called me a nautical Nazi Youth, and swaggered onto the speedboat."

I grin. "That's so . . ."

"Romantic?"

"Sad, actually. Really tragic. Like, what is this, a YA novel or something?"

Sam narrows his eyes in mock annoyance. "You're gonna pay for that."

And boom, we're kissing again, but this time he's trying to torture me. Kissing my neck slowly, so slowly, until I shiver uncontrollably, his bristles scratching my collarbone. Running the tip of his tongue behind my earlobe. Kissing just my top lip, then only my bottom lip, nibbling along my jaw. . . .

It's the sexiest, most excruciatingly divine thing that's ever happened to me, and I find myself gasping, genuinely gasping for air. At one point I actually moan, running my hands through his hair, until I realize I look and sound like something out of one of my goddamn romances, and I shut the hell up.

"Everything about you feels good," Sam murmurs a little while later. "You're just right."

"That's just what I was thinking about you," I say.

"I wanted to kiss you so badly that night we were in your bed. . . . God, I couldn't sleep. I just lay there, listening to you sleep-grunt all night like a baby hippo."

"I do not sleep-grunt! And you nearly did kiss me! The next morning . . . we were snuggling."

"We snuggled? God, and I slept through it? I will never forgive myself." Sam kisses me again. "I love your bottom lip. It's pouty and demanding, did you know that? It never wants to be left out of anything. But then, ah, your top lip, it's all innocent and hopeful. . . . It's so hard to choose my favorite."

"You really shouldn't play favorites. It's not fair."

"I know. And God knows what I'll do when I get to your perfect breasts, it'll be like a sexual *Sophie's Choice*. Okay, are you hungry? Wait, what am I asking. Of course you are. Come on, let's eat."

We head to the kitchen, holding hands. I don't think I've ever felt so happy. I feel like I must be glowing like the goddamn sun.

As Sam riffles through the big steel refrigerator, I take a moment to gaze out at the storm still raging outside, and around the apartment again. It's not at all what I expected from a couple of twentysomething guys sharing an apartment in Fort Greene. I figured it'd be some studio dump, all beaten-up bedbuggy Ikea sofas and dust bunnies. You know, dirty magazines and empty toilet paper roll in the bathroom and a crusty bottle of ketchup in the fridge. But it's serene, stylish, and very clean.

"This place is totally incredible," I say. "Is your friend Pete gay?"

"No, he's not, he just likes to do everything right," says Sam. He looks over his shoulder at me and grins. "How do you feel about grilled cheese?"

"I feel amazing about it."

Sam pulls out a loaf of sourdough bread, some cheddar cheese, and a huge block of butter. Then he takes a big frying pan out of a drawer and turns on the stove.

"This is going to blow your mind," he says, so intensely that I crack up. "Laugh it up, sweetface. Just you wait. I showed Vic how to do this the other day. He said it was the best grilled cheese he'd ever had, and he's been eating grilled cheese since before television was invented. First, we brown the butter."

"You want to burn the butter?"

"*Brown* it. Over low heat. You culinary philistine." Sam leans over to kiss me. "I take it back. You're not a culinary philistine." Then he looks at the pan, bubbling with three giant blobs of butter. "You need to keep stirring it while it bubbles till it turns brown and you can smell . . . ah. Perfect. Now, the bread." He puts four slices in the pan. "We let them hang out in there for a while. Come here again." I grin and lean in. God, I don't think I will ever get tired of kissing him.

After a few minutes, Sam leans back and looks at the pan. "Now we salt them, sea salt only, of course, I know how you feel about sea salt. Add some nice thick slices of cheese to two of the slices, flip the other two over as lids, and put the lid on the pan to let the cheese melt."

"And when do we kiss again?"

"We kiss . . . again . . . now."

Being with Sam is so sexy and giggly and easy. It feels just the way you always hope kissing will feel when you're growing up, you know? Effortless and intimate and romantic. It's just right.

There's a flash of lightning, and three seconds later the thunder claps louder than ever, like a gunshot going off, echoing around the apartment. I jump at the noise and pull Sam even closer to me.

"The storm is getting nearer," I murmur into Sam's lips.

"Are you scared?" he murmurs back.

"Right now, I'm not scared of anything."

Sam shifts his body slightly so he's leaning fully into me against the kitchen counter, and something changes. He's so much taller than me that I can barely reach up and around his shoulders. Isn't it so weird how guys are always taller than you think they're going to be? Or maybe I just think I'm a lot taller than I really am. I don't know . . . oh man, the kissing is good.

After a few minutes, I get the inevitable crick in my neck, and I hoist myself up so I'm sitting on the kitchen counter and we're kissing face-to-face. With my body pressed hard against his, I wrap my legs around Sam's waist and nuzzle his neck until I feel his breath coming out all shaky. I shiver inside with joy at the idea that I'm the person making him feel so excited.

Eventually, he can't take it anymore and pulls me hard against him with a little growl, kissing me even more passionately. This is different

212

kissing now, it's kissing with intent, serious kissing, kissing that's going somewhere, and I know where it's going and I want it so much but I'm scared, though I don't even know why, and I run my hands under his T-shirt and wrap my legs around him tighter and let myself imagine what it would be like to be naked with him, what this would be like if we were in bed, what it would be like to—

Then Sam pulls back and looks me in the eye.

"I really do love you, Angie James."

"I really do love you, too, Sam Carter."

"Now we eat."

So, somehow, we peel ourselves apart, take our grilled cheese sandwiches, and head back to the sofa. Then we eat, sitting sideways with our legs up and layered over each other like two inward-facing bookends. I'm sure he's feeling as tingly with desire and excitement as I am. Wanting someone this much is the sweetest torture in the world.

All I can think is, *God, you're gorgeous. You're absolutely perfect and I love you and know you and trust you, inside and out.*

And looking into his eyes, I know he's thinking exactly the same thing.

I smile and take another bite of grilled cheese sandwich, as a crack of thunder makes the building shake again.

"This is the best thing I have ever tasted in my damn life."

"Yeah," Sam says. "Told ya."

Suddenly, I have a flashback to eating grilled cheese sandwiches with a babysitter when I was a kid. My parents came home early from a party that night, fighting, and I heard my mother saying, "Angelique doesn't need to know!" and my father replying, "You're overreacting! She's a tough little thing!" and my mother yelling, "No! I mean it!" She told me the next day about boarding school, so I figured the fight was about that.

But, maybe it wasn't. Maybe she found out I knew about his affair with his secretary. And didn't want him to make me keep it a secret anymore.

When she told me about the divorce all those weeks ago, she said that I shouldn't be surprised "given what he's been up to over the years." I figured he'd finally come clean about his affairs, or finally gotten busted. But maybe she always knew about them and was trying to protect me from having to know, too. Because a child shouldn't have to keep secrets for—or from—her parents.

Boarding school was the first time I ran away from my problems. Though involuntary, it started a chain reaction of running away that never stopped. Something goes wrong, something's not working, and I leave. Get out. Walk away. Run. Always.

And now I'm running away from Brooklyn.

Is it the right thing to do? Or is it just what I've programmed myself to do as a knee-jerk reaction to every situation? Do I even want to leave now that I've realized how I feel about Sam? And what does he want? All he's talked about since I met him was getting out of here, getting on a yacht and sailing away. So what happens now? Are we a couple? I mean, we are, right? But I can't ask him. We just said I love you, but we also only kissed for the first time like an hour ago. I don't want to sound needy, or psycho, and most of all I don't want to break the weird spell that seems to have been cast over us tonight. The we're-the-only-people-in-the-universe spell.

I look back at Sam and find him staring at me, that familiar intense frown on his face.

"What are you thinking about?" I say.

"Just . . . happy we're being open with each other, finally," he says. "I feel like we have a lot to talk about. I need to tell you some things."

"Sounds gnarly. Okay. I gotta take a leak."

"Oh, wow. You are one classy lady."

I flick him the bird, and he pulls me across the sofa and on top of him for more kisses, until we're interrupted by another clap of thunder.

"Really. When you gotta go, you gotta go," I say.

"Is that from *Annie*?"

"I love that you know that," I say, and lean in to kiss him again before peeling myself off the sofa, as the apartment flashes white again and the walls practically shake with thunder. The storm must be nearly on top of us. Thank God we're safe inside.

On my way back from the bathroom, I notice that my feet are cold. So I duck into the room Sam went into earlier to get me the T-shirt and sweatpants. It's a large bedroom with a desk in one corner and a stack of clean clothes folded perfectly in a laundry basket on the bed. I pick a pair of socks from the top, and sit on the bed to put them on.

As I go to put the second sock on my foot, it drops to the floor, and when I bend down to pick it up I see a picture frame sticking out from under the bed. Probably a picture of Katie, his ex-girlfriend, I think to myself with a stab of jealousy.

I pull the frame out so I can take a good look at her, just as the thunder and lightning finally unite, shaking the entire building with their force.

You've gotta hand it to Mother Nature. She has a hell of a sense of timing.

Because it's not Katie in the frame.

It's a photo of Sam's college graduation.

He's standing next to an older couple who must be his parents. Sam looks younger, yet somehow tired and unhappy. His mom has a kind-but-sad face, very tan with a white-blond bob. And his dad has the same steady gray eyes as Sam, with silvery-white hair, and—

Wait a second.

Sam said he never graduated, he said his dad was dead. But that's clearly his father; the similarity is undeniable.

Suddenly, I realize I know that guy. It's the rich old guy that Cornelia was with at Minetta Tavern just a few hours ago. Roger Rutherford.

What the hell?

Then I look at the T-shirt Sam gave me to wear. It says Rutherford. It's his team T-shirt. Sam's last name is Rutherford. His dad isn't dead and buried in Ohio; Cornelia said he's one of the richest men in New York. This is Sam's penthouse apartment, not some mythical roommate, and Sam isn't a poor college dropout from Ohio slumming it as a boat boy, borrowing clothes from his roommate and trying to get to Europe on the cheap. He's another fucking spoiled New York rich kid with no sense of right or wrong.

And he's been lying to me. Ever since we met.

CHAPTER **34**

I walk out of the bedroom, still holding the picture, my hands shaking, my heart beating painfully, my chest aching with a pain that I know is only just beginning.

"Sam Rutherford." My voice sounds surprisingly strong and calm.

Sam looks over and I hold up the picture, just as the entire building shakes again. Outside the wind is shrieking and the rain is violently hammering against the window. But all I can see is Sam.

Our eyes meet.

And I know it's all true.

He lied. He lied about who he is, where he was from. He lied about everything.

After everything that's happened to me, you'd think I'd have learned that what you see is almost never what you get. That when it comes to instincts, mine can't be trusted. That I'm always, *always* wrong.

But I haven't. And realizing it again breaks me.

"*LIAR!*"

I throw the picture frame as hard as I can so it breaks, splaying across the floor in pieces.

Sam leaps up from the sofa. "No, Angie—"

I need to get out of here. For once, running away is the right thing to do.

Tears running down my face, I grab my purse, pull on my cardigan, coat, and shoes over the sweatpants and T-shirt, and stuff my dress and scarf in my coat pockets. I feel so hot and sick, I might pass out. Sam is now standing in front of me, desperately trying to explain.

"Angie, wait, I didn't, Angie! No, listen, you're overreacting, please look at me, I didn't want to talk about that stuff, about my family—"

"Fuck you!" I push past him. "I told you things I've never told anyone. Ever. I was so fucking honest with you! And you just . . . you lied and lied and lied!" My voice breaks.

"But no, Angie, I didn't lie. My parents are divorced, my mom is in New Mexico—"

"And your dad? He's dead, is he? How was it, dropping out of college?" I say, jabbing the button for the elevator. "Sam *Carter*! You even lied about your name!"

"No, Angie, it's my middle name—"

"And you pretended you didn't know New York. You grew up here! You probably know it better than anyone! You're not living on your buddy's floor; this is *your* apartment! That was *your* car service! And all that time we spent, counting our pennies, talking about how broke we were, what we'd buy if we could only get jobs—for what? All just to get laid? Just to trick me into bed? Or do you just like fucking with people?"

"No! Angie, it's not like that—"

"Bullshit!" I stab at the elevator button again violently. "More bullshit!"

"This is my brother's apartment, really, it is, I swear, but yeah, I do sort of live here, now, but I haven't lived in the city in a long time and my dad and I haven't spoken in years, I never—"

"Stop fucking talking!" I scream, putting my hands over my ears. "I trusted you! I am so sick of people lying and bullshitting me and just using me to get what they want!"

Sam looks like he's about to cry. "No, darling, no—"

Finally, the elevator arrives. I step in, ignoring Sam's pleas, and press the button for the first floor a dozen times. He tries to get in with me, but I shove him out of the elevator as hard as I can.

"Fuck off! Just fuck off and leave me alone! I never want to see you again."

As the elevator doors close, I see Sam's face crumple with misery. But I don't care. I mean it.

I will never see him again.

Then I collapse against the elevator wall, sobbing. If this is heartbreak, it's not a figure of speech: I'm in real, physical pain. Something inside me has broken and will never heal. My heart, no, my whole *body* hurts.

I finally get to the lobby and look through the glass doors. The storm is raging wildly, the wind howling, the rain coming down so hard and fast that I can hardly see out of the building, let alone across the street. I've never seen a storm like this.

But I have to get home.

So I take a deep breath and push the doors open.

The moment I leave the building the ice-cold rain hits me, like a solid wall of water.

The trees are whipping back and forth, almost touching the ground, and above the screams and moans of the storm, I can hear sirens and strange cracking sounds. Half the streetlamps are out, giving the whole street an eerie gap-toothed look, and the night sky has changed from gray-purple to a scary green-gray. There are no cabs, not a person in sight. . . .

Oh God, I don't think it's safe to be outside. But I need to get home to Rookhaven.

I need my friends.

I start running. The wind makes it feel like I'm being held back by invisible hands, and the wall of rain is sleeting down so hard it actually hurts.

At the corner I hear a strange squealing sound, turn and look behind me, and—in a split second so surreal that it's almost like I'm dreaming—I see an enormous tree fall over, with an agonizing lurch, across the street, crushing a car. Holy shit.

My heart beating with fear and adrenaline, I push on, ignoring the instinct that's telling me to get the fuck to shelter, listening only to the crazed voice inside me screaming, *Run away, run away. . . .*

Then the hail starts. Chunks of ice smashing down to the ground, but also hitting me sideways, and whipping straight from left to right, like pebbles in a blender, pinging off cars with an audible cracking sound. What the hell?

The sky is now flashing yellow and gray, debris whipping in circles, and the wind is shrieking all around me. . . .

Oh, my God. I'm in a tornado.

CHAPTER 35

I saw a documentary once about tornadoes in big cities. Everyone thinks they only happen in the Midwest, with old farmhouses getting ripped up and landing on witches, cows whipping around looking mildly surprised, all that sort of thing. But they can happen anywhere. And the tornadoes in a city like New York are, in a way, the most dangerous. Because everything—*everything*—becomes a weapon of destruction. Street signs, garbage cans, trees, cars . . . You name it, and the tornado will use it to kill you.

So I do the only thing I can think of: I run right back up the street to Sam's apartment building, around the side, and down a driveway ramp slick with rainwater to the underground garage. It's inch-deep in water already, freezing cold and pitch-black, but it feels about as safe as I can imagine.

I climb on top of a Hummer—a car I've been known to climb on before, funnily enough—and sit there shivering, listening to the storm rage outside.

My cell has no reception, so I'll just stay here until it's over. I lie back, staring at the concrete ceiling as tears stream down my face. They haven't stopped since I left the apartment. *Sam lied.*

I hear cracks and creaks and shrieks and thuds. My imagination quickly goes wild picturing all of Manhattan and Brooklyn flattened, every building smashed to smithereens, every tree uprooted, like something out of a movie—something that matches how I feel inside. *Sam lied to me. He lied and lied and lied. . . .*

I think back to every conversation we ever had, every chance he had to tell me he was a rich boy just like Stef's gang. Instead he said he was from Ohio, that he'd dropped out of college, that his dad was dead. . . . Why? *Why?*

Then, just like that, everything goes quiet. The storm is over. The rain has stopped. But the ramp leading down here has become a fast-flowing river of water and leaves and garbage and—

Holy shit! I'm moving. The Hummer is floating across the garage. I look around wildly. The garage is flooding! Then again, of course it's flooding. It's a fucking basement. It's the first thing that floods. Thank God my bedroom is on the third—

Oh no.

Vic.

The moment I realize Vic could be in danger I climb down from the car, splash my way through the dirty storm water, trudge up the ramp to the street, and run as fast as I can toward Union Street.

Brooklyn is battered. Every single tree has been stripped of any early spring leaves, some ripped out of the earth and thrown across sidewalks and cars; skylights and chunks of roofs and iron gates are lying, bent and twisted, in the middle of the road; car windows are smashed in by hail . . . It's like a war zone.

It takes me forever to reach Carroll Gardens, but I don't even notice the wet sweatpants flapping around my shoes, or how numb with cold my hands are, or the storm-created chaos I pass along the way. I don't think about Sam, or my life, or my problems.

All I think about is Vic.

He's all alone. What if he fell? What if he's trapped inside? People drown all the time in flash floods. He's old; he's probably frailer than he looks.

Finally, I reach Union Street.

"Are the basements flooded?" I ask a woman coming out of her brownstone, just a few doors up from Rookhaven.

She stares at me, her eyes lit up in panic. "Boerum Hill is flooding! The storm drains gave way, it's three feet deep in water! My sister lives up there, and—"

"But what about our street?" I interrupt her. "What about *our* basements?"

She turns and looks back at her brownstone. "Oh . . . shit."

Immediately, the woman turns and runs toward her basement, and with a thud of dread, I sprint the last thirty feet to Rookhaven, going straight to the door underneath our stoop.

"Vic? Vic! Vic!" I pound my hands against his front door, slapping them so hard my skin hurts.

No response. I hold my ear against the door: I can't hear anything inside, but I'm suddenly sure, totally sure, that he's in there.

"VIC!" I scream at the top of my lungs, and then listen again. . . . I think I hear a knocking sound, but I'm not sure.

So I turn and run up the stoop, two steps at a time, fumbling in my clutch for my keys, and let myself into Rookhaven.

"Is anyone home?" I yell.

No response.

I run through the house to the kitchen and out onto our back deck, which is covered in broken branches and still-frozen chunks of hail. From the railing, I can see Vic's backyard: a swirling, churning mass of brown water, lit from our kitchen window. And it's surging toward his apartment.

Holy shit.

Rookhaven really is flooding.

Without pausing to even think about it, I take off my sodden coat and climb down over the fire escape railings, dangle for a few petrifying seconds, and land with a splash in the backyard. The dark, dank water comes up almost to my knees and is freezing cold and flowing fast. I wade, with difficulty, to the door leading to Vic's kitchen. I can see the water pressure changing as I get near the house and feel the pull on my legs: it's swirling, seeping in underneath the glass door, but still rising. . . .

I cup my hands over the glass door and try to look in: nothing but darkness, but again, I'm overwhelmed by the strongest feeling that he's in there. I knock frantically, screaming, "Vic? Are you in there? Vic! It's me, Angie! I'm coming in!"

I try to open the door; naturally it's locked. I look around for something to use to break it open and see an old flowerpot outside the kitchen windowsill. The flowers in it are destroyed by the storm anyway, so I pick it up and smash it hard against the glass of the back door.

The flowerpot shatters. The glass is intact. You've got to be fucking kidding me.

I look around again and see a little wood-and-metal stool that Vic sits on sometimes, floating in the dark water. I pick it up and, with all my strength, swing it as hard as I can against the back door window. It smashes clean through. Then I take off my cardigan and use it to pluck out the broken shards of glass, until there's a hole big enough to reach in and unlock the door from the inside.

As I open it, I'm swept into the pitch-black apartment so fast I fall over, landing face-first in the revolting floodwater. Oh, God, I hope no sewage pipes have burst; it stinks, this water *stinks*. Fighting panic, I push myself up, leaning against the wall to stand up.

"Vic?" I yell. "Vic?"

Nothing. I've never even been in Vic's apartment before, so I don't know where I'm going. I'm going to have to feel my way through the apartment inch by inch and find a light switch.

"Vic? Are you in here? It's Angie! I'm coming!"

Rookhaven is unusually wide for a brownstone, but also long, and from the back of the house to the front is a long way. Especially in the pitch dark. And even more especially in knee-high freezing floodwater.

Calling Vic's name the whole way, I edge through the kitchen, my hands groping wildly in the darkness. I can feel the edge of the counter, a fridge, a sink, and then a door. The water swirls around me, pulling and pushing me, rising by the second.

I wade through the doorway and down a hall. There is a room immediately to my left, and I shout Vic's name again. The hollow echo makes me sure it's the bathroom, the one that Sam's been helping Vic renovate, and Vic's not in there. *Sam*. My heart aches for a moment. But I need to find Vic. Nothing is important right now except saving Vic.

I continue slowly making my way down the hall, smoothing my hands up and down the walls looking for a light switch. Nothing! Where are the light switches in this damn house?

Then a space opens up in front of my arms. Thanks to light coming in the windows on the far wall, I can just see that I'm in the living room and can barely make out a door on the far right wall. The bedroom. He must be in there.

"Vic? Vic!"

It feels like forever, but I make it to the doorway and hear a funny buzzing sound that starts, stops, and starts and stops again. *Bzzz. Bzzz. Bzzz. . . .*

I peer around, trying to make out the shapes in the room. I think I can see a bed, and a person lying on it.

Suddenly, I hear a moan.

"Vic?" I say. "Vic, is that you? Are you okay?"

There's definitely someone here. The buzzing sound has stopped, and I put my hands out to the wall for the light switch.

Found it.

Just as I'm about to turn the switch on the buzzing starts again, and with it, a strange, tiny spark. For a brief moment the room lights up, and I can make out a bed, with Vic lying on it. The spark came from the base of an old lamp on a nightstand that's almost covered in the murky floodwater.

Oh, my God.

I snatch my hand off the light switch. I'm standing in three feet of fast-rising water that's about to touch live electricity.

I could be killed at any second.

CHAPTER 36

I do the only thing I can think of.

I reach out to the nearest piece of furniture, a tall dressing table, and climb on it. My clothes are wet and heavy, but the adrenaline is rushing through me and I don't even notice.

"Vic? Vic, it's Angie. Are you okay?"

"Girlie?" I can hear Vic's voice, soft and breathy. "I was fixing the lamp. I was—"

"Did you get an electric shock?"

Vic tries to reply, I think, but all that comes out is a sort of wheezy sound. Fuck! Does he have asthma? The water is about to cover his bed, too. If it does, he'll be killed.

My mind is racing. Could an electric shock cause a heart attack? Does Vic have a pacemaker that could have short-circuited or something? I don't even know. He's about eighty years old; an electric shock probably isn't the best thing that could happen to him no matter what other health conditions he might have.

"Where can I turn off the electricity, Vic? Where's the fuse box?"

"Kitchen," he wheezes. "Above the icebox."

I jump off the dresser, landing with a splash in the still-rising flood-water. It's midthigh now; in just a minute or two it'll cover his bed!

With agonizingly slow progress, I swim-jog down the hallway back to the pitch-darkness of the kitchen. There, I find the refrigerator, and the fuse box above it. I open the door and feel my way along the little switches. What am I doing? I can't remember doing this ever before, in my whole goddamn life . . . but I remember seeing my dad doing it once, when the Christmas tree lights blew out all the electricity in the living room at my grandmother's house. He just flicked the one switch that was facing the wrong way back to the same side as the others.

So, since all these fuses are turned on, and all the switches are facing the same way, all I need to do is turn them back the other way in order to turn them off. Right? Right.

I quickly flip each switch one by one with a satisfying click. When I'm all done, of course, nothing happens.

But now I'm less likely to be electrocuted. So let's call that a plus.

I make my back to Vic's room, my heart pounding with cold and adrenaline and fear.

He's still breathing but now seems to be unconscious. "Vic! Please wake up!" I shake his shoulders, my voice high with panic. "Vic! *Please!*"

I try to pick him up, but I can't budge him. He's over a foot taller than me, and though he's skinny, he still weighs a ton. If I got him off the bed into the water, I could never support him, he'd just sink through the water to the floor. He would probably drown. But I can't leave him here, either. He needs medical help. God! What am I going to do?

He doesn't stir. I put my ear to his mouth—the way Sam did to Coco when she overdosed—to see if he's still breathing. But I'm trembling so hard from the cold I can't feel anything.

Shit. I don't know what to do. I just . . . I don't know what to do.

At that moment I hear a voice at the door. "Vic? Vic! It's Julia, are you okay?"

"Julia! Help me!"

Another voice. "Vic? It's me, Sam!"

What the fuck is Sam doing here?

"Angie?" Julia's voice is high with stress and panic. "Where are you? Where's Vic?"

"He's in here, in the bedroom!" I call. "He's unconscious; I think he was electrocuted or something!"

"How did you get in?"

"I broke in the back door when I saw the flooding, but listen, you need to call an ambulance, okay? Vic's in bad shape and the water's still rising in here."

"I'll call 911!" shouts Julia.

Then I hear Sam's voice, but louder, and I can see the shaky whiteness of a flashlight in the living room. "Angie? Where are you?"

Seconds later, Sam wades into the bedroom. The flashlight is so bright that I shield my eyes. "How long have you been here? Are you okay?"

"I don't know, a few minutes? Vic was conscious before; he told me he was fixing the lamp. I think a lightning strike caused a surge of electricity or something." I ignore Sam's second question.

"Angie, we have to talk—"

"Now really isn't the fucking time, Sam," I snap. "We have to help Vic."

"I was so worried about you out in the storm, I've been combing the fucking streets—"

"Not now! Help me carry Vic out of here!"

In silence, we carry Vic through the floodwater to the front door, where there are two steps up to street level. Thank God Sam is here: Julia and I could never have supported the weight of Vic alone. Outside, the water hasn't even risen as far as our stoop. Rookhaven—our part of Rookhaven—is fine.

We gently place Vic on the sidewalk, lying flat, his head resting on Sam's coat, and I crouch next to him and hold his hand.

Sam checks his pulse and his breath, the way I did earlier.

"I did that already, he's breathing," I say. "But I think it's getting weaker."

Sam checks Vic's hands. "Does he have any injuries? Electric shocks can burn the skin. Can you smell anything? You should be able to smell the burn."

"No," I say. People get *cooked* by electric shocks?

Julia comes bounding back down the stoop.

"Oh, Sam, you are the best, thank you."

"Are you okay?" I ask her.

"Fine, I just got home from work and ran into Sam, he came to check on Vic, and Vic gave me a spare set of keys for emergencies. . . . I was stranded in the office all evening watching the storm. It was insane! I've never seen anything like it! Where were you?"

I can feel Sam looking at me and purposely don't glance up or reply. Instead, I just keep stroking Vic's hand. He stirs, his eyes opening slightly.

"Vic, it's me, Angie, I'm here with Julia—"

"Uncle Vic!" Julia kneels down, clasping his other hand.

"Little Julia? And Sammy?"

"I'm right here, boss," says Sam. "There's an ambulance on the way."

"That's good news." Vic smiles weakly. "Damn electricity."

He closes his eyes and sighs deeply, his exhale coming out in shaky gasps.

"How did you know Vic was in danger, Sam?" asks Julia. "I mean, it's nice to see you! I was just, um—"

"I've been working for Vic for weeks, remember?" says Sam. "Once I saw the floodwater, I wanted to check up on him."

"Wow, that's so good of you!"

A voice interrupts. "Are you okay? Oh, my God, Vic?" I look up, and there's Pia standing with Coco and Madeleine.

"He's fine, I think, we don't know. . . ." I say. "Where have you guys been?"

"We just got back," says Pia. "We were stuck in Manhattan."

"I was with Ethan," says Coco, sounding tearful. "Oh, gosh, poor Vic."

The girls crouch down and start whispering to Vic, but my attention is on Julia and Sam. Something's just not adding up.

"So, um, anyway, Sam?" says Julia. "Is your friend's place damaged? It's in Fort Greene, right?"

"It's fine," says Sam, checking his phone. "Have you checked the rest of Rookhaven?"

"A few broken windows, but that's about it. So, uh, aside from biblical weather, how was the rest of your day? What have you been up to?"

I turn away. I can't look at Sam, that lying scumbag, or see Julia treating him like he's a friend, like she likes him. . . .

Wait a second.

I thought their date on Saturday night was a total bust. So why is Julia still sounding so happy and sort of, I don't know, excited to talk to him? Does she still have a thing for him, after all that Sam said about the date being terrible? Well, I can put a stop to that.

"He's not who you think he is," I snap, looking up at Julia. "He's not Sam Carter. He's a liar."

Julia looks at me, confused. "What do you—"

"He's from New York, not Ohio. He's not some poor college dropout, he graduated from Dartmouth and his family is loaded. And his name is Sam Rutherford."

Julia looks from me to Sam a few times. "I don't—"

"I tried to explain," says Sam. "Carter is my mother's maiden name, and—"

"Oh, my God," says Julia, putting her hand to her mouth and backing away from Vic and Sam. *"Rutherford."* She's staring at me. At what I'm wearing. The Rutherford T-shirt that is obviously way too big for me. And she knows me well enough to know I've never worn sweatpants in my life.

Julia backs away. I follow her, unable to say anything, feeling a desperate sense of panic and shame.

"You've been with him—How could you—You knew how I felt—" Julia is staring at me in total shock, almost whispering. No one else can hear us.

"No, no, it's not what it looks like, I mean, please, Jules, listen!" There's a note of desperation in my voice I've never heard before. Then I say the three little words said by treacherous friends everywhere. "I can explain—"

At that moment, the ambulance arrives, and we're distracted by paramedics running out to treat Vic. We try to comfort him as they load him on the stretcher.

"You'll be fine, Vic, everything will be fine," I say, covering his hand with both of my own.

"This is overkill," Vic grumbles as they slip an oxygen mask over his head.

"I'm going with Vic." Sam jumps in the ambulance, oblivious to the drama between Julia and me. "I'll call his family on the way to the hospital."

Seconds later, they're gone.

Julia turns to me again, her face blank and pale, the words coming out slowly, as though every new thought gives her pain.

"You knew how I felt about Sam. You *knew*. But you've been with him for the past three days. That's why you haven't been home. That's why I haven't heard from him. . . . Oh, my God, I bet he left to meet you on Saturday night. He left the bar just after you, you must have texted him."

"No, Julia, that's not what happened. I—"

But she's not listening. "You knew he was the first guy I've liked in so long, and you ruined it. Just to spite me. Of all the evil, bitchy, mean things to do—"

"No, that's not true, Jules, I promise! It just, oh God, it just happened tonight, I thought I had feelings for him, but I don't, he's just a liar, and he told me your date was a total failure, he said that there was nothing between you, I thought you didn't like him anymore, and—"

"And you didn't even think to talk to me about it? I thought you were my *friend*!" Tears fill Julia's eyes, and she turns and runs into the house.

I turn to Pia and Coco, trying not to sound hysterical. "What the fuck? Sam said nothing happened between them. Was that a lie, too?"

"They didn't kiss or anything," says Pia guardedly. "But . . ."

"She likes him, Angie." Coco is distraught. "She's liked him for weeks. How could you *do* this to her?"

And Coco runs up the stoop. I stare after her.

And the front door to Rookhaven slams shut.

Today I've been fired from the Gap, propositioned by a multimillionaire, found out my father's getting remarried and starting a new family, run through New York in a rainstorm, fallen in love with the guy I thought was my best friend, discovered he was a liar, had my heart broken, survived a tornado, saved a man's life, and accidentally betrayed one of my best friends.

But it's the shocked disappointment of Coco, the sweetest person I've ever known, that truly destroys me. I want to collapse right here, into a tiny ball, and never get up again.

I am a bad person.

I sit down on the stoop, my hands shaking with cold and shame, my breath coming out in hiccup-y gasps. I am too overwhelmed to even cry. Pia sits down next to me and sighs, then puts her arm around my shoulders. Her unspoken loyalty to me right now, even though we've barely crossed paths in weeks, is the only good thing in my entire existence. I rest my head on her shoulder and she kisses my forehead, a motherly gesture that is so tender and loving, it actually makes me feel worse. I don't deserve it.

Everything is fucked.

Then I remember.

"What time is it?" I ask Pia.

She looks at her phone. "Just past midnight."

"Happy birthday."

"Happy birthday."

CHAPTER **37**

"So, you're really moving out?" I ask Pia at 7:00 the next morning.

She nods. "I think so. I mean . . . yes. I am. I want to be with Aidan. I'm going to talk to my boss today, ask if I can work from San Francisco; we have an office out there. . . . But I haven't told the girls yet, so don't say anything, okay?"

Pia and I are in the sunlit kitchen having coffee. Lots of it. I didn't sleep last night. Not because of Sam, or my dad, or even the big black future-shaped hole in my life, but because when I close my eyes, all I can see is Julia looking at me like I'd just stabbed her in the heart.

Oh God, I feel so bad.

Guilt is different from heartbreak. Like heartbreak, guilt is inescapable, it's pervasive, it takes over your every thought. But where heartbreak makes you ache with tears, guilt just makes you, I don't know, *itchy* inside with shame and regret. And it feels like it will never go away.

"I'm leaving, too," I say. "I'm going to L.A. That whole Julia and Sam thing just gives me all the more reason to leave. I've totally fucked up everything here, you know? And I think I should start over. Today's my twenty-third birthday, and it's time I grew up."

Pia nods. "I understand. L.A. isn't that far from San Francisco. We can still meet up on weekends and stuff."

"Come on. You and Aidan won't be living in some couple-tastic dreamworld? Taking long weekends in Napa, going to Lake fucking Tahoe to waterski? Hiking? I'm pretty sure hiking is compulsory if you live in California."

Pia grins and covers my hand with her hand. "Ladybitch, I promise you. I will never hike."

"Doesn't it scare you? Leaving everything you know to move in with a guy?" I ask.

"Scare me? No . . . I love Aidan. Love isn't scary."

Yes it is, I think, but don't say aloud. Instead, my voice comes out in a tiny mumble. "But what if he changes his mind?"

"You think Aidan will change his mind?"

"No, no . . . I just mean, you know. Theoretically. This whole love thing . . . it can just go away, just like that. One minute you're safe and happy, the next minute it's over and you trusted someone you shouldn't have."

Pia stares at me, but I can't meet her eyes. I feel quiet and cold inside.

"You can't be scared of that," Pia says softly. "You have to just . . . hope."

Hope is for innocents and losers. I think of my mother, always hoping things would get better with my father, hoping he'd stop lying to her and come home. . . . How naive can you get? But then I think of Pia, who took so many huge risks last year, always hoping that the perfect combination of optimism, hard work, and luck would see her through. And it did.

Oh God, I don't know. If I try to figure out the world by looking at people in my life, I just get more confused.

I take another sip of my coffee and glance over at Pia. "I'm going to miss you, ladybitch."

"You are?"

"Of course I am," I say. "I'm happy that you're happy, of course, and

Aidan is great and everything, but ... I mean, I really missed you the last few months when you were hanging out with him all the time. Imagine how much I'll miss you when you're living in a whole other city."

"You did?"

"You're surprised?"

"It's just that ... you never act like you need me. You never act like you need anyone."

I'm stunned. "Pia, you saved my life when I jumped out of a taxi on the Brooklyn Bridge. You saved my life every time you invited me on vacation with your parents, because mine were such fuckups, and I felt so safe with you guys." I take a deep breath. "And you saved my life when you got me into Rookhaven. You just always save me. You're like ... my life preserver."

Pia reaches out and gives me a huge hug. "I love you."

"I love you, too."

"God, we are lame," she says, tears in her eyes.

"I know," I say, that familiar painful lump forming in my throat. I'll probably never live with Pia again. And I didn't even really make the most of it while I could. I just got drunk and did whatever I wanted and acted like I didn't care about anything or anyone.

I'm such an asshat.

Pia seems lost in her own thoughts. "Sheesh, I don't know. I should be happy I get to be with Aidan all the time once I move. . . . So why do I feel so depressed?"

"Birthday blues."

"Yeah. I fucking hate birthday blues."

It's strange to have the same birthday as your best friend. Pia and I are so similar. We both act before we think, have a history of bad decisions with men, same silly sense of humor. But we're so different, too. She's a people person, a charming drama queen, a gung-ho-we-can-do-it type, a caring and loud and loyal friend. I'm a loner, I'm tougher, I'm more stubborn, I internalize everything, I'm dreamy and quiet.

And I'm clearly not a loyal friend.

I hate that about myself.

I haven't seen Julia this morning. I think she went into work before I got up. Coco came into the kitchen briefly to pack her lunch, but wouldn't even make eye contact with me, and Madeleine headed off for her morning jog half an hour ago without saying anything, either.

I guess I deserve it.

When I think about how everything in my life seemed complete and certain and perfect for just a few minutes last night, and how I was wrong *again,* and how everything about Sam—the guy I thought I loved!—was a huge lie, I feel a dry, empty sadness deep inside. My friendship with Sam didn't ever truly exist. My heart aches so much, I can't imagine ever feeling good again.

Then I think about how Julia looked at me when she found out I'd been with him, and Coco's reaction, and I am overwhelmed with a tidal wave of guilt and regret. I betrayed my friend.

And that feels worse than heartache.

"I need to make it up to Julia," I say to Pia. "I need to show her how sorry I am."

Pia sighs. "Look ladybitch, it only just happened. She'll get over it. Give her time."

"But I'm leaving for L.A.! I don't have time!"

"You did the crime, you do the time," says a voice, and Madeleine walks in from her jog, pink with sweat and health and exercise and all those things I will never care about.

"Thanks for your support," I snap. "I didn't know she liked him that much. He said nothing happened. I didn't *know.*"

My voice cracks, and I bury my head in my hands. Please, God, don't let me cry in front of the girls.

"Oh, waaaaaah," says Madeleine, stretching against the kitchen counter.

"Stop it, Maddy," says Pia. "It's not funny."

"Sorry," she says, and sits down at the table. "Angie, don't cry, okay? I'm sorry."

"You're so goddamn bitchy all the time," I say, trying hard to control my goddamn tears.

"I was just trying to be cute," she says. "You always make snarky little comments like that."

I look up. "I do? I don't mean to. I'm not thinking about what I say to other people most of the time. I'm just sort of, I don't know, trapped in my head."

"Me too," says Madeleine. "It's a living hell."

This statement is so dramatic and at odds with Madeleine's usual understated manner that Pia starts laughing. I try to smile, but my face feels like it's made of concrete. Heavy and gray.

"How is Vic?" asks Madeleine.

"Fine," says Pia. "Julia texted me. He's staying in the hospital for a few more days."

"Oh, hey! Happy birthday!" says Madeleine. Pia and I both make "let's not talk about it" headshakes. "Sheesh. Okay." Then she turns to me and clears her throat. "Angie, um, I haven't thanked you for what you did at the bar on Saturday night. For starting the dancing, when I was singing? I was so nervous, you know, and self-conscious, but once I saw you dancing, it was like . . . like I remembered how to enjoy myself."

"You're an amazing singer," I say. "Really. You're so talented. Plus, you know, I wanted to show off my amazing dancing skills. I mean, skillz. With a Z."

"Actually, you're a pretty terrible dancer." Madeleine grins. "But a good person."

And boom, tears rush to my eyes again. "I am not . . . I'm not a good person." My voice is all shaky. "Everything I do is always wrong. I'm bad, I do the wrong thing, I'm a bad friend, I'm such a bad friend. . . ."

I hold my hands over my face, fighting back tears and regret and misery. Pia puts her arm around me, but this time, I pull away. I can't bear to lean on her. I don't deserve her support.

"Stop with the self-pity," says Madeleine firmly. "Just fix the situation. It's within your control to fix it. Apologize."

"But what do I say?" My voice is croaky with misery. "I'm sorry I kissed that guy you like? This goes deeper than that for her. You know it does. This confirms everything bad she's ever thought about me."

"Just open your mouth and say how you feel," says Pia.

I stare at the kitchen table so long that it starts swimming in front of my eyes.

"I feel like I need a grand gesture or something," I say. "Like, I don't know, I need to show up at Julia's work with a balloon saying 'I'm sorry.'"

"Hell no, don't do that," says Madeleine. "She works in an investment bank, that shit will get her killed. . . . Oh, my God, is that the time? I have to get to work!"

"So do I," says Pia. "I want to stop in and see Vic at the hospital first, too." She turns to me. "See you at home tonight, ladybitch? Maybe you should try to brainstorm some ideas about how to make up with Julia!"

"Brainstorming. For fuck's sake. Such a corporate whore," I say.

Pia winks and flicks me the bird. "Later, ladybitch."

After the girls leave, I try to do just that. I sit at the table and try to make a list of ways to let Julia know I didn't betray her, that I really do value her friendship so highly, that I'm sorry I hurt her.

But I can't think of anything.

So instead, I make a list of things that I wish I could change about my life. In no particular order:

Not talking to my mother
Dad's marriage and baby
Lack of career
Lack of money
No idea what to do with my life
Everything that happened on the yacht
Soho Grand night (??)
The fight with Sam
Hurting Julia

As far as I can see, it's only in my control right now to change two of those things. The first. And the last.

So I pick up my phone and call my mother's cell phone. She answers on the second ring.

"Angelique?"

"Hey, um, yeah, it's me."

"Oh honey! Happy birthday, darling! I was just about to call you, but I didn't know if you'd—I mean, I am so happy to hear from you!"

I don't know what to say. . . . What was it Pia told me? *Just open your mouth and say how you feel.*

"I'm so sorry I walked out on you that day, when you told me about the divorce," I say. "It was a rash and, um, immature reaction. I should have stuck around to talk to you about it. And I'm sorry I've been ignoring your calls."

"Oh, darling . . ." My mother's voice is soft with emotion. "I understand. I should have broken it to you more gently, and not in public. Your father had just called me that morning and, well, I was in shock, you see—" She takes a deep breath.

"He's getting married. And she's pregnant." My voice is totally flat. "I know. I ran into him last night." Was the Minetta Tavern just last night? It feels like so long ago.

"I was hoping he'd call you to tell you. . . . I've been so worried about it. I should just have told you."

"No, it's okay. You shouldn't have to do his dirty work for him." And neither should I. "How do you feel about it, Mom? Are you okay?" I can't remember the last time I said that word. *Mom*. I always called her Annabel. I de-Mommed her. Like a punishment. What a brat I was.

"I am. I really am!" Her voice suddenly brightens. "We were finished a very long time ago. . . . And my life is good. I've decided to stay in Boston, all my friends are here and he doesn't own the city, does he? I'm renting the most darling little apartment and I fill it with flowers twice a week, because who can be miserable when they're surrounded by flowers? And I've been so busy with volunteer work. We're throwing a domino party for charity!" She starts laughing with glee. "Can you imagine? Isn't it wild?"

"Sounds killer . . . but why are you friends with those women?" I ask. "The rich bitchy socialite women."

"Honestly, darling? I like them because they're always *doing* something. I know an awful lot of women my age who just do nothing with their lives. They just watch TV and gossip. It's depressing. And, well, they pay me very well to help organize their functions. I'm not relying on your father ever again, in any way, shape, or form. It feels wonderful."

My mother likes to work. Revelation.

"Now, I didn't know what you wanted for your birthday, so I simply transferred fifteen hundred dollars to your account. A little birthday surprise."

"No, no, I don't need that," I say quickly. "Really, Mom, I swear—"

"Too late, it's all done! Come on, if there's one thing I remember about being twenty-three it's that I never had enough money. . . . So what else is new with you, darling? How's Pia?"

And boom, we start talking, *really* talking, for the first time in years.

I tell her all about Rookhaven, and my roommates, about how I've been trying to get a job and working at the Gap. . . .

"And boys?"

I sigh. "I'm failing there, too."

"It's not called failing, darling. It's called living. Just keep trying. It's the trying that makes it fun. If you want to go to L.A., I think it's a wonderful idea. The most important thing to me is that you're happy."

I think about that for a moment. . . . Okay, maybe she shouldn't have sent me away to school without asking, but she thought she was doing the right thing. She was only trying to make me happy.

While I did everything I could to make her unhappy. But I know I can't fix that in one phone call. It'll take time.

She continues. "I'm so glad you rang. I didn't know whether you wanted to hear from me; I've been thinking about you so much."

"Me too, Mom." I pause. "Maybe you could come out to L.A. to see me. Or I'll come to Boston and see you."

"Of course! I would love that! Anytime. I love you."

"I love you, too, Mom."

As I hang up, I'm smiling.

Who can be miserable when they're surrounded by flowers. . . .

I have an idea.

CHAPTER **38**

"I can't *believe* you get to live in that brownstone." Edward claps his hand over his mouth in disbelief. "Do you have any idea how lucky you are?"

I look up at Rookhaven. "It's nice, huh?"

"Nice? Amazing is what it is. You're brand-new to the city and you land a place like that? Do you know what my first apartment here looked like, before I met Adrian? It had bloodstains in the bathtub, Angie, and the remnants of chalk body outlines on the floor."

I crack up. "I know, I know. I was lucky."

"And you're talking about leaving," Edward says, opening the back of his truck. "You're out of your cotton-picking mind."

I'm standing outside Rookhaven with Adrian's boyfriend, Edward, the guy I met in the Gap, next to his floral delivery van. His second van is right behind us.

And we're going to fill Rookhaven with flowers for Julia.

The moment I got off the phone with my mother this morning, I texted Adrian to get Edward's number, then called him and explained the situation. Together, we tracked down every hydrangea—Julia's favorite flower—in New York City. Enough to fill the hallway and living room and every bedroom in Rookhaven. And every other place I could think of.

It cost over half my birthday money, even though Edward got me a serious discount. Never underestimate the cost-cutting power of a florist on a mission. But it was worth it. It's going to look *amazing*.

Edward's even loaning me vases. And two of his delivery boys to help unload and arrange the flowers. He won't take any extra payment for his help, either.

"It's for a good cause," he scoffed, when I tried to protest. "I told you that you need your friends to survive in this city! You do whatever you can to hang on to them. Anyway, I owe you. We got you fired from the Gap, remember?"

Even with four people, it's backbreaking work to unload and arrange all the flowers and vases perfectly. Every time I climb the stoop, I glance down to Vic's apartment. The front door is open. I hear occasional thumps and shouts, and there's a big generator outside, with hoses going in and out. I guess they're pumping all the water out. I wonder if Sam is in there, helping to fix everything. But if he is, he's avoiding the front door.

Well, good. I don't want to see him anyway.

An hour later I'm sweaty and pink, and Rookhaven is transformed. Huge pots bursting with hydrangeas line the stoop, and inside, every room is overrun with gorgeous blooms, nestling in vases of every height and size. After the longest, coldest winter I can remember, it's like the house exploded with spring.

And when Julia gets home from work tonight, she'll see her favorite flowers everywhere she looks.

Maybe that will help her to consider forgiving me for being such a bad friend.

"Thank you," I tell Edward, when the place is done. "I could not have done this without you."

"Not a problem, sweetface," he says, triple-cheek-kissing me good-bye. "By the way, my heartbreak radar is going bananas around you. You wanna talk about it?"

I gaze at him. My body is so tired of making tears that I can't even muster up a throat-lump. "I think if I started talking about it, I would break into little pieces."

"Oh, honey." Edward sighs and gives me a huge hug. Man, I am really into the hugging thing these days. It's so goddamn nice.

I head upstairs to take a long shower and dress. Later, when Coco gets back to Rookhaven from her preschool, I can hear her mewing with delight as she walks up the stoop. When she walks into the front hall, her jaw drops. "Wowsers! Oh, my God! This is so awesome! Who did this?"

"I did," I say, from my vantage point by the kitchen door.

Coco's smile drops when she sees me. Sisterly loyalty trumps friendship. Every time.

"It's for Julia," I say quickly. "I want to tell her that I'm sorry about Sam, I'm sorry that I hurt her. You know, he told me they were just friends, that the date was terrible. And I had this crazy evening, um, anyway, no excuses, but I thought I had feelings for him. And we didn't sleep together, we just kissed."

Coco looks at me for a few seconds, narrowing her eyes suspiciously. "I always wondered why you didn't *like* like him. You get along so well, and he's so, you know, gorgeous."

"We were just friends. I swear. Last night, I thought that maybe there was something more there. . . . But I was wrong. He's a total sociopath. He said he was Joe Normal working on yachts to make ends meet, and it turns out he's just the kind of rich, entitled, lying fuckpuppet I've been trying to avoid."

"Why?"

"What?"

"Why did he lie?"

"Because that's what people do. People keep secrets and people lie."

"No, I mean . . . why would he lie to you? He's been working on yachts for years, right? It's not like he was doing it just so he could lie if he ever met a girl called Angie who hates rich boys."

I stare at Coco, trying to cover up my genuine surprise. "Are you telling me that everything isn't all about me?"

She giggles.

I take that as a sign of forgiveness. "Coco, I swear I would never try to hurt Julia. . . . I'm going to write her a little note, okay? Can you give it to her when she gets home?"

"Where are you going?"

"I'm going to visit Vic at the hospital."

Plus, I want Julia to see the flowers, read the note, and then decide if she forgives me without me being there. When you're angry at someone, sometimes just seeing them is enough to make you blow up. This is like sneaking in the side door and asking for forgiveness.

It takes me a while to write the note. I'm just not used to expressing how I feel. But finally, it's just right. I hope.

> *Julia,*
>
> *I'm so sorry about Sam. I don't know how much you want to know, but this is the truth: he told me that you and he had a bad date, that you were just friends. I'd just found out some stuff about my dad. I was upset, he was there, we kissed. I thought I had feelings for him. I was wrong.*
>
> *I would never, ever intentionally hurt you, and I hate that I caused you misery. Our friendship is the only thing I'm proud of since coming to New York. I really hope it isn't over.*
>
> *I'm sorry.*
>
> *A x*

Then I pick up my little gold clutch, the one I made all those weeks ago, and walk to the hospital. It feels good in my hand, this clutch. I guess I have to leave Drakey and my sewing machine behind when I leave. . . . I hate that. But I can just get new ones in L.A., right?

Today is the first time in ages that I can remember the afternoon sky being blue, truly blue. Like the storm ushered winter out and washed everything clean. It felt like the cold would last forever this year, but it never does. Spring always arrives eventually. I should really stop being surprised by that.

"Knock knock . . ." I whisper, at the entrance to Vic's hospital room. Vic is lying in bed with the *New York Times* crossword, wearing pale blue pajamas. "Why are you doing the crossword?" I ask. "What, you like being stressed out?"

"Girlie! Hiya . . . What, you mean this?" He gestures to the newspaper. "It reminds me of my wife. Eleanor did it every day, from 1942 when it started, and she was just a teenager, until the day she died. So every day I try to do it, just like she would, and I say to myself, damnit, Eleanor always knew how to make my head spin."

"She sounds smart."

"She was smart. And difficult and wonderful." He folds the paper up and puts it on his little sliding hospital table. "Like all the best things. Take a seat."

"How are you feeling?" I ask. It's weird seeing Vic in pajamas. He looks almost more vulnerable than he did when he was lying unconscious, fully dressed and soaked with floodwater, outside Rookhaven last night.

"I'm fine," he says. "Enough voltage went through me to start a car, can you believe that? From that damn lamp. I was paralyzed. . . . It threw me onto the bed. Next thing I know, you were there. My little guardian Angie."

I laugh. "No one's ever called me that before."

"You ever been electrocuted?"

"Nope."

"It's strange." Vic's voice is suddenly hoarse. "For a few seconds, the entire world flips. I knew what was happening, but I couldn't move, I couldn't do anything about it. . . . I feel like I'm still catching my breath."

There's an impatient knock on the door. A nurse. "Excuse me, visiting hours are over."

"This is my granddaughter."

"She signed herself in as a friend."

"Well, we're a friendly family. I have five granddaughters. They're very important to me."

I turn to Vic and he winks at me. But he does look tired.

"I should go, anyway," I say. "You rest. Will you be coming home tomorrow?"

"I promise." Vic smiles at me, his craggy old face creasing up. "You

244

be good to that boy of yours, you hear me? He's a keeper. One of the good ones. He stayed with me in the hospital all night, you know that?"

"He did?" I'm surprised, though I shouldn't be. That's just the kind of thing Sam would do.

But he's not my boy.

"Didn't leave my side until my niece turned up this morning. You know, I've never seen a storm like that in Brooklyn. People could have been killed. I'm just glad luck was on our side."

I walk out of the hospital, Vic's words ringing in my ear. *One of the good ones.*

Ha.

For a few seconds the other night, my entire world flipped, too. For a brief moment, I loved Sam and Sam loved me, and everything made sense. I thought it was real. The kind of easy, warm, true love you always read about in romance novels. (Well, I always do, anyway.) For the first time in my life I felt . . . full. Complete.

And why *did* Sam make up all those lies? He must have a reason. I could find out right now. I could talk to him, I could let him explain. . . .

But I won't. First, it would upset Julia, and second, I have to go buy a plane ticket to L.A. with the rest of the money from my mom. It's time to start over. I won't have any spare cash, but I'll get a job as soon as I land—at the goddamn Gap if I have to—and figure it out from there. Life *will* change.

My phone is ringing. I look at it: Cornelia? What does she want?

"Hello?"

"Angie! Sweetie. Emergency! I need you. The Met Ball is tonight, and I picked up this fucking douchebag PA in France who just left me high and dry, the hairy bitch. I'll pay you twice the usual; I just need you to organize the car and things like that. How quickly can you get here?"

I look at the time. It's 5:00 P.M. "I'm in Brooklyn. I'll be there in thirty minutes."

"I am so fucking sick of everyone living in Brooklyn. Make it faster!"

And click, she hangs up.

CHAPTER 39

Cornelia lives in a loft apartment in the West Village. It's all boutiques and trees and tiny cafés, the kind of picture-perfect Manhattan neighborhood that makes you feel a mixture of longing and resentment.

She's also going through her "downtown intellectual slum" phase, or at least that's what her mother told my mother. (Cornelia's mother is a Boston society doyenne who married Cornelia's much older and very rich father, moved to New York, and had Cornelia and her brother. She moved back to Beacon Hill in Boston two years ago, about a minute after he died.)

The loft was professionally decorated, naturally, and it's perfectly disheveled arty chic. Piles of books (that she hasn't read) everywhere, lots of bijou Paris flea-market finds resting on $15,000 side tables, thick plush carpets and big fat sofas, you know the drill. Slightly overstuffed with things, slightly too impeccable, and all with that immaculate spar-kle you only get with a full-time housekeeper.

I'm buzzed in and arrive to find the loft in a state of uproar.

"FUCK!" I can hear Cornelia screaming from her bedroom. "This is a FUCKING nightmare! Why does this shit always happen to me?"

"Hi, Cornie!" I call. "It's me! Angie!"

I quickly kiss her makeup artist hello. His name is Keith. We bonded last year during the holiday season, when Cornie went out every single goddamn night and I was the idiot running around picking up the right shoes and trying to help her borrow the right jewelry and making sure she had spare Spanx and extra MAC Face and Body Foundation and ugh, *everything*.

But the pressure of that is nothing compared to tonight. The Met Ball is a $25,000-a-seat gala held every year to celebrate the opening of the Metropolitan Museum's fashion exhibit at the Costume Institute. For the fashion world, it's like the Oscars plus Christmas plus New Year's Eve combined, and everyone who is anyone attends, from designers to *Vogue* editors to models to fashion-aware celebrities, and even sports stars, all wearing the most exquisite, glamorous dresses you've ever seen in your goddamn life. If you're into fashion, the Met Ball is your mecca.

"Hi, sweetie," Keith whispers. "We're in for a *rough* night."

"Angie!" screams Cornie. "Come here! Fuck!"

I run through the living room and down the tapestry-lined hallway into the pristine white-on-white master bedroom, through a walk-in closet (which, honestly, is bigger than my bedroom and would make you cry with envy) to the dressing room, where Cornie is staring at herself in the mirror while getting her hair blow-dried by Bibi, her personal hairdresser.

"Bibi, stop," she orders, clicking her fingers. "Angie. Lauren just texted me. That bitch Olivia is wearing the same Zac that I was going to wear. Little whore. I need to speak to Zac about it. Get him on the phone."

"Um, okay—" I walk back out to Keith. "I need Zac Posen's number."

"Well, only *Cornelia* has *that*." Keith has a habit of speaking in ital-ics. "She's *freaking out*. She *only* got a ticket because this *Rutherford guy* is on the *board* or some shit." He lowers his voice. "This is *way* out of her league."

"Angie!" Cornelia is screaming. "Do you have Zac yet?"

Suddenly, I understand why she's hysterical. Cornelia's been swimming around the lower echelons of the socialite food chain for a couple of years. She's rich, but not superrich. She has a car service but not a permanent driver, a hairdresser but not a stylist. She's ambitious: she wants to be a Page Six name, have a purse named after her, open a lifestyle boutique in the Hamptons, and launch a makeup line in Japan. Tonight is her chance to climb up the society ladder. This is a job interview.

I march back into Cornelia's dressing room and try to sound authoritative and like I'm not lying. "Can you give me his new number? I only have his old one."

"Get with the now, Angie, he changed it, like, six months ago." Still gazing at herself in the mirror, Cornelia hands me her cell. "Tell him if Olivia is wearing the pink then I need to know, because I have it in the yellow, and tell him to tell me if Lauren is lying to me because I will fucking cut that bitch dead tonight."

I nod and back out of the room while it's ringing.

Finally, on the eleventh ring, it goes to voice mail.

"Hello, this is Angie James calling for Mr. Posen on behalf of Cornelia Pace. She has an urgent query about a dress for the Met Ball this evening. Can you please call me back?" I leave my number and hang up.

Who am I kidding? Zac Posen is never going to call me back. He doesn't care what Cornelia is wearing. She's not important enough.

Then I remember. Candie Stokes dresses all the top-tier socialites. And if she doesn't dress them, she'll still know what they're wearing, that's her job. And though she'd never answer a call from me, her third personal assistant sure as hell will.

So for the second time today, I call Edward.

"Edward!"

"Angie! Sweetface! Are the flowers okay?"

"They're perfect! So perfect! But, um . . . I need your help again. Can you please, please call the assistant you always speak to at Candie Stokes's office and find out who is wearing Zac Posen to the Met tonight? I know it sounds weird, but I'm with Cornelia Pace, and . . ."

"Ooh! I love a socialite emergency! Of course I will! But only if you promise not to move to L.A. I wanna be BFFs!"

Tears flood my eyes. He's so lovely. But I have to leave. The chaos of working for Cornelia is a great distraction, but I know that the minute I'm alone, thoughts of Sam will lurch back into my head and I'll just start crying again. It happened twice on the subway over here, and I looked like a total freak. I need a fresh start.

I can't say anything, but Edward doesn't notice. "I'll call you in three minutes! Stand by the phone!"

As promised, three minutes later he calls back. And the news isn't good.

I walk back into the dressing room, where Keith is now prepping Cornelia's skin with a lymphatic drainage massage. She's convinced it makes her cheekbones stand out.

"Cornelia, Olivia is wearing the pink. Natalie and Anna are wearing Zac, too. And I found out what all Candie Stokes's other clients are wearing tonight." I hand over the list. "Voilà."

"Oh, Angie, you are the best!" She reads the list and looks up, a note of panic in her voice. "Those bitches have taken everything. I have nothing! Oh, my GOD!"

She gets up off the chair and makes a bloodcurdling wail, then sinks to the floor, her hand clutching at her hair. "ARRRRRRRRRRRRRGHH!"

I exchange a glance with Bibi and Keith, who are their usual mute passive selves. Someone needs to take charge of this situation.

"Cornelia, calm down. We can come up with a solution," I say. "Okay, so all the big guns are gone. Let's call someone newer. A designer who is up-and-coming."

"I don't want to wear up-and-fucking-coming!" Cornelia is lying on the floor, screaming into the carpet. "I want to wear Oscar de la fucking Renta! Or Armani fucking Privé! Or Atelier fucking Versace! Or—"

"What about that guy who used to do the cutting for Vera Wang?" I interrupt her before she can insert "fuck" into every couture brand in existence. "I read in *Women's Wear Daily* that he just started out on his own."

"Vera and I had a fight when she wouldn't design my dress for junior prom the way I wanted it. I fucking hate that bitch and I hate everyone who works for her," says Cornelia, her voice muffled by the carpet.

"Okay . . ." I rack my brains for a second. There's someone else, I know there's someone else. "Wait! I know! Sarah Drake! She worked for Narciso Rodriguez, you know?"

"I love him." Cornelia flips over. "But he has those bitch actress groupies who always wear him."

Man, I am tired of Cornelia calling every other woman in the world a bitch. "Well, she started her own label, Drake, about six months ago. I met her intern Philly Meyer in Starbucks when I was, uh, interviewing in the Fashion District! We're Facebook friends! I can get in touch with her in ten minutes."

Cornelia looks up at me, her pale blue eyes shining with hope.

"Do it."

And it works. By 6:30 P.M., Philly Meyer is couriering three dresses straight from Sarah Drake's atelier on Thirty-seventh Street to Cornelia's apartment. The dresses are on loan, for free: it's good PR for Sarah Drake. Cornelia isn't exactly A-list or even B-list, but anyone going to the Met Ball has fashion cachet today.

Thank God Cornelia is sample size. I guess all that coke is good for something.

She tries each dress, one by one, and parades out in front of Bibi, Keith, and me.

The first dress is called, according to the Sarah Drake–branded name tag that came with the delivery, The Bettina. It's pale pink and strapless, making her look like an upside-down tulip, and not in a good way. It would be perfect on someone edgier, but not Cornelia. She's too white-bread.

"Amay-zing!" sing Bibi and Keith. Jeez. So not true.

"No. A bit garden-y," I say. Cornelia nods obediently and takes the dress off. She trusts my opinion? That's a surprise.

The second dress is called The Shadow. It's black, sleeveless, and divinely dramatic with a high neck, but her shoulders aren't broad enough to carry it off, so it just sort of hangs down from her face, making her look like a bat-nun hybrid.

"Ohmygod!" chorus Bibi and Keith.

"No good for photos," I say. "Drowns your body."

Again, Cornelia nods and obeys.

The third dress is called The Angel. And it's just right. It's an ivory column dress, extremely fitted with angular, slightly futuristic details, and elongates Cornelia's figure perfectly, giving her an elegance and class that, between you and me, she sure as hell doesn't possess in real life. She looks like Grace Kelly, if Grace Kelly was in *Blade Runner*.

"Wow! Like, wow!" Bibi and Keith are orgasmic with joy.

"That's stunning," I say. "Shoes?"

"I want to wear the Louboutins," Cornie says, looking at me slightly pleadingly, like I have to give her permission. I glance down: they're burnished gold and absolutely beautiful.

"Fine. Bag?"

Cornelia promptly opens drawers containing over fifty evening bags. But none of them work. They're all the wrong color, too big, too last season, too shiny, too tacky . . .

"I can run to Christian Louboutin," I say. "Give me ten minutes—"

"Your clutch!" Cornelia interrupts. "The gold clutch I saw you with in the Minetta Tavern. Where is that?"

"Next to my coat . . ." I say, confused. "You want to borrow my clutch?"

"Yes. It's perfect! It's a talking point! It's all soft and bunchy; it'll be perfect next to the angularity of the dress! And because it's not a big label, I'll look effortlessly eclectic and unassuming, like those bitches who always end up on the best-dressed lists . . . not like I've just thrown money at the whole thing, because that's so tacky, you know?" Cornelia does her best imploring face. "Please, Angie? Please?"

"Um, okay, sure." I grab my clutch and empty the contents into my coat pockets. "It's yours for the night. Now, we have thirty minutes until the car gets here. Keith, work your magic. Bibi, fix the hair. Cornelia, can I get you a Red Bull?"

"You're acting weird," Cornelia says a few minutes later, as she's having foundation painstakingly brushed into her pores.

"I am?" I say. I'm crouched on the floor next to her, rearranging the two rejected dresses in tissue paper so they can be returned crease-free. "How?"

"Maybe not weird. But you're . . . I don't know. Different. Confident. Kind of take-charge. I mean, you were confident before, but not like this. . . . Before, I was never sure if you'd do something I asked you to do, or just walk away."

"Ha," I say. Without any mirth whatsoever.

"I guess you should never underestimate the life-altering power of a little scandal, huh?" Cornelia raises an eyebrow at me knowingly, then glances at her phone as she gets a text. "Oh, for fuck's sake . . . It's Roger. Some family crisis. He's going to have to meet me there."

"Family problem?"

"His son." My heart stops for a second. Sam? "He's going for some big job at a bank. Roger wants to have a drink with the chairman, to try to win him the job."

That's pretty obnoxious. And she definitely can't mean Sam. So maybe he does have a brother.

"How old is his son?"

"Twenty-five, twenty-six, I don't know. His name is Pete," she says, then lowers her voice. "Rog actually has *two* sons, but the other isn't talking to him."

Sam! My Sam! I mean, not my Sam, but, oh never mind.

"No kidding. Why?"

"I don't know. Something to do with the ex-wife. She was a fucking hippie, apparently. Always taking the boys to South America or Africa or whatever to do volunteer work. So pretentious. Just throw a fundraiser, you know?"

"Right on . . ." I say, staring into space. So Sam is the product of a genuinely philanthropic mother and an overachieving, overbearing father. Huh. "Is, uh, the other kid a banker, too?"

"Nah. He's traveling the world, finding himself, or something ridiculous like that. I think he wanted to be a doctor, but Rog wanted him to go into finance or law, something normal, you know? So they had some big fight."

Who the fuck wouldn't want their kid to be a doctor?

Suddenly, I remember something Cornelia said before she started talking about Sam's father. Something that didn't make sense.

"What did you mean before? When you said 'the life-altering power of a little scandal'?"

"I just mean . . . you know, Angie." Cornelia lowers her voice, as though Keith weren't standing four inches away from her applying individual eyelashes to her eyelids. "The *bar*. The *tape*."

I look up at her, totally confused. "What bar? What tape? What are you talking about?"

"The tiny secret bar in Hell's Kitchen. It's called Angie's Secret. They play the sex tape in the bathroom the whole time. I heard about it from that little sleazebag, what's his name, that guy you hang around with? Steven, or Stef—"

But I'm not listening anymore. Instead, I've grabbed my coat and am heading straight for the door, every part of my brain and body and soul blazing with fury.

The Soho Grand night.

Now I know what happened.

CHAPTER **40**

"That evil little fuckwit. We'll destroy it, okay? And cut his balls off. I'll be in Manhattan in half an hour. Don't kill anyone until I get there." Pia hangs up without waiting for a response.

Which is lucky, since I'm not sure I could say anything more right now. I just told Pia the truth about the Soho Grand night, about not remembering anything and waking up with three thousand dollars in an envelope. Pia, being Pia, didn't seem shocked at all. She just loaded her metaphorical shotgun and is coming with me to the bar to reclaim the tape.

I'm striding up Hudson, my face burning, my pulse racing, my stomach churning with an almost overwhelming need to vomit, or pass out, or scream.

There's a *sex tape* of me, taken when I was too out of it to know what the fuck I was doing.

Which means I had sex with—well, with someone—in the Soho Grand that night, and he taped me.

It's playing in that secret bar under the café in Hell's Kitchen.

They called the bar Angie's Secret in the end. After me.

Just like I asked them to.

I wonder who it was. Maybe it was one of the guys I met that night, one of the bar owners . . . Busey. Or Emmett.

Suddenly, I have a flashback to being in the back of a cab with Emmett. He gave me a keybump of coke. And then he kissed me. I remember tongue. Lots of tongue.

Yes. It was him.

Oh God. I am overcome with a sickening shame. I feel like I've lost something I can never get back. I wonder what I did on the tape, how bad it was . . . I mean, it shouldn't be a big deal, right? Everyone has sex! The existence of the human race is testament to the fact that everyone has sex. And every low-level celebrity and reality TV star has a sex tape. Hell, I'm pretty sure most of them make a sex tape to try to boost their fame quotient. They would probably just shrug this off. Or be proud of it, even.

But I'm not like that. I don't want fame. I don't want notoriety. I never did. I just want a job that will be the start of a real career and a life of which I can be proud. I'm fed up with people taking advantage of me, and yeah, maybe it's partly my fault for being immature and thoughtless and making so many stupid decisions.

But enough is enough.

As I argue with myself in my head, I'm marching through the West Village. The sky is getting dark, and this is postcard New York in April: beautiful buildings with yellowy lighting in the windows cut out against the dusk sky, trees kissing overhead, the twilight making everything magical. Everyone is walking home from work, thinking about their careers and love and sex and food and family and money and fashion and fun and all the things that New Yorkers are obsessed with. . . . God, I love it. I don't want to leave.

So what *do* I want? I keep walking until I reach the cobblestoned Meatpacking District, which reminds me of being in New York when I was about nineteen and dancing on chairs in those Sunday brunch places. I would so not do that now. I don't want that life. That's just not who I am anymore.

So who am I?

I feel like I'm still trying to find out.

My phone rings again. It's Pia.

"Where are you?"

I look up. "Thirteenth and Ninth?"

"Stay there."

A couple of minutes later, Pia comes zooming around the corner in Toto, her pale pink SkinnyWheels food truck, and screeches to a halt on the cobblestones in front of me.

Julia is next to her in the front seat. She opens the door and quickly climbs out of the truck.

Our eyes meet, and I feel, if it's possible, even sicker with apprehension. "Hi, Julia . . ."

"Angie, thank you for the flowers," Julia says. "I've never seen anything like it. I think it's the most romantic thing anyone's ever done for me."

I start laughing despite myself, feeling momentarily filled with relief. "Oh, Jules. I am so sorry I hurt you. I swear it wasn't deliberate."

"You didn't, not really," she says, leaning in for a hug. "Angie, the date with Sam *was* a total washout. There was no, I don't know, connection, no sexual tension; I knew it was a failure . . . but I wanted him to like me anyway. I wanted it so badly. I'm just tired of being single."

"I understand," I say. "I'm just tired of being me."

Julia smiles. "Let's go nail these assholes, shall we?"

"Yes," I say. "God, yes."

I climb into the truck, next to Pia, and Julia climbs in after me. Pia reaches back and knocks twice on the hatch behind her head. A double knock comes right back. I frown quizzically at her.

"Maddy and Coco," she says. "They're hiding back there. It's kind of illegal, but you know, they really wanted to help."

"Oh, my God, you guys are the best. I don't deserve this," I say. "Did Pia tell you? About the Soho Grand night? About the money?"

"I did," says Pia. "I hope that's okay."

"Of course it's okay," I say. "I don't want any more secrets from you guys. You must think—"

"We think you're our friend, and bad shit happens, and we're going to fix it," says Julia. "We're all in this together."

We smile at each other for a second, then she reaches down and turns on the radio. After a few seconds of loud static, it starts playing Blondie's "One Way or Another."

"Toto has such great taste in theme songs," says Pia, patting the steering wheel approvingly.

By the time we get to Westies, at the corner of Tenth and Forty-sixth, screaming along to the radio the whole way, I'm feeling better. I can do this. With the girls by my side, I can do anything.

We get out of Toto and stand in a group on the sidewalk for a moment.

"I can never thank you enough for this," I say. "You must think I'm an idiot."

"I promise we don't," says Madeleine. "And personally, I think you should question whether this was sex with consent."

"I don't think we'll know without watching the video," I say. "And I don't want to."

"We've all been drunk, and we've all had sex, we've all made mistakes," says Julia. "Could have been any one of us."

"It could easily have been you since you have, in fact, made a sex tape, and you weren't even drunk," points out Pia.

Everyone gasps, and Julia shrugs. "That was a long time ago, P-Dawg. My experimental phase. And I destroyed the evidence, anyway. It won't, like, pop up when I run for president."

Madeleine cracks up. "You had an experimental phase?"

"Enough!" says Pia. "Let's focus on the problem at hand."

"I'm focused." Coco makes a snarling sound. "Let's get these fuckers."

The five of us stalk into the café, all trying to look as angry and mean as we can, past the greasy counters and ancient cupcakes. I open the door at the back of the room and we march down the old cabbage-y stairwell, past the velvet curtain, and into the bar.

It's been weeks since I was last here, the night that started with a bad mood and a bad friend and ended in . . . blackout. But it feels like a lifetime ago.

The bar looks kind of like a stage set now, the way bars always do when they're empty, the lights are on, and you're sober. It's just the same as it was that time I met Stef here, with one change: above the bar, in a cursive script, is *ANGIE'S SECRET* spelled out in pink neon.

Looking at it makes me feel sick.

Leading the way, I walk straight to the back of the room, where there's a tiny unisex bathroom.

It's locked.

"Shit!" I say.

"Don't worry," says Madeleine. "I can pick locks."

"Where the fuck did you learn how to pick a lock?" asks Pia.

Madeleine arches an eyebrow. "You don't know everything about me, Pia. So it looks like a single-pin pick will do fine. Anyone got a bobby pin?"

Pia takes a pin out of her chignon.

"And I just need . . ." Madeleine runs to the bar, picks up a knife, throws it down, then grabs a corkscrew. "Aha!" She hurries back. "Give me two minutes."

But all she needs is thirty seconds. Click, click, click, the lock is done.

"Hurry," says Pia. "It's, like, 7:30. Even the latest of the late-night bars probably need someone in early to set up."

"Okay, okay." I open the door and look in the bathroom. It's just a communal sink with a huge mirror and two toilet stalls. I can't see a TV screen, or a DVD player, or even a laptop, anywhere.

The girls push past me. "Did you find it? Let's get out of here!"

"It's not here," I say, feeling a lump of desperation in my throat. "There's no screen, there's nothing. Anyway, what am I even thinking? They would have made copies of any tape. . . . It's digital, it's probably on the Internet. I can never destroy everything. There'll always be a copy somewhere. What were we thinking, driving up here like fucking vigilantes?"

Julia is frowning. "Something's weird about this room. . . . Look, why is the mirror angled up? Mirrors are usually angled down so that it's flattering to the person looking at their reflection, right?"

I gaze at the mirror. "So?"

"So . . . it's like it's designed to reflect something high on the opposite wall. You see?"

"What are you, Nancy fucking Drew?" says Madeleine.

Julia doesn't respond. Instead, she turns around and looks at the blank opposite wall, then swivels back to the mirror, and looks up.

And then I see it. There's a hole the size of a quarter in the wall above the mirror.

"It's next door," she says. "The camera. It's projecting the movie onto the wall and reflected in the mirror. So that when you're in the bathroom, you can see the movie, no matter which way you're facing."

We all file out of the tiny bathroom. Next door to it is another door . . . the janitor's closet.

"Hairpin! Hairpin!" says Madeleine, holding her hand out like a surgeon in an operating theater.

"Fuck the hairpin," Julia says, and kicks the lock on the door, very hard, with all her strength. On the third kick, I can hear wood splintering, and the door falls open.

Inside is a bucket full of cleaning products and a few crates of mixers. And when we look up, a tiny newly made shelf containing a vintage-looking movie camera.

"That's a Super 8 home movie camera," says Pia. "Aidan has a bunch of movies his folks made of him when he was a baby; it tapes and plays back from the same machine. . . . Super 8 has that grainy old-fashioned look, you know? It's totally popular again."

"Oh, good," I say. "So I was filmed having sex without my knowledge, but at least I look cool?"

"Well, it's unlikely that those losers bothered to transfer the film to digital, so that's a bonus."

"Get the fucking camera and let's go already," says Julia.

I reach up, knocking the camera off the shelf. It clatters to the floor.

"Oops. I think I broke it," I say, making a pretend-anguish face at the girls.

Julia grins and stamps on it so hard it breaks into three pieces. "Oops. I think I broke it more."

"Okay, can we do this back at Union Street?" Pia interrupts.

Everyone files out as I pick up the broken camera, and then they all turn around and walk back into the bar.

The other girls are frozen in front of me.

I look at them in confusion. "What are we waiting for? Let's go!"
Then I see why they're not moving.
Emmett, Busey, and Stef. Blocking the exit.
"Hello, Angie," says Stef. "Looks like you've discovered our secret."

CHAPTER 41

"How could you *do* that to me?" I stride right up to Stef. "You *filmed* me! Having *sex*! Do you really fucking hate me that much? What did I ever do to you?"

"Hey, it wasn't me, babe!" He puts his hands up and takes a step back. "I was as surprised as you were. Well maybe not *as* surprised . . ."

"I don't believe you."

"I swear."

I turn to Emmett and Busey, feeling like I might collapse from stress and anger. "You evil assholes," I stammer. "I could have you arrested."

"You're overreacting," says Busey, his chubby cheeks wobbling with every word. "It's really a beautiful movie. Very sixties, very classic. You should be proud."

I gasp, feeling like I've been hit.

"I thought you were into it." Emmett looks bored. "I set the camera up while you were in the bathroom. You never even noticed.... You were pretty wild."

I try to speak, but only a choking sound comes out, and tears flow down my face. I can't bear this. I can't. I don't know what to do.

"You piece of shit," says Julia. "How *dare* you take advantage of Angie like that! How *dare* you show a sex tape in your disgusting bar, like she was some kind of porn star!"

Busey smirks. "If the shoe fits—"

"Shut the hell up," says Pia, her voice low and threatening. "Don't you dare say that shit about my best friend, you fat fuck."

"We're leaving," Madeleine adds. "And we're taking the camera."

"By the way," Coco says, "my boyfriend works for the Department of Health, in the Bureau of Food Safety and Community Sanitation. Bet you twenty bucks you'll lose your liquor license and be shut down within the month."

"What liquor license?" Stef says under his breath, then looks up and sees that we all heard.

Coco looks at him, then back at Busey and Emmett. "I'd say you're pretty screwed, assholes."

Coco is one tough broad when she wants to be.

Just as we reach the curtain, Julia stops, turns around, walks back to Stef, and slaps him, once, very hard across the face.

"Hey—"

"That's for everything you did to my friend. She's a good person. She didn't deserve it."

When we get up to the street, I feel a heady euphoria. Victory! But before I can celebrate, I need to do one thing.

With shaking hands, I find the latch and open the camera, slip my finger into the film, and pull it all out by hand. Ribbons upon ribbons of film come out, quickly spooling in a huge pile at my feet. I start jumping and stamping on it, and then all the girls join in, laughing with the sort of relieved hysteria that you get when you've just escaped a scary, ridiculous, weird situation.

"We're throwing this film off the Brooklyn Bridge," says Julia. "And then we're going home. I need a drink."

"We really shouldn't litter," says Coco. "We'll cut it into tiny pieces at home instead."

"Let's get pizza," says Pia. "My treat."

I know what she's thinking. It's confession time. Pia and I are leaving Rookhaven.

As I'm getting into Toto the food truck, I spot Stef's car parked just down the street. His red Ferrari 308 GTS. The thing that means the most to him in the entire world.

I have an idea.

Without pausing, I stride into the deli next to the café, buy a two-liter bottle of Coca-Cola, walk over to the car, open the gas cap, open the Coke bottle, and pour every last drop of sugary, engine-frying Coca-Cola into the gas tank. Glug, glug, glug.

"What the fuck are you doing?" shouts Pia from the truck.

I don't reply. When every last drop is in the tank, I turn around and walk back to the truck, smiling to myself. Stef's precious car is fried.

Revenge. Is. Awesome.

Then we drive back to Rookhaven, sit down at the kitchen table, order pizza from Bartolo's, open a bottle of wine, and attack the film with scissors.

"No vodka tonight, Angie?" Madeleine teases me, as she slices up frame after frame. "No cucumber, no sea salt? No cigarette tucked between your lips?"

I smirk at her. I finally understand Madeleine. She's trying to be funny. It just comes out as bitchy sometimes. "Not tonight. Tonight, I want to toast to you guys. Thank you. I could not have survived that without you."

We all raise our glasses and clink, with all the obligatory intense-eye-contact-or-seven-years-bad-sex stuff.

Then the pizza arrives, and after we all take our first bite, Pia and I exchange a glance. It's time to tell everyone.

"I'm moving to San Francisco to be with Aidan," she says.

"I'm moving to L.A. to be with myself." I raise an eyebrow. "God, that's depressing."

"What?" Julia, Madeleine, and Coco exclaim in unison.

"Why?" Coco is distraught. "You're leaving? Both of you?"

"I just . . . I'm miserable without him," says Pia. "If you love someone, you want to be with them. Right?"

"What about your job?" asks Julia. "They're letting you work from San Francisco?"

"Um, no," says Pia. She looks up guiltily. "I asked my boss today. She said that she needed me here in New York, with the rest of the company."

"So you quit working at Carus?" Julia is horrified. "That's it?"

I'm stunned, too. Pia didn't tell me that her boss said no to the proposed San Francisco move. She'd walk away from her perfect career— when it's so impossible to find a job right now? Let alone one as amazing as hers?

"Not yet," Pia admits. "I couldn't bring myself to actually resign. After she said no to the move, I said, oh of course, I was just wondering if it was an option, yada yada. . . . But I will. Tomorrow."

"*How* could you quit the job that you worked so hard to get?" I slam my palm on the table so hard that everyone jumps. "You *earned* that job, Pia. You went through hell to get it."

"And we went through hell with you!" points out Madeleine.

"Oh man, I know, I know . . ." Pia looks at the ceiling in anguish. "I love my job. I mean, I *really* love it, and I've only just begun to realize my potential. . . . And I'm good at it! Finally, for once, I'm actually good at something. It's where I'm supposed to be, I'm sure of it . . . but I also feel like I'm supposed to be with Aidan. I love him."

"I guess you have to choose," says Madeleine. "Work or love?"

"I hate that!" says Pia. "Why should I be the one making sacrifices? Why can't he give up his stupid job to stay with me? What fucking decade are we living in?" She takes a slug of wine and sighs dramatically.

"And what about you, Angie?" Julia turns to me. "You're just going to fill Rookhaven with flowers and leave?"

"Just when we were finally getting to know you?" adds Madeleine.

"Come on, you guys," I say, looking at them uncomfortably. "You know I'm never going to make a life here. A real life. I can't get a job. And I can't keep working at places like the goddamn Gap or be a personal slave to rich bitches like Cornelia or that psycho bitch photographer, you know? I need to feel like I'm on the right track, like my life has direction, a purpose. And I don't."

There's silence. No one seems able to argue with me. This makes me crumble a little bit inside. I sort of hoped—half hoped, maybe—that one of them would tell me she didn't want me to go, that they simply wouldn't allow it. But why would they try to argue me out of anything? It's never worked before.

"What about Sam?" asks Julia.

"Sam is a liar." I stare at my plate. Talking about my emotions makes me feel so fucking awkward. "I have no feelings for him. I thought I did, and I was wrong, he's a liar. I was, you know, projecting." Yeah. That's a good word. I'm just not completely sure what it means.

"He's crazy about you, you know," says Julia.

I look up. "What?"

"On our date he kept mentioning you, or asking if I knew where you were, because he hadn't been able to get in touch with you. . . . I swear we only turned up at the bar because I said you were there and he in-sisted we go. Our date wasn't a real date; it was just dinner with a guy who happened to be into one of my friends."

"Oh," I say in a tiny voice, trying to process all this. "Well, he should have been up-front with you. Why did he go out with you, if he wasn't interested? He's still a bastard."

"He's not. I saw him when I got home from work tonight. He's been cleaning up Vic's place. He said he was sorry, that he thought we were on the same page with being more friends than anything else. He said he thought he'd be able to get you and his brother Pete to come to din-ner, too. Make a happy little foursome. He was about to tell you all about his family stuff. He never liked me like that."

"Ouch," says Pia. "Jules, that bites."

"No, it's fine," says Julia, rubbing her temples and frowning. "He was so honest, I couldn't even be upset. . . . I don't even know if I liked him all that much, either. I just wanted to like *someone* so badly. . . ." She sighs. "I would really like a boyfriend. That's all."

There's a long pause.

"So, Sam has a brother?" Pia says finally. "Do they look alike?"

Jules cracks up. "I know! That was the first thing I thought, too!"

We all eat in thoughtful silence for a while. I'm thinking about Sam, trying to figure out how I feel and what I should do, but there are just too many emotions jumbled inside me. Too much has happened in the past twenty-four hours. I feel like I could get into bed and sleep for a week. And I still need a job. I need a real life, a life that's heading somewhere. That's the bottom line.

"God, I love Bartolo's," says Julia, when the pizza is all gone. "But it always leaves me in the mood for something sweet, you know?"

"I know!" says Madeleine. I frown at her. Madeleine practically never eats sugar. "I could really do with, hmm, let me think, something pink and white, with icing, and candles. . . ."

Suddenly I notice Coco is at the fridge, pulling out a cake. "Ta-da! For Pia and Angie! Birthday cake!"

"I thought I wouldn't get a cake this year!" Pia is delighted. "Happy twenty-third birthday to us!"

Coco lights the candles, everyone sings "Happy Birthday," and then Pia and I take deep breaths, close our eyes, and blow out the candles.

"Don't forget to make a wish!" shouts Julia.

I wish to create a life that will make me happy.

The wish comes, unbidden, into my head. If I'd had time to think about it, I would have wished for something more specific, like a job that pays $150,000 a year and a house with a private chef and a rooftop goddamn swimming pool.

Or even just a job. But that'll never happen in New York. So I guess my wish will take me to L.A.

Then I open my eyes and look around at the girls. They're my family now. I don't want to say good-bye to them.

This is what it all boils down to: I don't want to leave, but I feel like I have to.

What the hell am I going to do?

CHAPTER 42

I barely slept last night.

Again.

I have that dull exhaustion faceache behind my eye sockets, you know the kind I mean? The kind that can only be relieved by about twenty-four hours of sleep and then a gallon of espresso. But it won't be happening here. Every time I closed my eyes last night, a kaleidoscope of images rushed through my brain. Everything that's happened, everything I wish I could erase, everything I wish I could ask Sam, everything . . .

A few things have become clear, in the restless thinkfest that was my night.

First, I was wrong.

(Again.)

Yes, Sam lied about who he was and where he was from.

But he obviously had reasons. His father, his mother . . . I don't know the full story. But I should have stuck around to find out. I should have given him the benefit of the doubt. Just like I should have stuck around with my mom that day she told me about the divorce, and I should have stuck around Rookhaven the night that Julia and I had the fight in the kitchen. But I didn't. My instincts said run.

So I ran.

I'm always led by instinct. Ruled by it, really. I always thought it was just who I was, I thought it was part of my personality. Unpredictable. Mercurial. Sometimes it's not such a bad idea, like getting away from the yacht in Turks. But sometimes—more often—it is.

So is it a bad idea, leaving Brooklyn, when I can't get a real job in New York? Or is it logical? I honestly can't tell what's rational and what's crazy anymore, or what's smart and what's stupid. There are too many choices. It's all too confusing, and I have this terrible fear, deep down inside, that I'll make the wrong choice and always regret it.

And now, it's Wednesday morning. Everyone else in the world is getting up, going to their jobs, earning money, having a life that's worth living.

Except me.

I need some air.

So I get out of bed, take a very quick shower, and pull on jeans, my studded Converse, and a white blouse. I got up at 3:00 A.M. and finished altering the neckline. It's so pretty. Maybe it'll bring me luck.

Then I grab my old Zara leather jacket, and throw my keys, money, phone, and lip balm in the pocket, since Cornelia still has my damn gold clutch, and leave Rookhaven without running into anyone else. I walk slowly down Union Street as the sun rises, getting that quiet buzz you feel when you're the only person awake and the world feels like your secret. Brooklyn seems fresh and clean and full of promise.

I walk down Smith Street and end up back on the corner of Smith and Atlantic Avenue, in the New Apollo Diner, the same diner I went to the morning after Pijiu, when I thought Julia and Sam had . . . well, you know.

That day I stared at my menu, thinking about Sam. I thought about the time we spent together, about bursting into tears in front of him after watching *Kramer vs.* goddamn *Kramer,* about him helping me hand out CVs and lattes. About how I was sure, totally sure, that we were about to kiss that time on my bed.

And I just kept telling myself, *No, he's just your friend.*

What would have happened if I had kissed him that night he slept over? Why did I decide that he had to be my friend and there was no alternative?

But I don't want to go.

There. I said it. (In my head, anyway.)

The events at Angie's Secret last night made me realize the girls are my family now. We're all in this together.

But if I don't go to L.A. and stay here, I'm right back where I started. No job, no career, no money, no options.

No Sam.

I have a huge urge to call Sam and ask him to forgive me for flipping out and charging into the storm like King Lear with tits. I want to ask him to explain his situation to me, why he didn't want to be honest about who he was and where he was from. I'm sure he had good reasons for lying. But I just can't. He hasn't even tried to contact me. And even though he lied, I can't judge him. I don't know his backstory, I don't know what it's like to be him. Just like no one knows what it's like to be me.

When did life get so complicated?

Though, when you think about it, has life ever been simple?

Finally my pancakes arrive, and I can't eat *and* think about life-changing decisions, so I pour maple syrup all over my plate, grab the *New York Post* that someone left on the table next to me, and stare at the cover as I stuff the first sweet bite into my mouth.

Oh, my God.

CHAPTER **43**

It's Cornelia. A mug shot. On the cover of the *New York Post*.

She was arrested. She's wearing The Angel dress and staring into the camera, looking spoiled and sullen.

Next to it, another shot of Cornelia in the dress, jumping on the back of an NYPD police officer, I guess just before she was arrested. She looks stunning. Crazy, obviously, but stunning. That dress rocks.

"CORN ON THE COP!" says the headline.

And then I see it. Down low, in the bottom corner of the front page, is a close-up photo of my clutch! My gold clutch! The one I made from the secondhand scarves I picked up months ago down at Brownstone Treasures. What the? I quickly read the story.

> Blond, beautiful . . . and busted. Manhattan so-
> cialite Cornelia Archer—great-great-granddaughter

of Randolph Archer, founder of Standard Oil—was arrested for smuggling two grams of cocaine into the Costume Institute Gala at the Metropolitan Museum last night.

Security guards noticed Archer's erratic behavior and called the NYPD, leading to a struggle in front of hundreds of shocked style stars, including Anna Wintour, Beyoncé, and Jennifer Lopez.

As Archer, wearing The Angel dress by Drake, was escorted from the gala, her Prada gold clutch was thrown to the floor in front of hundreds of waiting paparazzi, spilling its contents for all to see: lip gloss, cell phone . . . and two grams of cocaine.

Archer awaits sentencing today.

Oh. My. God.

They thought my bag was Prada.

Heart racing, I pick up my phone with trembling hands and call Pia.

"Ladybitch?"

"Cornelia, last night, my clutch, front page of the *Post,* oh, my God," I stammer.

"What? Slow down."

I can't sit still, so I get up and start pacing the diner while I explain.

"Wow," she says. "Your clutch is a drug mule!"

I pause for a second and crack up.

"Let's get practical," says Pia. "What do you want to do? I bet you could spin this to your advantage, you know, career-wise."

"Yes, um—" I'm trying to think. What do I want to do? Then I notice I have a call waiting from a withheld number. "Pia, I have to go, there's a call. . . ." I take the other call. "Hello?"

"Angie! This is Philly Meyer! From Drake!"

"Hey . . ."

He sounds slightly hysterical. "Cornelia Archer was arrested last night! And—"

"I know."

"We need The Angel back! The ivory column dress! It's the sample, it's the only one we have, and we've already had two requests for it, from *W* magazine and French *Vogue*. This is huge, you know? *Huge*. Everyone at the Met Ball saw the dress. It's the only thing anyone is talking about." Philly lowers his voice. "Sarah Drake is *freaking out*."

"Okay . . ." My brain is spinning. "I can get it back. I'll call you back."

"Hurry!"

I quickly stuff half my pancakes in my mouth at once, throw down some money, and leave. How do I do this? I can't just show up at Manhattan Central Booking and demand the dress.

Think, Angie, think. . . .

When you're arrested, you call a lawyer. And Cornelia being the Upper East Side WASP that she is, she would have called a family lawyer. Someone she could trust. So that's probably the best way to contact her. If I can get in touch with her lawyer, I can get to the dress. And my clutch. Unless it's being held as evidence. (Poor innocent clutch.)

So I call my mother to get the cell number of Cornelia's mother, legendary socialite CC Archer. The cell she only gives out to friends.

"Are you sure CC will want to hear from you, darling?" asks my mother. "She can be a little . . . difficult. And if her daughter's in a scandal, well . . ."

"I can handle it, Mom, I promise, I'm just going to ask her one question," I say. "I'll call you later this week to explain everything."

Then I call Mrs. Archer, introduce myself, and ask if she can tell me the name of her daughter's attorney.

"Why?" CC says suspiciously.

"Because I need my clutch back," I say.

"This hardly seems important right now," she snaps. "This whole silly affair will just blow over soon enough, you can have it then. And Chester won't be taking any calls."

"Chester?"

That's a pretty obscure name for an attorney. Not to mention fucking ridiculous.

"Tell your mother not to hand out my private cell number. Using this number is a privilege, not a right. I am displeased."

I fight the urge to say, "Blow me," and instead put on my cheeriest voice and say, "I'll tell her you asked after her. Thanks so much!" and hang up.

I immediately Google "Chester attorney Manhattan" on my phone. I scroll down and click on a *New York Post* entry from a couple of years ago, when a certain Chester Newland defended one of the Kennedy clan against a drunk-driving charge. And got him off.

That's just the kind of pedigree that would impress the Archers.

I find his number and dial.

CHAPTER **44**

Chester Newland's unusually chatty receptionist tells me he is currently at New York City Criminal Court. Getting Cornelia out as quickly as possible, I guess.

Next, I call Philly Meyer and tell him I'll be able to get the dress back this morning.

"I need it, like, *now*. Sarah is freaking. You better get it back," he says. "I'm not kidding."

Man, he's tense.

It's a quick twenty minutes to the criminal court in Chinatown. My guess is that they're posting bail right now, arguing that Cornelia has no prior record and all that jazz, and she'll be out in minutes.

And for once in my life, I'm right.

Just as I arrive at Centre Street, I see a gaggle of paparazzi going nuts.

It looks like a feeding frenzy you see on a nature show: they're running and jostling violently, shouting the same things over and over again.

"Cornelia! Here! Over here!"

"Cornie! Are you a drug addict, Cornie?"

"Cornelia! Are you out on bail?"

In the middle of the mass I catch glimpses of Cornelia, still wearing The Angel, with sunglasses she picked up from somewhere. She looks pale and tired but surprisingly dignified, carrying her gold heels and walking with the perfect posture of the terminally self-assured. She's flanked by two large bodyguard types in suits and a short bald guy in a suit. Chester Newland, I'll bet.

I can't see my clutch. . . . God, what if they had to keep it for evidence or something?

A black limo is waiting on the street, so I hurry to the car, ahead of the paparazzi.

"Cornie, it's me! Angie!" I say, over and over again, hoping she'll look up. But she's concentrating too hard on ignoring the jibes of the paparazzi while looking serenely beautiful.

Then the bodyguards shove me out of the way, the driver opens the limo door, and Cornelia gets in. The door slams after her, and thanks to black-tinted windows, I can't even see in! Shit!

The bodyguards are holding the paps back, and just as I'm sure that all is lost, that the limo is about to drive away with Cornelia and the dress and my clutch, the back window winds down one inch.

"Angie?"

"Yes! Cornie, it's me! I have to talk to you!"

"Oh, thank God!" Cornelia sounds like she's about to cry. "Chester! Get her in, get her in!"

And boom, like magic, the paparazzi are moved and the car door opens for me and I climb into the back.

Cornelia immediately leans forward and hugs me. I'm so surprised, and touched, that I simply hug her back. Imagine the trauma of being arrested for drugs. Imagine the embarrassment. I'd be so mortified; I'd be so—

"Isn't this amazing?!" Cornelia squeals, her eyes shining. "Keith and Bibi are waiting at my mother's house to sort this whole mess out." She gestures to her face. "And then I'm going to La Grenouille for lunch with my mother, so I can show the world I'm not guilty." She pauses and looks over at Chester. "You told the paps La Grenouille, right?"

She's not mortified at all. She's just thrilled to be the center of attention. How weird.

"Cornelia, I'm not here to—" says Chester.

"Did Roger call?" she interrupts. "No? Fuck him. He didn't even show last night. Asshole, putting his kids first. I can do better now, anyway. Angie, call Patrick, remember him? Tell him it's me and I need a date to Le Bernardin tonight."

"No," I say.

"What?" Cornelia looks at me in shock. "What do you mean, 'no'?"

"I can't be your PA today, Cornelia. I have to get that dress back to Sarah Drake, and I need my gold clutch back. Do you have it, or is it being used as evidence?"

"The case was dismissed due to police tampering with the evidence," says Chester, clearly relieved to have the conversation back on familiar ground. "Here." He pulls the gold clutch out of his bag. I grab it quickly. Thank God. My poor little drug mule. And "tampering"? Who'd they have to bribe to get *that*?

"No, Angie! I need you today!" says Cornelia. "You can courier the dress back later. I'll change at my mother's house. I can borrow one of her Chanel suits."

"Where does she live?"

"She lives at Seventy-ninth and Park." Cornelia sighs. "God, I miss our place on Fifth. Divorce is so selfish."

We're only just passing through the East Village now. It'll take me forever to get all the way up there, get the dress, do whatever else Cornelia orders me to do, and get back to the Fashion District to give The Angel to Sarah Drake.

"I can't do it, Cornelia." I try to sound as forceful-yet-polite as I can. "I have to get the dress back to Sarah Drake, now. Please, come with me to her atelier now. We can get you something else to wear, it'll be—"

"Be seen out in public again, in the middle of Manhattan, strolling around in this like some kind of trashed fucking starlet? I don't think so." With every block we get farther away from the courthouse,

Cornelia's officious attitude grows. "I need to wear it when I'm getting out at my mother's building, so the paps can see how close I am to my family, and then I need to change and go to lunch and let everyone see me."

Chester clears his throat. "Actually, Cornelia, I think you shouldn't be seen in public in that dress again. Period. Not at your mother's apartment, not anywhere. From now on, you need to look like the most innocent girl in the world."

Cornelia pouts. "So what the fuck am I supposed to do?"

And that's how I end up in my bra and panties in the back of a limo pulled over on East Thirty-fifth and Madison, while Chester and the bodyguards and driver stand outside the car and Cornelia and I swap clothes.

"This is a cute outfit." Cornie looks over the white top and jeans I hand her. "Where are these from?"

"Erm, I customized the top myself, and the jeans are just H&M," I say, shimmying into the dress.

Cornelia wrinkles her nose. "How adorably fiscally sensitive of you."

"Um . . . thanks."

Cornelia straps her sky-high gold shoes back on and opens the car door. "Okay, you can go now."

"Wait!" I say, struggling to cover my boobs before anyone outside the limo can see. "Can you zip me up?"

I step out of the limo, still wearing my white studded Converse and carrying my clutch and leather jacket, and start walking. The dress is a tight fit for me, and way too long, so I have to hitch it up with one hand.

Then I put my sunglasses on, hold my head high, and walk—or, let's face it, swagger—west along Thirty-fifth Street, in the dress that made the cover of the *New York Post* this morning.

No one even looks at me twice, of course. This is New York City. I could French kiss a rat while shooting up and no one would flinch.

Fifth Avenue, Sixth Avenue, Broadway . . . and then I'm in the Fashion District. They even call the stretch of Seventh between Thirty-fourth and Forty-second "Fashion Avenue," did you know that? I walk up it toward Thirty-seventh Street. Bizarrely, it's here that people start staring at me. Maybe recognizing the dress from the *Post,* maybe wondering why a girl would wear an evening dress that's so obviously worth thousands of dollars at 10:00 A.M., maybe just wondering who designed it. It *is* a stunning dress and an amazing piece of craftsmanship, after all.

I take out my phone and call Philly.

"What's the exact address?" I ask.

"220 West Thirty-seventh, seventh floor," he says. "I'll meet you in the lobby."

"Um, no, I'm going to have to come up," I say.

"Why?"

"You'll see."

I hang up and head to 220 West Thirty-seventh. A nondescript building, one that I'd usually walk past without even wondering what was upstairs. I walk past the security guard, dozing with a Dunkin' Donuts coffee by his side, and take the elevator to the seventh floor. I suddenly feel unaccountably nervous. I never got this far when I was actually applying for jobs. I'd send my résumé, e-mail, call . . . but I never got into the actual design studios.

The elevator opens on a shabby hallway, and I look around nervously. One door is labeled with the name of a Pilates studio, the other is blank. That must be her.

I knock.

About ten seconds later—such a long time to stare at a door!—it opens, revealing Philly Meyer, the intern slash DJ slash milliner I met at Starbucks that time, the guy who gave me Drakey. It's kind of strange to see him in person again; thanks to Facebook I know he's just gone through a breakup, sells his hats at the Brooklyn Flea, DJ'd last weekend at a bar in Washington Heights, and is totally obsessed with the crème brûlée donut at Doughnut Plant, but thinks it's making him fat. But I haven't seen him in person once since we met.

"Wow," Philly says, looking at me, and opens the door wider, so everyone in the studio can see me.

I glance around quickly. Two guys and a girl standing together over a cutting table, another guy on the phone, and in the corner, working at a huge architect-style desk, is Sarah Drake.

Thirtysomething, dark blond hair, glasses, no makeup. She looks impressive and intimidating, but somehow normal, like she needs coffee and maybe forgot to brush her hair this morning. It's kind of blowing my mind. I guess I've built up the idea of what someone who works in fashion would look like, you know. Not someone on the periphery, not trying to break in, not blogging about it, but someone *really* doing it. But she looks kind of normal. Smart and sharp and cool, yet normal.

Sarah looks up at me and for a second, it feels like everyone in the room stops breathing.

"The Angel," says Sarah finally.

I look down at the dress. The Angel dress. There's total silence.

"Well, that's one way to wear it."

I suddenly feel embarrassed. Who the hell am I to wear this dress with my dirty Converse and my Zara leather jacket? "I'm sorry, I didn't have any choice, Cornelia had nothing to change into; we swapped clothes in the limo—"

"And you walked it here from where?"

"Oh, just a couple of blocks, I didn't sweat in the dress or anything, but um, but otherwise it would have taken me another two hours; she wanted to wear it back to her mother's house on the Upper East Side. . . ." I trail off.

"I get it," Sarah says. "I appreciate the effort to get it to me on time. Punctuality is my thing."

"Punctuality!" chorus the boys at the cutting board. Everyone in the room grins, clearly this is an inside joke.

"Where's the clutch from?"

"From me," I say. "I mean, I made it. I was just playing with some old scarves."

Sarah walks over to me and takes the clutch. "Nice work. Where did you train?"

"I taught myself," I say. "I don't know much, I just, you know, I do what I like, I need to learn, really, I know I have so much to learn—"

"Okay." Bored of me, Sarah puts the clutch down and turns to Philly. "The Angel. Clean it, steam it, get it to *W*."

"But I have to run The Dahlia over to Julianne Moore!" Philly is panicking again. "Her PA just pulled it for a movie premiere tonight!"

"I can take care of The Angel!" I say quickly. "I know how to do that. I can do it. It's really no problem, I, um—"

Sarah narrows her eyes at me for a moment, thinking, then nods.

"Okay. That would be great. Thanks, Angie."

I clear my throat, feeling kind of foolish. "Can I, uh, can I get something to change into once I take the dress off?"

Sarah grins and throws me a gym bag from underneath her desk. "Hope you like spandex."

CHAPTER 45

By the time the day is over, I feel like my world has shifted on its axis. Not a lot. Just a little. But enough to make me dizzy.

First I clean, steam, and courier the dress to *W*.

Then I help one of the other designers fold a particularly complicated dress for shipping to Japanese *Vogue*. (Say what you like about the Gap, but it sure as hell taught me how to fold.)

After that I offer to sort out the chaotic button drawers for another of the designers; answer phones; do a coffee run and stuff a sandwich in my face while on my way back; dust the shoe shelf; refold the samples because they were in total disarray; act as a fitting model for Sarah for a jacket she was tweaking; arrange three returns for dresses Sarah loaned out to other celebrities for the Met Ball; Google, print, and clip all the Sarah Drake press from last night; and silently kneel and help as Sarah fits a couture wedding dress for a private client, a Korean heiress.

It was, in other words, the best day of work—no, the best day, *period*—that I have ever, ever had. Everything just felt . . . right.

Being near clothes all day, seeing Sarah Drake's next collection taking shape, is magic. Her design style is sort of old Hollywood meets sci-fi, like if Hitchcock were directing *Alien*, angular and very glamorous. I adore it.

I only make one false move all day. When the wedding dress is being fitted, I notice the fabric has pulled, very slightly, around the sleeve. I point at it, silently, so Sarah can see without the Korean heiress noticing. She gives me a total death look and ignores me.

Apparently pointing out a flaw in the dress is a bad idea. Good to know.

My heart kind of sinks after that misstep. I wait till the Korean heiress has left and then go over to Sarah's desk, bobbing awkwardly, feeling a little bit sick with nervousness at what I'm about to ask.

But I have to do it. This is the first real opportunity I've ever had to get the job I want. I can't fail now.

"Um, Sarah? Thank you for letting me help out today."

"No problem, you've been great," she says, without looking up from her laptop.

I take a deep breath. "I know you already have one intern, but I was wondering if you could keep me in mind if you ever need a personal assistant, or anything like that—"

She looks up at me, a little smile on her lips. "We do. Judging by the press The Angel got last night, and the volume of e-mail I've received today, we're going to need another pair of hands, effective immediately."

"Okay," I reply coolly, trying not to clap my hands and jump up and down. "I mean, great! What, um—"

"I'll work out the money tonight and we can talk about it tomorrow morning. It won't be great, but being a junior assistant is better than being an intern, and whenever I ask you to get me lunch or a coffee, I'll pay for you to have the same, too. I don't do slavery."

"Wonderful!" God! I feel all hot and burny inside! "That's so amazing! Thank you!"

"Cool. See you here tomorrow at 9:00 A.M.," she says.

"I won't be late, I promise." I am grinning so hard my face hurts a little bit. "Punctuality!"

"Right," she says, her face breaking into a genuine, huge smile for the first time today.

"Oh! And I'll wash your gym clothes tonight and bring them back in the morning."

"Don't rush," she says, waving her hand. "Gives me an excuse not to work out. Where do you live, by the way?"

"Brooklyn," I say. "Carroll Gardens."

"Oh yeah? I'm in Boerum Hill. Brooklyn's the best, isn't it?"

I smile. "Without a doubt. The best."

I never understood what people meant when they said they *floated on air,* but now I do.

Because I float home to Rookhaven.

I feel like my body is moving without me having to think about it. I feel light and free and happy. So very, very, *very* happy. I want to skip and sing and punch the air and jump for joy and hug the people next to me. I have a job. Ajobajobajob.

It's just past seven o'clock when I get home to Union Street, still wearing Sarah's gym clothes with my studded Converse and leather jacket, smiling joyfully at everyone I see and noting, with delight, that almost everyone smiles back.

I run up the steps at Rookhaven, past the vases of hydrangeas blooming beautifully, into the flower-filled front hallway, and shout as loud as I can.

"I got a joooooooooob!"

Immediately, I hear four screams from all over Rookhaven as everyone rushes out to meet me. Coco from the kitchen, Pia and Julia from the living room, Madeleine from upstairs.

Pia: "What? What? What happened? I've been trying to call you all day!"

Julia: "Pia told us about the purse thing! In the newspaper!"

Madeleine: "Where are you working? What are you doing?"

Coco: "I'm so happy for you!"

So we go into the kitchen, and I tell them everything. About stalking Cornelia, about getting the dress back, about walking across Manhattan to Sarah Drake's design studio. And then I tell them about the job.

"It was just the best day," I say. "I mean, I wasn't doing anything important, you know, but she gave me a job, a real job, and she's going to pay me and everything. So I must have done something right!"

"That is so awesome, ladybitch," says Pia. "I am so proud of you."

"I'm proud of me, too!" I say. I take a cigarette out of the pack and try to prop it between my lips, but I'm smiling so hard it keeps falling out. I put it back in the pack. Then I remember. "Hey! Pia! Did you resign today?"

Pia bites her lip, pausing before her answer for as long as humanly possible. "No. I couldn't do it. My life is here. My job is here. I love New York, I love Brooklyn, and most of all I love Rookhaven. I realized it when we got back last night. Being with all of you guys is where I'm supposed to be right now. . . . I don't know what will happen with Aidan, but this is my home."

"Damn, woman, you give a good speech," says Julia.

"I thought you were allergic to the word home," says Madeleine.

"I had a slight intolerance. But I've grown out of it."

"I decided the same thing this morning," I say. "I realized I didn't want to leave Rookhaven, no matter what. Right about the same time that I saw the cover of the *New York Post.*"

"Cornelia is a piece of work, huh?" says Julia. "I wonder if she got papped outside Le Grenouille just like she planned."

"I'll check," I say, taking out my iPhone. I Google "Cornelia Archer" and a couple of gossip site images immediately come up from her lunch with her mother. They're both wearing Chanel, two little peas in a pod. Well, I guess Cornelia got the job she wanted, too. She'll be a socialite wild child for a while. Until someone else comes along to replace her.

Then something farther down the Google results catches my eye. From Fashionista, a fashion industry news site.

EXCLUSIVE! Met Ball scandal clutch designer revealed!

What the hell?

I click on it, trying frantically to read the entire thing all at once, and then force myself to slow down so I don't miss a word.

Mistakenly identified as Prada, then Miu Miu, then Rodarte, the gold silk clutch at the center of socialite Cornelia Archer's Met Ball drug scandal is by up-and-coming designer Angie James.

The clutch, a hand-sewn gold silk palm-strap pochette, was dropped by socialite Cornelia Archer as security questioned her about her erratic behavior. Cue: two grams of cocaine spilling onto the floor in front of fashion's A-list, cementing Cornelia's position as fashion's newest bad girl, and the clutch as the most talked-about bag of the night.

But who is Angie James? Word has it she worked as muse to Dutch food photographer Anouk Brams, quit in an epic show-down at the end of last year, and has since gone underground. Our sources—and our instincts—tell us a collection is coming.

I read it again: once to myself, and then out loud to the girls.

"This is amazing. . . . Which one of you did this?" I say, staring at them. "Ladybitch? Is this you?"

"Nope," says Pia. "Swear to God."

"Julia? Maddy? Coco?"

"Like we would even know how to do something like that," says Julia.

Suddenly, a lightbulb goes on over my head. I can only think of one other person in the world knows I made that clutch.

It was Sam.

CHAPTER 46

Sam's not answering my calls.

So I'm going to him.

I march into Sam's Fort Greene apartment building, feeling a mixture of excitement and apprehension. I tell the doorman my name, and he picks up the phone.

"There's an Angie James here? . . . Okay."

He escorts me to the elevator and inserts his key to give me access to the top floor. At least Sam wants to see me, that's a good sign, right?

I take a second to check myself out in the elevator mirror. I changed out of Sarah Drake's gym gear, obviously, and quickly showered and put on what, I hope, is a perfect did-you-do-my-PR? outfit: a white silk top, my best jeans, my leather jacket, and boots. I was shaking so much, thinking about what I was about to do, that I could hardly even do my eyeliner right, and ended up wiping most of it off.

As I wait for the elevator to reach the penthouse, feeling breathless with nerves, I try to think, yet again, about what I'll say. I want to apologize for running away, I want to ask him why he lied to me, I want to thank him for telling the world the clutch was mine and find out how he did it, and I want . . . I want . . . I want to say something I'm too scared to even think.

In the end, I settle on four words.

Please, can we talk?

The elevator gets to the top, the doors open, I take a deep breath and prepare my best smile, and . . .

That's not Sam.

A guy who is not Sam, but who reminds me very much of him, is standing in front of me. Same blond hair as Sam, but pale blue eyes rather than gray, and slightly shorter.

"Angie. I'm Pete. I'm Sam's brother." He even sounds like Sam. Just a lot less friendly.

I step slowly into the apartment, looking around. We're the only ones here. "Where is Sam?"

"No idea. I just got home. All of Sam's stuff is gone, and he's not answering his phone. I figured you might know where he is."

I stare at Pete and realize he's wearing the same perfectly cut suit that Sam wore that day in SoHo when I was handing out lattes and CVs. And the same shoes: J.M. Westons.

So they were his roommate's shoes, just like he said. That wasn't a lie.

"This is your apartment," I say eventually.

"Yes," he says.

So that wasn't a lie either. It's not Sam's apartment.

"Can I ask you a few questions?"

"Knock yourself out," Pete says, looking at his phone.

"Sam's been sleeping on your floor."

"He has a bedroom. But he's been staying here, yes."

"Did he graduate from Dartmouth?"

"Yes. He majored in applied math." So *that* was a lie. Ha! "But he got into Dartmouth Medical School and then had to drop out before the semester started." Ah. So it wasn't a lie. Shit. "Why?"

"Just . . . trying to figure something out. And your dad . . ."

"Is coming here, now, to try to find Sam." Pete is very terse now, clearly warning me off the topic of the history of Sam and his dad. "So let's go find him."

Discovering that all of Sam's so-called lies were, in fact, not lies at all has left me reeling. They were just secrets.

What's the difference between a secret and a lie, anyway?

"I really don't know where he might be," I say, as we wait for the elevator. "Sam and I mostly hung out at my house, you know, we couldn't do much. . . . We were broke." Pete shoots me a funny look. Ah. He doesn't quite get the concept of broke.

"Where did you go most often when you did go out?"

"Wherever had free bar food that night."

Pete gives me that confused look again. He's never gone to a bar for free food.

"Wait!" I say. "I know where he might be! He was working for my neighbor. Vic."

"Vic? What does he do?"

"Uh, he's like, eighty-something years old. He does whatever the hell he wants."

"So what was Sam doing for him?"

"He fixed up his kitchen and bathroom; I think he helped knock through a bedroom wall. . . ."

Again, the look. Clearly Sam's old life didn't include helping Brooklyn octogenarians renovate their homes.

We get outside the building, and I glance up and down the street. "I think we can get a cab up that way, and if we can't, we can get a bus—"

Then a town car pulls up in front of us, and Pete opens the door for me. It's the same town car that Sam picked me up in at the playground in the rain that night. Of course. Pete has a permanent driver. This is Roger Rutherford's son, after all.

"Um, so, why do you live in Brooklyn?" I ask Pete, after giving the driver directions. "You do something finance-y, I'm guessing, a banker or something, so how come—"

"How come I don't live in Manhattan with all the other bankers?" he says, raising an eyebrow. "Don't judge a book by its cover, Angie."

"You're a book?"

Another death stare. Wow, Sam's brother is an arrogant fucker. Sam isn't exactly lacking in confidence, either, but somehow . . . somehow with him, it's an open, warm self-assurance. He's kind. And sexy. And funny and silly and gorgeous and everything I want and need and love. . . .

God, I miss him. I hope we can find him. I hope he hasn't just flown to some Caribbean island to get lost for another three years.

I stare out the window, trying to collect myself. I feel kind of panicky and wired. I was so nervous on the way up to the apartment in the elevator, all that adrenaline is still pulsing around my body, and this situation is so bizarre.

Then a new thought occurs to me.

What if he doesn't even want to see me?

I clear my throat. "Look, I don't know if I should come with you, okay? I don't know if Sam wants to see me. We kind of had a fight."

"I know," Pete says, flicking some fluff off his knee.

"You know?" I'm suddenly tired of Pete's clipped arrogance. "What the fuck do you know?"

"I know my brother told you he was broke because he didn't want to deal with all the inevitable Rutherford questions, and because it's just not part of who he is right now. I know he left a job because he wanted to see you again, and I know he stuck around in New York for way longer than he wanted to, just to be near you."

"Oh," I say in a small voice. "I didn't know that."

Pete looks over, frowning. "He's completely in love with you, Angie. Of course he wants to see you."

"Oh," I say again.

But inside, I'm exploding.

"Sam called in a couple of favors earlier today with a family friend who works at some fashion website. They called our father, who called me, wanting to know why I'd been keeping Sam a secret from him for the past few months."

"Why did your dad think that you'd know he was back?"

"Sam's my only brother, Angie. He's my best friend. Just because we're doing different shit doesn't mean we're not simpatico."

Simpatico. What a banker word to use. Sam would never use a word like that.

"Anyway," he continues. "We have to find Sam, now, before Rog does, and get him to leave the city."

"Leave?"

"My dad wants to kill him, Angie."

"You mean like . . ."

Pete looks over at me. "I mean like kill him."

CHAPTER 47

"I haven't seen him," is the first thing Vic says when he opens his front door. If I weren't freaking out right now, I'd laugh: Vic is a terrible liar.

"I don't believe you," says Pete.

"I don't care." Vic tilts his head so that the few inches of height difference between them looks like a lot more. He looks at me. "You should know better than this."

"Vic, it's really important we find him," I say. "This is Sam's brother."

"You're Pete?" Vic's face changes, just a fraction of warmth creeping in. "Okay, come on in."

Pete and I walk into Vic's apartment. It's surreal being back in the room that was waist-deep in floodwater a few nights ago. There's no furniture, the carpet has been ripped up, and there's a muddy, chemical smell from whatever they are using to clean the place.

"I was just packing up some things. I'm going to Jersey to stay with my niece until the fix-up is finished," says Vic. He turns around and stares at Pete for a few seconds, then gives him a little nod. "So what do you want to know?"

"Where is Sam?"

"He got a job."

"Where?"

"Some yacht he was talking about, something going to Europe," says Vic. "One of the crew dropped out at the last minute, Sam got the call. He stopped by first to say good-bye."

"Why didn't he tell me?" Pete asks.

Vic shrugs. "Didn't want you to have to lie to your father."

Well, obviously Sam never had a problem confiding in Vic.

Once we're outside, I turn to face Pete. "Now we go to the North Cove Marina."

"Are you sure he's leaving from there?"

"I'd bet my life on it. No, better than that. I'd bet my job on it."

Pete looks at me funny again. I have the feeling he thinks I'm a little nuts.

The drive over the Brooklyn Bridge is largely silent. Pete doesn't bother to make conversation, he just keeps drumming his hands against his thighs, fidgeting, biting his thumbnail, putting the window down, then up, then down.

"Stop it! Just stop it!" I finally snap, just as we reach Manhattan. "You're so fucking tense!"

Pete looks at me, his jaw clenched. "I need. To find. My brother."

"You're being a total drama queen. I need to find him, too. Your dad isn't going to kill him."

"Really?" Pete pauses for a very long time, staring at me, and then seems to make a decision. "Look, Angie, because of Sam, our father had to fork over more than half his money to our mother in their divorce settlement. Sam had been spying on him, taking photos of Rog, uh, playing around. Gave them to our mom."

"So?" I say. "Your father cheated. Sam did the right thing." I wonder if that's what I should have done when my dad asked me to lie. Probably.

"Well it turned out she'd cheated on him, too," snaps Pete. "She'd been having an affair for years. So, actually, Angie, Sam did the wrong thing. He judged the situation before he knew the entire story."

"Oh."

"Dad found out. Epic fight. It got . . . it got pretty bad. So Sam dropped out of college, went a little wild, then took off and didn't come back. We're less than a year apart in age, we're best friends. But I only know half of what's going on with him. Sam always does what he thinks is right."

"Like keeping secrets from me? Even though I was supposedly the reason he came back to New York?"

"Yeah. Probably. He told me he thought he was busted one time. This guy we went to school with, Lev? He ran into him at some dinner party at your place."

"Lev? Julia's coworker? The guy who called Sam 'Ruthy' at the surprise party?"

"It's an old school nickname," says Pete, grinning to himself. Then he assumes his scowly-mean face again. "Anyway, thanks to you, my brother has been a fucking mess the past few days."

"Sam lied to me." I know I sound defensive, but I can't help it. "I told him everything about me, about who I was, and he lied."

"He didn't lie to you, Angie. He just didn't tell you everything. It's not the same as lying. He was trying to figure out the right time. . . . You don't get to know everything about everybody right away. None of us do."

I stare at him. Maybe that's true. I might never tell Sam or anyone else outside of Rookhaven the whole story about the Soho Grand night and everything that happened with Hal and Stef. It's my life, it's my past, and it belongs to me.

So by judging Sam for doing the same thing, does that make me a hypocrite?

Pete sighs. "Sam's problem was he never thought he did the wrong thing. Ever."

"He does now, I think. . . . He regrets doing that stuff," I say, thinking back to our conversation on my bed at our sleepover. "He told me something about your parents' divorce one time. . . . I think he regrets fighting with your dad."

"He said that?"

"He said he acted like a penis. No, wait, that wasn't it, not a penis—a dick."

Pete laughs for the first time tonight. "Yeah, that's pretty true. . . . Sam has always been the principled one, always the guy who did everything right. The ultimate good guy." Wow. The opposite of me. "But he could be kind of a dick sometimes, too. Self-righteous. And stubborn. If he decided to do something he had a hard time going back on his word." Okay, maybe not the total opposite of me. "What can I say? We were brought up to be arrogant."

"I wouldn't call him arrogant," I say. "Self-possessed, yes. Cool under pressure."

"I think the last three years have changed him. He used to care more about principles and less about people."

"He cares about people now!" I suddenly want Pete to know how amazing I think Sam is. "He looked after my roommate, Coco, and Vic, and, um, and me. . . ." A tear-lump swells in my throat and I can't say anything else. He did look after me. And I had stupid tantrums about romance novels and ignored his calls and sulked when he asked Julia out, and he still looked after me. He loved me.

Pete's too wrapped up in his own world to notice my tears. "Well, now he wants to start somewhere with nothing and end up sailing across the world." While we've been talking about Sam, Pete has stopped fidgeting, loosened his tie, and undone his top shirt button. He's calming down and warming up, and somehow, reminding me more of Sam. "It's symbolic. Or some shit like that. Whatever, I don't fucking get it. . . . And then he's going to apply for scholarships to medical school in the fall."

"Scholarships?"

"Yeah. He won't take money from either of our parents, and he won't take it from me, either, though I keep telling him there has to be some benefit to me becoming fucking mini-Dad." I glance at Pete, but he's not actually being bitter, he's just being honest.

God. I wish Sam had told me a tiny bit of this stuff. Though maybe the clues were there all along. I just didn't look. Too busy thinking about myself.

And now my brain is turning over and over, thinking about the difference between doing the right thing and the wrong thing, between being a good person or a bad person, between secrets and lies. It's so confusing. . . .

The thing is, everyone thinks they're making the right decision when they're making it. It's only later that our mistakes become clear. And then we either make amends and fix those mistakes and deal with the aftermath, or we don't. Either way, life moves on.

Perspective is a bitch, but at least she's consistent.

We reach lower Manhattan. Endless skyscrapers light up the night sky. Millions of tiny twinkly lights, millions of people . . . Goddamn, this city is big.

And then we're finally here.

North Cove Marina. The place where yachts meet skyscrapers, where Manhattan meets the deep blue sea.

Pete and I jump out of the car and hurry toward the pier, and as we get closer, I can just make out two figures. They're screaming at each other. And then I realize who they are, and suddenly, I forget how to breathe.

Sam.

And Roger Rutherford.

CHAPTER **48**

At first, I can't make out any words. Just two extremely angry male voices shouting over each other. Even from twenty feet away I can see Sam is upset—oh God, I hate that. I feel almost sick at the idea of him being miserable.

Pete immediately charges between them and starts shouting, too, but I hang back, right at the end of the pier. It's horrible to watch, an almost violent fury between them. I can't imagine my father or mother ever screaming at me like that. It's like Sam's father really hates him. No wonder Sam wanted to leave.

"Don't you dare tell me you didn't know—"

"I was standing up for what I thought was right, goddamnit—"

"You were picking sides and being a pain in my ass—"

"I told you I never wanted to see you again, I meant it—"

"STOP IT!" Pete shouts so loudly that my ears hurt.

Sam and his father turn to Pete, their faces consumed with anger.

"Dad, back off, Jesus Christ!" says Pete. "What, you thought you'd come down here and bully Sam back into the family?"

"I thought I'd—"

"I'm still talking! And Sam, do you think maybe you could apologize to the old man for causing him so much trouble over the years?"

"I was doing what I thought—"

"But it wasn't right. It wasn't black or white, Sam, nothing ever is!"

"I don't need this! Fuck! This is why I left in the first place!"

Sam throws his arms up in the air, and then turns around, walking quickly away from his family, down the pier toward me. I've never seen him so worked up; he looks like he wants to cry and scream and run, all at once. I know that feeling; hell, that feeling has ruled me for years.

And then, when he's about fifteen feet away, Sam sees me and stops walking.

"Angie?"

I can't hang back anymore. I rush toward him, wrap my arms around him.

"I'm so sorry," we say in unison.

Then I lean back and kiss him, over and over again. My brain, my heart, my body is in free fall, and the only thought in my head is *Sam*.

Right this second, all I want is to make Sam's life easier and happier. I want to take away every sadness in his life, to make everything better for him, in every way possible.

It's the strangest feeling, this love. It's overwhelming. I want to protect him and be protected by him. I want to talk to him and listen to him. I want everything he wants to come true for him. It's not like anything I've ever felt before . . . it's whole. Complete. It will always be a part of me, it will never go away. But we don't have time to talk about it right now.

All we have time to do is kiss.

So in every kiss I try to tell him that I love him, that I hope he forgives me for running away, that I understand his past was his past and he didn't want to talk about it. I try to tell him that I know him so well, I love every inch of him, and that I know that I've only just breached the surface of him, of who he is and what he wants and what he's capable of doing with his life. I want to tell him that he's my best friend and my love, like no one else ever has been or will be again. And with every kiss, I feel like he's telling me the same thing.

"Oh, Angie, I'm so glad you're here, so glad," he whispers, leaning his forehead against mine. "I'm sorry. I should have told you everything."

"No, I'm sorry I wouldn't listen, I was wrong—"

"I wanted to tell you, it was killing me, really—"

And then I'm absorbed again by the warmth and sureness of his lips against mine, his lovely Sam-smelling skin, the truth and strength and *rightness* of him.

I pull back. "The clutch—it's all over the blogosphere. . . . That was you, right? You told the world it was mine."

"I pulled a favor with an old friend of my dad's."

"And that's what got you busted," I say, looking past him at Rog and Pete. "Helping me."

Sam smiles. "You're so talented, Angie, you just need one tiny break."

"I got one," I say. "I got a job today. A real one. In fashion." Even saying the words makes me smile so hard my cheeks hurt.

"Oh, Angie, that's amazing, I'm so happy for you—" Sam pulls me back in for more kisses.

Then I break away, glancing back at his father and brother, who are still talking angrily to each other. "You have to talk to them. You know you do. You don't want it to be like this."

Sam stares at me, smiles, and nods.

We kiss a couple more times, then once more for luck, then Sam takes my hand and leads me back down the pier. And for the first time in days, I feel quiet and calm inside.

"Angie James, this is my father, Roger, and my brother, Peter."

I nod at them, slightly awkwardly, given I know exactly who they are and that they have no goddamn interest in me right now.

Then Sam turns to his father. "Dad, I'm sorry I took those photos, I'm sorry I took sides. I just didn't like seeing Mom upset; I thought it was the right thing to do. I was wrong. I regret . . . everything."

Roger looks, immediately, like someone has pressed his deflate button, all that belligerent self-absorption disappears. "I understand, Sammy. I do. You've always been such a good kid, always sticking up for the little guy. . . . But what I don't understand is how you could not talk to me or your mother for three years. Three years, and nothing! Not a word!"

"I didn't think you'd want to hear from me. I thought you'd probably be happier without me around."

"Oh, Sammy . . . Never. I haven't been happy since you left. You're my *son*. No matter what else happens."

And just like that, the fight is over. Roger seems to have aged ten years in ten seconds and just looks like a sad old man, and Sam looks like, well, a sad young man. They stare at each other in silence.

"Your hair's turned gray," Sam says finally.

Roger grins. "I'd like to blame you for that, but I think your mother has the honor."

"Ha."

"Have you spoken to her?" asks Roger.

Sam shakes his head.

"I have," says Pete. Roger looks at him in surprise. "I didn't tell you, Dad. I knew you'd freak out."

"Well, I've been talking to her, too," says Roger eventually. "She's very happy out there, away from all this. . . ." He gestures to Manhattan, to the lights and sparkle and wealth towering over us. "She misses you, though, Sammy. She talks about you a lot, you know. She's been having some knee problems and been laid up a lot, so she's had a lot of time to think. . . . We started talking again because we were both so worried about you. Pete wouldn't tell us anything except that you were fine and figuring life out for yourself."

Sam looks away, and for a second, I think he's about to cry. Three years without even talking to your mother or father. And meanwhile, his parents are just getting older, and frailer, and lonelier. The minute that you think you don't need them anymore, that's when they need you.

"I'll call her," Sam says. "Tell her I think about her all the time. Tell her I'll call her, I don't know when I'll get phone access after tonight, but I'll call her."

Suddenly, from across the water, we hear a tiny speedboat approaching.

Sam turns his head. "That's my boss, we're about to go," he says, his face creasing in distress. "Dad, Pete . . ."

Pete leans forward to hug Sam, with a few back slaps for good measure.

Then Sam turns to his father. I don't think Rog is the physical affection type, but then he surprises me and leans forward, hugging Sam tightly. He whispers something in his ear, and Sam nods and then pulls away.

"I'll be in touch, okay? I promise."

Sam looks at Pete again and gives a funny little brotherly salute. Then he takes my hand, leading me down toward the end of the pier, where the *Peripety*—the yacht that will take him all the way to the other side of the world—is waiting for him.

We finally reach her, just as the little motorboat pulls up alongside and the captain jumps out carrying a box of supplies.

"Hey, Sam! This is the last of it. All good to go?"

"Yes. Good to go." Sam nods, his face assuming that professional crew member mask I remember from the day I met him. "Can I get two minutes?"

"You got it." The skipper climbs aboard the *Peripety* and disappears belowdecks.

The yacht that looked so big the first time I saw it now seems tiny. He can't sail across the ocean in this. It's not safe. I mean, she's not safe.

I turn to Sam. "Please, please be careful. Please. Nothing can happen to you, okay? I need you to be alive."

"I promise. If I could, I'd call you six times a day, but the cell reception on the Atlantic is really shit."

Sam pulls me to him and kisses me again. Then I pull away. I have so many questions.

"So you can't use a phone on board? What about e-mail? How long will it take you to get to Greece?"

"Three weeks, maybe four . . . The guy who owns the yacht won't be meeting us until June. Then we're sailing around the Greek Islands with him. Returning by September. I'm applying to schools. Some of them aren't that far away, Angie, we'll work it out—"

"Wow." Five months away. Five months is a long time. And then he won't even be living in Brooklyn anymore. Suddenly I feel a desperate panic in my chest. What if he forgets me? What if this is it?

There's a shout from the yacht. "Sammy! Let's go!"

"So no e-mails? No phone calls? Nothing?" I can't stop my voice from rising in distress. "I'll miss you so much."

"I'll miss you more." Sam kisses me again. "I'll be able to text sometimes, and whenever I get the chance to use the Internet somewhere, I'll e-mail you, okay?"

"The yacht doesn't have Wi-Fi?"

Sam laughs and kisses me again, and I try to empty my brain so all I think about is how this feels, this kiss, this feeling of his lips on mine and his arms around me, so I can have it at my mental fingertips to remember anytime I want, until the moment I see him again.

"This is for you, by the way. Happy birthday." Sam hands over a tiny gift-wrapped box. "I've had it for weeks. . . . I was going to give it to you for your birthday and tell you everything. Open it later."

I take the gift and smile at him. "I love you."

"I love you, too."

One tear runs down my cheek, and Sam wipes it away gently with his thumb. Then he gives me one last kiss, turns, and walks quickly away.

I'm overwhelmed with panic. Oh God, that's it. He's leaving.

A second later, Sam turns around and rushes back to me.

"One more," he says in a low voice, pressing his lips against mine. "Just one more, I couldn't let that be the last kiss. I couldn't take it." I start laughing and crying at the same time and kiss him back. Between kisses he whispers: "I'll stay. Say the word and I'll stay."

"No way," I say, tears running down my face. "This is yours. This is what you want now, it's what you need. You have to go. Just go."

And we kiss again, and then again. And then he turns around and, without looking back, walks to the end of the pier and climbs aboard the yacht. I watch for a few minutes as the skipper shouts instructions to him and the rest of the crew. Sam does everything quickly and confidently, with an air of intense concentration.

What feels like seconds later, the yacht finally pulls away into the darkness, and I watch the gap widening between me and him.

I stare after the yacht, my heart pounding, tears in my eyes, and a sadness deep in my stomach. But above all that, I know, I *know* this is the right thing. I need to stay here to find my future. He needs to leave to find his.

Please turn, Sam. Please look at me. Just one last time.

Then, just as I think that's it, I won't see his face again, Sam turns around and smiles at me, his face lit up by the flickering lights of the marina and the skyscrapers above us, and even from this distance, I can see he mouths "I love you."

I mouth it back. "I love you."

When the night has finally swallowed up the *Peripety,* I turn around, tears still wet on my face. I take a few deep breaths, looking up at the city above me.

I feel strangely okay and calm inside. Sam will be back.

And meanwhile, I have my own life to live.

I walk slowly back to Pete and Roger, a tiny smile on my face. When I get to them, Rog finally looks at me properly. "Haven't we met before?"

"I met you the other night at the Minetta Tavern," I say. "With Cornelia."

"Ah, Cornelia. The naughty yet ambitious socialite," Rog says, nodding. "I don't think I'll be hearing from her for a while. She's got bigger fish to fry."

"Dad, you wanna go grab a bite?" says Pete.

"I'd love that," says Roger. He turns to me. "Care to join us?"

"No, uh, thank you, I have to get home," I say. "I need my friends."

"Take my car service," says Pete. "I'll go with Dad."

"Oh no, I couldn't, really."

"Look, it's the least I can do, Angie," he says in a low voice, as Rog strides ahead. "You're the reason I found Sam. Without you, they'd have killed each other."

And so I say good-bye to the Rutherfords and get into the town car.

"Brooklyn, please. Union Street. Just up from Court."

The driver nods, and seconds later, we're heading across Manhattan toward the Brooklyn Bridge. Toward home.

Then I unwrap the little gift Sam gave me on the dock.

It's a tiny square box. Inside is a small pair of sapphire stud earrings. And a note.

Happy Birthday, Angie. These earrings are the color of the
Caribbean sea you dived into the first day we met. You probably
hate them. Your taste in jewelry is just one in the long list of
things that I want to know about you, and don't . . . yet.
I love you.
Sam

I put the earrings on and smile, feeling that happy warmth inside again. Sam will be back.

There's just one thing I need to do. I take out my phone and quickly text my dad. Despite the way he behaved, he's my father. And he probably needs me as much as I need him.

Let's meet up this weekend. I think we should talk. A x

Then my phone rings. A number I don't recognize.

"Hello?"

"Angie James?"

"Speaking . . ."

"Hi! This is Edie Jansen. We met a month or so ago, when you were handing out your CV with a free latte outside Maven? That was you, right?"

"Uh, yes?"

"I was the girl wearing Marni for H&M!"

"Oh! Hi!" The pointy-faced chic girl, the one who actually talked to me!

"Great! God, I have been looking everywhere for your CV, you would not believe the day I had, but in the end Cynthia had it, isn't that amazing? She was impressed with your ingenuity and kept it this whole time! Okay, so I saw on Fashionista that Cornelia Archer's clutch bag was designed by you, right? We want to know if you'd be interested in a hookup with one of our clients. It's a tiny fast-fashion brand called Serafina; it's only small-time now but it's—"

"Yes," I say. "I'm interested."

"Can you come in for a meeting tomorrow morning?"

"I'm working with Sarah Drake right now." I try to sound as official and efficient as I can. "Can you do six forty-five P.M.?"

"Yes! *Love* Sarah Drake. We'll work around you. That would be perfect! Okay, *ciao!*"

I hang up and put my window down, looking out at the city nightscape as we drive over the Brooklyn Bridge. I feel more calm and sure than I ever have in my life.

I am exactly where I am supposed to be. I have a job. I have a passion. I have best friends. I have true love. I have a life. I have things to look forward to and people to care about. I am never alone. I am happy.

This is where everything begins.

ACKNOWLEDGMENTS

The problem with writing these acknowledgments pages is that everything I write sounds clichéd. So let's pretend it doesn't, okay? Okay. Good.

Thanks to Vicki Lame and Dan Weiss at St. Martin's Press, and my agents, Jill Grinberg and Laura Longrigg for—oh, everything.

Thanks to all my friends. And all those times you [insert meaningful friendship-related event HERE]. And Hawk, for giving me exact instructions on what would give Coco an overdose. He's one hell of a fun doctor.

Thanks to everyone who read *Brooklyn Girls* and e-mailed me to tell me you loved it. You guys are my spirit animals. (I don't really know what that means, but it sounds funny.)

And most of all, thanks to my lovely little family for being perfect. I love you.

READ ON TO FIND OUT WHERE IT ALL BEGAN

Brooklyn GIRLS

PIA

Out **NOW!**

CHAPTER 1

Never screw your roommate's brother.

A simple rule, but a good one. And I broke it last night. Twice.

Oopsh.

At least the party was awesome. I'll try that excuse if Julia is pissy. And if her house is trashed. Which I'm pretty sure it is.

I'm not exactly surprised. I like parties, I'm good at them, and it was August 26 yesterday. And on that date, I always drink to forget. This year, I did it with whips, chains, and bells on.

My bare ass keeps brushing against the wall as I squish away from Mike. Don't you hate that? Doesn't random hookup etiquette demand he face the other way? I wish he would just leave without me having to, like, talk to him.

I wonder what Madeleine, his sister, would say if she found out.

She'd probably ignore me, which is what she always does these days. I wish Julia hadn't asked her to move in.

Julia, my best friend from college, inherited this house when her aunt passed away. So Julia invited me, her little sister Coco, and Madeleine to move in. And then we needed a fifth, so I asked my friend Angie. We're a motley crew: Coco's the Betty Homemaker type, Angie's all fashi-tude, Julia's super-smart and ambitious, and Madeleine's uptight as hell. And me? I'm . . . well, it's impossible to describe yourself, isn't it? Let's call me a work-in-progress.

We moved in two weeks ago. It's a brownstone named Rookhaven, on Union Street in Carroll Gardens, a neighborhood in the borough of Brooklyn in New York City. None of us has properly lived in New York before.

Carroll Gardens is a weird mix of old people who've probably lived here forever, young professionals like us who—let's face it—can't afford to live in Manhattan, and a bunch of yupster couples with young kids. There's a real neighborhood village vibe with all these old, traditional Italian bakeries and restaurants next to stylish little bars.

I like stylish little bars.

I like my bedroom, too. I've had a lot of bedrooms in my life—twenty-seven, if you count every room change at boarding school and college—but never one quite like this. High ceilings, windows looking out over the front stoop, wall-to-wall mirrored closets. Okay, the mirrors are yellowed and the wallpaper is a faded rosebud print that looks like something out of an old movie. It just *feels* right. Like this is how it's supposed to look.

That's kind of Rookhaven all over. If I were feeling nice, I'd call the décor vintage and preloved. (Old and shabby.) I'm just happy to be in New York, far away from my parents, in the most exciting city in the world, with a job at a SoHo PR agency. My life is *finally* happening.

Can I be honest with you? I shouldn't have slept with Mike. Not when things are already, shall we say, complicated with Madeleine. Casual sex only works when it's with someone you can never see again. But, as I said, it was August 26 (also known as Eddie Memorial Day, or Never Again Day). And on August 26, shit happens.

What is that damn ringing sound?

"I think that's the doorbell."

Gah! Mike! Awake! Right here next to me. I peek through my eye-lashes. Like Madeleine, he's ridiculously good-looking. I guess it's their Chinese-Irish DNA. Good combination.

"Erm . . . someone else will get it," I murmur. My breath smells like an open grave. Not that it matters. Because I don't like him like that. Even though last night I—ew. God. Bad thought. But hey! So what? So the whole sex thing was a bad idea. There is no reason to feel stupid Puritan guilt about one-night stands. I am a feminist. And all that shit.

The doorbell goes again.

"Pia . . . Come here, you crazy kitten," Mike says, pushing his arm under me.

"I better get the door. It could be someone important!" I say brightly, slithering down around him and falling onto the dark green carpet with a thump.

I wriggle into my panties, trying to look cool and unbothered as I put on the first T-shirt I see. It belonged to Smith, a guy I dated (well, slept with a few times) in college. The back says, "I brake for cheerleaders . . . HARD."

I pull on my favorite cutoff jean shorts and Elmo slippers and stuff my cell phone in my pocket.

"I'm glad you brake for cheerleaders," says Mike. "They're an endangered species."

"Um, yup, totally!" I say, and slam the door behind me, cutting him off.

Mike! God! Nightmare!

I close my eyes, trying to remember last night. It's worryingly hard. I was feeling meh after Thompson (this cockmonkey I've been dating, well, sleeping with) ignored my text (*Hola. Bodacious party. Bring smokes if you can* . . . Good text, right? Ironic use of passé slang, trailing ellipses rather than a lame smiley face, etc.). And rejection is not a good look for me. Not on August 26.

So I drank more. And more. And then more.

I remember dancing. On a table, maybe? Yeah, that rings a bell. . . . And I think I was doing some '80s-aerobics-style dance moves. The grapevine. Definitely the grapevine. I was having fun, anyway. I don't usually worry about much when I'm having fun.

And Mike was doing one-handed push-ups, really badly, and making me laugh, and then I stumbled, and next thing I knew Mike's lips were on mine. Now I *love* kissing, I really do, and he is pretty good at it, and I was trashed, so I suggested we go to my room. And then . . . oh, God.

Nothing burns like hangover shame.

The person at the door is really dying to get in. *Dingdongdingdong-dingdong.*

"Coming!" I shout, picking my way over the bottles and cigarette butts on the stairs.

I hope it's not the cops. I don't *think* there were drugs at the party, but you never know. Once time at my second boarding school I thought that my boyfriend Jack had OCD, which was why he arranged talcum powder in little lines, and as it turned out— Wait. Back to the nightmare.

I open the front door and sigh in relief.

It's just a very old man. His face is like a long raisin with pointy elf ears, on the top of a tall and skinny body.

"Young lady, where is your father?" he says in a strong Brooklyn accent. *Fadah.*

"Zurich," I say, then add, "Sir." (And they say I don't respect my elders.)

"Are you a relation of Julia's?"

"Fu— I mean, gosh, no."

"Well, that figures. I didn't think Pete remarried, and you're definitely a half-a-something."

Seriously? "I'm a whole person, not a half. My mother is Indian, my father is Swiss. Please come back later." I try to close the door, but he's blocking it.

"I need to speak with Miss Russotti."

"Which one? There are two. Russotti the elder, also known as Julia, and Russotti the younger, also known as Coco."

"Whichever is responsible for the very loud party that went on till 5:00 A.M. and caused the total cave-in of my kitchen ceiling."

I gasp. He must live in the garden-level apartment under our house. My mind starts racing. How can I fix this?

"Oh, I am so sorry, I can pay for the ceiling, sir, I—".

"I take it that there were no parents present?"

"I think my roommate Madeleine has babysitting experience, does that count?"

"Don't be smart with me."

"I've never been called smart before," I say, twisting my hair around my finger, trying to get him to laugh a little bit. No one can stay angry after they laugh, it's a fact.

His expression warms slightly, then falls as though pushing the crags and crevices into a new shape was too much effort. "Just get Julia."

"Yes, sir. Would you like to wait inside?"

"If you think I want to see what this house looks like this morning, you've got another think coming."

"Is it think or thing?"

"It's think."

"I'll go get Julia."

I run up the stairs, jumping over the leftover party mayhem, and knock on Julia's bedroom door.

"Juju?" I peer in.

No Julia, just Angie and some tall English lord guy she met in London at the Cartier Polo (yes, seriously). I saw them making out in the laundry room last night after a game of "truth or dare," which Angie renamed "dare or fuck off." Man, I hope they didn't screw on the washing machine. My laundry is in there. I keep forgetting to take it out, and it goes all funky with the heat, so then I have to wash it again and— Oh, sorry. Focus.

"*Angie!* Wake the hell up!"

I shake her, but she just gives a little snore and buries herself deeper into the bed. She looks like a fallen angel with a serious eyeliner habit. And she's *impossible* to wake after a night out.

Julia will lose her shit if she finds out about this. She and Angie haven't exactly bonded. My bad: I talked Julia into letting Angie move in before they'd even met, because Angie's folks got her a job as a PA to some food photographer woman in Chelsea and she needed a place to live, and Angie's been, like, my best friend since I was born. (Literally. Our moms met in the maternity ward.)

Then Angie walked in, said, "It's a dump, but it's retro, I can make it work," and lit a cigarette. Julia was not impressed.

"Angie! Get. The hell. Up."

"Pia?" She peers up at me through her long white-blond hair. "I had to sleep here, there was a threesome in my bed."

"Ew," I say, grimacing, as I pull Angie onto her feet. "Help me. Major crisis."

"You're such a fucking drama queen. Hugh. Dude. Get up."

Hugh climbs out behind her unsteadily. He has a very posh English accent. "Tremendous party." *Pah-teh.* He's very handsome, like a young Prince William, with more hair.

As soon as he leaves, Angie licks and smells her hand to check her morning breath. "Yep, pretty rank. What's wrong, ladybitch?"

"Everything. We have to find Julia."

"Roger that." Angie's still wearing her tiny party dress from last night and slips on a pair of snow boots from Julia's closet. "You have a hickey on your neck."

"How old school of me." I grab Julia's foundation to dab over it. "Ugh, why is she wearing this shade? It's completely wrong for her. Sorry, off topic."

We head upstairs. Angie stares at her closed bedroom door. "God, I hate threesomes."

"Totally. It's just showing off."

Angie smirks, then karate kicks her door in. "Show's over, bitches! Get the hell outta my house."

Two girls I've never seen before and a tall dark-haired guy I vaguely recognize from college saunter out of Angie's room.

"Pia, babe!" says the guy, putting on his shirt. "I tried to find you all night! Remember that party back in junior year? A little Vicodin, a little tequila . . ."

I shudder. Now I remember him.

"Leave," snaps Angie. "Now."

"Bitch," he calls, walking down the stairs.

"Blow me!" she calls back, then heads into her room. "Fuck! I'm gonna have to burn the sheets."

I hear a hinge squeak. It's Madeleine, coming out of the bathroom in a pristine white robe, her hair wrapped perfectly in a towel-turban.

"Morning!" I say, smiling as innocently as I can.

She pads to her bedroom and slams the door. Typical. Good thing I didn't add, *"By the way, your brother is naked in my bed."*

I trudge up the last flight of stairs, finally reach Coco's attic room, and knock. Julia must be in here. There's nowhere else to go.

"It's me . . ." I open the door slowly.

Julia is sitting on the bed, still wearing her clothes from last night yet sportily immaculate as ever, next to Coco, whose blond bob is bent over a plastic bucket and—oh, God. She's puking.

"Coco!" I say. "Are you sick?"

"Clap, clap, Sherlock," says Julia.

"I'm fine!" Coco's voice echoes nasally in the bucket. "So fine. Oh, God, not fine." Noisy, chokey barf sounds follow. "Wowsers! This is green! Oh, Julia, it's green, is that bad?"

"It's bile," says Julia, rubbing Coco's back and glaring at me. Furious and sisterly, all at once. "I need to talk to Pia. Try to stop vomiting, okay?" She has a deep, self-assured voice, particularly lately. It's like the moment she graduated, she decided it was time to *act adult at all costs.*

"Maybe I'll lose weight," Coco's voice echoes from the bucket.

I follow Julia to the tiny landing at the top of the stairs, closing Coco's bedroom door behind us. I feel sick. Confrontation and I really don't get along.

"I am sorry," I say immediately. "I guess you're angry about the party, and—"

"You sold it to me as a 'small housewarming,'" interrupts Julia. "This place was like Cancun on spring break, but less classy."

I hate being told off, too. It's not like I don't *know* when I've screwed up. Or like I do it on purpose. And I never know what to say, so I just gaze into space and wait for it to be over.

"I *said* no wild parties. When we all moved in, that was the rule." God, Julia is scary when she wants to be. "What the fuck were you *thinking,* Pia?"

"It just sort of, um, happened. . . ." I say, chewing my lip. "And I'm sorry about this, too, um, there's an old dude at the door? He said his ceiling caved in? I'll pay for it! I have the money and—"

"Vic?" says Julia in dismay. "I swear to God, Pia, I can't live with you if you're going to fucking act like this all the time. I mean it!"

She's going to kick me out of Rookhaven?

"I won't!" I exclaim. "I'm sorry! Don't overreact!"

"Start cleaning up!" she shouts, thundering down the stairs.

She's going to kick me out. I thought I finally had somewhere that I could call my own, somewhere that wasn't temporary, and somewhere I might actually not have to wear shower shoes. Yet again I am the master of my own demise. Mistress. Whatever.

I walk back into Coco's room. "Can I get you anything, sweetie? I've got rehydration salts somewhere."

"No," she croaks, smiling cherubically at me from the pillow. "I had fun last night. You were so funny."

"Oh, well, that's good." What the hell was I doing?

There are hundreds of books on Coco's floor. I think they're usually in the bookshelves in the living room. They're all old and tattered, with titles like *What Katy Did* by Susan Coolidge and *Are You There God? It's Me, Margaret* by Judy Blume. I loved *What Katy Did*, I remember. The sequel, *What Katy Did at School*, was one of the reasons I thought boarding school would be awesome. Stupid book.

"Why are these here?" I ask.

"I didn't want them to get, um, you know, trashed at the party," says Coco. "So I picked up all the ones that my mom loved the most and brought them up here."

"It must have taken you a while," I say.

"Every time I made a trip, I had a shot. . . ." Coco starts puking again.

"Hey, ladybitches," says Angie, sauntering in with an unlit cigarette propped in the side of her mouth.

"For you, Miss Coco." Somehow, Angie has found an icy-cold can of Coke.

"Wow, thanks! I normally drink Diet Coke, but—"

"Trust me, Diet Coke is bullshit. Okay kids, I am officially over this post-party chaos thing. Let's clean up."

At that moment, my phone rings. Unlisted number. I answer.

"Hello?"

"Pia, it's Benny Mansi."

Benny Mansi is the director of the PR agency where I work. My parents know his family somehow and got me the interview back in June. I started working there last week. Why would he call me on a Sunday? Is that normal? Perhaps it's a PR emergency!

I try to sound professional. "Hi! What's up?"

"Are you aware that there's a photo of you on Facebook, dancing on a table topless and drinking a bottle of Captain Morgan rum?"

WHAM. I feel like I just got punched.

"Um, I—"

"Pia, we're letting you go before your trial period is over."

WHAM. Another hit.

"You're firing me . . . for having a party?"

"Captain Morgan is one of our biggest clients," Benny says. "As my employee, you represent the agency. You're also Facebook friends with all your brand-new colleagues. You were tagged, they saw it. I applaud your convivial approach to interoffice relations, but that sort of behavior is just . . . it's unprofessional, and it's completely unacceptable, Pia."

"I know." A wash of sickly cold horror trickles through me, and I stare at the yellowed glow-in-the-dark stars on the sloping ceiling in Coco's room. They lost their glow long ago. . . . Oh, God, I can't be fired. I can't be fired after *one week*. "I'm so sorry, Benny." Silence. "Did you . . . tell my, um, father?"

He sighs. "I e-mailed him this morning. I didn't tell him why." I don't say anything, and his voice softens. "Look, Pia, it's complicated. We made some redundancies a few months ago. So hiring you, as a family friend, really upset a few people, and that photo . . . my hands are tied. I'm sorry."

He hangs up.

I can feel Coco and Angie staring at me, but I can't say anything.

I've lost my job. And I'm probably about to get kicked out of my house. After one week in New York.

My phone rings again. It's my parents. I stare at the phone for a few seconds, knowing what's on the other end, what's waiting for me.

I wonder if Coco would mind if I borrowed her puke bucket.

I need to be alone for what's about to happen, so I walk back out to the stairwell and sit down. I can hear Madeleine playing some angsty music in her room on the floor below, mixed with Julia's placating tones and Vic's grumbly ones from down in the front hall.

Then I answer, trying to sound like a good daughter.

"Hi, Daddy!"

"So you've lost your job already. What do you have to say for yourself?"

My voice is gone. This happens sometimes. Just when I need it most. In its place, a tiny squeaking sound comes out.

"Speak up!" snaps my father. He has a slightly scary Swiss accent despite twenty years living in the States.

"I'm . . . sorry. I'll get another job, I will, and—"

"Pia, we are so disappointed in you!" My mother is lurking on the extension. She has a slight Indian accent that only really comes out when she's pissed. Like now.

"You wanted the summer with Angie, so we paid for it. You wanted to work, so we got you a job. You said you had the perfect place to live, so we agreed to help pay rent, though God knows Brooklyn certainly wasn't the perfect place to live last time I was there—"

"You have no work ethic! You are a spoiled party girl! Are you sniffing the drugs again?"

They've really honed their double-pronged condemnation-barrage routine over the years.

"Work ethic. Your mother is right. Your total failure to keep a job . . . well. Let me tell you a story—"

I sink my head to my knees. My parents have the confidence-killing combination of high standards and low expectations.

They also twist everything so it looks terrible. They told me if I got good grades they'd pay for my vacation, and that I'd never find a job on my own, *and* they offered me an allowance, so of course I said yes! Wouldn't you?

". . . and that is how I met your father and then we got married and had you and then lived— What do you say? Happily ever after . . ."

Yeah, right. My parents hardly talk to each other. They distract themselves with work (my dad) and socializing (my mother). They met in New York, where they had me, then moved to Singapore, London, Tokyo, Zurich . . . I went to American International Schools until I was twelve, and then they started sending me to boarding school. Well, boarding schools.

"Life starts with a job, Pia. You think we will always pay for your mistakes, that life is just a party. We know you'll never have a career, but a job is—"

"A reason to get up in the morning!"

"And the only way to learn the value of money. Do you understand?"

I nod stupidly, staring at the wall next to me, at the ancient-looking rosebud wallpaper. At the bottom the paper has started to peel, curled up like a little pencil shaving. It's comforting.

"Pia!" my mother is shouting. "Why are you not listening? Do we have to do the Skype again?"

"No, no, I can't, my Skype is broken," I say quickly. I can't handle Skyping with my parents. It's so damn intense.

"We are stopping your allowance, effective immediately. No rent money, no credit card for emergencies. You're on your own."

"What? B-but it might take me a while to get another job!" I stammer in panic.

"Well, the Bank of Mom and Dad is closed unless you come live with us in Zurich and get a job here. That's the deal."

"No way!" I know I sound hysterical, but I can't help it. "My friends are here! My life is here!"

"We want you to be safe," says my mother, in a slightly gentler tone. Suddenly tears rush to my eyes. "We worry. And it seems like you're only safe when you're with us."

"I *am* safe."

"And we want you to be happy," she adds.

"I am happy!" My voice breaks.

My father interrupts. "This is the deal. We're vacationing in Palm Beach in exactly two months, via New York. If you're not in gainful employment by then, we're taking you back to Zurich with us. That's the best thing for you."

The tears escape my eyes. I know I've made some mistakes, but God, I've tried to make it up to them. I studied hard, I got into a great college. . . . It's never good enough.

How is it that no one in the world can make me feel as bad as my parents can?

"Okay, message received," I say. "I gotta go."

I hang up and stare at the curled-up rosebud wallpaper for a few more seconds. Then, almost without thinking, I lick my index finger and try to smooth it down, so it lies flat and perfect against the wall. It bounces right back up again.

With one party, I've destroyed my life in New York City. Before it even began.

CHAPTER 2

When Julia comes back upstairs moments later, pink with fury, my stomach flips over. I hate fighting. And Jules is really good at it. She should have been a lawyer.

"You destroyed our neighbor's ceiling," she snaps. "Destroyed. A piece of plaster fell on his sister's head this morning. She's eighty-six-fucking-years old, Pia!"

"Is she okay? Oh, my God, I can't—"

"She's fine," says Julia. "It was only a tiny piece. But Vic is *pissed*."

"I'll pay for it, I promise!" I say. "I have, like, sixteen hundred dollars. He can have all of it." It's all I have in the world, and the last of the money from my parents, but I need to convince Julia not to kick me out. "I'm sorry, Julia, I didn't know it'd get so out of control."

"What were you *thinking*?"

"I just . . . I thought it would be fun, that everyone would have a good time." I can't tell her that I was drinking because it was August 26. I never talk about Eddie to anyone. Only Angie knows the story, only Angie saw me that day. "Seriously, Juju, I never meant to hurt anyone . . . or destroy the old guy's, I mean Vic's, ceiling."

"Vic and Marie have been here *forever*. Since long before I was born, or my mom," says Julia. "They're like family, okay?"

Suddenly, I understand. Her mom grew up here, and she died of breast cancer about eight years ago. Her dad has cocooned himself in silent grief ever since, and then her Aunt Jo passed away, so I guess Vic and Marie—and Rookhaven—are sort of a last link to her mom. No wonder she feels so protective.

"I'll fix the floor damage," I say, reaching out for Julia's hand. She doesn't resist, which I take as a good sign. "And I'll get them flowers to say sorry. Today. And I will not let anything bad happen to this house again. I cross my heart."

Julia takes a deep breath and leans against the wall, closing her eyes. She looks exhausted, and it's not just from the party. Her job—trainee in an investment bank—starts at 6:00 A.M. every day, and she doesn't get home until past 7:00 P.M. every night. It's step one in her plan to take over the world. She's so exhausted, she's actually kind of gray. And she's not even hungover.

"I had fun last night, by the way."

"What?" I say.

She opens one eye, a tiny grin on her lips. "It was a great party. I had fun. Right up until Coco started to do a striptease in the kitchen."

I clap my hand over my mouth. "No way."

"I carried her up here. Anyway, don't tell her. She doesn't remember. I always think it's better that way."

"Oh, I know," I say. "You never flashed an entire bar your Spanx on Spring Weekend."

"Totally. Goddamnit, I wish I'd been wearing a thong that night."

We grin at each other for a second, remembering. That's the Julia I know and love. The girl who works hard and plays hard, too. And the girl who always wants to make everything right. But I can't tell her what happened with my job and parents just yet. I need to process it (uh, pretend it didn't happen).

"Hang on a moment." Julia narrows her eyes at me. "Bed hair. Panda eyes. And stubble rash. Peepee, you got action last night!" she exclaims.

"I did not! And don't call me Peepee!"

"Have we made up?" coos Angie, peering out from Coco's room. She wraps her bare leg around the door, lifting one snow boot–clad foot up and down like a meteorology-loving stripper. "Are we all friends again?"

"Those are my boots," says Julia. "Why are you wearing them?"

"Are you planning on skiing soon? I think not." Angie sashays past us down the stairs. "It's August. I'll return them in pristine condition as soon as the house is clear of party debris, okay, Mommy?"

Julia rolls her eyes and heads downstairs. "Start cleaning."

Angie flicks the finger at Julia's retreating back.

"Real mature, Angie."

"Suck my mature."

"I'm hungry."

"You're always hungry. Let's clean."

Somehow, being hungover and giggling with Angie cheers me up and helps squash my what-the-sweet-hell-am-I-going-to-do-now thoughts. She keeps making little moans of dismay at each new inch of party filth, and pretty soon we've both got the giggles.

"When I have my own place, there will be no carpets," I say. "Carpets are just asking for trouble."

"Did anyone lose a shoe? And why did we invite someone to our party who wears moccasins?"

"Is this red wine or blood? No. Wait. It's tomato sauce. Weird."

"You wanna talk me through the hickey, ladybitch?"

I catch Angie's eye and bite my index finger sheepishly.

"You had the sex? You little minx . . ."

"With her brother," I whisper, pointing at Madeleine's door. "Bit of an oopsh."

Oopsh is our word for a drunken mistake.

"Oopsh I kissed the wrong dude, or oopsh I tripped and his dick landed in my mouth?"

I crack up. No one does crass like Angie. She looks like a tiny Christmas angel and acts like a sailor on a Viagra kick. "Or was it more like, oopsh, I'm riding his face and—"

"Too far! That's too far."

"Sorry."

"Don't tell Jules, she'd just have to tell Maddy, and it'd be a whole thing."

"Absolute-leh, dah-leng," she says, in her best imitation of her mother's British accent. "You were totally kamikaze last night."

"It was August 26. That's International Pia Goes Kamikaze Day, remember? Crash and burn."

There's a pause. "Oh, dude, I'm sorry. I totally forgot. Eddie."

I can't bring myself to look at her. Only Angie saw me that day, only Angie knows how bad it was. She always calls me a drama queen, but she knows that misery was real. You don't fake that kind of breakdown.

"I don't want to talk about it," I say.

Angie keeps cleaning. "Fuck him, Pia. Okay? Fuck him! It's been four years!"

I nod, scrubbing as hard as I can. It has been four years since we broke up. And I really should be over it. Then, thank God, Angie changes the subject.

"So I'm gonna move out to L.A. after the holidays," she says. "I don't really belong here in Brooklyn, you know?"

This news just makes me feel even sadder. There's no point arguing with Angie. She does whatever she wants. Instead I scrub harder and, stair by stair, stain by stain, we make it downstairs. Angie puts on some music, and we clean to the post-party-appropriate strains of the Ramones. I can hear Julia and Coco throwing out empty bottles in the kitchen and, every now and again, shrieking when they find something nasty. Oh please, God, no drugs or used condoms. Just spare me that.

"What time did the party finish?" I ask Angie.

"About five. Lord Hugh and I saw out the last of the party people just as the sun was coming up."

"He seems . . . Lordesque."

"He's very Lordesque." She nods. "He also knows his way around a washer-dryer."

"Did you guys do a"—I pause and grin at her—"full load?"

"Just a half load. Then we rinsed. Very thoroughly. Oh, look. Half a spliff. How nice."

We make it to the first floor, and help Julia and Coco finish up the kitchen, which primarily involves de-stickying every surface. Nothing does sticky like forty-year-old linoleum.

"That was intense," says Julia, wiping her forehead with her arm. "The laundry room flooded. That's what made Vic's ceiling collapse."

"I'll fix it," I say again.

"Oh, I know you will."

"I cleaned the bathrooms," says an icy voice. I look up, and see Madeleine, carrying a mop and bucket. "They were absolutely revolting."

"Thanks, Moomoo," says Julia. Madeleine rolls her eyes at Julia's nickname for her—she professes to hate it—and pushes past us to the sink, giving Julia's ponytail an affectionate tug. She's so nice underneath that cold-and-controlled exterior, just not to me, not anymore.

Okay, the Madeleine story, in brief: we were friends once. Really good friends. In fact, she and Julia and I were pretty much inseparable for freshman year. We're all very different, but somehow we just . . . clicked, in an opposites-attract kind of way.

Then, suddenly, at the end of freshman year, Madeleine got crazy drunk for the first time ever and, out of nowhere, told me she hated me. I was holding her hair back so she could throw up, and she just said over and over again, "I hate you. I hate you, Pia, I hate you." Then she passed out. The next day, I tried to talk to her, she shut down, and we've been in a cold war ever since. And now her brother is naked in my bed.

Hmm.

Between you and me, I wouldn't have moved in if I'd known Madeleine was going to be here, too. Jules was probably hoping we'd make up, that the five of us will become best friends and start swapping traveling ya-ya pants, or whatever. I can't see that happening. Particularly given that Julia's now busy making her own little cold war with Angie.

An hour later, the whole of Rookhaven is clear of party fallout, not including hangovers.

"Perfect," says Julia, smiling as she looks around the living room.

"C'mon, Ol' Rusty hasn't been perfect since the Eisenhower administration," says Angie.

"Don't call this house Ol' Rusty," snaps Julia. "If you hate it so much, you can always leave."

"Who said anything about hating it?" says Angie.

"I like it just how it is," I say.

"I *love* it. And I love Brooklyn. I'm a lil' Brooklynista." Angie smiles sweetly at us all.

"Can we get some food, please?" I say to distract them from their almost-argument. "I'm starving."

"I'm making French toast!" That'd be Coco. She's been trying to force-feed us comfort food since we moved in. "Everyone in the kitchen!"

"I'll just be a minute," I say.

Time to deal with you-know-who.

"Hey." Mike is groggily stretching in my bed. He looks a lot better clean-shaven and in a pressed shirt. "Where've you been? You wanna snuggle?"

I laugh. "Snuggle?"

"All the cool kids are doing it. C'mon . . ."

I put on my aviators and take a deep breath. "Mike, your sister will kill me if she finds out about last night. Let's just pretend it didn't happen, okay?"

"Okay. Fine." Wow, he's bratty when things don't go his way.

"I'm serious. She doesn't like me as it is."

"She doesn't?"

"No . . ." Suddenly I realize that talking to Mike about his sister being a bitch isn't the smartest move. "Um, you know. I'm probably misinterpreting it."

"Maddy's pretty hard to read," he says. "She never lets her guard down. Even with me, and I'm family. I think it's insecurity."

I fight the urge to roll my eyes. I am so sick of people blaming everything on being insecure. It's not a get-out-of-jail-free card, you know?

"Whatever. We're all in the kitchen. Wait ten minutes and you can leave without being seen."

"Why don't I just climb out the window and shimmy down the drainpipe?"

"That would be perfect! Do you think you could?" I say, just to see his reaction. "Kidding. See ya."

Thank hell that's over with. I have more important things to worry about. Like being unemployed, broke, and cut off from the so-called

Bank of Mom and Dad (pay interest in guilt!) with the threat of being forced to leave New York in exactly eight weeks.

If a kitchen could be grandmotherly, then this one is. It's huge, yet also 1960s-sitcom-rerun cozy. The kind of kitchen in which cakes and cookies and pies are always baking, you know? My mother *never* baked.

As we're sitting around the kitchen table, listening to Lionel Richie and eating Coco's amazing French toast with bacon on the side, I finally tell the girls everything. About the Facebook photo, work, and even my parents.

"In a nutshell, I destroyed Rookhaven, and I'm unemployed, unemployable, and broke," I say, pushing my food around my plate miserably. "I don't know what to do. Who gets fired after one week? I'm such a fuck-up. . . . If I don't get a job, my parents will make me go live with them."

"You can't do that!" Somehow, Angie manages to look cool even talking through a mouthful of bacon. "You'd never survive! Your parents can't make you do anything."

"Yes, they can!" I say. "I've never stood up to them. I just do what they say, and then avoid them."

"Sounds healthy," Julia says.

I shrug. Is anyone's relationship with their parents healthy?

"I can't believe you were fired!" says Coco. "That must have been awful." She reaches over to give me a hug. For the second time today, I have to blink away tears. I swear I want to cry more when people are nice to me than when they're mean.

"Yuh," says Madeleine. "Who would have thought dancing topless at a party would backfire like that?"

"I was wearing a bra!"

"Pia, it was a sheer bra."

"Stop it, Maddy." Julia forks another piece of French toast onto her plate. I notice she hasn't said anything about not wanting me to move out.

"Listen, I have loads of cash, you won't go hungry . . . or thirsty." Angie picks up a piece of crispy bacon with her fingers and dips it in a pool of maple syrup, and then lowers her voice. "And I think the laundry room flooding might have been our, uh, my fault. I'll help pay for it."

"I can loan you money, too," says Julia quickly, her competitive nature kicking in.

"Don't be crazy." I can't accept charity. I won't. "If I need money that badly, I'll go to a bank. Get a loan."

"Are you crazy? Take a loan? You'd have some bananas interest rate, and the loan would just get bigger and bigger and you'd never be able to pay it back! So you'd have no credit rating! It would destroy your life!" Wow, Julia is really upset about the idea of a loan.

"Okay, jeez, I won't go to a bank," I say. "Anyway, that's really not the point. The point is, I need a job. And I just have no idea what I could do."

"What was your major?" asks Coco.

"Art history."

"Art . . . historian?"

Everyone at the table giggles.

"Yes, I chose a very impractical major. No, I don't know why."

"Probably because it sounded cool," says Angie, flashing me her best I'm-so-helpful smile.

I raise an eyebrow at her. "Not helping."

"I could see you working at a fashion magazine," says Coco, hopping off her chair. "Who wants more coffee?"

"Me please!" say Julia and Angie in unison, and frown at each other.

"I'm not a writer," I say. "Anyway, it would be all *Devil Wears Prada*–y. And the models would make me feel shitty."

"Besides, it's really hard to get a job in anything related to fashion," says Angie. For a second, I wonder if she knows that from personal experience. Before I can ask, she picks up her phone to read a text.

"And I need to earn money, *now*," I say. And, I add silently, it's a fact: the cooler the job, the worse the money. My salary at the PR agency—not even that cool compared to working in, like, fashion or TV or whatever—was thirty-five thousand a year, which, if you break it down and take out money for rent and bills, works out to about twenty-five dollars a day. I mean, a decent facial in New York is at least a hundred and fifty. How could anyone ever survive on that salary and still eat, let alone have a life?

Julia is in fix-it mode now. "Let's make a list of your skills and experience. What did you do at the PR agency last week?"

I think back. "I pretended not to spend all my time e-mailing my friends, sat in on meetings about things I didn't know anything about, and watched the clock obsessively. I swear I almost fell asleep, like, twenty times, right at my desk."

Everyone (except Madeleine) laughs at this, though, honestly, it was kind of depressing. Am I really meant to do that for the rest of my life?

"If you need fast cash, get a fast-cash job, girl," says Julia. "Waitressing. Bartending."

I blink at her. "Manual labor?"

Madeleine makes a snorting sound of suppressed laughter. I ignore her. I said it to be funny. Kind of.

"With that kind of princess attitude, you're screwed," says Julia.

"I want a real job. Something that will impress my parents, which means something in an office. Something with an official business e-mail address."

"So e-mail your résumé to PR recruitment agencies in Manhattan," says Julia. "Then wow them with how bright and smart and awesome you are. Any PR agency in Manhattan would be lucky to have you!"

"Okay." I love having a bossy best friend sometimes. It makes decision-making much easier.